THE COLORS OF HEAVEN

THE COLORS OF HEAVEN

Short Stories from the Pacific Rim

Edited and with an Introduction by

TREVOR CAROLAN

Vintage Books · A Division of Random House, Inc. · New York · Toronto

A VINTAGE ORIGINAL, FIRST EDITION
NOVEMBER 1992

Introduction & compilation copyright © 1992 by Trevor Carolan

All rights reserved under International and Pan-American Copyright
Conventions. Published in the United States by Vintage Books, a
division of Random House, Inc., New York, and simultaneously in
Canada by Random House of Canada Limited, Toronto.

Library of Congress Cataloging-in-Publication Data
The Colors of heaven : short stories from the Pacific rim / edited and
with an introduction by Trevor Carolan. — 1st ed.
p. cm.
"A Vintage original"—T.p. verso.
ISBN 0-679-73885-1
1. Short stories—Pacific Area. 2. Short stories—Pacific Area—Translations into English. 3. Short stories, English—Pacific Area—Translations from foreign languages. 4. Pacific Area—Literatures. 5. Pacific
Area—Literatures—Translations into English. I. Carolan, Trevor.
PN6120.2.C64 1992
808.83′10895—dc20   91-58058
                    CIP

Canadian Cataloguing in Publication Data
The Colors of heaven : contemporary short stories from the Pacific rim
ISBN 0-679-73885-1
1. Short stories—Pacific Area. 2. Short stories—Pacific Area—
Translations into English. 3. Pacific Area—Literatures. 4. Pacific
Area—Literatures—Translations into English.
I. Carolan, Trevor, 1951–
PN6120.2.C64 1992   808.83′10895   C92-094648–8

Pages 317–19 constitute an extension of the copyright page.

Book design by Rebecca Aidlin

Manufactured in the United States of America
10 9 8 7 6 5 4 3 2 1

For my wife, Kwangshik,
without whose patience and encouragement
this book could not have been completed

. . . Truly, is anything missing now?
Heaven is here before our eyes;
this very place is the Lotus Land . . .

Hakuin Zenji

CONTENTS

Contents

INTRODUCTION

Few areas of the world, and still fewer epochs of history, have experienced such extraordinary change in so brief a time as East Asia since World War II. In four decades "the Pacific miracle" has transformed an exotic spread of former colonies, dependencies, and a devastated Japan, China, and Korea into a masterwork of unrivaled economic vigor. But Western understanding of Pacific Asia's fundamental human terrain has long been cloudy, and the Pacific miracle has yet to bridge significant cultural differences between East and West. Even as voices as diverse as those of former President Ronald Reagan and sociologist William Irwin Thompson have clarioned the advent of a new "Pacific Age," and, as global economic and technological advancement grows ever more linked to Asian-Pacific development, it is ironic to note how little real corresponding growth there has been in general Western awareness of Asian-Pacific culture. The raison d'être for this collection of nineteen stories, therefore, is to introduce readers to this still relatively unfamiliar part of the world as it is illuminated by its contemporary literature.

The short story came into its own throughout North and Southeast Asia as a staple feature of daily newspapers, and this remains the case today. Writers of the region took to the form enthusiastically some sixty years ago, shaping it to the strong anticolonialist liberation currents of the times. From Japanese-occupied Korea through to the then Dutch East Indies, East Asian authors were passionate in their embrace of nationalism, and a concurrence of artistic creativity and political activism has persisted in the region's literatures ever since.

In fact, the impetus for this anthology came during a 1985 meeting in Seoul with Kim Chi-Ha, the revered South Korean poet, playwright, and champion of human rights. Spared from a military government death sentence in 1974 only through immense international pressure, Kim, on being asked what might be done to improve the awareness of Western writers among Asian readers, deflected the question by replying that it would be far more constructive in the short term if something could be done to bring a greater awareness of Asian writers to the West. This would be instrumental, he maintained, in sparing other Asian writers the imprisonment and brutality he had been forced to endure repeatedly and would focus concern on the routine silencing of important Asian political voices.

As we spoke, with my wife translating, it was impossible to forget for more than a few moments the two secret policemen we had encountered earlier; they waited menacingly outside the door of the inn where we met. Kim's words needed no further elaboration. On my return to North America, I began an exhaustive search of contemporary Asian-Pacific literatures, the distilled essence of which follows.

These stories have been selected both for their acuity of vision and for the exacting ways in which they speak to their respective cultures. There are no predictable chestnuts here; each work offers unvarnished insight into the human condition of the Asian-Pacific Rim as it exists now. The stories are as contemporary and active in meaning as the epigram that begins the collection, with its suggestion (echoing Buddhism's Diamond Sutra) that there is no "final" nirvana, only ordinary life, here and now. These stories suggest that the only true images of Asia come from the color and flavor of its daily life.

The concerns embraced in this collection are by turn universal and ethnocentrically particular. They encompass the conflicts generated by clashes between new and traditional cultural values. "Progress," and "In the Mirror" examine the problems of new urban societies in developing nations; in "Chinatown," the difficulty of an emerging nation unsure of its place in the larger world order is explored metaphorically. We see the lingering effects of colonialism and liberation struggles in "Heartland" and "Shadow Play," while the changing roles of women, the young, and the disadvantaged are addressed in "Mala," "Snow Flurry," and "In the Footsteps of a

Water Buffalo." Others recognize new problems—pollution; hurried, haphazard economic development; and the injustice of political and social intolerance. And others still speak of unfamiliar customs: of polygamous "second families"; of extended, multigenerational households; or, in "The Festival of Graves" and "The English Language Teacher's Secret," of startling new reproductive ethics. Perhaps naturally, many of these concerns overlap, for underlying each story is the pressure constantly exerted upon Asian societies by the world's most successful export: Western materialist culture.

As any gathering from so vast a territory must be, what follows is a highly idiosyncratic selection. But one hopes that certain threads may be detected: from the highly developed Confucian/Buddhist sensitivities of Northeast Asia (roughly from Hong Kong northward) to the sensuality of tropical Southeast Asia. Readers will note also the inclusion of work from both Australia and New Zealand—nations that are not ordinarily thought of as being "Asian," but that increasingly view themselves as members of the Asian-Pacific community.

Regarding the translations, it remains a truism that works by Asian writers in English-language editions are still in short supply. Locating and funding capable translations remains a problem. Officially sanctioned translations are customarily outdated, of pallid subject matter, or unthreatening to the governments who fund them. Genuinely challenging material does not often reach a wider international readership. One result of this tacit censorship is the growing number of Asian authors who now write in English.

Japanese authors are an exception to the rule and enjoy an advantage in this regard. The United States' lengthy occupation of Japan following the Second World War, and its initiative in establishing Japan as a reliable Pacific bulwark against communism, offered the boon of fostering a Western awareness of Japanese culture greater than that of any other Asian nation and, arguably, this remains the case. Japanese writers were the first East Asians truly to adapt the Western short story form to their culture. Fine writing from Japan has long been available in first-rate translation, and, undeniably, the masterworks of Japanese novelists such as

Mishima, Kawabata, and Tanizaki kindled interest in further Asian writing. Works by many mainland Chinese and Taiwanese writers now steadily find their way into English—thanks in large measure to the growing number of capable Western translators, of whom several of the most distinguished appear in this volume. These works join the current stir of interest in writing from Korea, the Philippines, Indonesia, and elsewhere about the Pacific.

The West has been engaged in economic and cultural exchange with Asia from the time of the Greeks. Indeed, our very concept of "the West" arose as a symbol of differentiation from the culture of Asia, normally typified by Western civilization through several millennia as a cruelly despotic world: the word *Asia* itself is derived from a root meaning "alien."

There was a time, however (roughly 2,500 years ago), when both Occidental and Oriental philosophical traditions were remarkably alike. Heraclitus and the pre-Socratics of Athens would have—and given ancient trade routes, perhaps may have—found themselves in lively agreement with Lao-tzu and the early Taoists. History has provided few occasions since when East and West have been on as companionable terms. But with the immediacy of history hard upon our time, it is encouraging to note in the stories that follow how much Asian daily life, for all its differences and the thousands of miles that separate it from us, can still appear so familiar.

The gathering of this anthology came by circuitous paths, and there are many to be recognized for their help. I am especially grateful to the authors, translators, and publishers whose work follows; much of it was obtained under very awkward conditions. I particularly wish to thank Kim Chi-Ha, now living in greatly relieved circumstances, for his inspiration and example; likewise, the inexhaustible Gary Snyder, whose early encouragement was invaluable.

While I was researching the collections of the University of British Columbia in Vancouver and the University of Hawaii at Mānoa, I found useful periodicals including *Solidarity, Renditions,*

Japan Quarterly, Korea Journal, Cornell University Asian Papers, and *Mānoa.* For their assistance with materials, Pira Sudham, Huynh Sanh Thong of Yale University's Council on Southeast Asia Studies, Goh Poh-Seng, Faith Conlan of Seal Press, and Shusaku Endo and Yoshiko Kozu of Japanese PEN deserve sincere thanks. Others offering valuable help and advice were Alberto Manguel; Ivan Kats, Obor Foundation; Bill Hamilton, University of Hawaii Press; John McGlynn, Lontar Foundation; Peter Richards, Asia-Pacific Foundation; Rosemary Morse, Wheatland Foundation; Dr. Mansoor Marican; Akiko Kurita; Craig Tapping; Blanche d'Alpuget; Tim Curnow; Rosemary Wildblood, New Zealand Arts Council; Thomas Gething, University of Hawaii at Mānoa; Louise May; Professor Herbert Phillips, University of California at Berkeley; Lisa Muri; and Sulak Sivaraksa, Santi Pracha Dhamma Institute, Bangkok.

I wish to thank expressly my agent, Jan Whitford; Carolyn Brunton; and my editor, Jenna Laslocky, for their exemplary care and attention to this book. To all who contributed,

Nine Bows,

Trevor Carolan
Deep Cove, British Columbia
1992

THE COLORS OF HEAVEN

KUNIKO MUKODA

(Japan)

Born in Tokyo in 1929, Kuniko Mukoda graduated from Jissen Women's University and worked as an editor for a foreign-movie magazine before establishing herself as a writer of radio and television scripts. Prodigious in output, she wrote mainly in Japan's popular "home drama" genre, which depicts everyday family relationships. The optimism of her early work darkened as she began composing studies of families lacking in harmony and mutual understanding. A 1978 collection of essays, Letters of Apology from Father, *which recounts her own prewar, middle-class family experiences was especially well received, significantly enhancing her literary reputation; it is now regarded as a period document. Mukoda did not venture into fiction per se until 1980 with* Cards in Recollection, *thirteen stories (including "Doubt"), which received the Naoki Fiction Prize. "Doubt" offers much illumination into the complex web of Japanese family relationships and a privileged view of certain less exemplary aspects of contemporary middle-class Japanese life. Tragically, in 1981, in the midst of a personal literary renaissance, Mukoda met an untimely death in an airplane crash on Taiwan.*

Doubt

"I can't leave the sickroom." Shiozawa knows very well that he shouldn't leave the patient until someone comes to take his place beside the bed.

His father is asleep, his snores echoing in the private hospital room. He collapsed from a cerebral hemorrhage three days ago, shortly after his seventy-seventh birthday, and has been unconscious ever since. It is his father's second stroke, and Shiozawa has just been told there is little chance of recovery—that he should prepare for the worst. Because his father's heart is still strong for his age, the critical time should come between midnight tonight and dawn. Shiozawa's wife had waited there impatiently for him to come from work, and is now home to make preparations for the mourning clothes and the funeral.

All the others whom his father ought to see, Shiozawa thought, have said their good-byes—not that there were many others. His father had been stiff and narrow-minded by nature, and had grown even more cantankerous after his wife died. When the first stroke had paralyzed him a year ago, his dislike of contact with others increased. The flowers and get-well gifts in the room are mere formalities, acknowledgments of Shiozawa's position as a company executive.

Outside, the sky turns gray and darkens at last. In the encroaching darkness, his father seems to be fighting for a little more space in which to live.

"I'm his son. I've got to stay here by his bed," Shiozawa thinks. But he finds the room hard to bear. It is the stench. It rises from his father's mouth, which hangs wide open, almost unhinged. The whiskers have kept growing after his collapse, and the mustache—an incongruous bundle of spindly twigs—trembles slightly with every breath. The heavy odor fills the room. Since it comes from one of his parents, Shiozawa feels he should dutifully ignore it. But his father's smell is not just a sick man's bad breath. It is much more—the stink of rotting guts.

His father had always been a drudge, an elementary-school principal who had continued working as an administrator long after retirement age. A social drinker, but one who never went too far. "Your father is the only man I know who never gets his shirt collar dirty," Shiozawa's mother had once remarked. Unlike his father, she at least would have an occasional evening drink of sake. She had insinuated that there was something lacking in a husband who, even as a young man, had had so little sexual desire. Always thin, he looked in later life like a dried stick ready to be snapped in two. Passing him in a corridor, Shiozawa would think he resembled a cigarette holder, in both shape and smell.

"What is this animal stink? Can't a man die without such a foul smell?" Shiozawa has a hunch his father's time will be up earlier than the doctor predicted. "I can't leave my seat. The relatives all think I'm a good eldest son. I have to live up to their expectations. I won't take my eyes off him."

But the stench is unbearable. Shiozawa suspects that is why his wife hurried out as soon as he came in. She couldn't take the smell either.

"I've got to get a newspaper." The evening papers will have arrived at the hospital kiosk. There have been stories recently about an acquaintance of Shiozawa's, an executive of an affiliated company who is suspected of bribery. Shiozawa knows it is just an excuse, but he leaves the room anyway.

When he returns with the fresh smell of newsprint on his ink-smeared hands, his father's snores have ceased. He does not feel much grief at the moment. As he presses the buzzer to call the nurse, he is preoccupied with how he will explain to the relatives that he was not there at the end. His own stink overpowers him, and he presses the button harder, noticing, as he does so, that the dead man's stench has disappeared completely, as if it had never been.

"What shall we do about Nobu-chan?" His wife was phoning family members with information about the wake and the funeral arrangements. She looked up at him for an answer.

"I don't think we need to tell him." Nobuo was Shiozawa's cousin.

His wife came to Nobuo's defense. "But Nobu-chan doesn't seem to be in touch with anyone else in the family."

"He's not a child anymore. Why do you still call him 'Nobu-chan'?"

"He *is* twelve years younger than you, and—let's see—that makes him thirty-five."

"He's old enough to be respectable, but he hasn't settled down yet. That's why no one takes him seriously," Shiozawa rejoined.

"Not settled down"—it had been his father's favorite phrase. Every family has one or two members the relatives find unacceptable, and Nobuo was one of these: Not once had he held a steady job. He had formally enrolled at the university at one time, but had soon quit. Since then, every time the family saw him, he had a different job and a different address.

Nobuo had once claimed to be a show-business agent and had shown Shiozawa an album full of publicity pictures and photos of models in swimsuits. Shiozawa hadn't recognized a single one of the "budding talents." Another time Nobuo had said he was an "anya." Shiozawa thought that meant he ran a shop making the sweet bean filling for cakes, but Nobuo explained he was another kind of "anya"—a liaison between television companies and manufacturers, whose job it was to think up gimmicks for television commercials. For a commission, he had said.

Every time Nobuo changed his job, he changed his woman as well. Sometimes he appeared to be nothing more than a gigolo.

Once he seemed quite poor; even his face looked strangely different. Then out of the blue he had sent Shiozawa a large box of prime canned crab as a year-end gift. Shiozawa's thank-you note came back stamped "Address unknown. Return to sender."

"That's true, but Grandpa was fond of him," his wife was saying.

"Go ahead and tell him then, if you want. I wouldn't," Shiozawa wanted to say. But he swallowed his words and began looking through a bundle of New Year's cards to find Nobuo's most recent address.

The women in the family all liked Nobuo. He was not particularly handsome, but he was subtly attractive, and had a way with women. Shiozawa had noticed that when Nobuo walked into a room, it came alive. The women began to talk and laugh more.

Once—he didn't remember exactly when it was—his eldest daughter had returned from a friend's wedding and found Nobuo talking with her mother in the dining room. Like her mother, his daughter was the thrifty type. She would normally take off her kimono after a ceremonial occasion so she would not ruin it. But this time she did not change until Nobuo had left. She sat eating cakes and drinking tea in her best clothes.

"What's the use of showing off for such a man?" Shiozawa wanted to ask her. He noticed, however, that it wasn't just his daughter who acted that way. His wife, too, hovered attentively over the younger man. Apparently remembering a remark Nobuo had made many years ago, she offered him the choice bits of salted salmon: "You prefer the belly-meat, grilled medium, don't you, Nobu-chan?" He never heard such cheerful tones from his wife when they were alone together. It so happened that Shiozawa liked that piece of the salmon himself, and he was indignant that his wife should offer the delicacy not to him, but to Nobuo. What's more, she enthusiastically listened to everything Nobuo said, occasionally nodding and stealing self-conscious glances at her own face reflected in the black lacquered tea caddy she was fussing with, dabbing unobtrusively at her nose with her fingertips to remove the shine. Shiozawa did not fail to catch that.

"Whenever Nobu-chan's name comes up, you speak as if you hate him," his wife said.

"I don't mean to. I just don't want what happened before to happen again."

"Before? You mean what happened at the funeral?"

"That's right. I don't want any more money squabbles among the relatives."

"But you didn't actually catch him at it."

"Who else would do such a thing?"

Two years before, at the funeral service for a member of the main branch of Shiozawa's family, a condolence gift of ¥50,000 had disappeared. Nobuo had been seen coming and going at about the time. He had talked then as if he were doing well, but in fact he seemed broke. He had presented only a token gift—bundles of cheap incense in a splendid box. It was rumored that he had tried to borrow from a rich widow in the family and had been refused. Shiozawa, who was in charge of the service, was mortified. He was determined to search Nobuo's belongings, but his wife and the other women talked him out of it. They didn't want a blood relative shamed in the presence of the deceased.

Shiozawa refused to let the matter drop. He made clear his suspicions to Nobuo himself, but the young man remained unperturbed. Adding insult to injury, he gathered the unmarried women and children around him and made a vulgar display, imitating chorus girls with his long, thin fingers. As Shiozawa watched the nicotine-stained, finely tapered fingers going up and down like dancers' legs, he thought it almost obscene. "Consider the occasion!" he wanted to object. It was all he could do to control himself.

Now he was chief mourner. Perhaps it was wrong to feel this self-satisfied respectability, having just lost a father, but that is how he felt. The general-affairs section of his company came out in force and arranged the whole program—the ceremony at the funeral altar, the wake, and the ritual farewell to the deceased. It all reflected Shiozawa's position. Those relatives he was not ashamed of came, and his friends paid their condolence visits. He felt a twinge of guilt as he displayed the appropriate grief like an actor, but he told himself not to be concerned: "Every important occasion in life calls for this kind of performance."

A huge lacquerware container of sushi was delivered to the kitchen door. It came from a large shop near the station. Shiozawa was told that whoever ordered the sushi had given no name, but simply told the shop where to deliver twenty servings of the best quality. Shiozawa and his wife glanced at each other: Nobuo. That was his way when he was in the money. Make people wonder, then put in an appearance.

"This isn't a third-rate production of a traveling theater! Don't you try to upstage me!" Shiozawa planned to say. But then he noticed that the children had already started enjoying the sushi, and the opportunity was lost.

Nobuo turned up a little later.

"It'll be all right this time. He's wearing new shoes and a new suit," Shiozawa's wife whispered.

"Don't take your eyes off him. I can't afford to be shamed in front of the company's employees." Shiozawa was raising his voice without realizing it, and his wife had to hush him.

Nobuo bowed to Shiozawa with a look and air he assumed especially for such occasions, and walked ceremoniously toward the funeral altar. He presented a condolence gift and politely offered incense. He sniffed noticeably as he pressed his palms together in prayer. It was more than Shiozawa could bear. When the eldest son of the deceased is not shedding tears, why should a distant relative give such a studied performance? Looking closely at Nobuo's black suit, he saw it was not made of an appropriately plain fabric, but of a small fish-scale weave. That truly irritated him. Shiozawa summed up the poseur to himself: Here is a man who gets along in the world by ingratiating himself and courting favors.

Nobuo came up to him to express his condolences. Shiozawa kept his eyes closed, inhaling deeply the smell of incense and flowers. "Every corner of the house is filled with the sweet smell of incense, even the bathroom and the pantry," he thought.

Suddenly there was a commotion at the entrance to the house. Whispers spread: "The wife of the executive Kujiraoka has come."

"Former. The *former* executive."

"Just 'Mrs. Kujiraoka' will do." The voices were interrupting and correcting one another.

This was the widow of one of the company's former executives, Kujiraoka, who had died six months ago. He had lost his post the year before, handing it over in a sense to Shiozawa. Despair had driven him to a nervous breakdown, and his premature death was brought on by a combination of excessive drinking and sleeping pills. Shiozawa had presided at the funeral ceremonies. Now the widow, a frail figure, came to express her condolences and her renewed gratitude for the attentive way Shiozawa had managed things at that time. Compared with what he had done for her, she said, she could do nothing for him. She apologized and left quickly.

"Ku-ji-ra-o-ka." Just behind Shiozawa, Nobuo was muttering the name as if trying to remember something. To Shiozawa, the meaning was clear. "After all, Nobuo was there," he thought. "He heard me that night." Shiozawa felt a knife twisting in his back.

Shiozawa knew he had some small moral flaws. He would break the speed limit when the coast was clear. He would accept small illegal kickbacks if he felt absolutely sure he wouldn't be caught. More often than he cared to remember, he had indulged in safe little love affairs on business trips. Shiozawa disliked knowing that this other, shady side lived behind the facade of the reputable, respectable businessman, but he comforted himself: "Men are like that. Everyone does it some time or other."

Still, there was that one thing Shiozawa did not want to remember at all. He could not explain to himself why he had done it. One summer evening when his wife and children were at the theater, before he realized quite what he was doing, he had picked up the phone and dialed the villa of the company chairman. When the chairman's familiar hoarse voice came on the line, Shiozawa had covered his mouth with a handkerchief and whispered into the phone slanders about Kujiraoka—a house he had built with illegal commissions, some tawdry liaisons with women. But when he had put down the receiver after this one-sided conversation, Shiozawa sensed he was not alone; someone else was in the house.

Nobuo was standing in the kitchen, drinking water.

"You should come through the front door when you visit us."
Shiozawa could hear his own voice trembling.

"Are you home alone?" Nobuo's casual question was a relief.
But he had heard.

"I hear Nobu-chan brought ¥50,000 in condolence money."
His wife's voice came to him as if from a distance.

During the vigil in front of the altar, Shiozawa needled
Nobuo. It was after the company employees had gone home, and
only close relatives remained. The wake was taking place on the
second night, so most of them fell asleep from sheer exhaustion.
The only ones left awake were Nobuo, Shiozawa, and his wife,
and even she occasionally nodded off.

Alcohol was making Shiozawa increasingly testy. "The
¥50,000 you offered is too much for a man of your status, don't
you think? Or are you trying to make up for something you've done
in the past?" He was of course referring to Nobuo's embezzlement
of the condolence money at the other family funeral.

Nobuo just scratched his head and said, "I know I've caused
you trouble. I'll do what I can when I can," and he served Shiozawa
more sake.

"I don't like a man who borrows a little money on Saturday,
and conveniently forgets his debt the next day, just because it's a
holiday. If he needs money he should borrow it on Monday and
borrow enough so he'll remember. You visit us only when you
feel you're a big man and can pass around your engraved visiting
cards."

Shiozawa had to make Nobuo angry. Only then would he know
for sure whether his cousin had heard him slander Kujiraoka that
night.

"Where do *you* get off saying such a thing? Who do you think
you are?" If only Nobuo would say something like that, Shiozawa
would be free from this suffocating suspense. It was as if they were
playing Doubt, the card game in which one's cards have to be played
in numerical order. If someone suspects that another player is
putting down the wrong card, he can say "Doubt." If his challenge

holds up and it isn't the right card, the challenger gains the point. But if he's wrong, he takes a big loss.

Shiozawa knew that if a single word about what he did that night ever leaked out, his reputation would be destroyed: certainly his wife would despise him. But that would almost be a relief compared with this continual uncertainty about whether Nobuo had overhead the phone call. Shiozawa was calling "Doubt!"

But Nobuo ignored his provocations, got himself drunk, and fell asleep.

Shiozawa's father had taught him how to play Doubt. Even as a child, Shiozawa had been good at guessing, and his less imaginative father was often tricked. When Shiozawa was playing the correct cards, his father would say "Doubt" and lose the game.

One summer vacation, when Shiozawa was in the second or third grade, his father had made him wait for an hour in the dimly lit Tachikawa railway station. He had taken the boy along to Okutama for some fishing, a rare treat, and on their way home, he had been stopped at the wicket. Shiozawa sat on a wooden bench alone, being bitten by mosquitoes. After an interminable wait, his father emerged from the stationmaster's office. He suddenly looked very old.

His father had said nothing as they left the station. Then he had silently treated Shiozawa to a bowl of eel and rice. Shiozawa sensed that his father had played the wrong card. He had not paid the full fare and had been caught. Shiozawa also knew that he wasn't to tell his mother and younger brother and sister. But his father doubted: clearly he thought Shiozawa was one who told tales. Shiozawa suspected that was why, after that day, his father had never again opened his heart to him, and had never loved him as much as before.

Nobuo leaned against the altar dozing.

"Could it be that he didn't hear me after all? Or is he just pretending? The happy-go-lucky bum has me over a barrel. And there's not a damn thing I can do about it. Even if I call his bluff, I won't know the truth unless he turns his cards face up." Shiozawa could not stop his thoughts.

He saw again before him his father's stooped figure as they walked out of the railway station. "Father, a man of reputation, of character, compromised himself that summer evening. And I, too. . . . The rotten stench at my father's deathbed is mine, too. Nobuo may have caught wind of the odor of my living decay."

All at once, his father's memory overwhelmed him with abhorrence and nostalgia both. Shiozawa added some chips of incense to the burner, which had almost gone out, and he lit a new stick as well.

Translated by Dan Semour

YOSHIKO SHIBAKI

(Japan)

Born in 1914, Yoshiko Shibaki graduated from her native Tokyo's First Women's Higher School, studied English and typing at a YMCA Women's Academy, and worked for the Mitsubishi Centre for Economic Studies. Her early literary work attracted the critical attention of novelist Fumiko Hayashi, and in 1941 she was able to establish herself with the story "The Fruit and Vegetable Market," which won the prestigious Akutagawa national literary prize. Following World War II, Shibaki published The Coursing Sun *and* One Woman *(1946),* The Journeying Song *(1948), and several collections of short stories, which were marked by a deepening social consciousness and an unaffected narrative style. Her 1954 novel,* Susaki Paradise, *brought Shibaki further acclaim, and, in her short story collection* A Luminous Woman *(1955), she began to delve into the themes of "downtown" manners and human relationships that would become her trademark concerns. "Snow Flurry," with its tenuous portrayal of the emotional dislocations caused by rapid postwar urbanization, is emblematic of these themes. Her autobiographical trilogy,* Dried Bean Curds, The Sumida River, *and* Marunouchi Building Number Eight *(1960–1962), is now recognized as a significant history of women's life in the Meiji, Taisho, and Showa eras. Shibaki's other works include* Night Crane *(1964), a reexamination of Japanese cultural traditions;* Dyed Colours *(1965);* Katsushika Woman *(1966);* The Celadon Fulling Block *(Japan's Woman's Literary Prize, 1972); and* The Peony Garden *(1977). Shibaki died in 1991.*

Snow Flurry

It was almost dark when the train approached Shibuya Station, and Kanako gazed from the window to the streets below. The signal at the intersection leading to Dōgenzaka must have turned green, for throngs of people swarmed into the broad crossing, burying it beneath them. Watching the busy crowd move through the December city, Kanako had the feeling that in reality they were only being swept along meaninglessly. The train coasted to a stop at the station platform.

Kanako got off the train and made her way out into the station plaza to mingle with the vast crowd. The city street at night was like a gloomy river: refuse floating with the current, people were washed together and then engulfed. There were too many aimless souls in the city. People like her, without home or family, wandering about vacantly. Kanako did not consider apartments lined up like so many boxes inside wooden and concrete buildings to be homes. Nor did she think that simply living together made a man and woman family. Was that because she still had nothing in which she could find solace?

She walked toward Dōgenzaka until she came to the right building, then climbed the stairs to a small, second-floor restaurant. This was where she and Horie Nobutaka met for dinner once a month. Perhaps because it was still early, a window seat was vacant. As long as she could watch the stream of people passing by on the pavement, it did not matter if he was late. One after another, people seemed to materialize and then dissolve into the empty shadows. Today, as Kanako was leaving the Shima Design Studio after work, Shima had called out to her. It was payday and no one was working overtime in the normally busy studio. Of course the studio, which occupied a single room in a small office building, only had five employees, including Shima. Kanako was the only woman, and so her most important task was serving tea, but after her first year with the studio she had taken two years of night classes at a design academy and now was allowed to help with some of the real work.

"Everyone will be at my house for Christmas, right? Seki's bringing another guest. I'll introduce you to him."

Shima's long head of hair shook as he spoke. Seki was a friend who often visited Shima at the studio. Kanako looked up and smiled. Each year at Christmas the staff was invited to Shima's house and treated to the hospitality of his wife, Yoshiko, a brisk, lively woman and an excellent cook. Although Kanako always felt herself excluded from the workings of society at large, the ordinary world apparently did take notice of her now and then.

Customers began occupying the other seats in the restaurant, but there was still no sign of Nobutaka. This made Kanako think he might not come. He was always late, and as she waited Kanako could never rid herself of the feeling that he would not come. Both had apartments within walking distance of the same train station, but Kanako felt that one day Nobutaka might suddenly vanish from his. Although he was only a second-rate screenwriter, Kanako might be able to find him if she looked. But she had decided not to. Beyond that, she did not know. She simply lived with the constant feeling that he was going to disappear. The apartments in which they lived were just small boxes, and it would have made little difference had one of them moved in with the other. But Nobutaka had not asked her and Kanako had never brought up the possibility herself. From their conversations she knew vaguely where he was from and what his relatives were doing, but she had no intention of prying more information from a man who did not volunteer it. As for Kanako, she had nothing special she could tell him about herself. They were like rootless, aquatic plants adrift in the city, perhaps, or leaves floating on the stream—something of the sort—and in no sense contributing members of society. Kanako felt the emptiness of being without a home, without a place to return to, in the same way that she felt the loneliness of losing her parents at an early age and having no one to turn to. Sometimes she dreamed of a house and land she could claim as her birthright.

Kanako once told Nobutaka about her father, a low-ranking government official who had spent his life shuttling from one assignment to the next. Kanako had changed elementary schools four times, and even more clearly than her native Chiba remembered a house her father had rented on the outskirts of a town near the old highway in Gumma. The house had a small garden, in the corner of which grew a large paulownia tree. The house was more spacious than any Kanako had lived in before, and from its sunny veranda Kanako had had her first glimpse of the purple flowers put out by the paulownia. There was a large sunken *kotatsu* in the living room at which Kanako recalled sitting down to dinner in the winter with her parents and brother. It was the last time she had experienced the closeness of family life. Soon after moving from the house Kanako's mother had died of breast cancer. After that, Kanako remembered only houses ravaged by the wind. Her father died the year she graduated from high school; when her brother graduated the year after, he went off to college in Hokkaido. Kanako moved to Tokyo and found a job with a construction company. She quit three years later when she came to the Shima Design Studio. She had gone for an interview after seeing an ad in the paper, but wondered whether they would really be able to pay her a regular salary. Later she heard that a college student had said at her interview that she planned to use the income as pocket money.

The Shima Design Studio had started with three people whose chief work was designing containers for a dairy products manufacturer. With the commissions received from the manufacturer their work had stabilized, and now there were five employees. Their size meant that everyone was busy and put in a lot of overtime. The crushing work load was necessary for their survival. The reason Kanako had gone to night classes at the design academy was out of a desire to help in any way she could.

Nobutaka appeared at the top of the restaurant stairs. His thinness made him seem especially tall. His face was gaunt and he looked older than his age, but there was nothing coarse about him.

Despite his streak of nervous irritability, Kanako felt herself drawn to him the moment he relaxed and smiled good-naturedly. As he approached from the stairs, Kanako told herself that at last he had come, that she would see him again today; but to him she said nothing. They sat across from each other at the table, two leaves blown together by the wind.

"Why are you looking at me like that?"

Nobutaka's question came as a rebuff to her.

"It's nothing."

Kanako looked out the window to the pavement below. The street wore a brightly illuminated, end-of-the-year expression.

"There are so many people going by—because it's Saturday, I suppose. Harajuku must be even worse. Everyone brushing shoulders. Don't you hate brushing against other people?"

"What are you thinking about?"

He glanced at the street crowded with young people, but soon picked up the menu. Even though he never had anything special, he was very careful about choosing. Kanako would have whatever he ordered. It was enough to have him in front of her. She felt relieved not to be out there among the drifters.

For her graduation project at the design academy Kanako had decided to draw a luminescent butterfly, and she wanted a real specimen as a model. Somebody told her about a butterfly dealer on Takeshita Street, one block in from Omotesandō in Harajuku. She visited the shop on a Sunday. Takeshita Street, a mecca for Tokyo's youth, was even more crowded than Omotesandō. Displaying the latest fashions and accessories, stores on both sides of the street did a thriving business. Boys and girls strolled along arm in arm, licking ice cream cones. The butterfly shop was on the second floor of a building in an alley partway down the street. The name on the door said "Tropicana." The small apartment-turned-shop contained rows of butterfly lockers. After taking off his shoes and greeting the young proprietor, the customer examined the butterflies, which were classified and mounted in cases in the lockers. For the more common varieties, as many as twenty specimens would be carefully arranged together, beautiful as a kimono pattern. Large or rare specimens were mounted separately, one or three to a case. Never in her life had Kanako seen such a bewildering array of butterflies. The customer who had come in ahead of her was talking to the owner. The owner was saying that every summer he went to the South Seas to catch butterflies, and that this year he planned to go to Celebes. The owner was sitting in a cramped work space at a desk on which a swallowtail lay partly mounted, outstretched wings fixed by pins.

"Can you catch enough butterflies in the South Seas to keep in business?" asked the customer, who was a little older than the owner.

"Once I got lucky and netted a *Graphium androcles*, but it's such a magnificent specimen I can't bear to sell it. They use the forewings to fly, drawing their long, white tails behind them. Exquisite."

Showing his enthusiast's colors, the owner narrowed his eyes in delight.

"Do collectors ask you to go?"

"Sponsors provide money, but some specimens I wouldn't give up for even 300,000 yen."

The owner continued talking as he picked out a *Papilio ulysses* for Kanako. The customer glanced at the white butterflies Kanako was holding.

"*Anthocharis cardamines*—orange tips. They look like petals of snow when they fly," he muttered. The small, delicate butterflies had patches of vermilion on the white upper wings. Kanako asked for one of them, too. Some of the butterflies in the shop sold for just a few hundred yen, others for tens of thousands, and still others for hundreds of thousands. Kanako took the two butterflies in their small case and left the shop. There was a coffee shop on the corner. Once seated inside, Kanako unwrapped the butterflies she had bought, drawing from them a small measure of consolation. Even after butterflies were dead, their still forms and outspread wings remained beautiful. In butterflies people symbolized the joy of being reborn and soaring once more through the heavens. The idea for a design took shape in Kanako's imagination. A man came into the small coffee shop and sat down in the only empty chair, the one next to hers. It was the man she had met in the Tropicana. People might demonstrate their independence in various ways, but something in them submitted to the dictates of chance or fate. So it happened that Kanako met Horie Nobutaka.

Some high school students—boys and girls—were gossiping at the next table in the coffee shop. The topic was a female teacher, and they did not seem to care who overhead: "She's already an old lady of twenty-six, you know." "And she still thinks of sex." Kanako started and looked away. By that logic she herself was at an age bordering on life's dreary end. A thin, wry smile had also formed on Nobutaka's lips. Driven out by the raucous voices of the high school students, they left the coffee shop. Young people who could scarcely yet be called men and women strolled through the Harajuku street as if they owned it. Neither Kanako nor Nobutaka could escape feeling awkwardly out of place. The feeling seemed to draw them closer. At Harajuku Station they discovered that they both lived on the Tōyoko Line.

"Do you like butterflies?" Kanako asked.

"I used to chase them a lot when I was in junior high school."

"Do you have a collection?"

"A small one back where I come from, but only about ten cases here in my apartment. The ones here are all hairstreaks."

"What are hairstreaks?"

"Just small, ordinary butterflies. Not very interesting." .

"Even small butterflies are pretty in groups of thirty or forty."

"I had a little sister who used to like orange tips because they were so lovely."

He seemed to realize what he was saying and suddenly fell silent. Kanako thought his sister must have died very young. Since she already had two pretty butterflies, Kanako said, next she wanted a hairstreak.

"I'll give you mine. I don't need them—they're just taking up space," Nobutaka said.

Perhaps they had drifted together by accident, like two leaves hesitating in the still water of a river shallow. Had chance conspired in this way to bring together two people who neither made good company themselves nor especially desired the company of others? Intimacy came to them as a matter of course. At the time Nobutaka was writing screenplays in an apartment one station beyond the station Kanako used. Half his time he worked for a small production company, and for the other half he was essentially unemployed. Nobutaka would come to her apartment in the evening after he had finished writing and go back home the next day. Sometimes he would not come for a week. Kanako would wait and tell herself that this was how it was going to end. She could not blame him if he never showed up again. From the start there had been no promises about the future: they were simply two people who had formed an instinctive relationship at an age when words were unnecessary. After several days Nobutaka would come knocking on the door and Kanako would utter a small cry, or even close her eyes for a moment. Her room was so small. It was not a home, only a box. The time she and Nobutaka had together was a brief rest in the still water. And yet neither of them ever spoke of wanting or expecting anything more.

They started meeting in the city once a month on Kanako's payday. It seemed a modest way of satisfying their appetites. They avoided the areas frequented by the younger set, preferring the somewhat more adult Dōgenzaka. Nobutaka had a talent for choosing good restaurants and good food, and his table manners were excellent. When Kanako mentioned this to him, Nobutaka simply replied self-derisively that he was from the country.

Tonight he had stewed tongue. It did not agree with Kanako, and for once she did not eat much.

"It's delicious. Why aren't you eating?"

Nobutaka used a spoon to scrape up the last of his stew. For Kanako, it was enough that he was satisfied. The year would be over in just a few days. She did not know what next year might hold: another year on the aimless current. Nobutaka's work was not going anywhere. Beneath the window walked people who dissolved into the murky darkness."

"I got a letter from my mother."

He did not seem to know how to continue. Kanako kept silent. He did not have to say anything unless he wanted to.

"Did I ever tell you about my brother in the United States? His wife's going to have another baby, so he asked my mother to come and help out. She wrote to say she's going. After I told her she was getting too old for that sort of thing."

Kanako nodded. She knew Nobutaka always went back to spend the New Year with his mother.

"The house will be empty this year, so she wants me to look after it."

"Yes, an empty house isn't safe."

"There's nothing worth taking. Everything's so old."

Despite his saying this, Kanako could tell he planned to go back. She felt extremely envious of someone who had a house to go back to. Packed into Nobutaka's house would be all the important memories of his life. He had mentioned that his home was in a village in Shiga, east of Lake Biwa. Kanako did not have a home to go back to. She thought of the places she had been when her father was transferred, but she could not return to any of them. Kanako's brother had settled in Asahikawa in Hokkaido, and they no longer kept in touch.

"When I think of home, I think of the house in Gumma with the big paulownia tree. My mother used to peel persimmons for drying on the sunny veranda. I think it's good to have a house, even one that's run-down. I wonder if people have a homing instinct. Some place they go back to one day. A place they go to die."

Nobutaka did not answer. After a while he said coolly, "It doesn't get you anywhere to go around confirming the beginnings of a petty, insignificant life."

"Then do you mean to say you can cut yourself off from your roots and become a piece of city trash? But I know you don't really see it that way."

Kanako had lost her mother and her father and could not even remember where they were from. They had given up their home-towns before her. Her only place of refuge was a box, yet for the time being she had him. How long he would stay was something she did not know.

"Ready?" asked Nobutaka. He stood up first, an unwilling partner to her sentimentality.

The night street was stirring with activity as the year drew to an end. A night breeze was gusting, and Kanako raised the collar of her overcoat. The stream of people looked cold and black.

Shima's house was located in Setagaya. The reason everyone from the Shima Design Studio gathered there on Christmas was quite simple: it was customary for them to combine Christmas with the studio's year-end party. Shima's house gave Kanako her only contact with an ordinary family. Even though all of her studio co-workers were married, they lived in what Kanako called boxes; Shima was the only one who actually owned a house. Shima's wife called out a greeting even before she came to the door to welcome Kanako inside. Yoshiko was wearing an apron over a red dress, and smelled very strongly of home. The Shimas had two grade-school daughters.

Food and drink had been set out on tables in the adjoining living and dining rooms. In addition to the four staff members, two other male guests were there. Kanako started helping with the food, but the Shima girls took over from her and Kanako was steered to the couch.

"Today you're our guest," said Yoshiko brightly, filling Kanako's glass with beer. A woman who supported her husband from the sidelines, thought Kanako, turning her attention to the family's domestic state of affairs. The well-behaved children had had their party in the afternoon and soon withdrew.

Although Shima's work showed an uninhibited originality, at home he was reduced to the level of an ordinary husband, always referring to his wife as "Mama, mama." Kanako felt no attraction for Shima's domestic side.

When the party had grown lively under the effects of the alcohol, Kanako examined the faces of the two male guests. The man Shima's friend Seki had brought with him worked in the same office. Kanako leaned back in her chair and took another look at the man's face. He was of medium height and build, and had a gentle appearance. The Shimas probably heard he was planning to remarry and had thought of Kanako. If this meant that Kanako was being given the opportunity to make an ordinary match, the experience was her first. It even surprised her that she had been given the chance. Kanako had been told that the man had a child which his mother was raising. When Yoshiko had mentioned a little while ago that he was divorced, Kanako had not asked why. Her interest extended only as far as the situation itself and did not take in her prospective partner.

The food at the Shimas had a delicious home-cooked taste. Flattered by Kanako's saying so, Yoshiko returned the compliment by saying that she did not have Kanako's talent for design.

"My designs?" laughed Kanako. She did little more than help lay the groundwork for Shima.

"Kanako does make a great cup of coffee," said one of her colleagues.

"Her best point is her even temper—she never lets herself get hysterical."

Kanako looked at each in turn.

"On the other hand, nothing you do seems to make me very happy, either. That's what you're getting at, isn't it?"

"You certainly know yourself well."

They all laughed amicably. The male guest was looking at her. Shima called his name—Mr. Okabe.

"I understand your engineering work keeps you pretty busy, Mr. Okabe."

"I do more than my share in that respect, but I'm afraid I haven't been very successful in my personal life."

"We all feel the same way," agreed one of the men from the studio. Kanako was impressed by Okabe's forthrightness, and for the first time regarded him in a favorable light. If his personal life had been a complete success, it would only have made her feel insecure. No doubt the semblance of a home could easily be achieved when the child came first and the husband and wife could center their lives on him. Kanako, without a home or family, could not help feeling thrilled by this rare bit of good fortune that had come her way. Separated for whatever reason from his wife, Okabe seemed to have been through an anguishing and very private experience, for even though he was drunk he gave no sign of becoming light-headed. The men from the studio fairly radiated good cheer.

"You're not eating a thing," said Yoshiko with a glance at Kanako's plate.

"Yes, I am. It's delicious."

Kanako had not enjoyed her food for the past week, but the atmosphere at the party was delightful. Toward the end, Shima had them draw Christmas cards and handed out presents. Kanako drew one with the *Kōfuku no Tani* and received a pair of candy birds on chopsticks. She considered it a good omen and smiled. Okabe's card was the *Birth of Venus,* and his present was a white porcelain dish in the shape of a shell, with a figurine on the edge. He seemed genuinely delighted and repeated, "This is great." They clapped with each new present. A., the middle-aged man who did the studio's accounts, drew the *Hattōshin no Bijo.* He was rewarded with a narrow woman's belt. Everyone burst into laughter when, after opening the belt, he seemed to dismiss it with a wave of the hand.

The joyful Christmas came to an end. Saying good-bye to her co-workers, who stayed behind to continue drinking, Kanako left with the two male guests. Seki quickly caught a cab, and Okabe went with Kanako in the next one.

"That was a nice Christmas. I don't usually celebrate it, but for once I really enjoyed myself. The Shima Design Studio must be a nice place to work," Okabe said.

"It's cozy—a little like a cottage industry."

After answering, Kanako realized that it was the harshness of studio work that made the occasional fun so pleasant. For someone starved of companionship, the cheerfulness of the Shima household warmed the heart. Kanako and Okabe basked in the gentle afterglow. Kanako had the taxi let her off at the corner of the street leading to her apartment.

"Thank you very much."

"I hope I can see you again," said Okabe, and then the taxi sped away.

If this represented an opportunity for Kanako to reach shore, it was her first such chance. Walking down the dark street after she had watched the taxi drive off, Kanako found that she liked Okabe. Yet even the thought of marrying a man who, like Okabe, commanded the world's respect seemed presumptuous of her.

The day before, Kanako had gone to the hospital to have her stomach looked at. After examining her, the doctor announced, "I'd say that you're pregnant. You should see a gynecologist after the New Year."

It hardly seemed possible, and a mixture of emotions—surprise, confusion, shame—prevented any words from coming out. Kanako could not decide then and there whether to have the child or not. What Nobutaka would think was not the problem; rather, she had to get a firm grip on her own feelings and decide what to do. What would a drifter in the city do with a child? Where would the child belong? If it meant an increase in the number of homeless vagrants, would not having it be wrong? Still, bearing a child seemed to be her sole prerogative as a woman. Having met Okabe tonight in this wavering state, she thought she might like to have the child after all. She was weary of her rootless existence. One day she might suddenly find that Nobutaka had left her. He, too, was like a rootless weed.

There was a light on in her apartment. Kanako brought herself up short. Could it be him? He knew there was a party at Shima's tonight. When she opened the door she saw Nobutaka in the single inner room on the other side of the tiny dining room/kitchen. Leaning against the desk, he turned to look at her. He was there. Did her happiness come because he was the shore toward which she always seemed to be moving?

"I'm so exhausted. I felt lonely having so much fun."

Kanako came into the room and said hello to Nobutaka, sitting down in front him.

"Having fun made you lonely?" he asked, the shadow of a beard on his face. Kanako was in earnest.

"Christmas parties and year-end parties are all the same to us Japanese. And besides, we're not used to having fun and so we get tired when we do anything different."

"Not a very helpful trait."

Managing a smile, Nobutaka asked for tea. He never felt like making it himself when he was at her apartment. When Kanako had a cup brewed just right, he drank it down.

"You came back by taxi, didn't you?"

The question was offered casually.

"One of Shima's guests saw me home. Even something small like that creates a kind of bond between people. The next time I see him I'll thank him, and so on. I hate bonds that tie people together like that."

"Why?" he asked.

"I wonder. Because it makes you think you can cling to them. They're so oppressive. It's more refreshing to go your own way, even if there's nowhere to go."

"That's true."

Although Nobutaka had touched upon Kanako's feelings, he said nothing more. Stretching his feet out in front of the gas heater, Nobutaka told her that his mother had left for America, so he would be going back before the New Year. In Kanako's imagination, the empty house in the country merged with the house in Gumma with the paulownia tree. She felt guilty about visiting with no one there, but on impulse she asked, "Would it be all right if I came to your house? If it's too much trouble, I could just look at it from a distance and come right back."

"What good would that do?"

"I don't know. Just having a house where you were born makes you seem more real and dependable than me. If you made any scratches on the posts or walls, I want to see them."

Nobutaka was silent for a while, and then unexpectedly granted her request.

"Maybe we should have a look. Who knows when the house might not be there anymore?"

Kanako stared at him. In the man who was offering her this chance she could not help seeing a weariness of life in the city, a deep longing for home.

Never had Kanako imagined that she would be able to spend the New Year at Nobutaka's family home. Even though they had known each other for over two years, Nobutaka was not one to talk about his birthplace or his relatives. He had mentioned a village near Lake Biwa, it was true, but Kanako had never been near Lake Biwa and this would be her first visit to the Ōmi district.

On the morning of December 31, they left Tokyo for Ōmi-Yahata in Shiga Prefecture. From there they took a taxi, passing along the lively shopping street in front of the station and out into the surrounding fields. Kanako's heart pounded with excitement. Crossing a bridge over a shallow stream, she asked Nobutaka if he had played there as a boy.

"Mm-hmm, with my friends and my sister. We used to catch crayfish," he replied, looking out the window at the river. He had the car stop at a road marked by a small stand of trees. Kanako got out first and looked around. Among the trees stood a cluster of tranquil, aging houses. Opposite the grove lay a small field, and beyond that a fine old house enclosed by a black wooden fence. Birds were resting on the roof. There was a two-storied detached cottage in the compound, and behind the main house was what appeared to be the roof of a storehouse. It seemed to be the residence of the local landlord. The taxi drove off and Nobutaka started walking. Following a path through the field, he went up to the roofed gate of the house with the black wooden fence. Kanako's first thought was that he was going to pay his respects to the landlord. Nobutaka reached a hand around the gatepost to open the lattice door. Kanako noticed that the nameplate on the post read "Horie." Words failed her. After a time, she asked: "This is your house?"

"That's why I'm going in."

The gate door opened and Nobutaka started across the stepping-stones. The main building had a mezzanine floor; the birds on the roof were decorations. The entranceway was in the style of a samurai residence: two wooden doors that opened to the left and right guarded the porch platform. Behind them would be ordinary sliding doors as well. Kanako looked up at the structure, trying to take it all in. Nobutaka used a key to open a side door on the right and went in. Beyond the entrance vestibule was the living room, and to one side lay a spacious earthen-floored kitchen. The thick posts, the old kitchen furnace, the sink—everything made her think of the people who had worked there in years gone by. Numbly she took note of the servants' room and the large storage area still further in.

There was a *kotatsu* in the drawing room; Nobutaka's mother had cautiously turned up the edges of the quilt. Nobutaka guided her into the house. There must have been a caretaker, for the storm doors along the front corridor were open and everything looked clean. Passing through an imposingly formal guest room and bedroom they came up to a decorative cabinet, which Nobutaka opened to reveal a lacquered Buddhist family altar. Following what appeared to be his usual practice, he sat and struck the altar bell, head bowed. Kanako followed his example. The picture of Nobutaka's father showed a man in his forties, in Western clothing, dignified in bearing and handsomer than his son.

So here she was inside the empty house, sitting vacantly in front of the family altar on mats which had not yet absorbed any of the warmth from the room's heater. She could think of nothing boastful in all the conversations she had had with Nobutaka which might have suggested this house to her. He had not given the slightest hint of having grown up in such a prominent family. Why? Was it from distrust of someone poor like herself?

He saw that the color had left her face.

"What's wrong? Are you cold?"

She shook her head, but she was freezing. Nobutaka calculated how many days his mother would be gone.

"A deserted old house isn't very inviting. Doesn't it seem eerie? It's usually brighter and warmer than this."

He looked past the open sliding doors into the garden. A red pine stood in the well-tended garden, and the magnificent stone lantern and landscaping stones were in keeping with the tasteful elegance of the house.

"This house was built over a hundred years ago. It's still in pretty good shape, I imagine because my mother looks after it so well."

The wood wore a quiet sheen and the glass was spotlessly clear. Nobutaka explained that while his family had given up much of its land in the postwar land reform, the tenants still came to help their former mistress.

"This is quite a family you were born into. Why did you hide it from me? Why didn't you tell me?"

"What, the precious son from a good family winding up a hack screenwriter? Come on," he replied sardonically. Then he shifted his gaze to the alcove and the transom.

"Lots of successful merchants come from this part of the country—it runs in the blood. Quite a few of them run major Japanese companies. This house belonged to my mother, and my father— her cousin—took her name when they got married. My father worked in textiles, but he died when my older brother was still in junior high school. If he had lived ten years longer maybe things would be different."

"You must have some memories of him."

"I was just in elementary school and my father was too busy to spend much time at home. I wonder if he really cared about his family. The house was put up by my great-grandfather toward the end of his life."

"Your great-grandfather!"

Kanako felt mingled envy and hostility at the distinguished background of a man she had believed to be no different from herself.

"What a wonderful family tree you have! The Hories have a house and property, even a mother who can testify to it all. Are you sure that feeling sorry for yourself as a failed screenwriter isn't just a pose?"

Kanako was seized with a desperate sense of inferiority. Nobutaka noticed the shock she had received.

"The reason I decided to show you the house was that it will soon be gone."

"The house will be gone?" she echoed.

The expression on Nobutaka's face turned dour. His brother had gone to America to try his hand at trade, but had run into problems. With things at an impasse, he had asked their mother to sell the house. Having her come to help with the new baby was probably just an excuse so that he could try to win her over. His mother, of course, was perfectly aware of that. And so, in her sixties, she had gone overseas on the first trip of her life.

"She must be quite a woman."

The image of a dignified, elderly woman came into Kanako's mind.

"My mother has lived in this house since she was born. She's never known anyplace else. She lives here with the spirit of the house—if she leaves she'll lose what gives her life meaning. Even when she visits my aunt in Kyoto she always comes back in less than three days."

"What about her son's place in Tokyo?"

"She wouldn't be able to give up Ōmi for life in Tokyo."

Acquainted now with the very real possibility of the house's demise, Kanako could not help feeling a sentimental attachment to it. What was Nobutaka going to do, she wondered.

"I'll let her do as she pleases. There's nothing else I *can* do, is there?"

He got up and invited her to come with him to the detached cottage. Built some time after the main house, it presented a refined appearance. From the rear corridor of the main house Kanako saw the storehouse, separated from them by a small garden. Nobutaka walked across the garden stepping-stones, which seemed to lead to the rear garden. Kanako considered the connection between the fine, undreamed-of old house and the history of Nobutaka's birth.

Here Nobutaka comported himself with total freedom. On the second floor of the cottage was the study room shared by Nobutaka and his brother. Nobutaka told Kanako that they used to fire air guns at passing birds from the bay window. As his words took him back in time, his facial expression too seemed to change for the better. The young woman in the picture on the small table in the main room would be his sister, Yuri. According to Nobutaka, she had died of leukemia when she was only twenty-one. She had been afflicted with the disease for more than two years; Nobutaka and his mother had nursed her. Nobutaka had quit his job in Tokyo and returned to Ōmi for the purpose. During a remission the three of them had gone on an excursion around Lake Biwa. The lake became a deeper blue the farther north they went. They went as far as Cape Sugaura. Yuri shyly said that she would like to wear an overkimono of the same shade of blue, with a white sash, at her wedding. Until she was eight Yuri had always said she was going to marry Nobutaka when she grew up. Nobutaka, five years older, would laugh and tell her she would soon change her mind. Even after the Biwa excursion, Yuri was in and out of the hospital until her death. The main room of the cottage had been her sickroom.

Various deaths had been inscribed upon the old house. The spirits of those who had died had waited restlessly for Nobutaka's return. Kanako was not repelled by the thought. She had the feeling that at any moment the door of the storehouse would swing open and there would appear the father who had died so soon. Left among the attachments of the dead, how had Nobutaka felt when he returned to Tokyo?

A visitor called from the distance. Nobutaka went out and Kanako, lacking the courage to remain alone, followed after him. An old local resident was standing on the earthen floor in the waning light. He exchanged familiar greetings with Nobutaka and set a bundle on the threshold, apparently in response to a request from Nobutaka's mother. Kanako waited diffidently in the corridor shadows.

"How long will you be staying?" the man asked.

"I plan to be here for about a week."

"If you need anything at all, don't hesitate to ask."

The man politely excused himself and left. He was the one who had been entrusted with caring for the house. The bundle contained New Year's dishes in tiers of lacquer boxes, rice cakes, dried persimmons, and sushi. Kanako felt ashamed that she had not had time to bring anything with her from Tokyo. She was also worried about spending the New Year in a house this large. Every time Nobutaka left her side she grew uneasy. The mezzanine of the main house had a view of the grove of the neighboring Shinoda Shrine, and Kanako was curious to see it. Nobutaka seemed to take on new life as he climbed the ladder ahead of her.

"Shall we pay a New Year's visit to the shrine tomorrow? The god is famous for his fire festival. Once when my sister was sick she said she wanted to see the fire festival, so I carried her up here piggyback. At night the pine torches crackled and lit up the sky, and we could hear all the excitement."

Nobutaka was more talkative than usual. He was trying to relate to Kanako the different memories he had of the house and the people.

"Which room are we going to sleep in tonight?"

"Which would be best? Wherever you like."

"Let's sleep in the next room. Not apart, because I've never stayed in a house so big and it makes me nervous. How did you ever manage it?"

"Stupid. It's my home."

He forced a laugh.

"Your apartment in Tokyo must seem terribly small."

"It's true that I always had this house to come back to. The thought of losing it makes me glad I have someplace to go in Tokyo. Now it's all I have."

Kanako realized that she and Nobutaka shared the feeling of being washed like dirt toward the same city river.

That night they slept beside each other on quilts laid out in the guest room. Kanako thought that it might be the only time in her life she slept in such a big room in a building that was not an inn. She slept with her pillow next to the family altar; perhaps that accounted for the dream she had. Dawn seemed to be near, and in the dim light of the garden, next to the great stone lantern, stood an elderly woman in a black coat. Kanako knew that it was Nobutaka's mother. The woman stood there in silence, as though to reproach Kanako for her impertinence in inviting herself into the house while its owner was away. Kanako grew tense and apologized: I'm sorry . . . please forgive me . . . I'm leaving right away. I promise not to disturb the quiet solitude of this neatly ordered house.

After a while Kanako awoke, but in her dream she did not remember the woman in the black coat going away. Kanako caressed herself with her hand, starting at her breast and moving down. Was it so insolent that, for the sake of the life she had conceived, she wanted to look closely at the house Nobutaka's great-grandfather had built? What would he say if he knew? Kanako waited patiently for the faint glimmer of daylight, feeling her resolve gradually strengthen.

Nobutaka stirred and opened his eyes wide. He asked Kanako if she was awake, then reached for the cigarettes near his pillow, lit one, and took a puff.

"You were dreaming, too."

"It's not easy to sleep under a big roof."

Nobutaka said he had dreamed of carrying his sister up to the mezzanine on his back. Having mentioned it to Kanako was probably the reason. A long time ago, he went on, he had read this story. There was a villa on a plateau at which people would gather every summer to have a good time, but eventually it became as neglected and desolate as an abandoned hut. The owner died, the villa was put up for sale, and some workers came to tear it down. On the mezzanine, from which the ladder had been removed, they found a mummified body.

"It was a frightening story. I'd forgotten, but it must have buried itself in my memory. I guess novels can stay with you that way."

Kanako guessed he was haunted by the notion of leaving his sister's mummy up on the mezzanine, and she could not help feeling closer to him than ever before.

"In an old house you can sense ghosts lurking in the shadows of the black beams, in the attic, around the kitchen furnace. I'd like to talk to them if I could."

"You'd be too frightened."

Yet Nobutaka did not think she was lying.

"I'm glad you brought me here. I'll never forget it."

Kanako closed her eyes. Nobutaka felt the cold on his shoulders, shivered, and burrowed under the covers. They were awake, but there was nothing to do. Staying in bed seemed a nice, quiet way to greet the New Year.

They went back to sleep, waking again only after the sun had risen. Kanako got up and began getting dressed. Nobutaka, keeping warm under his quilt, said, "New Year's Day. Shall we go to Lake Biwa later on?" Would it be all right if they ran into someone he knew? Kanako went and opened the hall curtains. Last night they had gone to bed without shutting the heavy storm doors. Sunlight streamed through the window, but when Kanako opened it and took her first look at the old house's garden in the morning light, she caught her breath in surprise. Even though the sky was blue, there were flakes of snow dancing lightly on the wind. It was as if a flock of tiny, white hairstreaks had taken flight.

"It's snowing. It's lovely—come and look."

Her voice brought Nobutaka to the veranda. The small, delicate flakes became a pattern dyed into the surrounding scenery.

"A snow flurry. Come to think of it, you hardly ever see one on a clear day in Tokyo."

The snowflakes dancing in the morning sunlight added a thin, fluttering accent of color to the garden of the old house. Admiring the beauty of the flurry, Kanako took the Ōmi morning into her heart.

Translated by Mark Jewel

O CHONG-HUI

(Korea)

"Chinatown" is a story so poignant it stands on its own as a resounding metaphor of Korean history from 1953 onward. Its author, O Chong-Hui, is one of the outstanding Korean writers of fiction in the twentieth century, and perhaps the country's most important living female writer. She was born in Seoul in 1947, and made her literary debut in 1968, when she won a newspaper literary competition while still a college student. She has since won two of Korea's most prestigious literary awards, the Yi Sang Prize (1979) and the Tongin Prize (1982). Unlike an earlier generation of Korean women writers, who gained recognition in large part because of their gender, O and several of her contemporaries have won praise solely for their literary accomplishments. From a Korean perspective, O's three dozen stories and novellas are marked by profound emotional depth and often (as in "Chinatown") by the innovative use of nameless first-person narrators, who lend a dispassionate yet barely restrained tone and intensity to the narrative. The emergence of Korean women from a rigid Confucian social structure remains slow, and in O's fiction independent-minded women both in and outside the family must contend with the frustration and repression of their aspirations, abandonment, and isolation by society. Focusing on strains and rents in the fabric of modern Korean family life, and on anomalies such as young girls who can only dream of growing up to become prostitutes for the resident GI population, O continues to probe the deepest recesses of the national psyche, and of lives bereft of emotional support in the face of violent dislocation—a condition repeatedly visited upon Korea from without in this century.

Chinatown

Railroad tracks ran west through the heart of the city and ended abruptly near a flour mill at the north end of the harbor. When a coal train jerked to a stop there, the locomotive would recoil as if it were about to drop into the sea, sending coal dust trickling through chinks in the floors of the cars.

There was no lunch waiting for us at home during those winter days short as a deer's tail, so we would throw aside our book bags as soon as school was over and flock past the pier to the flour mill. The straw mats that covered the south yard of the mill were always strewn with wheat drying in the sun. If the custodian was away from the front gate, we would walk in, help ourselves to a handful of wheat, leave a footprint on the corner of the mat, and be on our way. The wheat grains clicked against our teeth, and after the tough husks had steeped in our warm, sweet saliva, the kernels would emerge, sticking like glue everywhere inside our mouths. About the time they became good and chewy we would reach the railroad.

While we waited for the coal train we blew big bubbles with our wheat gum, set up rocks we had gathered from the roadbed and threw pebbles at them, or hunted for nails we had set on the rails the previous day to make magnets.

Eventually the train would appear and rattle to a stop with one last wheeze. We would scurry between the wheels, rake up the coal dust, and then hook our arms through the gaps in the doors and scoop out some of the egg-shaped briquettes. Usually, by the time the carters from the coal yard across the tracks had made their dusty appearance, we had filled our school-slipper pouches with coal—the bigger and faster children used cement bags. Then we would nestle the coal under our arms and hop over the low wire fence on the harbor side of the tracks.

We would push open the door to the snack bar on the pier and swarm to the table in the corner. Depending on the day's plunder, noodle soup, wonton, steamed buns filled with red bean jam, or some such thing would be brought to us. And sometimes the coal was exchanged for baked sweet potatoes, picture cards, or candy. In any event, we knew that coal was like cash—something we could trade for anything around the pier—and so the children in our neighborhood looked like black puppies throughout the year.

Some people called our neighborhood Seashore Village, others called it Chinatown. The coal dust carried by the north wind all winter long covered the area like a shadow, and the sun hung faint in the blackened sky, looking more like the moon.

Grandmother used to scoop ash from our stove, apply it to a fistful of straw, and polish the washbasin to a sparkling sheen before doing Father's dress shirts. But even when the shirts were hung to dry deep inside the canopy away from the dusty wind, they had to be rinsed again and again and starched a second time before they could be worn.

"Damned coal dust! What a place to live!" Grandmother would say, clicking her tongue.

A certain reminiscence would invariably follow. I had heard it so often that I would take over for Grandmother: "Let me tell you about the water from Kwangsŏk Spring. Now this was in the North before the war, you understand. When I used that water, the wash turned out so white it seemed almost blue! Even lye wouldn't get it that white."

When we returned to school after winter vacation our homeroom teacher would take all the Chinatown children to the kitchen next to the night-duty room. There she would have us strip to the waist, assume a pushup position on the floor, and take a merciless dousing with lukewarm water. Then she would check for coal dust behind our ears, on the backs of our necks, between our toes, and under our fingernails. If she gave us an affectionate slap where the gooseflesh had erupted in the small of our backs, we had passed inspection. We would giggle as we slipped on our longjohn tops flecked with dead skin.

Spring arrived, and with it the new school year. I was now a third-grader. My homeroom had classes only in the morning, and early one afternoon I was on my way home with Ch'i-ok. We had our arms around each other's shoulders.

"I'm going to be a hairdresser when I grow up," Ch'i-ok said as we passed a beauty shop at a three-way intersection.

Her voice reminded me of yellow. It had been worm-medicine day at school, and our teacher had made us come to school on an empty stomach. I wasn't sure if it was hunger, the medicine, or the smell of boiling Corsican weed, but everything seemed yellow— the sunlight, the faces of passersby, the blustery breeze that crept under my skirt and made it flutter.

Except for some makeshift stores, both sides of the street were virtually barren. Here and there the skeleton of a bombed-out building stood like a decayed tooth.

"Somebody said it was the biggest theater in town," Ch'i-ok whispered as she pointed out the one remaining wall of a building in ruins. Plastered in white, it resembled a movie screen or the curtain of a stage. But it too would soon be coming down. A row of laborers were taking aim at it with pickaxes, and in a moment the great white wall would roar to the ground.

Other laborers were removing the reusable bricks and reinforcing rods from a wall already demolished.

"The area was bombed to kingdom come," Ch'i-ok said, mimicking the adults and repeating "to kingdom come" over and over.

Diligent as ants, the residents had reclaimed the devastated areas and were rebuilding their houses. Pots of Corsican weed boiled on heaps of coal briquettes in stoves made from oil drums.

Ch'i-ok and I constantly stopped to spit big gobs of saliva.

"Feels like the worms took the medicine and went nuts."

"Uh-uh, I think they're peeing."

Whatever it was they were doing, it didn't make us any the

less nauseated. The froth from the Corsican weed, the smoke from
the coal, and the smell of plaster mixed with the seaweed smell of
the Corsican weed were one big yellow whirl.

"I wonder why they use Corsican weed when they're building
a house," Ch'i-ok said. "One whiff and I get a splitting headache."

The arm looped around my shoulder dropped like a dead weight.
I dawdled along, drinking in the smell of the Corsican weed. That
yellow smell had been my introduction to this city, the very first
understanding I shared with it.

My family had moved here the previous spring from the country
village where we had taken refuge during the recent war.

"If your father could only get a job," Mother used to say while
she was spraying her tidy stacks of tobacco leaves with mouthfuls
of water. She would leave home at dawn, a sack chock-full of the
leaves strapped to her back, and return looking half dead two or
three days later.

"I don't give up easily, but I've had it with this damn tobacco
monopoly. Unless you have a license, you're always getting searched
by the police. If your father could only get a job. . . ."

Father's job hunting consisted of looking up friends and class-
mates from the North who had immigrated to the South or had
somehow managed to flee the war. Finally he got a job in the city
selling kerosene.

The day the moving truck was to come, we ate breakfast at
daybreak and then camped beside the road with our bundled quilts
and our household goods tied up roughly with cord. Lunchtime
came and the truck hadn't arrived. The endlessly repeated farewells
with the neighbors were over.

Toward sundown, while we were plumped listlessly on the
ground, fed up with playing hopscotch and land baron, Mother took
us to one of the local noodle shops and bought us each a bowl of
noodle soup. The two oldest boys and I had changed into clean
clothes before going outside that morning, but by now our runny

noses had left a shiny track down our sleeves and on the backs of our hands.

It was dark now, but Mother, sitting on the bundled quilts with our baby brother in her arms, kept glaring toward the approach to the bridge, waiting for the truck.

Long after sundown the headlights of the truck finally appeared near the bridge. "It's here!" Mother shouted, and we children bounced up from our seats on the bundles. The truck briefly stopped. Mother rushed over, and the driver's assistant stuck his head out the window and shouted something to her over the roar of the engine. Mother returned and the truck left. My brothers and sisters and I looked at each other in bewilderment. The dark outlines towering above the high railing around the back of the truck were cattle. We could tell from the sharply bent horns and the soft, damp sound of their rumination, which flowed through the gloom.

"They'll be back after they unload the cattle. He arranged it that way because we pay half price if we use an empty truck going back to the garage," Mother explained to Grandmother.

Grandmother nodded with a reluctant expression that seemed to say, "I suppose you two know what you're doing." We had never seen her disagree with Mother and Father.

A good two hours passed before the truck reappeared. After delivering the cattle to a slaughterhouse in a city ten miles away, the men had had to clean the muck from the truck bed.

Mother and the baby squeezed between the driver and his assistant after the rest of us and our baggage had been piled in back. As the truck started out, we heard the faraway whistle of the midnight southbound train.

I stuck my head out from the bundles and watched our village recede into the night and blend with the hill behind it and its grove of scrub trees. They all undulated together, no larger than the palm of a hand, a darkness thicker than the sky. Finally they converged into a single dot that bounced up and down in counterpoint with the rear of the truck.

We crossed the township line and soon we were barreling along a bumpy hillside road. Those of us in back, stuck among the bundles like nits, kept bouncing up in the air like wind-up dolls. It was as if the truck had lost its temper at the driver's rough handling. I could see Grandmother fighting to keep from crying out because of the jarring. With each bounce I felt certain we would fall headlong into the river below, so I squeezed my eyes shut and drew my four-year-old brother close.

Though it was spring, the night wind prickled our skin like the tip of a knife. It swept across the river, raked my scaling skin with its sharp nails, and gradually removed the smell of cow dung from the truck bed.

I suddenly recalled the soft, damp sound of the cattle chewing their cud in the darkness. "Do you think all those cows are dead now?" I asked my big sister. But she kept her face buried between her raised knees and didn't answer. Surely the animals had been slaughtered, skinned, gutted, and butchered by now.

The moon kept us company, and after a while my little brother shook his fist at it: "Stupid moon, where you goin'?"

One or another of us always had to urinate, and so the truck stopped frequently. We would knock on the tiny window between the cab and the truck bed, and the driver's assistant would stick his head out the passenger window and shout, "What do you want!"

"We have to go to the bathroom," one of us would say.

With a wave of his hand the man would tell us to go where we were, but then Grandmother would raise a fuss, and the driver would reluctantly stop. The assistant would lift us down one by one and then bark at us to do our business all together. We shuddered in relief as we squatted at the side of the road. It took us a long time to empty our bladders.

Whenever the truck entered a different jurisdiction, which seemed to happen at every bend in the road, there was a checkpoint. A policeman in a military uniform would play his flashlight over the truck. Mother's tobacco peddling had left her with barely enough spunk to lean out the window and yell, "Help yourself, but all you're going to find are a few lousy bundles and some kids."

All night long the truck hurtled across hills and streams and through sleeping towns, and after stopping once for gas, breaking down twice, and going through a checkpoint at every turn in the road, we finally reached the city at daybreak. The streets seemed to perk up at the roar of the truck's old engine.

At the far end of the city we arrived at a neighborhood that seemed to keep the sea barely at arm's length, and here we were lifted down from the truck along with our bundles. After chasing us all night the moon had long since lost its shine and was hanging flat like a disk in the western sky. The truck had stopped in front of a well-worn, two-story wooden house. The first floor had sliding glass doors that opened onto the narrow street like those of a shop. "Kerosene retailer" had been painted in red on the dusty glass.

This was the house where we would live.

The blast of fresh cold air made my teeth chatter. I was supposed to be looking out for my little brother, so I put him on my back.

While the truck had rattled through the city we had craned our necks from among the bundles and gazed out in curiosity and expectation. The city was different from what I had dreamed of in our country village. When I thought of the city we would end up in, I thought of the rainbow-colored soap bubbles that I liked to blow from the end of a homemade straw, or I imagined the Christmas trees from some strange land that I had dreamed of but never seen.

Our street was lined on both sides with identical two-story frame houses that had tiny balconies. The squeaky wheels of bicycles ridden by seafood vendors on their way to the wharf and the footsteps of people going to work at the flour mill filled the shabby, filthy street with a disordered vigor like that of chickens flapping their wings at dawn. The vendors and mill workers squeezed past the truck, which had planted itself in the middle of the street, avoided our carelessly discharged bundles, and headed up the gentle hill that began at our house.

I was lost in confusion. Everything was different from the country village we had just left, but had we really moved? Was this really our new home? It had a dreamlike smell that filled the sky like an evening haze. It was like a once-familiar dream now forgotten, leaving only its sensation. What was that smell?

Father shoved open the door of the kerosene shop and barked at the driver that he hadn't followed the terms of the agreement. The driver shook his fist at Father and pointed back and forth at the rest of us and our belongings. Curious and apprehensive, we could only gape at them.

You could see the bluish marks where the razor had scraped my neck between my gourd-bowl haircut and the yellow rayon quilted jacket that was losing its batting. A little nine-year-old whose skin was flaking all over, I looked around our future neighborhood with a strangely uneasy feeling, my brother still riding on my back.

The neighborhood had awakened at our noisy arrival, and heads with rumpled hair began poking out through windows and doors.

The dozen or so identical frame dwellings that lined each side of the street ended abruptly with our house. The houses that faced each other on the hill above also had two stories but were much larger. Some were white, others were blue-gray like faded ink.

The houses on the hill were spaced apart, except for the first one, which practically touched our house. A broad wall enclosed the lot of that first house. The door and all the windows I could see were too small and tightly shuttered. I wondered if it was a warehouse—no one could have lived there.

With their steeply slanting roofs and the pinched ridgelines that contrasted with their bulk, these Western-style houses looked strange and out of place to me. Perched on the hill that stood alone like a distant island amid the swarm of people on their way to the wharf, the houses had an air of cool contempt. They faced the sea, their orifices shut tight like shells, but they seemed somehow heroic even in their shabbiness, for they left you wondering how old they were and what their history might have been.

The truck started up but didn't leave. The driver hadn't been paid as much as he wanted, and for a moment he rested both arms on the steering wheel and shut his eyes as if he were about to enter a protracted battle.

"What's all this damn commotion so early in the morning? Are the Northerners invading again?"

A blunt, hard voice flew over our heads, ringing in my ears, and knocked out the menacing roar of the engine with a single stroke. Mother and then my brothers and sisters and I looked up to see a young woman on the balcony of the house across the street. Her legs were exposed to the thighs and an army jacket barely covered her shoulders. Her dyed hair swung back and forth across her back as she went inside.

My big brother was running among the wheels of the truck. Father grabbed him by the scruff, hauled him out, and rapped him on the head. Then he took a look at us standing in a bunch. "Well, well, well," he chuckled as if in amazement, "we've got ourselves a platoon here."

Sunlight began to break through the dawn clouds, but still the sleeping houses on the hill kept their shutters tightly closed. The bluish gloom in the sky, driven from here and there throughout the city, gathered ominously above the hill like clouds before a storm.

When the darkness had vanished, the smell I had first noticed began to trickle through the delicate rattan blinds of the night and then rose from everywhere in the streets like a deep breath at last exhaled.

All at once the smell dispelled my confusion and the neighborhood seemed familiar and friendly. I finally understood the true nature of that smell: it was a languid happiness, an image colored by our refugee life in the village we had left the previous night, the memory of my childhood.

Later that year, around the time the dandelions were blooming, I became chronically dizzy and nauseated and had to sit on the shoe-ledge of our house, spitting foamy saliva while my little brother crawled about in the yard putting dirt in his mouth. It seemed Grandmother cooked Corsican weed all spring long. Whenever she forced a bowl of the broth upon me, I would drink it reluctantly, shaking my head in disgust, and then sink into a strange, languid stupor that felt like spring fever. The whole world was yellow, and regardless of the time, I would always ask Grandmother whether it was morning or evening.

"Are the worms stirring, you little stinker?" she would retort with a hearty laugh.

One day, while I sank into the familiar yellow stupor, as if I were walking into a forgotten dream, the two-story houses on the hill suddenly swooped close, one of the shutters opened, and the pale face of a young man appeared.

Mother became pregnant with her seventh child. Only fresh oysters and clams could soothe her queasy stomach, so every morning before school I would take an aluminum bowl and set off over the hill for the pier. I would dash by the firmly shut gates of the houses on the hill, sneaking glances at them out of curiosity and vague anxiety, for these were the houses of the Chinese. When I had run a mere twenty steps down the other side of the hill, the Chinese district suddenly ended at a butcher shop and the pier unfolded before my eyes. I would stop to catch my breath and look back, and about that time the shutters of the shop would clatter open.

I went to this shop every week to buy half a pound of pork. Mother would place some money in my hand and send me on my way, always with the same warning; "If he doesn't give you enough, ask him if it's because you're a child. And ask him to give you only lean meat, not fat."

The butcher was an unmarried Chinese who had a growth the size of a chestnut on his cheek. It looked as if someone had given him a terrific punch. Long hairs trailed from the growth, as if pulled by an unseen hand.

The first time I went to the shop, I found the man stropping his butcher knife.

"Are you only giving me this much because I'm a child?" I

blurted. By standing on tiptoe I was just able to get my chin over the counter as I stuck out the money.

The man turned and looked at me, baffled.

Afraid he would cut the meat before I could finish saying what Mother had told me, I snapped, "She told me to ask for lean."

Stifling a laugh, the butcher quickly sliced the meat for me. "Why only lean? I can give you some hair and skin too."

Next to the butcher shop was a store that sold such things as pepper, brown sugar, and Chinese tea in bulk. It was the only general store in Chinatown. The people from our neighborhood occasionally went to the butcher shop for pork, but didn't shop at the general store. We had no use for dyes and firecrackers, and we didn't need decorative beads for our clothing and shoes.

The store's shutters were opened only on one side, and even on bright, sunny days the interior was dark and gloomy, as if enveloped in dust.

But in the evening the Chinese flocked there, creeping like dusk through interlocking alleys. The women had great thick ears and wore silver earrings. They tottered on bound feet, baskets over their arms, and their heads bobbed, the tight buns looking like cow dung.

While the women shopped, the men sat in the chairs in front of the store and silently smoked their long bamboo pipes before creeping back home. Most of them were elderly.

We children parked ourselves in a row on the narrow, low curb, tapping our feet on the street and pointing at the men.

"They're smoking opium, the dirty addicts."

And in fact the smoke scattering from the pipes was unusually yellow.

Now and then the elderly men gave us a smile.

Our families lived right next to Chinatown, but we children were the only ones who were interested in the Chinese. The grownups referred to them indifferently as "Chinks."

Although we had no direct contact with the Chinese in the two-story houses on the hill, they were the yeast of our infinite imagination and curiosity. Smugglers, opium addicts, coolies who squirreled away gold inside every panel of their ragged quilted clothing, mounted bandits who swept over the frozen earth to the beat of their horses' hoofs, barbarians who sliced up the raw liver of a slaughtered enemy and ate it according to rank, outcaste butchers who made wonton out of human flesh, people whose turds had frozen upright on the northern Manchurian plains before they could even pull up their pants—this was how we thought of them. What was inside the tightly closed shutters of their houses? And what lay deep inside their minds, seldom expressed even after years of friendship? Was it gold? Opium? Suspicion?

"Let's do our homework here," Ch'i-ok said when we arrived at her house. She looked up toward the quilt and the blanket stretched over the side of the second-floor balcony. This was a sign that Maggie was out. If she were in, she would have been in bed, beneath the blanket. I hesitated, glancing across the street at our house. Mother and Grandmother referred to Ch'i-ok's house as a whorehouse for the GIs. Our house was the only one in the neighborhood that didn't rent out a room to a prostitute. These women threw open their doors to the street and thought nothing of letting the American soldiers give them a squeeze. Stained blankets and colorful underwear festooned with lace hung in the sun on the balconies, drying from the free-spirited activities of the previous night.

"Scum!" Grandmother would say, turning away from the sight. To her way of thinking, women's clothes, and especially their underwear, should be hung to dry inside the house.

Ch'i-ok's parents lived downstairs, and Maggie rented the big room upstairs with a darky GI. Ch'i-ok had to go through Maggie's room to get to her own, which was small and narrow like a closet. When I went to get Ch'i-ok for school in the morning I always encountered Maggie lying in bed with her hair disheveled and the huge darky sitting hunched in front of the dresser trimming his mustache with a tiny pair of silvery scissors. Maggie would beckon me in with the slightest motion of her hand, but I always remained outside the half-open door to the room, peeking inside while I waited for Ch'i-ok. The thick flesh of the darky's chest looked like molded rubber and his eyes were smoky. He always mumbled when he spoke, and he never smiled at me. What a gloomy man, I thought.

"Can't you call me from the street?" Ch'i-ok once asked. "The darky doesn't like you going up there."

But every morning I walked up the creaky stairs and called to Ch'i-ok while hovering outside Maggie's room.

"Maggie said she won't be back until tonight. So we can play on her bed," Ch'i-ok cajoled me.

I thought for a moment: Mother had a bad case of morning sickness and was probably lying in the family room, looking vexed at everything. My older brother had likely gone outside to catch mole crickets. And I knew that as soon as I walked in, Grandmother would tell me to piggyback my baby brother, who had just been weaned, and then shoo us out of the house.

And so I followed Ch'i-ok upstairs. Jennie, Maggie's daughter, was asleep on the bed. Curtains kept the sun out, making the room dim.

Ch'i-ok opened the storage cabinet, located a box of cookies, took two of them, and carefully replaced the box. The cookies were sweet and smelled faintly like toothpaste.

"That's so pretty," I said, pointing to a bottle of perfume on the dresser.

Ch'i-ok turned it upside down and pretended to gently spray her armpits with it. "Made in America." Again Ch'i-ok reached inside the cabinet and rustled around. This time she produced two candies.

"It tastes so good," I said.

"Mmm, because it's made in America," Ch'i-ok answered in the same blasé tone.

Jennie was now wide awake and watching us.

"Jennie, aren't you pretty? Now we have to do our homework, so why don't you go back to sleep for a little while?" Ch'i-ok spoke softly, brushing Jennie's eyelids down with her palm, and in an instant the little girl's eyes had closed tightly like those of a doll.

Everything in Maggie's room seemed marvelous. Ch'i-ok let me feel each of the things for just a moment, and every time I exclaimed joyfully as I caressed it. Then we replaced each item, leaving no sign that it had been touched.

"I have an idea."

Ch'i-ok reached inside a cabinet at the head of the bed and took out a gourd-shaped bottle half full of a green liquid. After making a line with her fingernail on the side of the bottle to mark the level of the liquid, she opened the bottle, poured a small amount into the cap and handed it to me.

"Try it. It's sweet—tastes like menthol."

I quickly drank it and returned the cap to Ch'i-ok. She filled it and then gulped it down. The level of the liquid was now about two fingers below the mark, so Ch'i-ok made up the difference with water, capped the bottle, and returned it to the cabinet.

"Perfect! How was it? Tasty, huh?"

The inside of my mouth was refreshingly warm, as if I had a mouthful of peppermint.

"Now don't tell anyone," Ch'i-ok said as she removed a velvet box from among some clothes in one of the dresser drawers.

Everything in Maggie's room was a secret. The box contained a pearl necklace long enough to make three strands, a brooch adorned with garishly colored glass beads, some earrings and other jewelry. Ch'i-ok tried on a necklace made of thick glass beads and studied herself in the mirror.

"I'm going to be a GI's whore when I grow up," she said decisively. "Maggie said she'll give me necklaces, shoes, clothing—everything."

I felt as if I were dissolving and the tips of my fingers and toes had gone to sleep. I was short of breath and couldn't keep my eyes open. Was it the darkness of the room? I imagined that the peppermint was leaving a white trail every time I breathed out. I drew aside the curtain covering the door to the balcony. Seething yellow sunlight entered the room, illuminating the dust and making the room look like a greenhouse. I touched my burning cheek to the doorknob and peered outside. Once again I saw the two-story house in Chinatown with the open shutters and the face of the young man looking my way. A mysterious sadness, an ineffable pathos began undulating in my chest and then spread over me.

"What's the matter? Are you dizzy?" asked Ch'i-ok, who knew what the green liquid was and how it affected you. She snuggled up beside me against the door to the balcony.

I shook my head, unable to understand, much less explain the feeling I got from that face in the second-floor window, and at that instant the wooden shutter thumped shut and the young man disappeared.

The glass beads of Ch'i-ok's necklace clicked together, their colors dancing in the sunlight. Ch'i-ok took one of the beads in her lips. "I'll be a GI's whore."

I drew the curtain and lay down on the bed. Who could he be? I tried fretfully to revive my memories of a forgotten dream. I knew I had seen him the previous autumn at the barber's. I had had to sit on a plank placed across the chair because I was so short. I had instructed the barber as Mother had told me:

"Please make it short and layered on the sides and back, but leave the top long. I'm ugly enough already, so a gourd-bowl haircut won't do."

But when the barber had finished, I looked in the mirror to find I still had a gourd bowl.

"Too late to complain now. I'll do better next time—promise."

"I knew this would happen! Why can't you concentrate on cutting hair instead of gabbing with everybody?"

The barber jerked the plank away from under me. "What a smart-alecky little girl. That's no way to talk. I'll bet that yap of yours was the first thing that came out when you were born."

"Don't you worry about how I should talk. And I'll bet you're a hair chopper because you came out with scissors around your wrist."

The other customers roared with laughter. I looked around with a triumphant air. The only ones who weren't laughing were the barber and a young man sitting in the corner with a bib around his neck. The young man was studying me in the mirror. He's

Chinese, I suddenly thought. Although I had seen him only at an angle from across the street, never close up, his inscrutable gaze had given me that impression. I removed the towel around my neck and tossed it in front of the mirror. Then I stamped to the doorway, put my hands on my hips, and turned back: "Until the day you die you'll be nothing but a hair chopper!" And then I ran home.

Father was constantly at work on our house, as if to compensate for the privations of our refugee life in the country village—the entire family crowded into a single rented room, and before that the many sleepless nights he had spent keeping the children warm in his arms under a bridge or inside a tent. He got rid of our tiny yard, adding a room and a veranda to the house in the way that girls who have just learned how to sew might add secret pockets to the inside of a book bag or the underside of their clothing. And so a mazelike hallway appeared in the house, long and narrow like an ant tunnel.

Along with the hallway there materialized a place where I could hide and no one would find me—the back room next to the toilet, which was filled with old clothing, household stuff, and other odds and ends. The day of the ill-fated haircut, I ran inside the house, sneaked into this room, and pressed my face against the narrow mouth of a jar, hoping in vain that the sorrow sweeping over my bones like a strong current would empty into it.

Several times after that, usually when I was hunkered down in front of Father's shop waiting for the evening newspaper, I sensed that the young Chinese man had opened his window and was looking toward me.

"Jennie. Time to get up, Jennie—your mom's here," Ch'i-ok said in a affectedly sweet and gentle tone. Jennie opened her eyes and sat up. Ch'i-ok went downstairs and returned with a washbasin full of water. Jennie didn't cry even when the soapy water got in her eyes. We combed her hair, sprayed some perfume on her, and changed her into some clothes we had found in the closet. Jennie's father was white and her mother Korean, and at the age of five she still hadn't begun to talk. She couldn't feed herself, much less put on her own clothes, and when she was fed, the food would trickle out the side of her mouth. Whenever the darky was there, Jennie would be moved to Ch'i-ok's room.

Grandmother occasionally saw Jennie on the balcony or outside the house. "Whelp!" she would say, looking at the girl as if in amazement, her eyes filled with the hatred she reserved for fur-bearing animals. She frightened me whenever she stared at Jennie like that. Some time ago our house had become infested with rats, and so we had gotten a cat. The cat bore a litter of seven kittens in the back room, and Grandmother fed it seaweed soup to help it recover. Then she stared right into the cat's eyes and repeated several times, like a refrain, "Kitty had some baby rats, seven baby rats." That evening the cat ate all seven kittens, leaving only the heads. Then it yowled all night long, not bothering to clean its bloodstained mouth. As if she had been expecting this, Grandmother wrapped the seven tiny heads in newspaper and sent them down the sewer drain.

Mother used to tell me that Grandmother was so fastidious and cold because she had never had children of her own. She was actually Mother's stepmother. I had once overheard Mother whispering about Grandmother to an elderly woman who was a distant relative: "They'd been married only three months when her husband had an affair with his sister-in-law—can you believe it? That's why they separated and she decided to come live with us."

Jennie was like a doll to Ch'i-ok. Ch'i-ok could give her a bath and change her clothes every half hour, and never get a scolding from Maggie. To Ch'i-ok, Jennie was sometimes a baby, sometimes a sick little girl, sometimes an angel. I envied Ch'i-ok with all my heart, and it must have shown on my face.

"Don't you have a sister too?" Ch'i-ok asked me dubiously.

"She's my stepsister."

"You mean that's not your real mother?"

"My stepmother," I lied with a lump in my throat.

Tears gathered in her eyes. "Well, well. Somehow I had a hunch. Don't tell anyone, but I have a stepmother too."

There wasn't a soul in our neighborhood who didn't know this.

I linked my little finger with Ch'i-ok's and we promised to keep each other's secret.

"So, does your mom spank you and tell you to get lost and drop dead?" I asked.

"Yeah, when no one's around." Ch'i-ok lowered her pants and showed me her bruised thighs. "I'm going to run away and be a GI's whore."

How often I wished I really were a stepdaughter, so I could run away whenever I pleased.

Mother was still carrying baby number seven. None of us children in this poor district next to Chinatown believed that babies were brought to earth in the arms of an angel in the middle of the night. And they didn't emerge smiling brightly from their mother's belly button. Everyone knew a baby came out screaming from between the naked legs of a woman.

We were watching some GIs in T-shirts take target practice with knives on one of the tennis courts at the army base. The knives sliced through the air toward the concentric circles on the target. They had a piercing glint, like silver needles, a flash of light, a man's prematurely white hair. Whenever a knife whistled to the black spot dead in the center of the target, the men howled like animals and we gulped in terror.

A white GI had been taking a step back every time he hit the center of the target. He took aim once again, but as the knife was about to spring from his hand, he suddenly pivoted. The knife ripped through the air toward us. We flattened ourselves with a shriek in front of the wire fence surrounding the base. I felt a warm wetness between my legs. A moment later we lifted our pallid faces. The chuckling GI was pointing at something a short distance behind us. We turned and looked. A black cat lay rigid on its back with its legs in the air, the knife stuck in its chest. The cat was as big as a small dog. It was probably one of the strays that were always getting into the garbage cans on the base. Its pointed whiskers were still trembling as we crowded around it. Suddenly my big brother picked up the cat and ran off. The rest of us set out after him. My wet underpants chafed.

Brother stopped, panting, when we were out of sight of the Americans' barracks. Then he looked down at what he was holding. He shuddered and dropped the cat, which fell to the ground with a thud.

"How come you brought that thing?" one of the children demanded.

Thus challenged, my Little Napoleon of a brother pulled the knife from the cat's chest and wiped the blade on the grass. It was sharp and pointed like an awl. He folded the blade with a snap and put the knife in his pocket.

"Go get me a stick," he said.

One of us snapped off a branch from a tree we had planted the previous spring on Arbor Day and returned with it.

Brother took off his belt and looped it around the cat's neck, then tied the end to the branch. We paraded down the street with the cat splayed out behind him. The cat's paws dragged along the ground, and its weight bent the branch on Brother's shoulder like a bow.

By the time we reached Chinatown the long summer day had begun to wane. As the sun slanted toward the horizon the cat's shadow seemed to grow endlessly from its midsection.

The flour mill workers walked past us on their way down the hill, their hair frosted with flour, their empty lunchboxes rattling.

We walked toward the wharf, treading on each other's gigantic, frightening shadows and the shadow of the long, black carcass of the cat. And then I saw him again. The second-floor shutters were open, and he was watching our procession. I couldn't fathom his gaze, but I thought I saw sorrow, anger, and perhaps a subtle smile.

When we reached the wharf Brother put the branch down and removed the belt from the cat's neck. Spitting in disgust, he cinched the belt around the waist of his pants, which constantly threatened to fall down. Then he dropped the cat into a mass of garbage, empty bottles, and rotting, white-bellied fish washing up against the bank.

As we often did when the sun was going down, we decided to go to the park. There we would usually lie on our stomachs on the endless expanse of steps and look up the hoop skirts of the GIs' whores, exclaiming at the bare legs inside the bloated framework of whale tendon. Or we would loll on the grass and bellow one of the old standards that an aging prostitute might sing to herself:

When I look back, I see every step of my youth stained with tears,
When I look back at my regrettable past, I hear the bells of Santa Maria.

But this time we walked up silently, one step at a time, toward the sky.

At the highest point in the park stood a bronze statue of the old general whose landing operation here just a few years before was already inscribed in legend. From this spot the entire city could be seen.

Boats and ships were moored at the pier, their flags fluttering like confetti. The jaws of a crane bit into their cargo again and again. At a distance from the pier floated something that looked like an islet or a huge old carp—probably a foreign freighter.

The bell from the Catholic church behind us kept tolling. It was the sound that had been tugging at us ever since—no, even before—we had thrown the cat into the water. Producing endless ripples at precise intervals, confined to a single tone, simplifying every desire and temperament into one basic harmony, the sound of the bell evoked in my mind the awesomeness of a peal of thunder heard on a summer evening upon being awakened from a dream, the mystery of train wheels rumbling through the deep of the night.

"A nun must have died," said one of the others.

We all thought that a nun was dying peacefully whenever the bell tolled on and on like this.

Across the railroad tracks a black stream spewed from the smokestack of the flour mill, surging into the sky above the war-ravaged city like dust rising from a battlefield.

The intense bombardment from the warships during the landing operation would long be remembered in the history of warfare, the grown-ups liked to say. About the only structures to have remained intact were the old frame houses in our neighborhood, which had been seized from the Japanese at the end of World War II, and the two-story houses on the hill in Chinatown.

The sunlight lingered in the western part of the city, but Chinatown was being saturated with darkness, as if the smoke were smothering it. Perhaps it was the dust carried by the north wind from the coal yard, settling there like ash.

Here at the highest point of the city we had a commanding view of Chinatown and the colored blankets and lace underwear on the balconies of the sooty houses seized from the Japanese. These were the scenes, the underside, the mysterious smile of this city. Part of me would always be weighed down by these images. To me, Chinatown and my neighborhood were the flooded stern of a listing ship about to sink.

Torches, lit too early in the evening, flared at the public playfield in the eastern part of the city. The flames swayed as if they were flickering remnants of the wind in the last traces of the sunlight. A crowd of people cried out, "Czechoslovakia go home! Poland go home! Puppet regimes go home!" All summer long, one member from each household would report to the playfield as soon as the sun had vanished, and the throng would shout these slogans while stamping their feet. Grandmother would return from these rallies and groan all night long from the pain in her lower back.

One day at morning assembly our principal had explained why the people were protesting: Czechoslovakia and Poland, satellites of the Soviet Union, had forsworn their obligations as members of the neutral-nations peacekeeping force by digging for U.N. military secrets to pass on to the communist side.

If I buried my head between my knees, the outcry from the playfield would become a distant hum, like the sound made when I blew across the narrow mouth of an empty bottle. It was the sound of the earth groaning deep below the surface, a faint ripple foreshadowing a tidal wave, a lingering breeze licking the roofs of houses.

At home I found Mother retching beside the drain in the yard.

For the first time I empathized with the brutish life that women must live. There was something pathetic and harrowing about Mother's retching, and this symptom of her pregnancy made me plead silently with her to produce no more brothers and sisters for me. I was afraid she would die if she gave birth again.

I couldn't get to sleep until well into the night. My older sister had bound her emerging breasts with a waistband that Grandmother had torn from a skirt. The breasts were sensitive even to the touch of her sheet, so she tossed and turned, embracing them tightly and moaning. As I lay awake, I counted each time the night guards tapped their sticks together to signal their approach, and I tried to count the number of wheels of the freight trains that passed by. At daybreak I went to the wharf. The dead cat was nowhere to be seen among the garbage and rotting fish washing up against the bank, nor was it beneath an abandoned boat I spotted drifting a short distance offshore. Perhaps some children in a distant port were dragging its shapeless body around at the end of a pole.

Autumn drew near, but the bedbugs flourished as never before. When the sun shone full on the balcony, we would take the tatamis outside to dry and scour the wooden floors of our rooms for the eggs. Though our pajamas had elastic cuffs, the bedbugs would manage to crawl inside, making us itch and producing the smell of raw beans. The electricity stayed on until midnight, and so we usually went to sleep with the lights on because they kept the bugs away. But when the lights went out at twelve the bugs would swarm from the straw of the tatami or from cracks in the floor and launch their all-out attack.

One night, while I was half asleep and scratching away at the bugs, I was awakened by a thunk—it sounded like a block of wood being split. Before I knew it my older brother had thrown on his pants and was down the stairs like a bullet. The sudden hubbub from the street told me something had happened. My heart quickened, and I went out on the balcony. The electricity had been off for some time, and it was pitch dark outside, but I could make out the noisy crowd that had filled the street between our house and Ch'i-ok's. The neighbors' sliding glass doors scraped open, and peo-

ple appeared on the balconies above, shouting for news. Among the
hum of voices the word "dead" came to my ears like a revelation.
The word passed from mouth to mouth like a round. Some people
reacted by shuddering in disgust, others poked their heads through
the layers of onlookers. My chin trembled as I looked across the
street and saw that the door to Maggie's room was open. The darky,
dressed in an undershirt, looked down on the street from the balcony, his hands resting on the railing.

A moment later I heard the wail of a siren and saw an American
army jeep. In an instant the crowd had separated. Maggie lay in
the street, drenched in the brightness of the jeep's headlights. Her
long, thick hair covered her face and was strewn every which way,
like solar flares. "He threw her into the street," somebody said.

The darky was drunk. The MPs dressed him in his uniform,
and as they loaded him into the jeep, his shirt unbuttoned, he
chuckled.

The next day I found Ch'i-ok feeding water to Jennie, who
had the hiccups. She patiently wiped the moisture that trickled
from the corner of the little girl's mouth. But no amount of water
would make the hiccups stop.

"They'll put her in an orphanage," Ch'i-ok said. She sounded
a bit sulky, as she had the day she told me that Maggie would go
to America in the spring—the darky had decided to marry her.

Maggie had looked happy then. Once I had found her washing
the darky's feet as he sat on the edge of the bed. Her dyed hair
was piled high on her head, and as I stared at the clean nape of
her neck she turned to me. Without makeup she seemed to have
no eyebrows. She gently beckoned to me, saying, "It's okay. Come
on in."

"Jennie went to the Catholic orphanage," Ch'i-ok told me with
a fierce scowl two days later. Her eyes were red and puffy. A younger
sister of Maggie's had come to pack up the dead woman's belongings.
Maggie's room remained empty for quite some time. But I didn't
go up there to do homework or to play with Ch'i-ok anymore. Instead
I called to her from the street on my way to school every morning.

I became more and more convinced that Mother wouldn't survive another birth, but her stomach continued to swell almost imperceptibly beneath her skirt. As it turned out, the one who failed was Grandmother, whose stinging hands and pungent, vicious curses had seemed to make her healthier by the day. One morning she collapsed while doing the laundry, and she never recovered. My baby brother, who had practically lived on her back, became my big sister's responsibility.

After Grandmother began needing a bedpan, Mother and Father agreed to move her to the countryside, where Grandfather lived.

"A stroke can last twenty years," Mother whispered to Father. "It can melt a rock." And in a slightly louder voice, "When you're old, there's only one place to be, and that's next to your husband, whether you love him or hate him." Finally, in a loud tone, "We'd better reserve a taxi for her."

Grandmother became like a baby. As Ch'i-ok had done with Jennie, I would go into Grandmother's room when no one else was home and comb her hair, feed water to her, and sometimes gently feel to see if her diaper was wet.

The day Grandmother was to leave, Mother dressed her in clean clothes. "She still has her figure because she never had children."

Father went with Grandmother to the village where Grandfather lived with Grandmother's younger sister and their children. "I don't feel right about it," Father said falteringly when he returned. He sighed. "I don't think they'll be happy with her. She'll be a thorn in their side. You know, it's amazing—I thought she wouldn't recognize anyone, but then she spread her jacket, took Father's hand, and placed it on her chest. She must have been so frustrated. Makes me wonder what it means to be man and wife."

"There was a lifetime of bitterness inside that woman," said Mother. "But didn't I tell you? We did the right thing sending her there."

Mother decided to open Grandmother's clothing chest. Grandmother had never let anyone else in the family touch it, and so we craned our necks to follow the movement of Mother's hands. One by one she removed the neatly folded articles of clothing piled inside and placed them on the floor. Out came Father's old long underwear, which Grandmother had hemmed for her own use, and the Japanese-style baggy pants that she had worn around the house. And there were clothes made from fabrics woven in traditional ways, such as sheer silk and rough, thick, glossy silk. As Mother's outstretched hands continued to produce clothing that Grandmother had worn but once or twice in her life, I realized that she wouldn't be coming back, that the days she would wear such clothes were gone, and I felt as if a chill wind had swept through the depths of my heart. When had she worn such clothes? And for what special occasion had she saved them deep in the chest?

The last article of clothing was an otter vest. Mother then groped along the bottom of the chest and took out something small wrapped tightly in a handkerchief. With bated breath we fixed our eyes on Mother's nimble fingers.

With a quizzical expression Mother looked inside the handkerchief. A jade ring broken in two, a tarnished copper belt buckle that seemed about to crumble, a few nickel coins from the Japanese occupation, several buttons of various sizes that might once have been attached to clothing, some pieces of colored thread—these and other things she found there.

"Really, Mother! Saving broken jade is like saving bits of pottery." Clicking her tongue, Mother rewrapped the objects in the handkerchief and tossed them into the empty chest. She set aside the long underwear and other underclothing to use as rags, and moved the rest of the clothing to her own chest. The otter fur was of high quality, she said—she would use it as a muffler.

The next day I sneaked into Grandmother's chest and took out the bundled-up handkerchief. Then I went to the park and walked sixty-five paces from the statue of the general to some trees—one step for each year Grandmother had lived. I found myself beside an alder—the fifth one into the grove—and I buried the bundle deep beneath it.

Toward the end of winter word arrived that Grandmother had died. It had been just the previous summer that she had left in the taxi. Mother, who was in her ninth month, did something uncharacteristic: she began crying while caressing Grandmother's clothing chest, now stuffed topsy-turvy with the children's threadbare clothing.

All evening I hid among the odds and ends in the back room, where no one could find me, and when everyone had gone to bed I went to the park. The sky was black, but I found the fifth alder tree without even having to take the sixty-five steps.

The damp handkerchief, buried for two seasons deep in the ground, stuck to my palm like rotten straw. I brushed the dirt off the pieces of the ring, the tarnished belt buckle, and the coins and held them tenderly in my hand. They felt exactly the same as before. They were warm now, but the cold would soon return to them.

I returned the objects to their burial place beneath the tree. After I had tramped the dirt down and brushed off my hands, I started walking toward the statue, concentrating on taking even steps. At the count of sixty I was there. I began to wonder. Surely it had been sixty-five steps the previous summer. Did this mean I would reach the tree in fifty paces the following summer? And a year later, or ten years later, would one giant step take me there?

Since it was still winter and late at night, I could climb up on the statue without any disapproving looks from others. And so I clawed my way onto the pedestal, then climbed onto the binoculars that the general held against his stomach. From there I looked down on the city sparsely dotted with lights. The outcries of the previous summer, swelling like dust from a battlefield, were gone. Now it was still. As I strained to listen to the sounds flowing gently in the darkness, I felt as if I were tapping an undiscovered vein of water in the deepest part of the earth.

The sea was a black plane. I drank in the wind that had been blowing all night from the East China Sea, and the seaweed smell it carried. I saw the oblong light framed by the open shutter of the two-story house on the Chinatown hill, and imagined a pale face revealed there. I felt the soft breath of spring hiding in the chilly air.

Something was budding in my warm blood, something unbearably ticklish.

"Life is . . .," I murmured. But I couldn't find the right word. Could it be found, a single word for today and yesterday, with their jumble of indistinguishable, all too complicated colors, a word to embrace all the tomorrows?

Another spring arrived and I became a sixth-grader. My older brother was raising a puppy he had brought home one day. With Grandmother gone, the dog had the run of the house, pooping and shedding anywhere it pleased.

I had grown the better part of a foot in the past twelve months, and since the previous year I'd been carrying around my older sister's oxford-cloth school bag embroidered with roses.

All winter long my rat pack and I had sneaked coal from the freight trains, and as always we had run wild through the streets. Occasionally I had closeted myself in the back room at home to read popular romances and such.

One Saturday—the day we had no afternoon classes—I was on my way home from school. "Tomorrow's worm-medicine day, so be sure to skip breakfast," our teacher had reminded us the day before. "The worms won't take the medicine on a full belly."

There was much less house rebuilding now, but Corsican weed was still being boiled and the smell still seemed to dye the air yellow.

In the simmering yellow sunlight I frequently stopped to spit. "Feels like the worms are going nuts," I muttered once again.

I saw Ch'i-ok mixing permanent-wave solution in a can in the beauty shop at the three-way intersection. Her father had lost a leg in a conveyor belt at the flour mill and had left the area with his wife the previous winter. Ch'i-ok had remained with the people who ran the beauty shop. Every day I passed by the place on my way to and from school and saw her through the glass door. She would be sweeping the hair on the floor while pulling down her small sweater, which was constantly riding up her back and revealing her bare waist.

I walked past the beauty shop. The yellow sunlight filling the street looked like thousands of feathers soaring up in the air. When was it? Shaking my head in irritation I tried to revive a distant, barely remembered dream. When was it? I continued toward home, and when I arrived I looked at the open window of the two-story house on the hill. He was leaning partway out the window, beckoning me.

I started up the hill, drawn as if by a magnet, and he disappeared from the window. A moment later he heaved open the gate to the house and emerged. His yellow, flat-nosed face still wore that mysterious smile.

He offered me something wrapped in paper. When I accepted it, he turned and went inside. Through the open gate I could see the narrow, shaded front walk, the unexpected sight of a sunny yard, and the sunlight dancing and darting on the limpid skin of his feet with every step he took.

At home I went into the back room, locked the door, and opened the package. Inside was some bread dyed in three colors, which the Chinese ate on their holidays, and a thumb-size lantern decorated with a plastic dragon.

I hid these things in a cracked jar that no one used. Mother was in labor in my parents' room, but instead of looking in on her I went upstairs. I sneaked into a storage cabinet, as I did when playing hide-and-seek. It was midday, but not a ray of light entered. While listening to Mother scream that she wanted to die, I realized that the church bell had been tolling and I fell into a sleep that was like death itself.

When I awoke, Mother had pushed her seventh child into the world after a terrible labor. A sense of helplessness and despair came over me in the darkness of the cabinet, and I called out to her. Then I felt inside my underwear, and finally I understood the humid fever that had been closing about me like a spider web.

My first menstrual flow had begun.

Translated by Bruce and Ju-Chan Fulton

BEI DAO

(China)

Bei Dao ("North Island") is the pen name of Zhao Zhenkai, one of contemporary Chinese literature's most cogent, unsparing writers. Born in Beijing in 1949, Bei Dao attended the city's Fourth Middle School, then considered China's finest preparatory school. When his studies were derailed by the Cultural Revolution, he joined the Red Guard movement for a time but left in disillusionment. Allowed the rare privilege of travel in 1970, he visited several coastal and central areas of China. Bei Dao's writing began during this period and was first published in 1972. He took part in the historic Tiananmen Incident of 1976 and within two years became a key figure in China's fledgling Democracy Movement as the coeditor of an influential but short-lived "wall poster" magazine, Today. *His work there made him a national literary figure; however, his reputation was justly consolidated through both his poetry and his fiction. The poetry—known as "shadow poetry"—was notable for its abstract quality. Younger readers, however, recognized this ambiguity as a mask, as a defiant symbol. Bei Dao's poetry drew the predictable ire of China's sinecured literary hacks who contended that its highly personal nature ignored the officially cherished dictate that art and literature serve the interests of the state. Politically contentious though it may be, Bei Dao's vision—poetic or fictional—needs no decoder ring, as "13 Happiness Street" affirms. Its Kafkaesque nature is rooted in the ghastly bureaucratic stranglehold on everyday Chinese life.* Waves, *a collection of Bei Dao's short fiction, was published in 1987. He currently lives in exile in Stockholm.*

13 Happiness Street

I

A late autumn morning. The street was bleak and desolate. A gust of wind rustled the withered yellow leaves on the pavement. The dreary, monotonous cry of an old woman selling ices could be heard in the distance. Fang Cheng pulled his old black woolen coat tightly around himself and kicked a stone on the ground. It wedged itself in the iron grate in the gutter with a clunk. The call from his sister just now had been really too fantastic: young Jun had been flying his kite in this street yesterday afternoon, yes, this same bloody street, when all of a sudden, he had disappeared without a trace, in broad daylight! His sister's sobs, followed by the beep signaling the line was disconnected, had upset him so much that his head was still ringing. Sun, the section head, was sitting opposite him at the time and had given him an inquisitive glance, so he had put down the receiver and done his utmost to look normal.

Across the road, a row of locust trees had been sawn down to the roots, the trunks lying across the pavement. A yellow Japanese forklift was parked by the side of the road. Four or five workmen were busy attaching hooks to the sawn-off trees and loading them onto a large truck to the tooting of a whistle.

Fang Cheng approached the old woman selling ices. "Such fine locust trees, how come . . ."

"Ices, three cents and five cents." The shriveled mouth snapped shut.

"Comrade . . ."

The old woman's strident voice robbed him of the courage to repeat his question. He crossed the road to the truck. A young fellow who looked like the driver was leaning against the front mudguard smoking.

"Excuse me, what's going on here?"

"Don't you have eyes in your head?"

"I mean, what are you sawing the trees down for?"

"Who do you think you are, going around poking your nose into everything? Are you building a house, and you want us to leave you a log for the roof beam? I'll tell you straight, I can't even get one for myself." Flicking away his cigarette butt, the driver turned around and climbed into the cab, slamming the door behind him.

Fang Cheng bit his lip. A middle-aged woman carrying a string bag was walking past. He caught up with her. "Excuse me, where did you get those turnips?"

"At the greengrocer's over the way."

"Oh." He smiled politely and walked with her for a few steps. "How come these trees have been cut down? Such a shame."

"Who knows? I heard that yesterday a kite got caught in the trees and some young rascal climbed up to get it. . . ." She suddenly fell silent and hurried off nervously.

A long shadow slipped across the ground.

Fang Cheng swung around. A man wearing a leather jacket pulled a green army cap over his eyes, gave him a swift glance, and walked past.

It was only then that Fang Cheng noticed the high outside wall exposed behind the stumps of the felled locust trees. The plaster was so old that it had peeled off in places, showing the large solid brick underneath. He took a deep breath, inhaling petrol fumes mixed with the sweet scent of locust wood, and walked back along the wall. Before long he came upon a recess in the wall enclosing a gateway guarded by two stone lions. The red paint on the door had faded and was covered with a layer of dust, as if it hadn't been opened for a long time. On it was a very ordinary plaque with the words "13 Happiness Street," and beneath it a cream-colored buzzer. Fang Cheng went to press it, but it wouldn't budge. On close inspection he realized it was molded from a single piece of plastic and was purely decorative. He stood there bewildered.

As he drew back a few paces, trying to get a clearer view of the whole gate, he bumped into an old man who happened to be passing by.

"Sorry. Excuse me, who lives here?"

He stopped short. The terror that welled up from the depths of the old man's eyes made Fang Cheng's legs go weak. The old man stumbled away, his walking stick beating an urgent and irregular rhythm as he disappeared into the distance.

A young boy walked by, absorbed in whittling a branch from one of the locust trees with a penknife.

"Hey, where's the neighborhood committee office, young man?"

"Turn at the lane over there." The boy sniffled, pointing with the branch.

The narrow lane twisted its way through the shoddy makeshift houses. From time to time Fang Cheng had to walk sideways in order to prevent the boards and exposed nails from catching and tearing his overcoat. At the entrance to what looked like a rather spacious courtyard at the far end of the lane two signboards were hanging side by side: Neighborhood Committee and Red Medical Station. Both were covered with the muddy fingerprints of children.

He pushed open the door of the room on the north side of the courtyard and stuck his head inside.

"Did you bring the certificate?" asked a girl busy knitting a jumper.

"What certificate?"

"The death certificate!" she said impatiently.

Everything in the room was white: the sheet, the folding screen, the table, the chairs, and also the girl's lab coat and pallid face. Fang Cheng shivered. "No, no, I've . . ."

"Listen, if we don't sign it nobody's going to let you hold the funeral service!"

"I'm looking for someone."

"Looking for someone?" She looked up in surprise, lifting her hair back with one of her knitting needles. "Don't you know what is proper?"

"But this is . . ."

"The Red Medical Station."

Retreating into the yard, Fang Cheng noticed a dense crowd of people in the room to the south. He walked over and knocked on the door.

"Come in," a voice said.

Inside about a dozen people were seated around a long wooden table, all staring at him in silence. The light inside the room was so dim that he couldn't make out their faces, but judging from their heavy, bronchial wheezing, most of them were old women.

"Has it been signed?" The question came from a woman at the far end of the table. From her voice she seemed pretty young; she'd be the chairwoman or something.

"No, I . . ."

"Then they're still alive and breathing," she broke in sharply.

A howl of laughter. One fat old woman laughed so much she started gagging, and someone thumped her on the back.

"I'm a reporter," Fang Cheng explained hastily.

Instantly the room fell deathly silent. They gazed stupidly at each other, as if they were not too sure what he meant.

The chairwoman was the first to break the silence. "Your papers."

Fang Cheng had barely taken out his press card when it was snatched away by the person near the door. The card in its red plastic cover was handed around the table for everyone to look at and comment on. As it passed from hand to hand, some of them shook their heads while others spat on their fingers and rubbed it. Finally, it reached the chairwoman. Gripping the card, she studied it carefully, then got the old man in glasses beside her to read it aloud. At last she gave a nod.

"Hm. Have you come to take photos?"

A buzz of excited confusion filled the room. Dull eyes flashed, people nudged and tugged at each other, and one old woman who had fallen asleep propped against the table actually woke up. It was as if something that they had been waiting a lifetime for was finally about to happen.

"You can take our picture now, we're in the middle of our

political study," the chairwoman said haughtily. "Sit up everyone, and don't look into the camera!"

They all sat up straight, and there was a loud rustle as they picked up the newspapers on the table.

"Hold on, I haven't brought my camera. . . . I'm here on another matter. I'm trying to find out who lives at Number 13 Happiness Street."

"How come you never breathed a word of this earlier?" said the chairwoman, obviously quite put out.

"You didn't give me a chance. . . ."

"All right then, what do you want to know?"

"It's about Number 13 Happiness Street. . . ."

"Someone alive and kicking? That's none of our business. On your way then, and next time don't start gabbling away at us again, these old bones can't take all the excitement."

"Whose business is it?"

"Quiet! Let's get on with our meeting. Now, where were we? Oh yes, this case involving Dumb Chen from over in the Fourth Xiangyang Courtyard. He'll live on in our hearts forever and all that, but people have started asking why he's still being issued with a face mask every winter. . . ."

"Maybe his corpse is still breathing."

"We'll issue you with a caldron to lie in when it's your turn to go to heaven, so you won't have to straighten that hunchback of yours. . . ." A strange rasping sound came from the corner.

They started to quarrel, their voices getting louder and louder. Fang Cheng took advantage of the confusion to slip out. When he reached the gate he breathed a long sigh of relief, feeling that he had actually almost died himself.

He took a wrong turn. The buildings inside another compound were being pulled down, and clouds of dust filled the air. A crowd of children pressed around the entrance, peering inside. In the yard the workmen were chanting as they swung a wooden pole against the gable of the house to the east. A structure like a well was under construction in the middle of a stretch of rubble.

"What is this place?" Fang Cheng asked the children.

"The local housing authority," a young girl replied timidly.

Stepping over a pile of lime, Fang Cheng ran into a young fellow carrying a bucket of cement. "I'm a reporter, where is your foreman?"

"Hey, Wang. . . ."

A head popped out from a scaffold. "What is it?"

"The newspaper again."

Wang leapt down nimbly and put down his trowel, wiping his forehead and muscular neck with his sleeve. "Well, you lot are on the ball all right, it's our first go at this particular innovation. . . ."

"Innovation?"

"Sounds as if you're here about cadres doing manual labor again. Your paper's carried that news a good half dozen times already, and the only thing they ever change is my name. If you fellas keep it up it won't be long before I'll have trouble figuring out what I'm called. Take a look at this job. What'd you reckon?"

"What exactly is it?"

"A house, of course. The latest style."

"Actually, it looks like a . . ." he bit back the word "tomb."

"A blockhouse, right? But it doesn't have peepholes in the sides."

"What about windows?"

"They'll all be on the roof." Wang rubbed his hands in glee, flicking off small pellets of mud. "Ideal in case of war, keeps out robbers, protects you against both wind and cold, it's got lots of advantages. It's something we learned from our ancestors."

Our cave-dwelling ancestors, Fang Cheng smiled wryly.

"The thing is that houses like these are cheap, you can build 'em by the dozen with premixed concrete. They're easier to make than chicken coops, and they're more solid than a blockhouse. If this catches on, you and me'll both be famous. For starters I'll get a new house and sit in an armchair at the bureau office. But don't put any of that in your story. Here, take a look at the blueprints. We're in the middle of a demolition job, so the air's not too clean. Hey, Li, are you taking the shovel's pulse or what? Look lively now and bring a stool over here. . . ."

Fang Cheng felt a bit dizzy. "It's all right, I'll look these over back at the office. By the way, do you happen to know who lives at Number 13 Happiness Street?"

"Dunno, that's not our business."

"Whose is it, then? Whose business *is* it to know?"

"Don't blow your top, let me think about it for a second . . . you could try asking around at the bureau, they've got a big map there, it shows everything down to the last detail."

"Good, I'll try them."

"Do us a favor while you're at it, take this blueprint with you and give it to the director. We'll get a pedicab to take you."

"No need, but thanks all the same."

"This time be sure you don't get my name wrong," Wang shouted after him.

Fang Cheng staggered out and stood in the middle of the road, staring at the sky.

II

The secretary darted out from behind the door, her heels clicking. "Director Ding will be very happy to see you, Comrade Reporter. The other seventeen directors would also like to talk to you, at your convenience of course. Director Ma would like to give you his view on the question of the revolutionary succession; Director Tian wants to give you a rundown on his war record; Director Wang would like to discuss the simplification of Chinese characters. . . ."

"Which one of them is the real director of the bureau?"

"Here we make no distinction between the director and assistant directors, we simply list them all in alphabetical order."

"I'm sorry, but I'm a bit pressed for time. I'm here on another matter. Anyway, how do all the directors know I'm here?"

"They were at a board meeting together just now."

"Am I breaking it up?"

"Don't give it another thought. They've been at it for nine days already. They were only too glad to take a break."

The director's office was thick with smoke. A pudgy old man with a healthy-looking complexion standing beside the conference table extended his hand to Fang Cheng with a broad smile. "Welcome, have a seat. Look at all this smoke, it's a form of collective murder. . . ."

"What?"

He waved his arms around in the air in an attempt to disperse the clouds of smoke. "The fact that I'm an optimist has been my salvation, let me tell you. Have you heard of a medicine called 'Anliben'?"

"No."

"It's a miracle drug used overseas for people with heart trouble. Does your paper ever send you abroad?"

"The chances are pretty slim."

"Then could you ask someone to help me get some?"

"I'll see what I can do. Do you have heart trouble?"

The director immediately looked glum. "I'm an old man, getting past it. Who knows, maybe the next time you come it'll be Director Ma sitting in this seat. . . ." He cleared his throat. "But let's get back to the matter in hand. Major political campaigns bring about major changes, and major changes promote further political campaigns. In the current quarter we've completed 158 percent of our work plan; compared with the same period last year. . . ."

"Excuse me, Director Ding, I haven't come here on a story."

"Oh?"

"I want to make some inquiries about a house. Who lives at Number 13 Happiness Street?"

Beads of sweat appeared on Ding's shiny red face. He pulled out a handkerchief and wiped his face. "You're not trying to trick me with some difficult question, are you? A big city like this, how could I know every house on every street by heart, like a production chart?"

"I heard that you've got a big map here. . . ."

"Yes, yes, I almost forgot." Groping for a small bottle in his pocket, he poured out a few pills and popped them into his mouth. "What do you think of the chicken-blood cure?"

"I haven't tried it."

He pressed a button on his desk and the red curtains on the wall parted slowly. He picked up a pointer, whipped the air with it energetically, and went up to the map. "How about the arm-swinging cure?"

"I'm sure it helps."

"Yes, it's very effective. Happiness Street . . . Number 30 . . . a coal depot."

"I'm after Number 13."

"13 . . . 13 . . . come and see for yourself, my friend."

It was a blank space.

"How come it's not marked?" Fang Cheng asked in surprise.

Director Ding patted him on the shoulder. "Look carefully, there are quite a lot of blank spots on this map. No one knows what these places are."

"No one knows?"

"Nothing to be surprised about. It's just like all the blank spots in our knowledge of medicine."

"Not even the Public Security Bureau people?"

"Why don't you go and see for yourself, we open out onto their back door; it's very handy. What do you think of gadgets like pacemakers, are they reliable?"

"Pacemakers? I don't know much about them." Fang Cheng felt around in his pockets and fished out the blueprint. "This morning I went to the local housing authority and Wang, the foreman, asked me to give this to you. It's the innovation they've been working on."

"That fellow's too active for his own good. He's like a bloody magician, always coming up with some new gimmick. There's still a lot of major business here we haven't had time to get around to yet." Ding frowned, rolled up the blueprint, and threw it into a wastepaper basket in the corner. "It's thanks to people like him that there's never a moment's peace and quiet anywhere."

The secretary appeared at the door.

"A message for all directors. The meeting is about to resume."

Fang Cheng showed his press card to the guard standing at the opening in the iron fence which surrounded the Public Security Bureau. "I want to see the director of the bureau."

"Interrogation Room I."

"Uh?"

"Up the stairs, first door on the right."

"I'm a reporter."

The guard looked at him blankly, not bothering to reply.

Fang Cheng went up the stairs, and with the help of the faint light in the corridor found a door with a brass plaque nailed to it: Interrogation Room I. He knocked. No one answered so he pushed the door open and went in. It was sumptuously furnished, with a red carpet on the floor and some leather chairs set around a tea table. It was not in the least like an interrogation room. He heaved a sigh of relief and sat down.

Suddenly three or four policemen came in through a small side door, escorting a man in a gray Mao suit. The man was of medium height, and his swarthy face was like an iron mask, cold and stern. A policeman wearing spectacles moved to his side and whispered something in his ear. He nodded.

"This is Director Liu," Spectacles said by way of introduction.

"Please be seated." The director's voice was deep and harsh. He and Spectacles moved to the chairs opposite and sat down. The other policemen stood at either side of them.

"Director Liu, there's something I would like to ask you," said Fang Cheng.

"Just a moment, first I've got a question for you." After a moment's pause, Liu proceeded. "If I gave you five matches to make a square, how would you do it?"

Fang Cheng stared at him in astonishment.

"Now, don't be nervous."

"I'm not nervous." He thought hard, but his mind was a complete blank.

Suddenly, Liu gave a harsh laugh, and turned smugly toward Spectacles. "This is typical of ideological criminals, they always try and find a way to use the extra match. Ordinary criminals are another case altogether. . . ."

"You have a thorough grasp of the psychology of the criminal mind," offered Spectacles obsequiously.

"This is an outrage!" Fang Cheng protested.

"Don't get excited, young man, and don't interrupt me when I'm talking." Liu turned to Spectacles again. "The important thing to note here is that by using psychological tactics you can force the criminal's thinking into a very small space, or shall we say a surface, where he can't possibly conceal himself, and then he's easily overwhelmed. Do you see what I am saying?"

Spectacles nodded. "But . . . but how can you tell he's a criminal? From the look in his eyes?"

"No, no, that's all out-of-date. Ideological criminals can easily disguise their expressions. Listen, everyone you confront is a criminal, and don't you ever forget it."

"Everyone?"

"Yes. That's what class struggle is all about."

"But . . . then . . . that's . . ." Spectacles spluttered.

"All right, you ask too many questions. I have no alternative but to put you down as ideologically suspect." Rudely cutting Spectacles short, Liu turned and looked sternly at Fang Cheng. "State your business, young man."

"I . . . I want to make an inquiry about a house."

"Good, go on."

"Who lives at Number 13 Happiness Street?"

Director Liu froze, but in an instant a barely perceptible smile appeared on his lips. Spectacles, still looking crestfallen, opened his briefcase and took out some paper, ready to take notes. The two policemen stood next to Fang Cheng. The atmosphere in the room became tense.

"Your name?" Liu asked sharply.

"Fang Cheng."

"Age?"

"What do you take me for? I'm a reporter."

"Hand over your papers."

Fang Cheng drew out his press card and passed it to one of the policemen at his side.

"Examine it and take his fingerprints. Also, find his file and check his ideological status," ordered the director.

"What am I being accused of?"

"Prying into state secrets."

"Is Number 13 Happiness Street a state secret?"

"Whatever no one knows is a secret."

"Including you? You mean, you don't know either?"

"Me? There's a certain continuity to your case, you won't even cooperate during interrogation."

Fang Cheng sighed.

"Next question. . . ."

Towards evening, Fang Cheng was released.

III

The municipal library was empty except for the faint but pervasive odor of mold. Fang Cheng leafed through the catalog, finally locating the book: *A Study of Grave-Robbing Techniques Through the Ages.* He noted down the call number and rushed upstairs to the reading room.

A middle-aged woman with prominent cheekbones standing behind the desk looked at the slip and then studied him. "Are you an archaeologist?"

"No, I'm a reporter."

"Are you planning to visit some tombs for a story?" she said half jokingly.

"I want to uncover some secrets."

"What secrets can you possibly find in this book?"

"A place where life has ended can still contain all kinds of secrets."

"Doesn't anyone know what they are?"

"No, because even the living have become part of the secret."

"What?"

"No one knows anyone; no one understands anyone."

The woman with high cheekbones stared at him. "Good heavens, you must be mad."

"It's not me who's mad, it's heaven."

She turned away and ignored him after that. Nearly an hour later he heard the clickety-clack of the book trolley, and the book landed on the desk, raising a cloud of dust. Putting it under his arm, Fang Cheng went into the reading room and sat down at an empty desk in a corner. He leafed through the book, taking notes from time to time.

A pale square of sunlight moved slowly across the table. Fang Cheng stretched and looked at his watch. It was getting late. Before long he found himself surrounded by other readers. Strange, they were all concealing their faces behind thick books. Looking more carefully, Fang Cheng shuddered. They were all reading the same book: A *Study of Grave-Robbing Techniques Through the Ages.* He broke into a sweat and stirred uneasily in his seat.

As he slipped out of the library he was aware of a shadowy figure following closely behind. He went into a small lane and then suddenly turned back. The man didn't have time to conceal himself and they met head-on: it was the fellow in the leather jacket he had bumped into the previous morning on Happiness Street. As soon as he emerged from the lane, Fang Cheng made a dash for a trolley bus at a nearby stop. He jumped on board, and the doors closed behind him with a squeal.

When he got off the bus he looked around anxiously and only relaxed when he felt sure he had not been followed. He thrust his hands into his overcoat pockets and did his best to regain his self-confidence and courage.

At a crossing a boy ran past flying a kite. The string in his hand was taut and the kite danced in the air. A high place, of course! Jun had disappeared while he was flying a kite. It must have been because he had seen something from a high place. What an idiot I've been, he thought, why didn't I think of that earlier? How awful, he'd almost let himself be suffocated like a rat trapped in a hole.

He bought a pair of high-power binoculars at a secondhand store and set off in the direction of Happiness Street, working his way toward his target through a maze of lanes and alleyways. Finally he saw a tall chimney towering alone in a stretch of vacant ground, surrounded on all sides by broken bricks and rubbish.

He made for the boiler room at the foot of the chimney. A wizened old man was stoking the boiler as an airblower droned in the background. His tattered, sweat-stained work clothes were held together at the waist and swung back and forth in time with his monotonous movements.

"Can I interrupt you for a minute!" Fang Cheng called out.

The old man slowly straightened himself, turned his long, skinny body, and walked over to the doorway. His face was covered with coal dust and ashes.

"Who're you looking for?" he asked.

"I wonder if you could tell me where this leads to?"

"Heaven."

"No, what I mean is who's the fire for?"

"How should I know. They pay me, I do the work, that's the way it is."

"If they pay you, there must be some evidence for it."

"Ah, yes. Now where's my pay slip got to?" he said, patting himself up and down. "Must've used it to roll a cigarette."

"What was written on it?"

"Let me think . . . seems it might have run something like this. 'Burn enough to make a thousand black clouds.' Hah!" The old man grinned, baring his teeth. Against his grimy face his broken and uneven teeth seemed extremely white.

Fang Cheng took off his black woolen overcoat. "Can I trouble you to keep an eye on this for me? I'm going to take a look."

"You don't want to leave a note for your family?"

"What?"

"You're the twelfth so far. Just yesterday a girl jumped. . . ."

The old man went back to stoking the boiler. Tongues of flame shot forth.

Fang Cheng gazed up at the chimney, which seemed to lean

slightly. He went to the foot of the iron ladder and started climbing. The houses grew smaller and smaller and it got so windy that his clothes flapped around him. When he reached the last rung, he steadied himself. Hooking one arm through the ladder, he turned around and began to survey the scene with his binoculars. Rooftops, date trees, courtyard walls . . . all came clearly into view. Suddenly he stiffened, and the hand holding the binoculars began shaking. He couldn't believe his eyes. Finally, he managed to collect his thoughts and refocus the lenses. He searched carefully in every corner, but didn't see even a single blade of grass.

"Oh bloody hell . . ." he muttered to himself.

As his feet touched ground he heard someone calling out sharply behind him. "Don't move. Where do you think you're going now?" Not at all surprised, he brushed the dust off his clothes and turned around. The man in the leather jacket gave him a shove, and they walked toward a jeep parked some distance away.

Twisting his head, Fang Cheng saw the old man stoking the boiler while thick smoke continued to billow out of the tall chimney.

"Black clouds," he said.

IV

Fang Cheng was sent to the lunatic asylum.

When he looked at the people running in circles around the desolate grounds and the outside wall covered with weeds, he finally understood: so now he too was inside the wall.

Translated by Bonnie S. McDougall

ZHU LIN

(China)

A native of Shanghai, Zhu Lin is the author of three novels and numerous novellas and short stories published since 1979. Emblematic of the "lost generation" who graduated from high school in the late 1960s, Zhu Lin spent several years of governmentally imposed "rustication in the countryside" in Feng-yang County, one of the poorest areas of China's east-central Anhui Province. Her first novel, The Path of Life, reflects the psychological damage suffered by many of the young urbanites during their years of exile in rural regions during the Cultural Revolution and emphasizes the vulnerability of women in Chinese village society. Portraying a hostile, natural world whose menace is paralleled in human society by the exercise of unscrupulous, oppressive power, its tragic plot concerns the triangular relationship between a pure woman, a rapacious official, and an inadequate protector. Its use of rape as a metaphor for the relations between men and women (or ruler and ruled) is a recurrent feature of Zhu Lin's work from the early 1980s. As one might surmise given the vitriolic nature of "The Festival of Graves," despite her success Zhu Lin remains on the periphery of China's literary establishment and continues to have difficulty placing her work in national publications; nor has she traveled outside China. Not inclined to follow literary fashion, she persists with the revelations of social and political injustice and remains both suspicious and diffident toward authority.

The Festival of Graves

Rain beat down relentless and slate-gray in the howling wind. It poured through the bare branches of the trees and battered the stunted shoots of winter wheat. The world was cold and bleak. Only the shallow river rejoiced, gulping in the rain and turbid streams that swept down the channels between the fields. Then the wind died down and the rain stopped. Sunlight pierced the clouds like a magic sword, and the land shone. The river waters rushed in sparkling torrents, oblivious of the shriveled remnants of last year's waterweeds.

The trill of a bird wafted from the depths of the bamboo grove, breaking the long silence of winter. But people seemed unconvinced by this herald of spring, until they noticed pale yellow buds of forsythia on the sunlit slopes, and shepherd's purse spreading its carpet of fresh white flowers over the fields.

She surveyed it all coldly, and the stirring of new life filled her with an irrational dread. Each day the earth became more bountiful, and each day she felt more empty and alone. Here it was again, April 5, the Festival of Graves. Withered branches along the riverside thrust forth buds of white and red, peach and plum trees burst into bloom, and in the vegetable plots the rape plants flowered golden yellow. Bamboo shoots pushed like steer horns through the soil, and the leaves on the willow trees burst forth like blossoms. The waterweeds revived, and the waters embellished their vivid color. When she opened the door, a dazzling haze of green confronted her.

As she brushed her hair, she examined herself in the mirror. She saw a gray, lined face, eyes like dry wells, a sharp nose, and a puckered mouth. Worst of all was her chin, which looked as if it had been gouged away by a shovel. A few remaining teeth protruded between thin lips. It was the face of an old woman ready for the coffin.

Try as she might, she couldn't understand how age had crept up on her. Other women could watch their children and grandchildren grow, and sigh at the passage of time: "They're so big now, it's no wonder I'm getting on." But there was none of this for Huang Huizhen, who had been Director of Women's Affairs and served as the Commune's Party Secretary. She had not endured the pain of childbirth or known the pride and joy of being a mother and grandmother. Life seemed to have jumped from childhood to old age; for her, the fantasies of young womanhood had never existed. The past was reduced to a dim vision: the setting sun burning out like a last ember in the ashes, and the moon's pale crescent high in an inky sky. An old graybeard emerged from the gloom, singing a senseless riddle:

> From times gone by, who knows when,
> few survive three score and ten.
> Childhood slips by in a haze,
> dotage passes in a daze.
> In between is haste and hurry,
> days of toil and nights of worry;
> Once midautumn's come and gone,
> see the moon grow pale and wan,
> Past the Festival of Graves,
> flowers wither, blossoms fade . . .

She must have been six years old, squatting by a stream playing in the mud, kneading crumbs of soil into the shape of breadrolls, then crumbling them and starting again. The strange song had delighted her then. She looked up to catch a glimpse of the old man's face, but just then the last dim light of dusk died. Disembodied, the rasping voice sang on:

Round and round the seasons go,
the curfew tolls, the roosters crow . . .

There had been more besides, but she couldn't remember what.
Something about grave mounds, perhaps. Nor could she remember
who the old man was. An uncle, maybe a great-uncle, at any rate
someone from her family. It embarrassed her that not all of her
ancestors had been the simple commoners she would have liked
them to be, and that one of them might have sung a ditty like this.

Huang Huizhen couldn't understand why this vision had been
haunting her since the beginning of spring. Why should she be
remembering the events of childhood so late in life? At times she
felt she had dreamed it all. The graybeard couldn't possibly be any
relation of hers; he was probably just an old monk passing by. How
could she, a Communist, a revolutionary, and a materialist, indulge
in such delusions? Why could she not dwell on deeds from her past
that merited praise and brought her glory? Was this some ill omen,
warning her that she was not long for this world?

The idea of dying frightened her somewhat. She was already
sixty-six years old, and as the local saying went, "sixty-six, sixes
doubling, bean curd boiling hot and bubbling," meaning that when
you got to this age, the traditional funeral dishes of bean curd were
ready for your death. So the custom of the region was for all daughters to give their parents sixty-six cubes of pork in the Festival of
Graves in the year they reached sixty-six. It was said that, by eating
the sixty-six cubes of meat, the old folks could avoid illness and
avert the unfortunate implications of "bean curd boiling hot and
bubbling"; then, once this milestone had been passed, the parents
would live on for many more years. On this morning, people who
had survived sixty-six years would all wait anxiously for their daughters to come by. Those who had no daughter of their own would
make arrangements for a stand-in, who would chop pork into the
requisite number of pieces, and carry it ostentatiously through the
village.

Huang Huizhen would not, however, copy the practices of the
ignorant villagers. She was a woman of status and high revolutionary

consciousness who had always despised such customs as adopting stand-in daughters and eating sixty-six pieces of pork. She also knew some science, and realized that for older people, eating so much meat at a single sitting could be hard on their systems and certainly would not prolong their lives. Besides, there was the cost to be considered! Yet somehow this cogent reasoning did not completely reassure her.

On the morning of the Festival of Graves, she was unsettled. Outside, spring was bright and fecund, so that the festival to honor the dead became a celebration of life. The villagers were making the dumplings that were always eaten at the festival, kneading the dumplings in their sticky-rice coatings into various shapes, long, round, or angular. Pampered children stuffed them into their mouths. If they didn't like what they tasted, they spat them out, or ate the filling and discarded the slippery outer shells. Their grandmothers would grumble at their antics, but even when the little darlings tossed their leftovers to the chickens and ducks or played with them like mud pies, it didn't seem to affect the general good mood.

In Huang Huizhen's eyes, these unlettered rustics were no better than mother hens brooding on their nests. All they cared about was raising sons and carrying on the family line. After all these years of revolution, their consciousness was still so low that they cared more about trivialities, like the yield from their beans or the amount of weight a grandson was putting on, than they did about the great affairs of the Party and State. She found this vexing and painful. Huang Huizhen refused to pander to their primitive beliefs, or join in their merriment.

She looked silently around her at her four walls, hung with the pictures of her past. There had been times when she had enjoyed opening the windows and flooding the room with light, letting the crimson sunlight shine on her photographs and warm her heart. But later she had become nervous of drafts, and the windows had remained shut tight from that time. Now the photographs before her were yellowing and faded with age.

The damp cold chilled her to the bone. She had lived alone

since her husband's death, without even a dog or a chicken to keep her company. Now the place seemed uninhabited, a wasteland, without any babies crying or toddlers scattering their toys about.

Someone knocked firmly on the door. Startled, she sat up suddenly. Then, after a moment, the knock came again, still firm, and courteously insistent. She hurried to her feet, her heart fluttering with the thrill of hope. Could it possibly be that her daughter had come?

For she had a daughter. Not her own flesh and blood, but the child of her husband's first wife. Even though she was a stepmother, she had truly loved the child and cared for her. When the girl was young, she had taught her to sing "The Sky in the Liberated Areas Is the Brightest Sky of All," and told her tales of the Red Army's final surge to victory in the civil war. She wasn't one to coddle a child, but she certainly never treated her poorly. There had always been food on the table and clothes to wear. Not too many clothes, of course, and not much in the way of treats and toys, but what harm was there in raising the child in the tradition of revolutionary austerity? When her daughter married, she gave her two chests and some quilts as her dowry. What the girl actually wanted was a dressing table, but Huang Huizhen drew the line at that. Dressing tables were for the pampered young ladies of the bourgeoisie. How could a Communist Party cadre provide such a gift? When she saw how disappointed her daughter was, she spent a little extra on books; but the young couple seemed uninterested in the kind of books she gave them, and behaved most ungratefully. They did maintain appearances, however, and visited her at New Year's and on festivals.

Her daughter became pregnant soon after the wedding, and gave birth to a little girl. The young woman, her husband, and his parents all wanted to try again for a boy. The one-child family planning policy was in effect by then, and Huang Huizhen was Director of Women's Affairs. She tried several times to persuade her daughter to volunteer for sterilization, but the young woman would not consent, and began to avoid her. So Huang Huizhen went to the factory where her daughter worked, and impressed on them that they were not to make any concessions in this case because of her connections with officialdom. Her daughter's response was to stop going in to work. Six months later there was a general inspection by the birth control authorities, and all the women of the commune were ordered to present themselves for examination. Huang Huizhen's daughter was brought in, already heavily pregnant. The mother's face darkened with fury: "Take her away and abort it." People stepped forward to drag her off, but the young woman slumped to the ground, and wailed, "Mother, mother, I beg you, let me have my baby!"

Huang Huizhen remembered her daughter as a headstrong child, too proud to beg, who had seldom called her "mother." She couldn't help but be moved by such desperate pleading. But birth control was Party work. How could she let personal feelings interfere with duty? If she let her daughter off, how could she enforce the policy on other women?

When they heard that Huang Huizhen had refused to give permission for the baby to be born, her son-in-law and his parents, both of them in their sixties, came in and knelt before her. "Director Huang," begged the old grandfather, "if you'll only let her give birth, the whole family will kowtow and burn incense for you, and the child will remember your kindness all his life."

Such obduracy was exasperating. Huang Huizhen hissed through clenched teeth, "All right, if you want the child so much, pay the fine. It's a thousand *yuan*!"

In fact, the regulations stipulated half that. She only spoke as she did to get rid of them, since she was sure they couldn't raise the cash. But instead, her words seemed to galvanize them all like a shot of ginseng. They dashed off to borrow what they needed, and within twelve hours they were back to her with the thousand *yuan*. Not that it did them any good. Huang Huizhen was the kind of official who always has to take the lead in implementing Party policy, and never invites the disapproval of her superiors. She refused the money, and her daughter was hauled away to the clinic. An examination confirmed that she was seven months pregnant, and an abortion was ordered. But then—and nobody knew how it could have been done with so many watching eyes—someone slipped her a note and she announced that she had to go to the bathroom. People were sent with her, of course, and posted at the door. But when after several minutes she had still not emerged, they went in to find the room empty! Incredibly she had managed, as heavily pregnant as she was, to escape through a high, narrow window.

There must have been accomplices. It was a conspiracy. Huang Huizhen was livid. Her husband attempted to coax her as they lay together that night: the girl was his only family, and, besides, she was seven months gone, so why not just let her have the child? Such talk only made her more determined, and after a sleepless night she sent people out at daybreak to tie her daughter up and bring her in.

They strapped her to the birthing table and induced labor. To the astonishment of all, the seven-month fetus was born alive— and it was a boy. The doctor had no choice but to put the baby in an incubator. The daughter's in-laws were so overjoyed they lit incense, recited the name of the Buddha, and then came happily along to pay the fine. The hospital officials didn't know what they should do, so they went to Huang Huizhen to ask for instructions. Huang Huizhen ordered them to remove the baby from the incubator immediately. Naturally, before long, his life ebbed away.

Her daughter's in-laws wailed in anguish. Demented, the old father-in-law seized a knife and vowed to settle things with Huang Huizhen. If the authorities hadn't intervened on Huang Huizhen's behalf, locking the old man up for a few months on a charge of intended homicide, her own life might have been at risk. The ill will that this incident generated between her daughter and herself had endured for over ten years, during which her daughter never once visited her. The consensus of the village gossips was that the mother had gone too far. People felt that she had been so mean only because the girl wasn't her own flesh and blood. But that just wasn't so! It wasn't that there was any bad blood between her and her daughter. She was acting for the Party and the State, for the public good!

Time and time again she had considered going to see her daughter to explain, but the girl had become a stranger to her. Only today did she realize how much she longed to see her again. She shook convulsively as she reached for the door handle. Today is the Festival, she thought, perhaps my daughter will bring me sixty-six pieces of pork like the village bumpkins do.

But when she opened the door, it was a messenger, who told her that she should go to county headquarters for a Party meeting.

Despite her disappointment, she felt some slight comfort. At least officialdom hadn't forgotten her. Even if her daughter didn't bring her anything, the county would treat her to a meal—and a few pieces of pork would be nothing compared with the banquet that was certain to follow the meeting.

II

It was mild outside, the warm breeze redolent with pollen and honey. On this day, the Festival of Graves, there was a bustle of activity in the inlets and peninsulas on the banks of the winding river, for it was there that the commune's dead rested in their collective tranquillity. For many years, the graves had been neglected and overgrown. The dead passed their years secure in their coffins, spared the atrocities that the living committed against each other. Now, however, times were changing. In a period of affluence, people were more inclined to feel concern for their ancestors, and on this Festival day they brought offerings of fish and meat, wine and vegetables to the gravesides. Now that they had more to spend themselves, they worried that the dead might still be poor, so they burned silver ingots made of tinfoil. Strings of paper money, yellow, white, and green, hung from the trees by the graves, spinning in the breeze like colored lights revolving over a dance floor. Huang Huizhen had always turned up her nose at such superstition, but today she was a little less inclined to find fault.

She was quite warm by the time she arrived at the government office compound. Sweat beaded the tip of her nose, and her cheeks were flushed as if she had been drinking. Other old comrades were streaming in to attend the meeting. Some were being led along by their grandchildren, some were perched on the backs of bicycles pedaled by their sons, still others hobbled in leaning on their canes. In this company, Huang Huizhen seemed very sprightly to have come along unaided.

She had every reason to feel proud of herself. She had served a three-year term as Party Secretary of the Commune (or county, as it was now called). The two pines at the gate of the compound had been planted in those years on her orders. Since then, an orchard had been added, which shimmered with the pink petals of flowering cherries—trees which to her eyes were eminently lacking the resolute spirit of the pines. In those days . . . but a hero does not dwell on past exploits. Her back was straight and her head held high as she strode into the meeting hall.

Through force of habit, she surveyed the room as she entered. Nobody jumped up and exclaimed, "Here's Secretary Huang!" Nobody ran over with a stool, or poured her a cup of tea. It was as if she, their former Party Secretary, was invisible to them, like a bubble, like thin air. They just sat there chattering merrily away, gossiping or complaining about their sons and daughters-in-law. Irritated at their rudeness, she cleared her throat. At last some of them looked around at her, nodded briefly, forced a smile, and then went back to discussing all the things they had to do at home, and to comparing their various aches and pains. She stalked angrily over to a seat by the window, sat down, and did her best to ignore them. Of course she wouldn't join in—here they were, old Party members, hardly out of office, and they had turned into a pack of old gossips. Really, it was terrible. She wouldn't have tolerated that kind of sloppiness when she was Party Secretary. But the new Deputy County Head didn't seem bothered by it at all. He read through a Party document about carrying out rectification at the local level with a smug grin on his face, and then remarked to the chattering crowd in front of him, "Well, now I've put you in the know about the spirit of the document from Party Central. Considering the fact that you're all getting on in years, and it's been quite an effort for you to make it to County Headquarters today, I suggest that you have your lunch and then head home."

Huang Huizhen had understood perfectly well when she was summoned to County Headquarters that the meeting would only be a formality. Still, she was most displeased at what this wet-behind-the-ears official had to say. In her day, whenever Party Central had announced a new initiative or set forth key duties, she would invariably organize discussion groups and send feedback to the upper levels. Then she would select model peasants for everyone else to emulate, identify pacesetters in carrying out the new policy, and publicize their experience with the campaign. And what did you get these days? "Put you in the know." Indeed! "Have some lunch"! What does he take us old comrades for? Are we just wind-bags, lunch buckets? Others might be willing to accept it, but not Huang Huizhen. She had joined the Party in 1948, before this new Deputy County Head was even born.

Not that she didn't want a meal, of course. After the exertions of the morning, she had started to feel hungry. Besides, one of her reasons for coming was that she wanted to eat meat to make up for her disappointment over the "sixty-six cubes of pork."

The meeting hall was transformed into a dining hall, and young Butch, the chef from the county government offices, came in with some other youngsters to lay out the bowls and chopsticks. She couldn't abide that Butch. His class origins weren't anything to be proud of, and to make matters worse, he followed current fashions, growing his hair long like a girl, wearing jeans that hugged his backside, and talking in slang that made him sound like a gangster. He also took advantage of the fact that he and the new chief had been at school together and had been roommates when they returned to the village. Now he addressed the Deputy County Head uncer-emoniously as "Little Li." And not only did the official respond to this, but he even slapped the other on the back. "Hey, old pal, mind how you do your work today. Cook the meat as tender as you can, 'cause these old comrades don't chew so well."

Butch stared maliciously right at Huang Huizhen and snorted,

"Huh, they've eaten so well so long they've all rotted their teeth."

Little Li merely slapped him on the back to shut him up. "Cut the crap, eh?"

Butch grimaced and went off to another table. The Deputy County Head didn't pursue the matter, but turned to address the gathering. "Since the meal isn't ready yet, why don't you old comrades make some suggestions about how the county should do its work in the future?"

This lackadaisical attitude made Huang Huizhen's blood boil. What kind of Party leader was he? Where were the prestige and principles of a Communist Party member? She couldn't stand it any longer. Her face puffed and purple with rage, she rose abruptly.

"Since this is a Party rectification," she snapped, "I'll be blunt. Our present leadership is short on Party consciousness, it lacks principles, and its political standards are low."

The listeners looked at each other nervously, unsure of how to react. Working herself up even more, she picked up a newspaper off the table, rolled it up, and slapped the table with it. "When I was doing underground work, I was under the leadership of comrades who had headed south to fight the civil war, and in those days . . ."

Everyone was silent. They had heard this line from Huang Huizhen almost daily when she was Party Secretary. She would only have to mention heading south, and you knew a lecture would follow; like it or not, you had to pay attention, or you were in big trouble. This time, however, after a few seconds of bemused silence, there were snorts of laughter. Amid the laughter someone muttered, "Huh, heading south with the leader of the Red Army. I've heard that some of those women were sold into whorehouses and they haven't come out yet!" Someone else added, "What do the old whores think they have to brag about?" It was just as well the laughter was so loud, so that she didn't hear the last few words, or Huang Huizhen might have really had a fit. She was so furious as it was her mind was a blur. If it had just been common people being so impudent she could have borne it, but these were Party cadres. All of them had always been subservient and attentive to her, and now they were mocking her brazenly. Could the inconceivable be true—that their behavior toward her in the past was all a sham? At a momentary loss for words, she opened the newspaper in her hand, and saw the bold print of a headline: "Party General Secretary Visits Europe." There was a photograph beside the report. As she looked at it, and then at the others, the blood rushed to her head. Obviously everyone else had already seen it. She shouted, "Don't you laugh! I've got criticisms of the General Secretary as well. He's leader of the Party, but instead of doing rectification work, he's off on a trip overseas. That's the job of the Foreign Minister . . ."

Before she could finish, the tension broke, and the listeners began to howl with laughter. Butch called out for someone to rub his stomach and ease the pain of laughing. The laughter was so loud it threatened to blow the roof off. The new Deputy County Head hurriedly gestured them all to lay off. "Don't laugh, folks. A Party member has a right to air her opinions about the leadership."

He was trying to keep a straight face, but everyone could tell from the twinkle in his eye and the catch in his voice that he couldn't completely suppress his mirth. Butch found it hard to contain himself as well. Muttering, "crazy bitch" and rubbing his belly he headed back into the kitchen. "Hey guys, hot news! They've dug up a mummy from the tombs at Mawangdui who wants to take a potshot at the Central Committee!"

"What do you mean?" His young co-workers clustered round.

Butch couldn't resist the opportunity to do an impersonation. By the time he was through, everyone else was holding his sides as well. Then Butch shook his head. "It's hard to understand why," he said more soberly, "but they get old and the brain starts to go. Oh yes, I almost forgot, Little Li said to cook the stuff soft or the old monkeys won't be able to chew it."

"What's so hard to understand?" said an old cook who was chopping meat on the table. "You shouldn't make fun of her. In the old days, you'd have been called a rightist or counterrevolutionary for less than that." There was menace in his voice, but Butch's assistants were just a bunch of kids, without any real understanding of what the words "rightist" and "counterrevolutionary" signified. They just laughed at the old cook as if he too were some ancient relic. "You guys don't believe me?" He pointed to Butch. "His father talked too much and he lost everything."

That wiped the smile from Butch's face. His father had been framed and sentenced to labor reform in a coal mine, where he died when a mine shaft caved in. The case was determined by Huang Huizhen, and he had always hated her for that. He was a child when his father died, and his mother and others had lacked the education to explain very well the whys and wherefores of the case, or exactly why Huang Huizhen had taken it on herself to brand his father a counterrevolutionary. Over the years, those who understood better were reluctant to talk to him about it, preferring to leave well enough alone. So now that the old cook had raised the subject, Butch pressed him about what had happened.

"It's a long story," said the old man. "It was during the Great Leap Forward in 1958, and Huang Huizhen's husband—he was the boss of the commune in those days—told everyone to plant five hundred catties of seed on every *mu* of land and harvest a hundred thousand catties of grain from it. If you try to spread that many seeds onto a single *mu,* they'll rot, and most won't sprout. Huang Huizhen was pretty ingenious, though. She mobilized the entire village to paint old newspapers with paste, then stick the seeds onto it standing on their ends. When the newspapers were loaded with seeds, they laid them down in the fields and covered them with soil."

This had them all baffled. Someone asked, "Did they really plant their fields that way? Did the seeds grow?"

"Sure"—the old cook nodded—"a couple of shoots here and there, no more."

Butch understood where the story was leading. The cook's version wasn't really all that new to him, but the other youngsters still hadn't a clue. "So what's this all got to do with Butch's dad?" they asked.

The old cook pushed the cubes of meat to the side of the chopping block and continued slowly. "Butch's father was the teacher at the primary school at the time, and when there was something nobody else could understand, we would always go to him for an explanation. He said that what Huang Huizhen was doing was against the laws of nature, and he wrote a letter saying so to the authorities. He even sent an article to the newspaper, which was how he came to be dragged away as a counterrevolutionary. Nobody doubted his scientific knowledge."

He sighed. "That's all in the past now. Don't let it get you down, Butch. Just try and mind your manners a bit, don't shoot your mouth off all the time. You meddle in things that don't concern you and say things that shouldn't be spoken." To the others he said, "Take that business about criticizing the Party General Secretary. It's all very well for Huang Huizhen to talk like that, but if you'd breathed a word of it when she was in power she would have had you tied up and dragged off. Face the facts, we're not all equal, you have to give way."

The old man looked around, but Butch was gone. Then he saw him going into the hall bearing a tray loaded with food.

It was a splendid lunch. The pork was as tender as the new Deputy County Head had said it should be, and the chicken was falling from the bone. Butch had divided the food into individual portions, and placed the same selection before all the diners.

Only Huang Huizhen had an extra dish at her place, a bowl decorated with a blue floral design, full to the brim with bubbling white bean curd, fragrant with the tang of green onions, a rich sauce dripping down the side.

"How come she gets bean curd and I don't?" complained the person beside her.

Butch said, "Take it easy, just let her have what she deserves."

Huang Huizhen was starting to feel a little better. The spread before her was eminently superior to "sixty-six cubes of pork," and it looked as if she was finally getting some preferential treatment. But when she heard what Butch said, she realized the intent behind the bowl of "bean curd boiling hot and bubbling," and she trembled with rage. "How dare you!"

Butch stood to one side watching her, the tray still in his hands, the corner of his mouth curled in a half-smile of malice that made her shiver. Huang Huizhen's face turned from sallow to crimson, and then from crimson to white. She slammed down her bowl and stormed out.

How unfair it was! She had lived long enough, and she might as well die now that she was sixty-six, but she couldn't take any more of this insubordination! Who the hell did Butch think he was? How could he humiliate her like that? Just because he was friends with the new Deputy County Head . . . or maybe the Deputy County Head was behind it all. When the higher-ups had decided a few years ago that he should take over for her, she had put up a stubborn fight—why should they take her power away when she was in good health and prepared to redouble her efforts for the revolution? Besides, how could she stand it if her power was handed over to someone like that? A young guy in his thirties, born after she joined the Party. So cocksure of himself because he'd been to college. Always going on about incentives and efficiency. Surrounded by a pack of disco dancers! What direction was he dancing in?

He got the position anyway, though as a result of her efforts he was given the rank only of Deputy rather than full County Head, as the original plan had been. He must have set up today's embarrassing scene to get revenge on her.

But Huang Huizhen was still Huang Huizhen. Rattled as she was, a course of action came to her. She would pay a visit to County Head Zhu.

County Head Zhu wasn't like Little Li. He was a solid cadre of the old school. He had served under Huang Huizhen as office manager for the Party Branch Office, and she had seen to it that he was designated as one of the next generation of leaders. Years ago in her campaign to stop people like Little Li from getting power, she and Office Manager Zhu had busied themselves day and night with their investigations, collecting incriminating evidence, calling all kinds of meetings, busying themselves till their hair turned gray, and suffering who knows how many sleepless nights. It was Zhu who had composed their letter denouncing Little Li. They decided that their letter would have to be anonymous for the time being, because Little Li was the cunning type: he knew how to suck up to people, he always managed to get the credit when things went right and avoid criticism for disasters.

Naturally, the district authorities had taken the letter very seriously, and spent over a year investigating the Little Li affair. But then they ruled that the accusations were largely hearsay and slander. Huang Huizhen was appalled at the decision, and upset to think of the wasted effort. Little Li had been delighted and ready to celebrate his promotion. Then all of a sudden, the policy changed. The top leadership stopped promoting people several grades at once and went back to a system of letting them go up a step at a time. So Little Li rose only to Deputy Head, while the higher rank— County Head and County Party Secretary—went to the author of the anonymous letter, Office Manager Zhu. Even the darkest of clouds had silver linings, after all.

Now Huang Huizhen walked out of County Headquarters and followed the road toward the east. In a while she saw the birdcages hanging above the balcony of County Head Zhu's home. Her spirits revived. Zhu was the decent and generous sort. He would always let her have her pick of the cage birds. Once he had bought a talking parrot at considerable expense, and simply because she had admired it, he had sent his wife around with the bird as a gift that very evening.

She'd have a good talk with County Head Zhu. Not only did she plan to tell him what she thought of Little Li, and offer advice on how he should proceed, but she also intended to discuss the great affairs of Party and State. The land in the village was now being contracted out to families, and individuals were being allowed to hire laborers and exploit them. In the cities, foreign capitalists were being invited over to manage factories, entrepreneurs were opening businesses, and there were merchants and peddlers all over the place. The only thing missing from the 1940s were the foreign concessions. No, they even had them too, though they gave them a slightly nicer name: "Special Economic Zones." What did all this have to do with socialism? It wasn't just some fit of pique that had made her say she was going to lodge a protest against the Party General Secretary. But those people at County Headquarters . . . they were all cadres who had been nurtured by the Party, yet they were so unfeeling, they had mocked her . . . huh, go ahead and laugh! Just remember, she who laughs last laughs loudest, she thought. Someday the General Committee will regain its senses. Her only regret was that since she was getting on in years, sixty-six already, she might not live to see the day. County Head Zhu was younger, though—he'd be around when the time came. But then again, even he was fifty-eight, and would not outlast Little Li. In three year's time, County Head Zhu would be forced into retirement as she had been, and Little Li would take over. That prospect really made her feel anxious. She would have to suggest ways County Head Zhu could make his position more secure.

She hurried on toward his house. She didn't know if he would be in or not, so she peeped in through the high window that faced the road. He was in there having lunch, so she went up to the door and knocked. Nobody answered at first, so she rapped a little harder and called out, "County Head Zhu, Little Zhu!"

It wasn't Zhu who opened the door, but his wife, a forced smile on her face. "Oh, it's you . . . I'm so sorry, he's . . . he's not at home just now."

Not at home? But she'd just seen him eating his lunch! At a loss for words, she stared dumbly at the wrinkles etched into the woman's fat face, as if seeking an explanation in the pattern of their lines.

III

The river flowed quickly that spring. Broken stalks of winter wheat were whisked around in little whirlpools and swept along by the current. Huang Huizhen realized that fate had been as relentless and unfeeling to her as those cold waters, sweeping away all. What had it all been for, her life of struggle? She wasn't so sure anymore. Everyone had forsaken her, her colleagues had humiliated her . . . no need to dwell on that now. But County Head Zhu, Little Zhu, her protégé, her successor! She had cared for him, guided him along like a younger brother, and now he treated her like a stranger. He was there, she knew he was, but his wife said, "He's not at home," just like that—as if she'd been a supplicant pleading at his door.

She trudged along in a dream. Or perhaps it was the past which was the dream from which she was now waking. The wind blew chill against her, its cold cutting her heart, and she began to shiver uncontrollably, though oddly the flowers, grasses, and trees seemed to be absorbing warmth from the sun despite the cold, growing strong and spirited. Young women stepped out, dressed in their brightest and newest clothes, bearing woven baskets with the sixty-six cubes of pork for their parents. Courting couples strolled along arm in arm, the men in Western suits and leather shoes, the women with their hair flowing free over their shoulders. Huang Huizhen disapproved of all of this. It was a scene from another planet to her. And so confusing—had she awaked from a dream, or returned to one?

Huang Huizhen wavered, not knowing where she should go next. Everything before her was a blur, fields stretching as far as the eye could see, the setting sun fading like a last crimson ember dying in the ashes. High in the blue-black sky, the slender crescent of the pale new moon was rising. Out of the gloom came the old man, singing his senseless riddle:

> From times gone by, who knows when,
>   few survive three score and ten.
> Childhood slips by in a haze,
>   dotage passes in a daze.
> In between is haste and hurry,
>   days of toil and nights of worry;
> Once midautumn's come and gone,
>   see the moon grow pale and wan,
> Past the Festival of Graves,
>   flowers wither, blossoms fade . . .

She was six again, playing in the mud by the stream, kneading tiny fragments into the shape of breadrolls, then crumbling them and repeating the process. The strange song enchanted her. She looked up to see the old man's face, but in that instant the last glimmerings of dusk were covered by the curtain of blackness. The desolate sound of the rasping voice continued:

> Round and round the seasons go,
>   the curfew tolls, the roosters crow,
> See your dead before your eyes,
>   weeds grow yearly where they lie,
> Unattended, overgrown,
>   Hosts of grave mounds high and low . . .

Remembering now these last few lines, she felt a marvelous sense of relief. She saw that she had come to the bend in the river where the graves lay. How could she be here? This wasn't the road home. She was about to turn back when her eye lit on a familiar figure, a woman in a purple jacket, her hair permed, kneeling by a grave with a wicker basket in her hand. It was her daughter. She was lifting dishes out of the basket, making offerings to her father.

As Huang Huizhen watched, a sudden hope shone through her depression. If her daughter cared enough to make offerings to her father, perhaps she would pay a call on her as well. Why couldn't she get on with her daughter as the peasant women did with theirs, and live out her life in contentment? She almost called out, but she couldn't drop her defenses that far. Then it occurred to her that her daughter would have to pass by her house on her way home, so she decided to go first and make her a special meal.

Back at home, she rolled up her sleeves and got busy. Time was tight—she couldn't go out and buy fresh ingredients or grind glutinous rice into flour for the traditional dumplings. Fortunately, she had a well-stocked cupboard—cans of luxury food not available to mere peasants, sausage, dried meat floss, pressed chicken—and so it didn't take long to lay out a dozen plates of food and a bottle of red wine on the table. In case that wasn't enough, she filled bowls with melon seeds and candies, and even measured some malted milk powder into a glass, with hot water ready to add when her daughter arrived.

She would put on airs no longer. If her daughter would only come, she would give her anything; the dressing table of course, even a television! Her daughter might not agree to it all right away, so perhaps she would start off with some new clothes for her grand-daughter. Huang Huizhen resolved that she would not oppose her daughter even if she said she wanted another child; why, she would even make a contribution to help pay the fine. She had money, and what she would really like was a chubby little grandson making messes on the floor and wetting the sheets . . .

She waited until the dishes on the table were all cold, but still there was no sign of her daughter. Impatient, she went back to look for her. She rushed in a panic to the bamboo grove across the river from the graveyard. All she could see were the green grave mounds and the strings of paper cash fluttering like butterflies in the breeze. The pines, still without new growth, stood somber and dark, grief-stricken like widows. There was nobody there. Her daughter was gone.

Huang Huizen felt dizzy. The bamboo grove whirled around, the river flowing above her, dark yellow waves rushing at her . . . the world was turning upside down. She groaned and grasped a slim bamboo beside her. But it wouldn't hold her up, and she slumped to the ground.

Beyond the shade of the bamboo grove there was the red of peach blossoms and the green of willows. A sunset red as tulip petals caressed the fields. And in the fields, the golden rape, and snow white magnolia, the pink flowers of the broad beans . . . however fierce the wind might be, however hard the rain, the earth would come to life, the flowers bloom again.

Translated by Richard King

LI ANG

(Taiwan)

Women have made a significant contribution to arts and letters in Taiwan for the past thirty years, although it has been only with the emergence of the last decade's well-organized women's movement that they have achieved due prominence. Foremost among the newcomers has been firebrand author and social activist Li Ang. Born in 1952, she published her first novel, Flower Season, *at age seventeen, following it with "Mo Chun," a controversial story detailing a young girl's first sexual experience. Ang worked on behalf of several social movements, most notably that of single mothers, upon which she based a short story collection,* Their Tears. *She then traveled to the United States, where she earned a master's degree in drama at the University of Oregon. Returning to Taiwan in the late 1970s, she contributed the column "A Woman's Opinion" to the* China Times. *Then, as she says, "Finally, after three years of real involvement in social causes, I thought that writing stories could be my best contribution to society." In 1983 her novella "The Woman Who Killed Her Husband" won a national award; however, at the suggestion of the judges, the title was changed to* The Butcher's Wife *(available in translation by Howard Goldblatt); it became a hugely successful film in Taiwan. A devastating exploration of the unspoken domestic terror and sexual repression tolerated by women in traditional Chinese culture, Ang's novel inspired patriarchal outrage. Her other work includes two collections of short stories,* Mixed Chorus *and* The Mundane World. *Of the unexpectedly erotic perspective of "Curvaceous Dolls" Ang contends that "women writers must present a woman's worldview" and that they must explore creative areas "hitherto neglected by men," thereby establishing a new set of standards.*

Curvaceous Dolls

I

She had yearned for a doll—a curvaceous doll—ever since she was
a little girl. But because her mother had died and her father, a poor
man, hadn't even considered it, she never got one. Back then she
had stood behind a wall every day secretly watching a girl who lived
in the neighborhood carrying a doll in her arms. The way the girl
left her doll lying around surprised and confused her; if she had a
doll of her own, she reasoned dimly, she would treat it lovingly,
never letting it out of her sight.

One night as she lay in bed clutching the sheet to her chest,
obsessed with the idea of a doll, she figured out a way to get one
that she could hug as tightly as she wished. After digging out some
old clothes, she twisted them into a bundle, then cinched it up
with some string about a quarter of the way down. She now had
her very first doll.

The ridicule this first doll brought down upon her was something she would never forget. She recalled it years later as she lay
in the warmth and comfort of her husband's embrace. She sobbed
until he gently turned her face toward him and said in a relaxed
tone of voice that was forced and revealed a hint of impatience:

"It's the rag doll again, isn't it!"

Just when it had become the "rag doll" she couldn't recall with
certainty, but it must have been when she told him about it. One
night, not terribly late, he lay beside her after they had finished,
still somewhat breathless, while she lay staring at the moon's rays
streaming in through the open window and casting a fine net of
light at the foot of the bed. She had a sudden impulse to reveal
everything, to tell him about her first doll; and so she told him,

haltingly, blushing with embarrassment, how she had made it, how she had embraced it at night in bed, and how, even though her playmates ridiculed her, she had refused to give it up. When she finished, he laughed.

"Your very own rag doll!"

Maybe that wasn't the first time anyone had called it a "rag doll," but he had certainly used the word that night, and his laughter had hurt her deeply. She failed to see the humor in it, and telling him had not been easy. He could be pretty inconsiderate sometimes.

She never mentioned the doll again, probably because of his mocking laughter, and from that night on she began sleeping with her back to him, unable to bear facing his broad, hairy chest. Although it was the same chest that had once brought her solace and warmth, she now found it repulsive. It seemed to be missing something, although she couldn't say just what that something was.

Later on, her nightly dreams were invaded by many peculiar transparent objects floating randomly in a vast grayness, totally divorced from reality yet invested with a powerful life force. She seldom recalled such dreams, and even when she knew she had been dreaming, they vanished when she awoke.

It was a familiar feeling, the realization that she had obtained something without knowing what it was, and it worried her and drove her to tears. She often wept as she lay in her husband's arms, and he invariably blamed the rag doll. But it's not the rag doll! she felt like shouting. The rag doll had disappeared that night, never to return. But she couldn't tell him, maybe to avoid a lot of meaningless explanations.

The dreams continued, troubling her more than ever. She would sit quietly for hours trying to figure out what the floating objects were, but with no success. Occasionally she felt she was getting close, but in the end the answer always eluded her. The preoccupation took its toll on her husband; after being casually rebuffed in bed a few times, he grew impatient, and when he realized that things were not going to get better, he decided to take her to see a doctor. By now she was fed up with his bossiness and the protector's role in which he prided himself, but her dreams had such a strong grip on her that she finally gave in.

On the way, the oppressive closeness inside the bus made her regret going. She had no desire to open up to a doctor, nor did she think a doctor was the answer. As she looked over at her husband, a single glance from him convinced her that it would be useless to argue. Slowly she turned away.

Someone brushed against her. Glancing up, she saw a pair of full breasts, whose drooping outline she could make out under the woman's blouse. Her interest aroused, she began to paint a series of mental pictures, imagining the breasts as having nipples like overripe strawberries oozing liquid, as though waiting for the greedy mouth of a child. Suddenly she felt a powerful urge to lean up against those full breasts, which were sure to be warm and com-forting, and could offer her the sanctuary she needed. She closed her eyes and recalled the time she had seen a child playing with its mother's breasts. If only she could be those hands, enjoying the innocent pleasure of fondling a mother's soft, smooth breasts. Her palms were sweaty, and she wondered what her hands might do if she kept this up much longer.

Feeling a strong arm around her shoulders, she opened her eyes and found herself looking into the anxious face of her husband.

"You're so pale," he said.

She never learned how she had been taken off the bus, recalling only the extraordinary comfort and warmth of her husband's arm. She leaned up against him in the taxi all the way home, gradually reacquainting herself with his muscular chest. But she couldn't stop thinking about those breasts, so soft and smooth, there for her to play with. If only her husband could grow breasts like that on his chest, with drooping nipples for her to suck on! In a flash she realized what was missing from his chest—of course, a pair of breasts to lean on and provide her with sanctuary.

Later on, to her amazement, the objects in her dreams began to coalesce. Those unreal and disorderly, bright yet transparent objects took on concrete form with curves and twists: two oversized, swollen objects like resplendent, drooping breasts; beneath the translucent surface she could see thick, flowing milk. It's a woman's body, a curvaceous woman's body! she wanted to shout as the astonishing realization set in.

When she awoke, she experienced an unprecedented warmth that spread slowly from her breasts to the rest of her body, as though she were being baptized by the endless flow of her own milk as it coursed placidly through her body. Overwhelmed by such bountiful pleasure, she began to moan.

When she opened her eyes and glanced around her she saw that her husband was sound asleep. In the still of the night the moon's rays swayed silently on the floor beneath the window like a pool of spilled mother's milk. She began to think of her second doll, the one made of clay. Since her first doll was called the rag doll, this one ought to be known as the clay doll.

The idea of making a clay doll occurred to her one day when she had felt a sudden desire to hold the neighbor girl's doll. She had approached her, not knowing how to make her desire known, and after they had stared at each other for a few moments, she reached out and tugged at the doll's arm. The other girl yanked it back and pushed her so hard she fell down. Her cries brought the girl's mother, who picked her up gently and cradled her against her breasts to comfort her.

She had never touched anything so soft and comfortable before. She didn't know what those things were called, but she was instinctively drawn to them and wanted to touch them. After that, she lost interest in her rag doll, since it lacked those protruding, springy objects on its chest and could no longer afford her any solace. She thought about her mother. It was the first time in years that she truly missed her mother, who had left no impression on her otherwise, but whose bosom must have offered safety, warmth, and a place to rest.

The feeling returned: she longed to tell her husband about her clay doll, but then she recalled how he had laughed before, a humiliating laugh without a trace of sympathy, the sound coming from the depths of his broad chest, ugly and filled with evil. As she turned slightly to look at her sleeping husband, from whom she felt alienated and distant, a vague yet profound loneliness came over her, and she desperately missed her clay doll.

It had been raining then, and the water was streaming down the sides of a mound of clay near where she lived. She regularly went there with the other children to make clay dolls, but hers were always different from theirs. She molded small lumps of clay onto their chests, then worked them into mounds that jutted out. Most of the time she rubbed their bodies with water until they took on a silky, bronze sheen, glistening like gold. She fondled them, wishing that someday she could rub real skin as soft and glowing as that.

In fact, her husband's skin, which also had a bronze sheen, was as lustrous as that of her clay dolls. When she reached out to caress his body her hand recoiled slightly when she touched his hairy chest, and she wished fervently that a pair of soft breasts were growing there instead! Moved by a strange impulse she unbuttoned her pajama top and exposed her breasts, full like a married woman's, and let them rest on her husband's chest, praying with unprecedented devotion that her breasts could be transplanted onto his body.

The weight of her heavy breasts on his chest woke him, and with an apologetic look in his eyes, he embraced her tightly.

Whenever she did something like this she had no desire to explain herself, so he would just look at her apologetically and she would calmly accept what he did. But each time his chest touched her breasts, she felt a strange uneasiness, and a peculiar shudder, tinged with revulsion, welled up from the hidden depths of her body. At times like this she felt that the man on top of her was nothing but an onerous burden, and she was reminded of old cows in her hometown, which stumbled along pulling their heavy carts, swaying helplessly back and forth.

She couldn't imagine that she would ever be like an old cow, wearily and dispiritedly bearing a heavy burden that could never be abandoned. Her husband's body had become a pile of bones and rotting flesh that made a mockery of his robust health, although it was slightly warm and exuded an animal stench. It was an instrument of torture that made her feel like she had been thrown into a wholesale meat market.

She began to experience a mild terror; the concept of "husband" had never seemed so distant and fragmented. Before they were married, she had often stroked his shoulders through his shirt with something approaching reverence. Though powerful, they retained some of the modesty and stiffness characteristic of virgin men. They could be called young man's shoulders, not those of a grown man; yet despite the stiffness, the masculine smoothness of his well-developed muscles intoxicated her. After they were married, whenever she stroked his shoulders she noticed how all the roughness and sharp edges had disappeared; they had become a soft place where all her cares and doubts melted away. She then sank into a new kind of indulgence, a feeling of nearly total security that became purely physical.

Her mild terror helped her renew her love for her husband's body, and although she was partially successful in this regard, she knew that this renewal would not last for long, and that someday a new weariness would set in to make him repulsive again. The only foolproof way to avoid that was for him to grow a pair of breasts to restore the novelty and security she needed so desperately.

The following days were spent in constant prayer and anticipation of the time when breasts would grow on her husband's chest, there to await the hungry mouth of a child.

How she wished she could be that child's mouth, sucking contentedly on her mother's breasts just as she had once rubbed her lips against the breasts of her clay doll, a form of pleasure so satisfying it made her tremble. She still remembered the time she had hidden in an underground air-raid shelter and covered her clay doll's lustrous skin with kisses. She was like a mole wallowing in the pleasure of living in an underground burrow that never sees the light of day. She derived more gratification from this activity than any father, any neighbor girl's doll, or any neighbor girl's mother could ever have provided.

One question remained unanswered: had there been a struggle the first time she kissed the clay doll? She recalled the time she had raised one of her clay dolls to her lips, then flung it to the floor and shattered it, leaving only the two bumps that had been on the chest looking up at her haughtily.

But she never had to worry about being discovered in her underground shelter; she felt safe in that dark, empty space deep underground. Besides, kissing her clay doll like that was perfectly proper; there was nothing to be ashamed of.

How she wished that her home had a cellar, a room unknown to anyone else, or some dark place where she could hide. But there was none—the place was neat, the waxed floors shone, and there were no out-of-the-way corners. She was suddenly gripped by an extraordinary longing for her hometown, where the vast open country and sugarcane patches provided an infinite number of hiding places where no one could ever find her. She missed it so badly and so often that the thought brought tears to her eyes.

She finally decided to tell her husband that she had to go back home. He lay there holding his head in his hands, frowning.

"I can't for the life of me figure out where you get such ideas. Didn't you say you'd never go back to that godforsaken home of yours, no matter what?" he said contemptuously.

"That was before, things were different then," she said earnestly, ignoring the impatience in his voice. "Now all I want is to go home, really, I just want to go home."

"Why?"

"No reason."

"Do you think you can?"

"I don't know," she answered, suddenly losing interest and feeling that defending herself was both meaningless and futile. It was all so ridiculous that she turned away.

"Are you angry?" He gently put his arms around her.

"Not at all," she said.

She was genuinely not angry. She let him draw her close, but when her back touched his flat chest, the image of those vast sugarcane patches flashed before her, until the bed seemed surrounded by them, as far as the eye could see. "He has to grow a pair of breasts, he just has to!" she thought to herself, in fact, said it very softly, although he was so intent upon unbuttoning her pajama top that he failed to notice.

As in the past, his hands made her feel unclean. She had always believed, although somewhat vaguely, that the hands fondling her breasts ought to be her own and not his. The weak light in the room barely illuminated the outline of his hands, which she allowed to continue fondling her breasts. It was funny that she was aware of his hands only when they were in bed together.

But it hadn't always been like that. When she first met him, his hands had represented success and achievement; like his chest, they had brought her contentment and security. Then, once they were married, his hands had brought her unimaginable pleasure. And now all she could think of was how to escape them. The foolishness of it all made her laugh.

She knew that this was inevitable, that all she could do was pray for him to grow a pair of breasts. For the sake of domestic tranquillity and happiness, she had to pray with increased devotion.

From the beginning she knew that in a unique situation like this simply kneeling in prayer was hopeless. A more primitive kind of supplication was called for, a thoroughly liberating form of prayer. And so, after her husband left for work in the morning, she locked herself in the bedroom and pulled down the shades, stood in front of the full-length mirror, and slowly undressed herself. As she looked at her reflection in the slightly clouded mirror she fantasized that she was being undressed by an unknown force. She knelt naked on the cold hardwood floor, which was warmed by no living creature, put her palms together in front of her, and began to pray. Invoking the names of all the gods she had ever heard of, she prayed that a pair of breasts like her own would grow on her husband's chest. She even prayed for her own breasts to be transplanted onto his body. If the gods would only answer her prayers, she was willing to pay any price.

She derived immense pleasure from her prayers, and wherever her limbs touched the icy floor she got a tingling sensation like a mild electric shock. She looked forward to these sensations, for they made her feel more clean and pure than when she lay in bed with her husband, their limbs entwined. She began to pray in different postures, sometimes that of a snake wriggling on the floor, at other times a pregnant spider, but always praying for the same thing.

Her husband remained ignorant of what was going on, so everything proceeded smoothly, except that now a strange creature began to creep into her prayers; at first it was only a pair of eyes, two long ovals, their color the dense pale green of autumn leaves that have withered and fallen. In the dim light of the room they gazed fixedly at every part of her naked body with absolute composure and familiarity. She took no notice and remained on the floor, where she laid bare her womanly limbs. Those eyes, expressionless and filled with a peculiar incomprehension, watched her, but since the creature's very existence was dubious, it had no effect on the fervor of her performance. She embraced the icy floor and kissed it with the vague sense that she was embracing a lover sculpted out of marble.

The pale green eyes continued to keep watch, although now they were filled with cruelty and the destructive lust of a wild animal. At some point she discovered with alarm that she had fallen under the spell of the frightful sexual passion in those eyes, which she now believed belonged to a half-man, half-animal shepherd spirit sent down by the gods in answer to her prayers; moved to the point that she felt compelled to offer up her body in exchange for what she sought, she opened up her limbs to receive that mysterious man-beast. Under the gaze of those eyes, she lay back and exposed herself to their enshrouding vision. She had completed a new rite of baptism.

This may have been the moment she had been waiting for all along, for it surpassed her marble lover and her obsession with the hoped-for breasts on her husband's chest. She was rocked and pounded by the waves of a profound, unfathomable happiness, which also turned the pale green eyes into a placid lake, on the surface of which they rose and fell in a regular cadence. Her happiness was compressed into a single drop of water, which fell without warning into the pale green lake and spread out until every atom of her being had taken on a pale green cast. After that she felt herself reemerging whole from the bottom of the lake. When she reached the surface she discovered that she was a pale green mermaid with hair like dried seaweed blown about by the pale green winds. The water of the pale green lake suddenly and swiftly receded, as darkness fell over everything and blotted out the pale green eyes.

When she regained consciousness her first thought was that she had been defiled. Emerging from the chaotic spell of sexual passion, she slowly opened her eyes and was struck by the knowledge that her body, which she had always thought of as incomparably alluring, was in fact just another body; for the first time in a long while she realized that she was merely a woman, no different from any other woman, with neither more nor fewer womanly attributes. She lay on the floor, sobbing heavily and recalling the breasts she had hoped would appear on her husband's chest. An inexplicable sadness made her sob even more pitifully. She was living in a dream, an illusion containing vast, hazy, transparent, and mysterious things, with no way to bring them all together. She knew there was no way, even though she had tried before, and even though she once believed she had succeeded; there was no way, she knew that, no way she could ever bring them all together.

She stopped sobbing. Numbly, vacantly, and reluctantly she got to her feet and slowly, aimlessly got dressed, as she knew she must.

II

She lay there, her arm gently wrapped around her husband's neck as he slept on his side. She felt safe, for the darkness around her was free from all objects; it revealed nothing but its own sweet self—boundless, profound, and bottomless. She gazed at her husband's dark, contented eyes and smiled. She had known that sort of happiness before, and was consoled by the knowledge that it would soon be hers again. Feeling like a wandering child returning to its mother's warm embrace, she believed that any child who had come home was entitled to return to its mother's breast. Gladdened by the thought of the pleasure awaiting her and her husband, she continued to smile.

She couldn't say how long the smile remained on her face, but it must have been a very long time. Since emerging from the vast emptiness of her dream, she had begun to love her husband's flat, manly chest with an uncustomary enthusiasm. She gave herself over to enjoying it and caring for it tenderly, for now she was relieved of her burden of uncleanliness and evil. When her husband perceived this change in her attitude, he started to treat her with increased tenderness. And in order to assure her husband of her purity and rebirth, she began to want a child.

Her image of the child was indistinct. She had always avoided thinking of children, for they reminded her of her own childhood and caused her to experience overwhelming waves of pain. But in order to prove her ability as a mother and show that she no longer required a pair of mother's breasts for herself, she needed a child, whose only qualification was that it be a child, with no special talent nor any particular appearance; as long as it had a mouth to suck on her breasts and two tiny hands to fondle them, that was enough for her. Her only requirement for a child was that it be a child.

She told her husband of her decision. As he lay beside her he heard her out, then laughed derisively.

"You sure have some strange ideas!" he said.

His remark amused her. She could—in fact, she should—have a child. Which meant that *he* was the strange one. She realized for the first time that her husband could be unreasonable and think illogically. The idealized vision of her husband, who had always been the epitome of correctness and reason, began to dissolve, and she knew she could now dismiss that rational inferiority she had once felt; all she needed now was to await the birth of her child.

Her husband did not share her enthusiasm and was, in fact, decidedly cool to the idea. But she took no notice, intoxicated with the happy prospect of becoming a mother. She enjoyed standing naked on the icy bathroom floor and playing with her swelling, full breasts, pretending that it was her child's hands fondling the objects that represented absolute security—its mother's breasts. Her pleasure brought her fantasies that the tiny hands of the child were actually her own and that the mother, mysterious yet great, was actually an endless plain whose protruding breasts were a pair of mountains poised there for her to lay her head upon and rest for as long as she wanted.

Oh, how she yearned for rest; she was so weary she felt like lying down and never getting up again. Although the nightmares no longer disturbed her in their many forms, they still made indirect appearances. Late one night her husband shook her awake while she was crying and screaming in her sleep; her cheeks were wet with tears as he took her gently into his arms and comforted her. Deeply touched, she decided to reveal everything to him. More than anything else she wanted peace, complete and unconditional. So in a low voice she began to tell him about her clay doll, how she had made it and how she had played with its symbolic breasts. When she finished, he looked at her for a moment with extraordinary calmness, then reached out and held her icy, sweaty, trembling hands tightly in his warm grip.

A great weariness spread slowly throughout her body, and she closed her eyes from exhaustion. Her husband's attitude took her by surprise, for she had expected the same mocking laughter as before. But all he did was look at her with a strange expression on his face, a mixture of indifference and loathing, as though he were observing a crippled animal. She felt the urge to cry, but knew that the tears would not come; she felt like someone who had done a very foolish thing.

Maybe she had actually been hoping for her husband to react by mocking her again, for she remembered how he had laughed so cruelly when she told him about the rag doll; the rag doll had suddenly vanished from her dreams, and for the first time in her life she had known peace of mind. Now she was hoping he would laugh like that again to rid her of the clay doll, like amputating an unwanted limb to regain one's health.

She rolled over on her side, turning her back to the awkward look frozen on her husband's face, then closed her eyes and waited wearily for sleep to come.

In the haziness of her dream she was running on a broad plain, devoid of trees and shrubs, an unbroken stretch of flat grassland. She was running in search of far-off solace when she spotted two mountains rising before her, two full, rounded mounds standing erect in the distance. She ran toward them, for she knew that the solace she sought could be found there. But whenever she felt she had drawn near to them, they faded beyond her reach, even though she kept running.

She awoke and saw the moonlight at the foot of the bed, looking like a pool of mother's milk, and her heart was moved in a peculiar way. She yearned for those mountainlike breasts, and as her eyes began to fill with tears, she clutched a corner of the comforter and cried bitterly.

Suddenly, through her tears she saw something stirring in the surrounding darkness, rocking restlessly in the motion of her tears. Then, slowly it became visible in the form of a flickering thin ray of pale green light. She sat up in alarm, shutting her eyes tightly and squeezing the tears out and down her cheeks, cold, as though she had just emerged from underwater. Then she opened her eyes again, and there lurking in the darkness were those eyes again, pale green, cunningly long slits that were laughing with self-assured mockery. Oh, no! she wanted to shout, but she couldn't move. They stared at each other in the two-dimensional darkness, although she was sure that they were slowly drawing closer to her. The pale greenness was growing crueler and becoming an approaching presence of overwhelming power. There was no way she could back off, nowhere for her to turn, and nothing with which she could ward off the attack. And all this time her husband slept soundly beside her.

She had no idea how long the confrontation lasted. The pale green eyes stood their ground as they kept watch over her, sometimes revolving around her. The milky light of the moon grew dense, slowly creeping farther into the room. During one of the pale green

eyes' circuits around her, something else was revealed in the moonlight—the tail of an animal, covered with long silky black hairs,
suspended lightly and noiselessly in the air. She knew what to do:
she reached over to the table lamp beside the bed. The pale green
eyes did not stir; they kept watching her, smiling with consummate
evil, as though they were looking at her with a slight cock of the
head. She touched the light switch with her finger, but she knew
she lacked the courage to press it.

The pale green eyes knew it too, and willfully remained where
they were, watching her calmly with a mocking viciousness. All
she had to do was press the light switch to win the battle, but she
knew she couldn't do it, she simply couldn't. The pale green eyes
also sensed that the game was over. They blinked several times,
then started to retreat. And as they gazed into her eyes for the last
time, there was an unmistakable hint that they would be back, that
she could never escape them—for her there would be no escape.

From then on she often awoke from disturbing dreams late at
night, only to discover those pale green eyes keeping watch over
her quietly from afar or floating past her; they seemed to be evil
incarnate, and every time they appeared, her own past reappeared
before her with a stabbing pain. Needing a liberating force, she
began to wish even more fervently for a child.

She sought the sucking mouth of a child, for she knew that
the only time the pale green eyes would not appear was when a
mouth was vigorously sucking at her breasts. She wanted the con-
soling feeling of rebirth that comes with a child's greedy mouth
chewing on her nipples, knowing that it would be more wonderful
than her husband's light, playful nibbling during their lovemaking.
She wanted a child, one that could show the pale green eyes that
she had become a mother. In order to achieve her goal, she felt a
need to turn to a supernatural power for help, and that was when
she thought of her wooden doll.

She no longer derived any stimulation from stroking her husband's body or from the imaginary breasts that had once preoccupied
her. The chest that had filled her with such longing was now
nothing more than a mass of muscle, flat and completely ordinary.

As she recalled the breasts she had once hoped to find on his chest, she was struck by how comical and meaningless it had all been. She knew that no one could help her, that she had to find her own way out.

She had searched, ardently and with an ambition rooted in confidence, for a pair of breasts that belonged to her alone, not distant and unattainable like those on the neighbor girl's mother. Finally, in an abandoned military bunker, she had found a wooden figurine of a naked woman with pointed breasts, two even, curvaceous mounds on the doll's upper torso. This was the first time she had truly appreciated the form of those breasts she loved so dearly. Her clay doll's chest had been adorned only with shapeless bumps. As she fondled the exquisitely proportioned curves of the wooden doll she felt a heightened sense of beauty and a reluctance to stop.

Standing in front of the full-length mirror bare to the waist, she examined her own full breasts, finding them so alluring that she had a sudden yearning for them. Crossing her arms, she fondled them until they ached. She longed for them, she longed for those soft and lovely, yet dark and shadowy lines, she longed to rest her head on them, she longed to chew on those delightful nipples. She bent her head down toward them, only to discover that they were forever beyond her reach.

She would never forget the first time her lips had touched the nipples of the wooden doll and how much pleasure that had brought her. Those tiny nipples seemed to exist only for her to suck on, and since she could fit an entire breast into her mouth, she could thus possess it completely. She prayed to the wooden doll for a pair of real nipples to suck on or for a tiny child's mouth to replace her own and suck on her breasts.

She wanted a mouth that was devoid of sexual passion, and her husband did not fit the bill. So when the pale green eyes reappeared late one night, she climbed gently out of bed and began deftly unbuttoning her pajama top. As they watched her, the pale green eyes appeared puzzled for the first time. She unfastened her bra and began to fondle her breasts. The pale green eyes, quickly falling under her spell, moved toward her. Two long, gleaming fangs shone through the darkness. The taste of imminent victory was wonderfully sweet to her.

As the pale green eyes drew nearer, the gleaming fangs grew brighter. She dropped her hands to her sides, exposing her breasts to the approaching eyes. She imagined those fangs biting on her nipples and bringing her the same pleasure as a child's tiny sucking mouth. Overcome by this exquisite pleasure, she began to moan.

The pale green eyes were startled out of their trance. They quickly recovered their mocking attitude and retreated nimbly after a long stare that betrayed the remnants of sexual passion.

She believed that the pale green eyes, with their primitive lust, were capable of bringing her happiness and release. She craved them, and in order to have them she had to do as they dictated. The vast sugarcane fields of her hometown spread out around her in all directions, layer upon layer, dark and unfathomable.

She knew that there would be countless pale green eyes staring at her in the heart of the sugarcane fields, that there would be countless tails stroking her limbs, that there would be white feathers filling her vagina, and that there would be gleaming white fangs biting down on her nipples. But it was a sweet, dark place, boundless and eternally dark, a place where she could rest peacefully, a place where she could hide. She longed for all of this, she longed to possess it all, and nothing else mattered. She yearned for her hometown and for the sugarcane fields where she could hide. She shook her husband awake.

"I want to go back," she said with uncharacteristic agitation. "I want to go home."

The sleepiness in her husband's eyes was quickly replaced by a totally wakeful coldness. "Why?"

"Just because."

"You have to give me a reason."

"You wouldn't understand."

"Is it because of those damned dolls of yours?" he asked in an intentionally mocking tone.

"Since you already know, yes, that's it."

Her frigid indifference enraged him.

"Haven't you had enough?" he said angrily. "I forbid you from going."

"Do you think I really *want* to go back? I'm telling you, I have no choice, there's nothing I can do. I have to return."

She shut her eyes slowly, wishing she hadn't brought up the subject in the first place. Dimly she sensed that somewhere in the illusory, distant dreamscape the little girl's mother's breasts had exploded for some unknown reason, and a thick white liquid began to seep slowly out of them like spreading claws, snaking its way toward her. In her bewilderment, her first thought was to run away, but she discovered that she was drawn toward the thick white liquid, which was trying to detach her limbs from her body and suck them up into its cavernous mouth. Her feet were frozen to the spot. The meandering liquid drew closer and closer to her, until it was at her feet. It began to creep up her body and she could feel the snakelike clamminess and springy round objects wriggling on her skin, as though two dead breasts were rubbing up against her. The liquid climbed higher and higher, until it reached her lips, and just as it was about to enter her mouth it suddenly coiled itself tightly around her like a snake. The feelings of suffocation and pain she experienced were eclipsed by an immense sense of joy.

She knew that the stream of white liquid would never enter her mouth, and that she would always be searching and waiting. Yet she wanted to seize it, for she believed that it offered her the only hope of attaining a kind of solace, a truth that would allow her to offer up everything in tribute. In the dim light, she set off on a search, not concerned that her husband might oppose her, for she was convinced that this was her only way out.

When she opened her eyes he was gazing at her, his eyes filled with remorse.

"Work hard at it, no matter how long it takes and someday it will happen to you."

"Maybe," she thought, "but not if I go about it your way. I have to do it my own way." But that was a long way off. She leaned gently against his chest, recalling a naked mannequin she had once seen in a display window. "I'll possess her someday, and maybe I'll call her my wax doll!" she said to herself softly.

Translated by Howard Goldblatt

BO YANG

(Taiwan)

Kuo Yi-tung, who uses the pseudonym Bo Yang, was born in Kaifeng, China, in 1920. In the late 1940s he moved to Taiwan and began writing essays in the tradition of Lu Xun's social criticism. His principal targets were bureaucratic privilege and corruption. During the 1950s and '60s he wrote numerous articles attacking Taiwan's closed society and advocating human rights, democracy, and freedom. Although he also wrote fiction, Bo Yang's fierce journalism earned him the wrath of the Kuomintang government, which imprisoned him from 1968 to 1977 on charges of "defaming the leadership" and "complicity with the communists." An irrepressible rebel, he also managed to earn the censure of Taiwan's mortal political rivals in Beijing but he has remained a popular hero both at home and abroad. While imprisoned, he wrote poetry, and his Poems of a Period *contains some of his most poignant writing. In recent years he has been transcribing a monumental eleventh-century history of China, the* Zizhi Tongjian, *into modern Chinese. Bo Yang is the author of more than one hundred books, most of them reportage, for which he is best known. Among those available in English are the short story collections* Secrets *and* Farewell, *his very controversial essay* The Ugly Chinaman, *and a quite remarkable history of Southeast Asia's opium bandit country,* The Golden Triangle. *Bo Yang lives in Taipei with his wife, the poet Shiang-hua Chang.*

Dragon-Eye Rice Gruel

I

"Who is it?" I shouted.

Hsinchu. From the middle of November, the wind in this famous old town in Taiwan never ceases. All day and all night a continuous roaring, whistling sound fills the ears. It seems just like the scene of an oil refinery which has been bombed, with black grit constantly swirling around in dense clouds of smoke. From groves of trees where the branches of trees shake till they brush against the ground, there comes the grating sound of leaves and branches scraping against each other. The layer of dust covering the glass of the tightly closed windows gradually increases day by day. The sun is like the eyes of someone who has just been knocked out: through the daze, it manages, with effort, to open, but it lacks the strength to see the earth as clearly as it used to.

I knew Hsinchu fairly well. On the day that this story took place, I had already lived there for two full years. Human nature is basically lazy. When I first accepted a friend's invitation and came to teach at his school there, I only intended to stay for one semester, but at the end of the semester, I was getting on well with my colleagues, and I liked my students, so I decided that I might as well stay on and continue teaching there. There was only one thing I did not like about this ancient, placid town, and that was the fierce wind which inevitably blew every winter.

I would not say that my attitude to the wind had changed after living in Hsinchu for a long time, but one's body gets accustomed to any discomfort after a while. My method of coping with it was negative, as, apart from going to school to teach, I totally closeted myself up in my room. It felt as if I were shut inside a submarine at the bottom of the sea. Whenever I imagined that my walls were the hull of the boat, and just outside my door the world was as turbulent as ever, I congratulated myself on my good fortune to be wrapped up in such a warm room.

The day that Shih-ming came, we had just started our winter vacation. Though it was not yet six o'clock by the time I had finished dinner, it was already getting dark, so, turning on the light, I settled down in a rattan chair with its back to the door and started to read a book. I did not hear Shih-ming knock.

Someone who is accustomed to all the intricate customs and etiquette of living in a big city finds certain things not quite right when he comes to the sort of simple, country place where I was living, so Shih-ming simply pushed open the door himself. As the angry wind poured in, a burst of cold air stabbed me in the back, and the painting of a man fishing on a deserted river which was hanging on the wall was lifted up and wrenched around. When I looked over my shoulder, I saw someone's shadow. "Who is it?" I shouted.

"A traveler from afar. A visitor from Taipei."

"Shih-ming," I said. On seeing my old friend again for the first time in a long time, I jumped up excitedly and took his briefcase for him. "Why didn't you first write and tell me you were coming? You should have written me a letter. How come you managed to get the time off? Aren't you always extremely busy in your present job?"

He took off his coat, settled down in the one comfortable chair in the room, and lit a cigarette. I noticed that his face was pale. His cheeks were emaciated, as if someone had pared them with a knife, making his cheekbones stand out prominently, and his eyes peered out vacantly from deeply sunken sockets, accentuating his haggard look.

"Are you ill?" I asked.

"No," he replied. "I'm just exhausted."

"Of course you're exhausted. If you become chairman of a great, big hardware company when you're over forty, of course the work load is a bit of a strain. By the way, Shih-ming, you should get married. You can't tell me you can't find a suitable partner."

He did not answer me. He just shook his head to express his disagreement and then closed his eyes.

"What time did you get here?"

"This morning."

"Oh? What was the business that brought you here for the day?"

"I came to attend a funeral," he said hesitantly.

I brought out the camp bed from the cupboard and said, "You can sleep on my bed. You're tired, so we'll talk tomorrow. If you don't mind the cold weather, you can have a bath. I've just heated this big pot of water."

He grunted his assent. As he stretched himself, yawning, the remainder of a cigarette fell from his mouth onto the floor. He bent down, picked it up, and put it back in his mouth. Then he went into the bathroom.

While I was waiting for him to finish washing, I set up the camp bed and hung a mosquito net over it. In theory, a windy place should have very few mosquitoes or even none at all, but Hsinchu seemed to be the sole exception to this rule. In fact my house seemed to have become a veritable haven for mosquitoes, so I had to check the net over carefully. When I had finished getting all this ready, I settled down in the rattan chair and continued reading my novel.

Shih-ming's bath must have helped him regain his composure, for when he came out wrapped in my nightgown, he seemed to be in considerably better spirits. He sat down and combed his wet hair. Although the light was not very bright, I could see that almost a quarter of his hair had turned gray.

"Whose funeral was it?" I asked, encouraging him to go on.

"An old woman's."

"I never knew that you had a relative or friend like that."

"She was my wife."

I could not help laughing. A mouthful of tea gurgled in my

throat. With an effort, I blew out my cheeks and thus managed to prevent the tea spurting out, but as the boiling liquid passed down my throat, I cried out in pain. It felt like I had just gulped down a mouthful of strong plum wine.

"Please don't be like that," Shih-ming said, looking serious. He put the comb down on the table. "Yung-en, if you want our friendship to continue, please don't make such an awful face."

I have never seen him look so grave. I stared at him with my mouth wide open, and he clearly saw my expression of shock, or maybe of stupefaction.

"It was like this," he said with a sigh, lighting another cigarette. "I always concealed it from my friends, but now she has peacefully passed on. As her soul floats around in space and she looks down on me, her husband, I don't know if she will shed a tear or not. Yung-en, you know where I came from, don't you?"

"Honan, on the North China Plain."

"That's right, Honan. But do you know where I came from in my former life?"

"Shih-ming!"

"In my former life, I was born in Hsinchu and lived here until I died when I was twenty-five."

"Why don't you have a rest? You're too exhausted."

Sadly turning his head away to get out of the light, which, although not very bright, was shining straight onto his face, he inhaled deeply from his cigarette. The room seemed exceptionally bleak. The wind was still howling outside, and the windows shook ceaselessly.

"I remember everything very clearly," he said in a low, deliberate voice. "Ever since I was young, I've always dreamed easily, and in my dreams . . ."

II

"Yung-en, I forgot to tell you, right until I came to Taiwan, I didn't know that the *kuei-yuan* fruit that we had back home were also called dragon eyes. Back home, *kuei-yuan* were *kuei-yuan*, and only people who came from rich families or who were sick were able to eat them. At this point I should make it clear that I had never particularly liked *kuei-yuan*, and, although my family was fairly well off, the first time that I ate *kuei-yuan* was when I was twenty years old. However, ever since I was young, I have often dreamed of eating dragon-eye rice gruel."

"Listen," I said, "the sound of the wind is really loud. You should rest for a while."

"You mustn't think I'm talking rubbish. It's really true. Ever since I was young, I've dreamed of eating dragon-eye rice gruel. I can't say exactly at what age I started having this dream. I just remember that when I was in the fifth and sixth grades of junior school, I frequently dreamed that someone was inviting me to eat dragon-eye rice gruel. As you probably know, dragon-eye rice gruel is a sweet gruel made from white sugar, *kuei-yuan*, and rice.

"At first, my dream was very hazy. All I knew was that, in the misty darkness, there was a bowl of food in front of me, and I couldn't help wolfing it down. Then I abruptly woke up, and there was still a clear taste on the tip of my tongue.

"I once told this dream to my mother. 'You're a greedy child,' Mother said. 'When you don't eat your fill during the day, you dream up some strange story so that you eat during your sleep. It's sweet? And not thick? And what else? What on earth is this thing you're talking about?' At the time, I didn't know it was called dragon-eye rice gruel, so there was no way I could answer. However, the day after Mother laughed at me, in my dream I indistinctly heard a voice saying, 'The dragon-eye rice gruel is ready. Come and eat it!'

"That was the first time I had heard the words 'dragon-eye rice gruel,' but they stayed deeply etched in my mind, and as I grew older, they became clearer. The voice seemed to be coming from a hazy, stretched-out hand whose fingers were not clear. I could tell it was a female voice, but I still couldn't see anything. Ever since that time, although I didn't know what dragon eyes were, I knew what dragon-eye rice gruel was.

"Nobody could understand why I kept on having that dream. My mother soon stopped laughing at me. Many times she herself heard me making the sound of eating gruel while I was sleeping. She thought that I must have fallen into the clutches of some evil spirit, but, in every other respect, I was perfectly normal. At school, I always got good grades on my exams, and I was as strong as a train engine. But every now and again, I dreamed that that woman was calling. 'The dragon-eye rice gruel is ready. Come and eat it!' and the sound of her voice got more pathetic each time.

"Doctors could find nothing wrong with me. Mother specially went to Mount Sung and invited a famous Taoist priest to our house. He came furtively for fear the evil spirit would get wind of his arrival and leave. At noon that day, my family put up a thirty-foot-high Taoist awning. When the sun had just set behind the mountains, at just the time when ghosts and spirits come out, the priest mounted the rostrum and, holding a peach-wood sword in his hand, performed his magic ritual while I sat on yellow parchment paper inscribed with magic spells. I remember that he shouted out the following words: 'Lord of Heaven, quickly obey this order. Ai Shih-ming, first son of the Ai family, had no quarrel with you in his former life and has no quarrel with you in this life. Return to your cave before the third quarter of the first watch tonight. If you exceed the time limit, you will be beaten with this seal, which was given by his holiness, the Master of Heaven. Let this order be widely known.' After each incantation of the curse, he swished his peach-wood sword through the air above where I was sitting."

I gave Shih-ming another cigarette. He lit it, coughed several times, drank a mouthful of tea, coughed several times more, and then closed his eyes.

"I've probably caught a cold," he said, and then paused a moment before continuing. "I stood at her graveside for a long time. She didn't have any children, and she had no property, so there were just a few nephews and nieces from her clan and six coffin bearers attending her funeral. After she was buried, they all left. As I looked at the pile of earth, I knew that she would be at rest forever. Her coffin lies next to mine in the Nine Springs Paradise.

The strong wind drowned the sound of my shouting, but I knew that she could hear me calling her name. I let her down. I am a worthless coward. She must be standing anxiously on the edge of a cloud, waiting for her dearest husband to come and join her, but now she must have discovered that her husband is still peacefully living on this earth, and those vows of devotion were as meaningful as a puff of smoke. I don't know if she is happy or is weeping in her grief."

"Shih-ming," I said, "you've got a high fever, and you're talking crazily." I stood up. "Why don't you go to bed and get some sleep? We can continue talking tomorrow."

"You think I'm talking crazily? Well, I'm not. Wait till I finish telling you, and then you'll find that I'm completely normal except for the unbearable grief tearing at my heart. And how could there be no grief? When a devoted, loving couple are prized apart by death, what do they leave behind? In the land of the dead, there is some intangible blur. But people who are still alive think that they can prolong their marriages into the next life. Heaven, you gave us love. Why did you have to give us hatred as well? Why did you have to give us the bitterness of separation?

"Let me go back to the Taoist priest. He went on skipping and jumping about till the middle of the night before he stopped. The next day, he left, but he didn't manage to stop my dreams. I gradually started to take note of when I had them, and I discovered that I always dreamed of eating dragon-eye rice gruel on the fifteenth day of each month of the lunar calendar."

"You went crazy every full moon!" I said in surprise.

Shih-ming gave a listless laugh and then stared at me with wide-open eyes as he tapped his cigarette with the tip of his finger. "No," he said, "I didn't go crazy. I just dreamed about dragon-eye rice gruel, that's all. You needn't be afraid. Even if I had gone crazy every full moon, I wouldn't harm you today. Although today is exactly the middle of the lunar month, there is no moon in the sky, is there?"

"I didn't mean it like that," I said with difficulty.

"All these years, I've regularly had that dream, but it gradually became part of my life, and I didn't think of it as any trouble. Nobody, however, knew my secret except the people in my family. We are old friends, but I never told you, as I considered there was no need to. Judging from your reaction just now, I reckon I was right not to tell you.

"My dreams, however, became more and more intricate. They were no longer the hazy blur that they had used to be. In front of my eyes, there appeared an old town that I had never seen before, but my feet seemed to know exactly where they were going, as if I were returning to my home after just a couple of days' absence. I stopped in front of a gateway with peeling yellow paint and then went in without the slightest hesitation. Inside the house, everything was dark and empty. There was just a table, and on this table was placed a bowl of steaming-hot dragon-eye rice gruel."

I listened, staring incredulously.

"Afterwards, every time I had the dream," he said, "I always walked along those streets as I went to eat the dragon-eye rice gruel, and gradually even after I had woken up, I was completely familiar with the streets. I never saw anyone, but when I heard that voice, which seemed to be choked with tears, calling, 'The dragon-eye rice gruel is ready. Come and eat it!' I groped out for it in my dream.

"I don't know if other people are the same, but I tend to become one with my dreams. Every time the lunar calendar showed it was the fifteenth of the month, I always went to bed early and had a good, peaceful sleep. Yung-en, in the end, what is reality? What is imagination? When I woke up the next day, there was always the taste of dragon-eye rice gruel left in my mouth. It made me wonder, is my dream in fact real life? Is my everyday life just a dream?"

"Shih-ming, have you been to the hospital for a checkup? Maybe you're suffering from a nervous disorder."

"I wish I were, but I'm not. I'm in perfect health, and my job is going very well too. In telling you about this matter, I've compressed all that happened in about thirty years into a few minutes, so naturally you got the impression that it took over my life completely. In fact, it didn't cause me any particular trouble. On the contrary, it seemed to put my soul at rest, as every so often I could get a really good night's rest. Later on, when Mother passed away and I came to Taiwan, that dream took me back to my childhood. People's memories are always rather poor. Only the luckiest of people remember much about their childhood. Most people totally forget everything they saw, heard, and experienced in that lovely, golden era. But I can always remember the Taoist priest with his Taoist robes and boots as he ludicrously and energetically jumped up and down on his rostrum like a monkey, and the image which this gives me gets clearer the older I get. Every time I return to my childhood, I linger in my home village beside the choppy waters of the Yellow River, and I imagine myself once more as a child sitting on the yellow parchment paper inscribed with magic spells and waiting for the peach-wood sword to come slicing down."

"You still have your dream now?"

"No, I don't," he said.

"When did it stop?"

"Yesterday!"

"How did it stop? Was it sudden? Or did you have some sort of premonition it was going to stop?"

Shih-ming took a long, deep breath. Then he slowly threw the cigarette between his fingers into the ashtray and poured a little tea onto it. The remaining glow in the cigarette butt went out with a hissing sound, and the tiny wisp of smoke whose source was now extinguished threaded its way upwards until it dispersed at the level of our heads. The evening was getting chilly, and the wind still shook the windows. I filled up the teacups from the thermos flask.

"You could say it stopped suddenly, but then you could also say it didn't," he said slowly. "I used to think that I would always have that dream, but then I never imagined . . . oh, Yung-en, I could never have guessed what would happen. It was the autumn of my fifth year in Taiwan. I had already been promoted to my current position. In order to buy a load of scrap iron, I came to Hsinchu. It was the first time since I had come to Taiwan that I left Taipei, so of course it was also the first time that I had been to Hsinchu. It was getting dark as I got off the bus and went to look for a nearby hotel to stay in.

"I remember it exceptionally clearly. Early the next morning when I was going out to get some breakfast, I noticed the calendar in the hallway had the words 'Fifteenth Day of the Lunar Month' clearly printed on it. I smiled but took no particular notice. In the past, I had dreamed that lovely dream on a train, on a ship, in a hotel, and even in the deserted countryside, so I didn't regard it as anything out of the ordinary anymore. However, when I walked out of the hotel, before I had gone very far, I suddenly realized that at some time in the past I had already been to the place I was now in."

III

"You'd been there?" I asked blankly.

He held his teacup with both hands and gazed at the dark window as if he wanted to escape through it to the world outside.

"Of course I hadn't," he said. "That was the first time in my life that I had been to Hsinchu. Hsinchu is a beautiful name which I had heard of long before, and I knew that it was a town famed throughout the land for its wind, but I had never imagined that I would actually come here myself. I suppose no one can control his fate, nor can he choose the places he is fated to go to. So I had finally come to Hsinchu. As I started out of the front door of the hotel hoping to find a stall selling bean-curd milk or a shop where I could get some breakfast, I suddenly discovered that the roads of Hsinchu, which should have been totally strange to me, were completely familiar.

"Yung-en, I immediately asserted that I really had at some time or other been there. Without the least doubt I had been there, otherwise how could everything be so familiar? But when had I been there? After the first crossroads, there would be a stone lion in front of me. Correct. And then after the stone lion, there would be a half-collapsed ceremonial arch and a great, big banyan tree. Correct. In front I should make a turn. Correct.

"Then I suddenly realized. It was in the dream that I had been there! So the town in the dream was Hsinchu, and I was now in the scene of my dream."

"Shih-ming!" I said haltingly.

"You needn't worry. This all happened three years ago. I forgot about having breakfast. With my curiosity driving me onward, I followed the route in my memory and then, just as in the dream, I saw the yellow-painted front gate."

"Then the gate really existed!" I interjected.

"Yes," he continued. "The gate was exactly the same as I had seen it in my dream. I involuntarily paused and even started to get frightened. The gate was tightly closed, and the step in front of it was covered with fallen leaves. Dust filled the places where the paint had peeled away, and a spider was crawling along a fine thread hanging down from the lintel. I couldn't decide what I should do. Several times I almost turned around and went back, but I knew that that was impossible. A thirty-year-old mystery was about to be solved, and even if the danger threatening me had been greater, I would still have gone on. After hesitating for a long time, I knocked at the gate.

"A gray-haired old woman opened it. She didn't use a stick, but coming out to open the gate was enough to make her tired and short of breath. She was very thin and haggard. Her clothes were both tattered and dirty, the result of many years of poverty. Not waiting for her to ask what I was doing, I walked in, and she followed along behind me. Inside, there was a small yard which was overgrown with weeds interspersed here and there with piles of stone. Past the yard, there was a very old, broken-down house. It was built in the old Chinese village style, of blackened red bricks, which were covered with moss. It was impossible to tell how old the building was. The old woman was rather startled by the arrival of her unexpected guest, and after I walked into the house, she stood by the door as if glued there like a piece of paper.

"Just then, I noticed something. Hanging on the wall was an enlarged photograph of a good-looking young man. He was wearing clothes fashionable in the first years of the Republic, in the early twentieth century, with a high collar and buttons made of cloth, but these did not make him any less handsome. The photograph, however, was yellowing, and one corner had already turned white. On the table below this picture a bowl of steaming-hot dragon-eye rice gruel was ritually placed."

I asked Shih-ming why he did not ask the old woman any questions, but he cut me short with a wave of his hand.

"Of course I wanted to ask her questions, but to make her willing to talk was not that simple. Thinking quickly, I pulled out my accounts book and told her I was a new census officer from the county government. I said I had come to pay a visit and ask her for her help. She believed me. After talking for a while about other unrelated matters, I asked her who the man in the picture was. "My husband," she answered. "Where is he now?" I asked. "He's dead," she answered. "He died of consumption when he was twenty-five. That was forty-one years ago."

"Yung-en, her words sent a cold shiver through me. That year I was forty-one years old.

"Next I asked the old woman, 'Is the offering you have made dragon-eye gruel?' My words brought a spark of life back to her tired-out old eyes, and poured a little energy into her body, which looked frail enough to fall apart if you touched it. She slowly walked up to the table and then looked up at the young man with the tenderness of a young girl. With a gentle voice, she answered me, 'Yes, sir. When he was alive, he loved dragon-eye rice gruel, and because his lungs were not good, he had to eat it every day. I remember the day he died. As his head lay on my arm, I held him up with one arm and fed him dragon-eye rice gruel with the other. My tears splashed into the spoon. He lifted his face up and smiled at me. Then he closed his eyes and passed away.'

"As the old lady supported herself with her withered hand on the offering table, the only thing in the room that could still be called clean, the loose outer layer of skin of her hand trembled slightly. I guessed that in her mind she had already returned to the time she was a young woman. 'At that time,' she continued, 'I was just twenty-one, and we had been married for only four years. Sir, I can assure you that there's not a husband and wife on earth who love each other as much as we did. I got a fright every time he coughed, but then he died. It was because Heaven envied us. I vowed never to get married again, so I have stayed a widow for the rest of my life. After I die, he will be waiting for me, and we will become husband and wife again in our next lives. You know, sir, I graduated from a teachers' training college, so after he died, I supported myself by teaching at a junior school. My pay as a teacher never let me live comfortably, and I was finally too old to teach, but I've no complaints. I've kept this three-roomed, broken-down old house that was given to us by our forefathers, and I feel content so long as I can make an offering of the dragon-eye rice gruel that he loved so much every fifteenth of the month.'

"While she was talking, I noticed another photograph. It was a picture of the two of them together. The young girl was smiling radiantly. Her hair was in the style that was fashionable at the time, with a fringe that fell lightly over her forehead. She was more than just good-looking. She was enchanting, but in just forty-one years this beautiful young girl had turned into a pathetic old woman.

"I was about to say good-bye and stumble out when I suddenly realized that I was that young man. Originally we were that loving couple, and I had died in her arms. I had let her down.

"Afterwards, I thought about sending her some money to help her live out her old age a little more comfortably, but I couldn't think of an excuse to do it, so I kept on putting it off. The day before yesterday, which was the fifteenth of the month, I didn't have the dream, so I knew that something had happened. I immediately hurried to Hsinchu, and indeed, she had died. She had died while standing by the side of her stove, and on the stove a pot of dragon-eye rice gruel was about to come to the boil."

IV

"Yung-en," he said, "I'm really exhausted."

I did not know what to say to comfort him. I pulled him up from his chair and helped him onto the bed, where he buried his head in the pillow like a helpless orphan. I secured the mosquito net. Outside, the storm was still raging. As the wind blew past the electric lines, it emitted an anguished whistling sound, giving one a lonely feeling of homelessness. I stared at the light, but it could tell me nothing. My mind was blank. I was just nostalgic for my old hometown, which I had left so long ago. In my hometown, I had an elder sister. I switched off the light and groped my way to lie down on the camp bed. My head was heavy, as if there were a sandbag pressing down on it.

Translated by David Deterding

F. SIONIL JOSÉ

(Philippines)

One of Asia's preeminent literary figures, F. Sionil José is the Philippines' most widely read author in translation, and it is said he has more readers abroad than in his home country. Born to an Ilocano family on Luzon in 1924, José studied medicine before breaking into print in 1945 with a story in the Philippine-American. *He writes in English and edits* Solidarity, *an important journal of Filipino and Asian affairs to which he also contributes frequently. A prolific author, José credits Rizal, the Filipino nationalist martyr, as his principal influence, and his works customarily reflect a similar quest for moral order and abiding social justice. José's novels weave a dense tapestry of Filipino national life; a series of five books in particular—*Po-On; Tree; My Brother, My Executioner; The Pretenders; *and* Mass—*trace the social, political, and historical development of the Philippines through five generations of Spanish and American colonial influence and subjection, and onward to its stormy independence. With his wife, José runs his country's most celebrated bookstore and literary beehive in Ermita, Manila. He is also the founder of the Philippines Centre of International PEN.*

Progress

Marina Salcedo, Senior Clerk, second grade, hurried to her desk to examine the deductions in her pay envelope. It was the fifteenth of July and, on the morrow, she would leave for Manila to follow up her promotion that was five years overdue. She had been in the Ministry for twenty years and, during the last five years, the cost of living had risen so much she was sure that, without this promotion, her youngest son would not be able to go to college. And now, there was this mortgage to their house and lot, incurred three years ago when her husband was hospitalized, and the bank had notified them of its decision to foreclose. The house and lot were their only property and for almost two decades they had slaved for it.

The usual deductions were clear but still, she was thirty pesos short. Then she remembered the IOU of ten pesos that she got the other day from the paymaster and its interest. And, of course, there was her contribution of fifteen pesos for the visit of Minister Arcadio Guzman the month previous. It was their regional office that hosted the preparations and she was angry at herself that day for not being brash enough; she just had a small plate of rice and some fatty portions of the roast suckling pig. The Minister had brought along a large entourage, mostly security people who ate like hogs, as if his life was in extreme danger.

Everything was now accounted for, two hundred and sixty pesos—what she would bring to Manila. She turned to the far end of the hall, to the only air-conditioned office in the building. The girls there were not chatting. It meant the Chief was in.

She stood up, trim in the blue and white uniform of the Ministry, her wooden shoes a rhythm on the cement floor. The Chief's secretary told her to go right in.

The chief was reading a dog-eared copy of *Playboy,* which he did not bother to put away. Marina stood before him, waiting for his cue. He was fiftyish and balding.

"So you are leaving tomorrow, Marina," he said, his buckteeth showing.

"Yes, Sir . . ."

"Well, you can have the afternoon off—with my permission so that you can prepare. You will have only three working days in Manila. Do you think that will be enough?"

"I would like to have an extension of three days, Sir. If it is not enough . . ."

"No problem, Marina," the Chief said. "And by the way— when you are there, will you please buy me the latest gabardine material for a pair of pants? I will pay when you get back."

"Yes, Sir. Thank you . . ."

Gabardine material—it must cost at least sixty pesos. Last time, the Chief wanted a pair of Levi's; they had cost a hundred and twenty pesos. They had this ritual when she returned, his insisting that he pay, her refusal. After all, the Chief had been particularly nice to her. This afternoon off, for instance, the leave with pay. And he did not make any physical advances the way he did with the other female clerks.

The first trip of the Pantranco bus at six in the morning was always crowded but, on this weekday, there were few passengers and she had a whole seat to herself on the right side of the bus. In the flood of sunlight, the countryside was yellowish green with newly planted rice, the ditches were full of water, the water lilies were crowned with purple. The towns with their plazas decked with soft drink signs flowed by, children on their way to school. All through the valley, even where the hills were grassy for cattle, the land was stirring. The bus sang through ribbons of concrete, across new bridges of steel. This was progress under Martial Law which Marina appreciated—the new roads and the bridges that made travel to Manila so easy. Whereas it took a whole day before, it now took just ten hours.

She knew, however, of the tension in the villages in the Sierra foothills, the refugees who had swelled the towns. But in the capital where she lived, there was the usual commerce. Even her humdrum life had its blessings, she and her husband had finally built a house. Three children, one of them already married and scheduled to migrate to the United States, another about to finish college, and the youngest almost through with high school. No matter how she juggled the figures, she and her husband were wage earners and their savings were all eaten up by the increased prices of everything. They no longer cooked with kerosene and the firewood from the farm was not always dry. And it was a long, long time ago that they stopped using toilet paper in the house.

She had filed for promotion five years earlier and she had gone to Manila twice. Now, she finally had this notice that it would be processed.

Shortly before noon, they reached Cabanatuan. She did not leave the bus; she brought out the plastic lunch box which her daughter had prepared. The fried pork, hard-boiled eggs, and fried rice tasted very good. She felt embarrassed having to go to the restaurant and eating her lunch there without ordering anything. When she was through, she went down for a drink of water.

The bus pulled into its Manila station at dusk. She had difficulty boarding a jeepney at rush hour with her two bags. She got off at España and walked the three blocks to where her second cousin lived. They went to college together. She would probably sleep on the rattan sofa in their living room again but that was all right. Better than spend thirty pesos in a cheap bedbug-infested rooming house in Quiapo.

They were having dinner when she arrived and, like a good relation, she brought a stack of salted meat, a couple of mudfish which were still squirming, and a *ganta* of gelatinous rice which they could cook into cakes. Her nephews and nieces were in their teens and their cassette recorder was on, full blast. Her second cousin and her husband seemed happy to see her, although she could sense a hint of displeasure in her question, "When will you leave?"

"I won't be here more than a week," she said. "And I will be away most of the time. I will not be eating here for I will be spending my days in the Ministry, following up my papers."

She had breakfast with the family the following day. She was up at six at the same time the children were getting ready for school. They had kept her awake with their cassette recorder playing the Bee Gees. She just had a cup of coffee and a piece of *pan de sal* although she was urged to have her fill with the busy day ahead.

It was a hustle taking a ride in España early in the morning so she decided to walk to Morayta, where she could get a ride more easily. She arrived at the Ministry at eight-thirty and proceeded immediately to Personnel. It was always good to know someone in any office and she wondered if her colleagues way back were still there, like Mr. Tobias, who was once section chief. She looked around the broad expanse of desks, at the clerks chattering. There was no one she knew of consequence who could help. And Mr. Tobias had retired.

She wondered if she should go direct to the Minister; he had told her when he visited the valley that she should come and see him but she knew his saying that was just one of those niceties. Furthermore, he seemed incoherent then for he had got drunk again and she was sure he would not remember what things he promised. Now that she was in Manila, she realized this was a simple matter which should not be brought to someone as high up as a Minister.

She asked one of the clerks near the door who was in charge of papers of staff promotion and she was directed to the other end of the office.

She was a large, corpulent woman, in her early thirties, with bad teeth, stringy hair, and too bright a lipstick. Her uniform was one size small and her pendulous breasts seemed ready to burst out of it. She brought out a list from her drawer and went through it studiously, then, after a lot of shifting of papers, she looked at her with a smile pasted on her porcine face. "I am sorry, Mrs. Salcedo, but your name is not here. Maybe, the forms got misplaced . . ."

"But it cannot be,' Marina said, her voice rising. "I have the official letter from you last month." She quickly dug into her handbag and brought it out. "Here—and the file number . . ."

But the woman was adamant. She shook her head without the plastic smile leaving her face. "Mrs. Salcedo," she said coyly, "I will have to go through the files—stacks and stacks of them. I am very busy. I will have to ask one of the boys . . ." She opened her drawer close to Mrs. Salcedo. "Why don't you drop a twenty peso bill here for him . . .?"

For a moment, Marina Salcedo was shocked, not quite able to believe that this was happening to her since she worked in the same Ministry. Then she recalled how Anita Botong in her office did the same thing—a custom too entrenched now to uproot. She opened her handbag and dropped the twenty peso bill in the drawer. "Will I come back for it this afternoon then?"

"Oh, Mrs. Salcedo," the woman said sweetly. "You know how difficult it will be. Why don't you come back early tomorrow?"

"I am from the province . . ."

"Yes, I know. I will do all I can to help you . . ."

She had nothing more to do. It was almost ten so she took a jeepney to Quiapo and browsed around the textile stalls, asking the vendors what gabardine was, and which was the best brand. It was a humid morning and the fumes of a thousand jeepneys and buses choked her and tightened her chest. She ended up in one of the department stores where she did not have to haggle; the gabardine pant material cost her thirty-four pesos. From the store, she walked to the public market and compared food prices; they were higher than at home and she was complaining!

At noon, she went to a greasy noodle restaurant on the boulevard. The place was dirty, with scraps of paper on the floor, the tabletops awash with noodle droppings. She spent five pesos on a steaming bowl of noodles with strips of chicken; it tasted soapy but it was filling.

Back in the crowds of Quiapo, she remembered how her children had warned her about bag snatching in the heart of Manila and she hugged her vinyl handbag, the strap over her arm. She did not want to return to the apartment in Sampaloc and be a bother to her second cousin and rile at the racket of her nephews and nieces. She decided instead to have a fill of the shops at Avenida and the Escolta; she had not been to Manila for some time; the jostling crowds, the sweaty faces of people, the stench of alleys in Santa Cruz and the warren of streets behind Avenida—how vastly different was her life in the valley. She was about to cross to Escolta when an air-conditioned bus for Makati stopped in the traffic; she had read about this new bus. She boarded it, its air-conditioning quickly suffusing her.

Makati had really changed; the soaring glass-cased buildings, the wide streets. They were knocking down so many sidewalks and whitewashing the gutters. Manila was clean compared to what it was and Makati was cleanest. "It is like America," one of the Ministry assistant secretaries had remarked once when he lectured on the problems of urbanization. There was tremendous wealth here and he wondered which of the buildings belonged to Minister Guzman for it was rumored that he owned one, that its foundations were fertilizer. How could anyone in government own a building so fast? The reply to that question was that Minister Guzman had been very frugal; he took jeepneys instead of riding in taxis. If this was America, then her oldest son would see a lot of it and when he finally became an American citizen, he could petition her and her husband so that they, too, could share the bounty of that land of milk and honey. But the future was here, in Makati. If this is the future, was it necessary to emigrate?

The following morning, she was given another shock by the woman who finally found her papers. There was a missing form —a new one which she must get from Administrative, Form I 12, which she should fill in immediately and present to Personnel for endorsement back to Administrative. The section was on the fifth floor and the elevator was not working. She went out into the stairway, dirty with spit and cigarette butts. On the walls were posters proclaiming the goals of the New Society, the need for discipline, increased production. She was in charge of distributing them in her part of the province and there were still stacks of them in Property.

The man in charge of Form I 12 was very solicitous. "Oh, Miss, please come back tomorrow in the afternoon. We have run out and we are mimeographing a new batch."

"But I am from the province," she started protesting, then held back. She recognized it at once—the old ploy—and was irritated that it should also be done to her. The man's top drawer was open. She looked into her handbag and found a five peso bill—the smallest denomination there. She made a mental note, she should have two peso bills. She took one and dropped it into the open drawer.

"Please, I am really in a hurry," she said. "Do try and find one. There must be one lying around . . ."

The man closed the drawer with a smile, then went to one of the gray, rusting cabinets behind his desk. It didn't take him a minute to find one.

Marina studied it. It was one of those identity questionnaires. Maybe some intelligence people were again looking closely into the past associations of government employees. It was not enough that in each office there was an intelligence agent or informer like their new typist.

She filled in the form haphazardly. Under the heading *travel abroad*, she could not help but suppress a laugh. How many government clerks have ever traveled abroad? She had not even been to Mindanao or the Visayas. They would probably feed the form into that computer in Camp Aguinaldo and God knows what would happen after that.

Going over the dates of her schooling, her joining the service and all that, she mused over the fact that she had never really aspired for something higher. After all, there were women bureau directors, even assistant ministers, and she had a college degree. She had thought about it a bit and she was not one to indulge in self-pity. The truth of the matter was that she and her husband knew their limitations and also what it took to go beyond what they were. They had elected to live, for one, in the province and it was enough that, after all these years, they had their own home, a piece of land, and they could sleep soundly at night, bothered not by nightmares induced by misdeeds they may have committed if they joined the gods.

She went to the Chief of Administrative, not quite sure that the form she had filled up was done properly but what did she care? It would take some time before they would come across discrepancies and she could always explain. It was her second day and she did not have a single endorsement yet. Fortunately for her, the Chief of Administrative was in; they had met some eight years ago at a seminar and though she remembered him very well, his bald head, his aquiline nose and thin lips, Chief Bermudez did not seem to remember.

He had a reputation of being straight, a management expert, and she would certainly find out the veracity of that reputation now.

Her turn came and she stood up from her far chair and went closer to the glass-topped desk. Behind Chief Bermudez was the usual picture of the President and his Lady.

"Well, what is your problem?"

"My promotion, Sir," Marina said. "It is overdue." She placed the papers before him. With an experienced eye, Chief Bermudez studied the forms.

"Well, Mrs. Salcedo, everything here seems all right. You know the procedure. After I endorse it, you go to Finance to find out if funds are available. Ah, that is where the difficulty is. Then, if the funds are available, the Minister will sign it. And you have your hundred pesos a month—retroactive to the first month of the year. I will see to that." He returned to the form and scrawled something on the second page. "I know that you have been in the service long and I should not be telling you this—but we must be patient with the bureaucracy. To move it an inch," she remembered his lecture at the seminar, "we must push, and push, and push . . . without being pushy." He smiled broadly. "Good luck with Finance."

They were now alone in the room. "Is that all, Sir?"

"Why, is there something else that I have forgotten?"

Mrs. Salcedo, in her confusion, forgot to thank him. At the door, she decided that Chief Bermudez was a good man and she wondered how he would feel if she got him some gabardine material, too. After all, he made her raise retroactive.

She lunched at the Ministry canteen—just a stick of fried bananas and a bottle of Coke. At one, she was at Finance. Many of the girls were grouped at desks, chatting away. Others read newspapers or just stared blankly into the cosmos. It was an all too familiar scene and Mrs. Salcedo felt like she was back in the province. At the office of the Chief, she was told that he was not coming back; he was at Batasang with the Minister, attending a meeting on the budget.

She saw no sense in staying. She decided to see a movie; she had not been in an air-conditioned theater in five years!

The following morning, before eight, she was already at Finance. She noticed that the section had several pretty girls and they seemed to do nothing. Then, at eight-thirty, he arrived, Julio Lobo, one of the most powerful men in the Ministry. He was in a brown gabardine suit—she recognized the material at once when he passed her. Through the glass panel she saw that he had settled at his desk. She went in.

Chief Lobo was pouring over a batch of folders and checking out the figures with a small calculator. He looked up at her, his eyes bulging from their bags, his thick lips pursed in a smile. "Yes?"

Mrs. Salcedo did not waste words but she did not forget to tell him that she was from the province.

"You can leave your papers here," he said, still grinning. "I am in a hurry. There is this meeting at Batasang and I will not be back the whole day. Till five this afternoon. You can come back and see me then . . ." He nodded twice, indicating that the interview had ended.

Marina had a whole day free; the movie she saw the previous day was not very good and she wanted something to free her mind from the tension and frustration that had tightened her stomach and brought this pain to the back of her neck. But she was far luckier than some of her colleagues who, even after a week's time, had not cleared their papers from Administrative. Besides, it could be worse in other ministries; a teacher she knew, for instance, had to pay a thousand pesos just so she could obtain a transfer.

It had started to drizzle when she was at the foyer so she decided to stay in the building instead and visit Planning and Educational, where she had friends.

At three, she posted herself in the anteroom to Chief Lobo's office. All the typewriters in the section were new, unlike the antiques they had in the province. And the girls looked well dressed even in their uniforms. Their shoes were leather high heels, their faces made up as if they were ready for a party. She had bought a pocket book the other day for her daughter who liked to read novels and she tried going through the first pages but Irwin Shaw, for all his lucidity, could not hold her interest, nor the bits of conversation of the girls, about the disco they were going to that evening in Makati.

At quarter to five, Chief Lobo arrived, his expensive leather briefcase bulging with papers. Three girls went in with more papers, and a fourth brought him a bottle of Coke and some cookies. When they had gone, she went in. He remembered her. "Ah, Mrs. Salcedo—yes, your paper is still here. But I will work on it tomorrow, Saturday. Did you know I work even on Saturday?"

"No, Sir."

"Well, I do," he said, baring his teeth, yellow with nicotine. "So, maybe, tomorrow afternoon, I will finish it." He looked at his desk calendar then at her papers again. "At range 53, a hundred pesos a month. Why, that's one thousand two hundred pesos a year. Surely, you can afford to treat me to a forty peso dinner!"

"Yes, of course, Sir," she said.

"Well, then, my favorite Japanese restaurant is in Ermita. It is easy to find, at Padre Faura. I will be there on Sunday evening, at seven. It is a date? I will have your papers—all finished. I see no problem, really."

"Thank you, Sir," Mrs. Salcedo said. Forty pesos! If she did not eat, she could afford the meal. Maybe, she would spend eighty pesos. There would still be enough for her bus fare. And if the worst came, she could take her pay in Manila, although that might take some doing.

Saturday and the whole of Sunday morning, Marina Salcedo did not leave her second cousin's apartment. She was afraid that if she as much as stepped out of the door, she would spend unnecessarily. She made rice cakes, cleaned the back of the kitchen where they hung the washing and kept a few potted begonias and San Franciscos. Then she washed the living room till the cement tiles were rid of the mud that had caked and hardened, and, with wax, she polished the floor till it shone. She also washed the dingy walls with soap. When the family returned that evening, the place smelled clean and her cousin was both embarrassed and happy that she had worked so hard. Sunday morning, she helped with the washing and ironing and at two in the afternoon, she went to Ermita to locate the Japanese restaurant.

It was not difficult to find. At two-thirty, it began to empty but there were still foreigners inside, mostly Japanese and some Westerners. There was something forbidding about it. Automatically, she knew that air-conditioned restaurants were expensive and she wondered how much she would have to tip, too. She must be honest with Chief Lobo, tell him that she did not have all that money, that his real treat would come when she got the raise.

From the restaurant, she went to the Luneta as she called it still, and then to the Manila Hotel. That was where her graduation ball was held in 1955 and she had fond memories of it, her boyfriend who was to be her husband, as her date, and how they went to a motel that evening when the dance was over.

She gaped at the cavernous lobby, the fine hardwood panels, the gleaming marble floor; it was a crime to walk on those thick carpets, to sit on those sofas. She had never been before in such a luxurious place, with bellhops in their white uniforms. So, there was progress under the New Society as this hotel elegantly proved. She saw the coffee shop, the pretty hostess in a *terno,* but she could not afford even just a cup so she went back to the lobby and sat there, enjoying the air-conditioning and the parade of beautiful people.

At five, she went to the Park and listened to the Symphony concert; it was her first live symphony orchestra—and she marveled at the different sound that emitted from it. At six-thirty, she walked back to the Japanese restaurant.

Chief Lobo was there, in blue jeans and T-shirt, his stomach bulging, his sparse hair slick with pomade. He smelled of expensive cologne but when he raised his arm, the odor of sweat and unwashed body assailed her. He guided her to a stool. Before them, a long shelf with fish, eggplants, prawns and, beyond the shelf, Filipinos in Japanese coats broiling eggplants, strips of meat, and chicken wings. The place reeked with the smell of soy sauce and cooking oil. In the light of the red paper lanterns above the food shelves, Chief Lobo's face looked faintly sinister.

Marina Salcedo had difficulty saying it. "Sir, you know I am just a poor clerk in the province. I have only a hundred pesos—"

Chief Lobo's hand dropped heavily on her knee and he pressed it. "My dear woman," he said. "We are not going to spend all of that. I will just have tea and—*sashimi*—that's raw fish. Too much food is bad for me. But not fucking. So, after this, we go to a motel. That will be no more than forty pesos . . ."

Marina did not want to believe what she had heard. Then, it came to her—the gossip that the chief of Finance was a womanizer, that this was what he often extracted. This cannot be, this cannot be, I must talk him out of it, she told herself, anxiety knotting her chest. She ordered bean sprouts, which was the cheapest thing on the menu. There was no fork, no spoon, so Chief Lobo tried to teach her how to use the chopsticks.

"I have three children, Sir," Marina whined. "My oldest is married—and I have a grandson, the first."

"That's wonderful! But you know, you don't look like a grandmother yet. And your arms are not flabby." He looked hungrily at her breasts and Marina felt the blood rush to her face. "And you are full breasted. Well, I will see if they are still firm after three children."

"Surely Sir, with all those pretty girls in your office . . ."

"Ha! So you noticed," he said with a laugh. "But they lack maturity, practice. And they need to be taught. I don't want to be a teacher all the time. Like I always said, nothing like a beautiful and mature woman. Which you are . . ." Another pressure, this time, higher up her thigh.

"I am forty-five."

"But you don't look thirty-five!"

She followed him obediently to his car, which was parked farther up the street. It was air-conditioned. "It will take only an hour," he was saying as they eased into the Boulevard. "But if you enjoy it, we can make it two."

Her throat was dry. She must be good to him. The future was in his hands. "Sir, I cannot do it," she said in desperation. "Even if I wanted to . . . my period . . ."

He turned to her, grinning. The man could not be dissuaded. "Marina, I am not finicky."

Alone with him in the motel at last, she made one last entreaty. "Sir, please. I will give you half the money when I get it. I promise!"

Chief Lobo looked at her in surprise. "Stupid girl," he snarled. "It is not money I need," and he proceeded to unbuckle his belt.

When she did not move, he barked at her. "Take off your clothes, or I will rip them off . . ."

"My poor husband, my poor children," Marina moaned as he started pawing her.

———

She was back at the apartment at nine. Chief Lobo dropped her at the corner of España and she walked part of the way. She took a long shower, feeling dirty, feeling abused, and filled with a loathing that could not be vented. The feel of his hands, his foul breath, his greasy face close to hers, sickened her. She wondered how it would be in the morning when she would see him again. He did not even bring her papers as he had promised.

A listless night, and, when morning came, Marina felt like throwing up. But there was this job that must be done and after having gone through the trauma of the evening, there would be no obstacle now that she could not face.

Chief Lobo winked at her when she came in. She could not look at the fleshy face, the sensual grin. "We will go to the second floor where the Minister is," he said, rising and bringing with him the folder which she recognized as hers.

The Minister's office was huge, carpeted, the walls covered with blue wallpaper, some paintings, and behind his desk was a picture in color of the President and his Lady. At the other end were upholstered sofas. There were ornamental plants close by, a crystal vase with daisies on the coffee table.

Minister Arcadio Guzman was signing papers which a couple of secretaries unfolded before him. He was also in a light tan gabardine suit although, on closer scrutiny, she realized it was of finer material.

When he was through, Chief Lobo went to him with Marina's papers. The Minister turned briefly to her with the bleary eyes of a drunk and recognized her at once. He looked at the name on the papers. "Ah, Mrs. Salcedo. Yes, you led the singing of the National Anthem in the program. I remember. And this—of course, I am very happy to sign it." To Chief Lobo, "Are there funds for this?"

"Yes, Sir," Lobo said.

After the Minister had signed the papers, he turned to her again, "Mrs. Salcedo, how is it over there? What are your problems? It is not every day that someone from your region comes here to me, you know. And your region is pivotal in the program of the New Society. How are you coming along?"

Mrs. Salcedo appeared thoughtful. Was the Minister serious? She wondered how he could be drunk so early in the morning. She shook her head. "We have no problems, Sir. As far as I can see."

"Come now," the Minister said, coaxing her to be open. "Be honest. Only the truth will enable us to achieve results. We don't want to make constructions on air. Hot air. I want facts."

Mrs. Salcedo shook her head again. "Everything is fine in our region, Sir," she repeated.

"All right then," the Minister intoned. "But you must work hard. All of you. You must remember that we are here to serve the people, that we are building a New Society. The bureaucracy has this rare opportunity to prove its worth, to build a progressive nation."

The admonition was not just for her; it was also for the others in the room, clerks, favor seekers, hangers-on.

"Yes, Sir."

"We must all work together. Cooperation is the word. And innovation, too. Promotions are wonderful but they must be deserved. And we deserve it, only if we serve the people . . ."

After she had paid her bus fare, she had only two pesos left. She had made three *pan de sal* sandwiches with corned beef and they should last her till she reached home. It was a bright July day—the rains had passed—and it remained that way all through the Plain and till late in the afternoon.

It was past six and already dark when she got home. She decided to save on a tricycle fare and walk. She did not carry much anyway, just her handbag and this canvas bag with her clothes, the length of gabardine, the bargain Irwin Shaw novel, and two apples.

The houses thinned out soon after the bus station. They lived on the outskirts of the town, where they could raise vegetables and chickens and, now, the road was rutted and unpaved. There was no electricity and the houses were now far between. She had just made a turn at the fork of the road when a man burst from the shadows and grabbed her bag. Though shocked and afraid, she held on to it, determined not to let it go. But the man had brute strength; he pushed her and she fell, her face scraping the ground. Now, the man tore the bag away and, as he did, she shouted at him, "There's no money there—just my papers. My papers!" But she doubted if he heard for he had sprinted away and was gone.

She stood up slowly, dazed and hurt. Her house was still a distance and, now, she felt so weak she could hardly walk. She picked up the canvas bag with her homecoming gifts. It started to drizzle and her folding umbrella was in the handbag that was lost. She did not mind being wet—it was the loss of her papers that numbed her. All she would have done was show them to the pay-master; the raise was finally hers. She knew after all these years that neither letters nor telegrams to Manila would elicit duplicates of the papers. She would have to return and the bleak prospect of going through that calvary again enervated and frightened her.

Their house came into view, its tin roof, a dull gleam in the afterglow, above its shroud of avocado and *marunggay* trees. When she pushed the door open, they were eating supper and they rushed from the table to greet her. They saw the torn blouse, the dirt on her ashen face, her wet and disheveled hair. To their torrent of questions, she gave no reply as the dam broke and Marina Salcedo crumpled on her knees, the grief, the anger, torn from her in bitter sobs. No word of comfort, of solicitude, no embrace could stanch the flow.

JOSE DALISAY, JR.

(Philippines)

Jose Dalisay, Jr., was born in 1954 in the island village of Alcantara, Romblon. His family relocated to Manila, where he began university studies in 1970. Dropping out after a year, he spent the next decade raising a family and working in a variety of occupations, including journalism. He returned to the University of the Philippines to earn a B.A. in English in 1984 and stayed on to teach for two years. Dalisay won a Fulbright Scholarship to the University of Michigan at Ann Arbor, where he received his M.F.A. in creative writing, and he subsequently completed a PhD. in English at the University of Wisconsin, Milwaukee. He continues to write fiction in English but writes drama in his native Tagalog. His literary concerns are eclectic, covering a broad human terrain. "Heartland," for example, with its graphic imagery of the ongoing Filipino New People's Army insurgency, possesses a terrifying universality of life in much of the "developing" world. Dalisay has published two collections of short stories: Oldtimer *(1984)* and Sarcophagus *(1992). He has represented the Philippines at literary conferences in Bali and China. He lives near Manila and is a member of the English faculty at the University of the Philippines.*

Heartland

The dawn broke weakly, like a soldier of a defeated army rising at reveille, for nothing. The sun was a yellow smudge in the kettle-gray sky. It shimmered, shivered, and dissolved quickly in the wetness that crept over the encampment and everything in it; and the air, rich with vapor, carried the morning crisply into every tent— horses' dung; the grass, crushed where the caissons had rolled over it; alcohol and ether, festering sores, cordite, and burnt greenwood.

Ferrariz was seized in the middle of a dream by the sensation of a large ball of iron lodging in his groin, settling there, growing and pushing against the skin to break free. The pressure rose to his temples and raised a cold sweat on his head and thighs. He came to and recalled briefly what his dream had been about: Carmela, at the *baile*, teasing him to take her sister; he felt confused, distressed, and intensely alive. He got up from the cot and relieved himself in an enameled chamberpot in the far corner of the tent. It was a silly thing to drag along in a battlefield full of holes and craters of every sort, and where an incoming round could, in a flash, rip canvas and wood, flesh and bone, mind and memory apart so that nothing much really mattered upon the instant. But Ferrariz treasured the little comfort it afforded him, he was a discreet and well-mannered man, despite the raggedness of the war. The chamber pot reminded him of soft beds and spotless linen. He thought of his dream again, had difficulty remembering the scenes, missing a detail here and there, and then suddenly he lost everything, as if a rag had been wiped across his brow.

It happened most mornings, grieving him more than the shattered legs and nerves he saw to daily and tried to mend, often with little more than morphine. Blood came with the business; it meant nothing now, the corpses piled in the wagon behind the camp, bloated and dripping; the physical fact of death was the first lesson any surgeon learned. Army doctors saw the worst of it; masses of men threw themselves at each other and when their work was done were brought back in the beast-drawn wagons, the crippled standing over their fallen comrades, clutching at the sides for balance as the bodies shifted beneath them when the wheels slipped into a rut or struck a rock. The rest of the infantry straggled in a file behind the wagons. He met them calmly, the burial detail beside him; it was the easiest of his tasks to certify the dead. It was only a trifle more difficult to decide who among the wounded would be sent back to the fighting.

He saw through malingerers with a practiced eye. Their faces demanded pity and it was simple to refuse them. He did not have space enough in the extended tent they called a field hospital— when they had gathered enough men in to justify the status—for the genuinely injured. Only those who could not walk on their own two feet were temporarily excused. At least three men already lost their feet willingly; the nature of their wounds was suspect, but Ferrariz did not care to assist the work of the courts-martial.

He cared very little, indeed, for the War and the army he nominally belonged to. That the war itself was pointless had long been evident to him. The natives had staged a revolution, and their task was to put it down by sheer force and attrition, because nothing else seemed manageable. The battalion marched into the interior through towns and villages named after a brace of saints. Each little huddle in the wilderness looked more miserable than that before it. The stench of the wretched clung to the walls of the mud-floored shacks they entered, seeping from dark patches in the straw. With few exceptions they found the villages deserted and stripped of all things useful. Ferrariz remembered the old man in San Victorino, betel juice streaming from the sides of his mouth, blind to the world and reason; and the headman of Santa Fe, rushing to greet them with a crude copy of their own flag. After they had been shot, their villages were burned and the army moved on. Behind them, the natives reemerged from shadow and tropic foliage with fresh bamboo and palm from the mangrove swamps. In less than a day, villages were remade and pigs were slaughtered, to go with coconut liquor. The people feasted, danced, and slept fitfully when they had had their fill.

That, to a large extent, was the revolutionary war as the company of Dr. Ferrariz knew it. It was as fruitless as hacking through the undergrowth—the infernal tangle of thorns and weeds that turned a man mad over nothing—and hoping that it would grow no more, that the rest of it would wither from sheer shock.

There was a rebels' army in the mountains, with generals, colonels, and captains of their own. These officers wore uniforms for their men to respond to; the men wore what the women had packed into their bundles. They even wore, Ferrariz heard with amusement, banana leaves and *buri* fronds, and stole into camps disguised as such, ever keen to slit the throats of the unsuspecting. The rebels trained monkeys at this task; they turned snakes and leeches loose upon the sleeping; they colored streams and wells with the blood of the kidnapped, so the rumors said. The truth mattered little, the doctor knew; confusion, at least, kept the men alert. The dead kept coming, with lead in their kidneys, brains, and kneecaps. Ferrariz imagined the instant of clarity—no monkeys there, nor razor-edged palms, only guns spitting bullets of familiar, fateful caliber. The enemy was made up of regular men, no need to count their ribs.

Ferrariz himself felt no unusual passion for anyone or anything. He felt colder than those horse-brained officers all wrapped up in their war. But then he understood that it was in the natural order of things for men to quarrel violently and do murder within the species. The brain was imperfect; scars and strange secretions turned children against their own mother.

The doctor liked to think that he faced his duties with the proper detachment and consistency. Before the war he had served briefly with the poorman's hospital in the capital. He saw infants born with open skulls and bellies; he saw and memorized the progressive ravages of ulcers, consumption, and diseases of the flesh. He developed what people took to be judgment and efficiency. When a patient seemed more likely to survive, he slapped a compress to the man's head or prescribed him a placebo and sent him home happy. When he slipped beyond a certain point, Ferrariz drove a vialful of morphine into his arm and wished him good night. It was, he reasoned, the only sane and moral policy to apply. It kept his mind clear and his soul pure on the battlefield as far as he was concerned. The morphine killed no one; it simply eased what was left of life. His hands rarely shook and his sutures were neat, a surgeon's pride; but when he shaved and saw the tiredness in his eyes he knew that he was bored with and hated disease and injury and the consistency of it

They were five days deep into the heartland, in pursuit of a rebel band no more than a fourth of their size. The men rushed into the forests eager for contact, the heat of the crackling, choleric air in the soulless huts now far behind them. The first patrols found no one; those, more timid, who came after them met savage fire from anthills, aeries, mud pools, and the hollows of fallen trees, or so it seemed to their unfocused eyes. The first group turned and again met nothing but the sight of carnage and the terror of laughter and battle cries in some strange and native pitch threatening to return, to mock them as they moved their dead. With all these gaping wounds and little deaths Ferrariz had begun forgetting his dreams within a minute of his rising. It was extremely annoying to the calm and collected man, whose chamberpot tinkled with what he thought was a ball of iron.

They brought him back to camp shortly before noon, trussed up in the wagon beside the headless body of a soldier named Venegas. A bloody flour sack at Venegas's feet gathered fat bottle-green flies.

Quirino Venegas, twenty-four and husband to a cobbler's daughter in Cadiz, had stood sentry in the forward outpost the night before and, like a privileged few before him, had fallen to the spell of the fireflies. It was neither rumor nor the devil's work. On certain nights, given the rare agreement of weather, instinct, and the indulgence of predators, fireflies of a family gathered themselves into balls beneath the canopy, these luminescent hives throbbing in the night like low-hung moons in a mahogany-leaf sky. At times such a ball would move abruptly, or explode in a thousand curving, deathless sparks, as when Venegas approached. The ball recomposed itself at a safer distance, a beacon in the mists; and Venegas, giggling at his luck and thinking of the words he would be using in his letter to Cadiz, ran after the fireflies, rifle thumping wildly against his side, and saw the other.

Venegas froze, unslung his weapon, and tried desperately to peel back the fingers that seemed to be digging into his guts. A dry scream rose in his throat, stopping short of his teeth. The bush crackled nearby with the other's movement; the fireflies fled, faithless and fugitive. The soldier pressed his back to a tree and hugged his rifle as though it were the blessed cross. *Ave Maria, Madre de Dios.* The other was the enemy, because the only man with him on the detail was his good friend Simeon, who was sleeping at the post just then. Simeon had never seen the lights and would have enjoyed his story. But Simeon had already shot a rebel dead while Venegas had never seen them face-to-face, until that moment. A feeling welled in his breast, a kind of courage; he would get his own man, with a little pluck. He eased his breathing and his grip and waited for the enemy.

The shot took him in the guts below his heart, tearing tissue but no bone. He felt astonishment more than pain; that would come, but at the moment he groped for answers, and fell on his nose and mouth in the mud.

Boots sloshed his way, they stopped at his feet, moved to his side. Whoever he was took time to catch his breath.

The first jab of pain hit him when he moved; the booted one tried to roll him over with the rifle as a prod. Instead of provoking the man to use the thing again, the rebel helped his weight along and felt a fiery liquid shoot into his veins from somewhere in the middle of him; it did nothing against the chill creeping up from his feet. He tasted salt and oil at the mouth. His head dropped to a side, the man on the other. Opening his eyes by the barest fraction, he saw the bolo lying within reach. He moved and the soldier stiffened instantly, pressing the rifle to his jaw.

He lay still and closed his eyes. The soldier knew he was alive, but had not decided what to do with him, Venegas who had so recently bargained with his God and Virgin and who now commanded a captive's breath. The muzzle trembled against the skin of the rebel's jaw, then lifted; a boot creaked; the man was kneeling over him. The rebel marked by his captor's breathing the distance to his face. A hand searched his pocket and his neck for treasure, and paused, as though the soldier had only then realized that his enemy was in uniform, though barely a boy, whose eyes were those of a man, eyes which opened and stared at him suddenly as the boy reached for the bolo and with a cry of pain and fury lopped the head of Quirino Venegas off his shoulders.

It was the good soldier Simeon who discovered them that morning, the rebel and his headless friend. Simeon gaped and puked, and, these protests of the gut done with, Simeon turned loose his fury upon the body of the boy, who lay sprawled on his back, a dull brown stain on his chest, his cream cotton shirt wet with dew.

Simeon grabbed Venegas's rifle and shot the boy in the face with a click; its chamber was empty. Simeon raised the rifle high in the air and brought it crashing down on the rebel's mouth, drawing the crack of broken teeth and a barely audible moan.

Simeon screamed, throwing the rifle in fear as though it were the devil's staff. The boy was alive.

And Venegas's head, lying in the mud with its eyes on the river, carried the same look of terror and astonishment.

The Major joined Ferrariz and the burial detail at the gate, gathering his greatcoat about his shoulders. It was bound to rain. The clouds sat low and ragged on the mountains' backs, the angry riders of solidly unmoving steeds.

The Major was a small man even in his boots, although he seemed to have once been fuller of body, here and there. But he was no weakling; he absorbed energy and kept it quietly like a shrunken fig. A year in the tropics had stripped his body of all but the most essential things, excepting the large blue veins that snaked across his temples like a hero's wreath.

He was a spare and practical man all told. His one folly was his hair, the color of well-burnt ash, which was swept back, neatly on either side of a perfect furrow, plastered to his skull with a perfumed kind of gelatin. He kept this in a special tin, which served him as the chamberpot did the surgeon. Most of his men tucked crumbling letters into their knapsacks or taught their favorite song to others, until they cried. He preferred vanity to sentiment or even comfort on that score; it declared more, lifted his foot smartly forward. Ferrariz looked like a shabby bear beside him, rubbing his palms as if he had never seen winter in the old country. It was impatience rather than the cold, or troubled nerves. A thick beef stew was steaming in the officers' mess and the wagon was late. Ferrariz wondered if the Major had had his lunch; it was possible, for a few quick minutes, after chatting up the man Simeon. Ferrariz had stayed with the soldier without saying much, letting him babble on about the bodies in the mud, already convinced that Simeon had suffered no lasting damage and would be his own story's hero in a day or so of more fanciful retelling. The Major came in time to hear the simplest of it and had sent men to fetch Venegas and the body.

A drizzle fell and Ferrariz put a felt cap to his head. The Major, who always wore a cap in the open over his well-tended hair, glanced briefly at him and returned his gaze to the road.

Figures, schemes, and all sorts of mean and evil dreams were running through the Major's mind. In less than five days in the interior, he had lost nearly two dozen men against six bodies of the enemy left in the bush. He had inspected each of these six bodies, vexed to find all of them irretrievably and uselessly dead. He had poked the tip of his saber into the eyeball of one of them, just to be certain; something like the white of an egg oozed out. He flicked the dead man's collar aside and saw the scratch on the side of the neck. The killer had claimed the prize that went with such sweetly personal victories—a brass bauble of some sort, inscribed in a language he vaguely recognized as holy. The six were peasants; their feet were large, their cracked toes splayed wide apart.

The bodies of his own men also often returned shoeless, and even, when they had been left out for a time, disgustingly naked. But that was hardly the worst of things. Many of those two dozen lost their ears and noses as well, or else were cut up badly in the most unnecessary places. As the men had all been shot, it was to be assumed that the enemy was playing, on the side, a gruesome kind of sport. There was a man who returned—alive—without his hands, which had been severed neatly at the wrists, whose screams filled the night until the doctor's ministrations took effect. And now Venegas lost his head. The Major thought of the headless soldier running back to camp with nothing to scream through.

The Major stared at the wagon coming down the road, drawn by a native bull whose head swayed from side to side. The stupid man must have stuck his neck out like that.

Ferrariz dipped into his pocket for a handkerchief and blew his nose. The burial detail, two men leaning on their shovels, looked tiredly at the scene. Ferrariz shifted and folded the handkerchief absently. The taller of the two gravediggers pulled his shovel from the wet earth; it came off with a soft sucking sound.

The light rain slid off the polished brim of the Major's cap. He pulled it down slightly over his eyes, so that he faced a curved horizon. Before this posting, at the Academy, they said he possessed a certain charm, a light and even comic wit for the ladies, and a crushing knowledge of affairs for manly debate over brandy in the study. This was when he had taken on the habit of parting his hair straight down the middle so that, with the veins and his ample brow, full accent was laid upon his being a man of deliberate thought.

But in those monkey-infested islands the Major had few occasions for charm or repartee. Not until this morning, in the brief course of their campaign, had he felt the tingle in his body that he remembered went with the first day of any war and with moving smartly down the reception line of a grand ball.

He wished to meet the rebel and confirm the existence of their first live prisoner personally. If his man was right, they had an officer at that. Not that the Major cared for the native ranks; the poor coconut Napoleons and banana Wellingtons would never have heard of Clausewitz to begin with. But they quite possibly knew a few useful things that the dead took with them.

The wagon stopped before the party and the Major saw the enemy who had passed out on top of Venegas's body. It was a young face, as dark as they come, with high cheekbones, a squat nose, and a large jaw, a plain kind of face that told him nothing, yet. Ferrariz looked at the broken figure on the wagon floor and saw another face, one that had been terribly bashed in; its lips were cut and swollen; the jagged edge of a cracked tooth stared out of the open mouth; a cheek was turning black. It was a mess of gristle, dirt, and fluid—blood, saliva, mud, and rain—as if the boy had wandered coverless into a storm of rifle butts and leather heels. The surgeon glanced at the men who went with the wagon. They were looking elsewhere, one of them murmuring something strained, an enraged lament, to the tall gravedigger. The murmurer dealt a chop to the air and the gravedigger winced. No one was moving to get Venegas's body or his head in the sack.

The Major studied the boy's uniform. It was such a hopeless army. No name, no signs of rank but the rough cotton thing itself to distinguish the boy from his—the man sought and found the word—playmates. He was probably a corporal, the Major guessed, probably sixteen, they were that desperate. The boy had no fire-arms. He was such a poor rebel, but the Major was not going to be fooled. Tell that to Venegas, he thought.

Ferrariz coughed and the Major nodded. The doctor opened the boy's shirt and checked the wound, blue-black around the point of entry, deep red at the mouth. Ferrariz asked a question of the sergeant in charge of the wagon detail. The sergeant shrugged; the other soldier who had been murmuring tapped his arm quickly with a small and eager smile. Ferrariz leaned over the boy's body and pressed gently down the length of the other arm, suddenly en-countering nothing, and for a second he thought that someone, probably that soldier, had cut the arm off in half-hearted revenge. But there was little blood on the outside of the sleeve. Ferrariz pulled and eased the lower arm out from under the body. The arm flopped whichever way.

Shot, bashed, and broken. Ferrariz mentally ticked off the likely complications, the degrees of spoilage a body like this underwent. Attacks of delirium, the rot of gangrene. Worst of all—and remarking upon this, Ferrariz felt something close to sadness—the boy had nothing to live for.

"He's going to die," he said to the Major, turning aside politely and sniffing again into his handkerchief. The weather was awful; he was steaming inside his brown wool jacket. Give him an hour, he thought of the boy, who hardly seemed worth the wagon ride.

The Major looked intently at the body, saying nothing. Ferrariz crooked a finger at the two gravediggers, who dropped their tools and hurried over. They hauled the boy off the wagon feet first; they tried to hold him by the broken arm and the body sagged to the ground. The soldiers laughed. Venegas's raw neck stared at them, as if wanting badly to join in. Nobody was scared of Venegas anymore; they had taken their horror out on the boy. The doctor reached over for the sack and peered inside. The smiles vanished, and each man in his mind implored the doctor to keep the head where it was. Ferrariz was simply being curious, professionally. He had practiced all sorts of cuts and slices on cadavers before, but never quite so decisively. It seemed easier vein by vein.

"Make him live," the Major said.

Ferrariz realized with a start that it was not Venegas, of course, whom the Major wished to revive. Ferrariz toyed with the thought of stitching the soldier's head back on as a joke. It was insane but so was this other notion and he felt like telling the Major so.

But the Major was already snapping out orders to his men, now scurrying about like harried ants to produce the stretcher nobody thought would be needed.

A flush rose to the Major's cheeks, a flush that felt good. It was a day for men of deliberate thought.

Ferrariz was holding on to the wagon, his mouth half-open, the boy at his feet.

"It won't do," he said. "I can't save him."

"Bosh. Try, Ferrariz. It'll do you good."

"I'm telling you, this boy's . . ."

"Do it, you quack!" the Major shrieked and stalked away. Goddamned good-for-nothing chamberpot fancier. Two dozen men all goddamned certified dead with his goddamned flowery signature, the bloody incompetent quack.

Ferrariz trembled with his own anger, wishing at that moment to simplify things and drive a pick straight through the Major's skull. When the Major breathed his last, he swore, he was going to perform the autopsy by the book, beginning with shaving off that idiotic hairthing. Army doctors had trouble enough with diarrhea, syphilis, and footsores to have had to contend as well with the addled brains of martinets.

But the Major had turned to him again and spoke in a more even voice that was almost pleading.

"Save him. The boy could help us. Help save us all."

It was true. The doctor sighed forcefully to expel his anger and contemplated the enormity of the task.

After three days on the sickbed the boy came awake and screamed. The doctor, who was out watching the packhorses feed, rushed back to the tent upon being told the news.

Ferrariz had insisted on having the boy moved to his own place. There were ugly plots afoot, he was certain of it. The boy was enemy, bastard killer. He deserved other fortunes than to be nursed and guarded like the King's own son when the feet of privates were rotting in their cheap rotten boots.

The Major had agreed, securing the tent all the same with sentries who chuckled every time the chamber pot tinkled.

Ferrariz reserved notice of such little things; for three days he worked like a driven man, cleaning out and dressing the boy's wounds, setting the arm, packing cold compresses upon the swellings. He felt godlike in that mission. He unpacked his books from their mildewed boxes, brushed off the fungi, and reviewed and relived the passion of the way of healing. He watched miracles work themselves upon the boy and stood back amazed at his own handiwork. When he was through, when he faced nothing more than that penance of waiting for the boy to revive, Ferrariz realized that his eyes were wet. Not since he stepped into the University, knowing nothing, had he felt as much of an honest man.

Ferrariz knew what to listen for from far off. They were cries, not really screams—cries of fear, cries of pain, cries of misery. The boy was going to open his eyes to the sight of another face intent on drawing the life out of him. The surgeon had used the morphine sparingly, anxious to return feeling to the boy, no matter pain. What the boy was going to suffer most—and Ferrariz believed in the existence of a kind of instinct that told people of it—was the loss of the sense to live. The boy was going to meet the Major.

The doctor himself knew nothing certain of the Major's plans for the boy. Surely the boy was of no great importance? But he had killed, in a terrible way. But it was sheer animal reflex, surely, by no means an act of war? Surely the boy needed to defend himself from Venegas, as he needed to defend himself again very soon from a battalion of the man's friends? Perhaps the boy was going to be a hostage, yes, perhaps the Major thought that, too. Perhaps the boy was going to be traded for one of their lost men. Perhaps the boy was a native prince, and the Major had seen the secret signs, having studied him so closely.

Ferrariz found himself pleading for the boy's life in his thoughts and he grieved for his hopes, leaves in the wind.

His name was Makaraig; he was fifteen. That was all. He was a soldier in the Army of Independence. He pointed to his uniform. Of course. What of it? It was a cousin's, a captain's or other, he wasn't sure, he was a dunce about those things. It was very cold where they were staying, up there. That night. They had sent him out to fetch wood. He had borrowed the shirt with the long loose sleeves; the fabric was thicker. He had lost his way. How?

Makaraig thought deeply, trying to remember. He found it very hard to think of anything. The first questions were easy. He tensed up and tried to breathe. Pain bored through his chest; it was tightly bandaged but a rust red spot crept through the gauze and it hurt. The left side of him, too, felt thrice its size. His words slid out of lips he could hardly part and even then only with pain. Pain, he was all pain. And the man expected him to think.

The man—he had a funny beard, but Makaraig could not laugh—had fed him soup from a bowl, spoon by spoon through his savaged mouth. He tasted nothing but salt, but the warmth of it was good inside.

"How?"

The man's voice was unlike the others he had heard through the canvas. The man's voice was firm and his accent was all wrong but his was a voice the boy had come to be used to. It spoke to him at night, lulling him to sleep. It banished evil. "How?"

He saw them in the trees, the fireflies.

They were beautiful. They were like a dream. When you tried to touch them, they left you, laughing.

He had followed the fireflies.

And when Makaraig remembered this, he wanted to smile, but for the pain.

The tent's door flaps flew open and the boy, staring, began to wail.

The Major took no notice of it, addressing himself to Ferrariz, who still had the bowl and spoon in his hands. Drops of soup fell on the doctor's lap.

"Healthy dog, is he now?"

"Barely," Ferrariz mumbled, cleaning up. "He can't move."

"He's eaten," the Major said. He had his riding crop in his hand and he gestured at the bowl with it.

"You told me to take care of him," the doctor said, trying to sound very annoyed, but the plea showed through the hoarseness.

"He's going to save us," the Major said, pleasantly.

"He's already saved me!" Ferrariz shook violently.

The Major looked down at him with contempt.

"Don't be any more of a fool than you have to be."

Tears were streaming down Makaraig's cheeks. The Major faced him suddenly and struck him across the nose with the crop. Makaraig's mouth wanted to fly open but for the pain, the pain.

"No gift for speech, hm? Can you talk? Let's help you along, shall we?"

Makaraig's eyes rolled upwards. The Major was poking his crop down the boy's throat. Makaraig vomited blood and soup.

Ferrariz was sobbing into his palms, muttering a prayer.

"You puked," the Major accused the boy. "You goddamned puked on me."

"He's only a boy, for the Virgin's sake, Major! He lost his way Major please Major . . ."

The Major rested the tip of his crop gently on the spot of blood in the boy's belly.

"Get out, Ferrariz."

"He knows nothing, you ass!"

The crop whipped to the doctor's nose, barely grazing it. "Get out," the Major said, "or you are going to wish you had never seen this boy."

"You're going to kill him," Ferrariz whined on his way out.

"Troop strength, deployment, order of battle. These, baboon, are the basic references of military intelligence estimates . . ."

The door flaps closed behind the doctor. The rain was falling and the cavalrymen were hurrying their horses to shelter. A horse and rider passed Ferrariz and splattered him with mud.

"I'm sorry," Ferrariz said.

The rider slowed his mount, puzzled.

A scream rose through the tumult and the rider spurred his horse forward, as though to escape before it reached him.

"I'm sorry," Ferrariz said again, remembering Carmela, his chamberpot, and morphine.

SHIRLEY GEOK-LIN LIM

(M a l a y s i a)

Born in the historic town of Malacca, Shirley Lim won the Commonwealth Poetry Prize in 1980 for her first collection, Crossing the Peninsula. *In 1982 her short story "Mr. Tang's Girls" won second prize in the prestigious* Asiaweek Short Story Competition. *The story also appears in her collection* Another Country, *which was published in Singapore. Lim's books draw heavily upon her Chinese-Malaysian heritage, although, unlike those of many Chinese authors from Southeast Asia, they are refreshingly free of sentimental cant. They address, rather, aspects of life in the Chinese diaspora that are seldom spoken of—as in "Mr. Tang's Girls," which explores the difficulties experienced by women in the "second families" of polygamous men. Anthologized as both an Asian and an Asian-American author, Lim received a Ph.D. in English and American literature from Brandeis University and lives and teaches in California. She remains an observer of Southeast Asian life, however, and retains important links to the Pacific Rim's literary community. In 1989 Lim coedited* The Forbidden Stitch: An Asian American Women's Anthology, *which won the American Book Award.*

Mr. Tang's Girls

Kim Mee caught her sister smoking in the garden. It was a dry hot day with sunshine bouncing off the Straits. The mix of blue waves and light cast an unpleasant glare in the garden, whose sandy soil seemed to burn and melt under her feet. Everyone stayed indoors on such Saturday afternoons; Ah Kong and Mother sleeping in the darkened sunroom and the girls reading magazines or doing homework throughout the house. Kim Mee had painted her toenails a new dark red color; she was going to a picnic in Tanjong Bederah on Sunday and wanted to see the effect of the fresh color on her feet bare on sand. The garden behind the house sloped down to the sea in a jungle of sea-almond trees and pandanus; a rusted barbed-wire fence and a broken gate were the only signs which marked when the garden stopped being a garden and became sea-wilderness. A large ciku tree grew by the fence, its branches half within the garden and half flung over the stretch of pebbles, driftwood, ground-down shells, and rotting organisms which lead shallowly down to the muddy tidal water. It was under the branches hidden by the trunk that Kim Li was smoking. She was taken by surprise, eyes half-shut, smoke gently trailing from her nostrils, and gazing almost tenderly at the horizon gleaming like a high-tension wire in the great distance.

"Ah ha! Since when did you start smoking?" Kim Mee said softly, coming suddenly around the tree trunk.

Unperturbed, without a start, Kim Li took another puff, elegantly holding the cigarette to the side of her mouth. Her fingers curled exaggeratedly as she slowly moved the cigarette away. She said with a drawl, "Why should I tell you?"

"Ah Kong will slap you."

She snapped her head around and frowned furiously. "You sneak! Are you going to tell him?"

"No, of course not!" Kim Mee cried, half-afraid. There were only two years' difference in age between them, but Kim Li was a strange one. She suffered from unpredictable moods which had recently grown more savage. "You're so mean. Why do you think I'll tell?" Kim Mee was angry now at having been frightened. In the last year, she had felt herself at an advantage over her eldest sister, whose scenes, rages, tears, and silences were less and less credited. The youngest girl, Kim Yee, at twelve years old, already seemed more mature than Kim Li. And she, at fifteen, was clearly superior. She didn't want to leave Kim Li smoking under the cool shade with eyes sophisticatedly glazed and looking advanced and remote. Moving closer, she asked, "Where did you get the cigarette?"

"Mind your own business," Kim Li replied calmly.

"Is it Ah Kong's cigarette? Yes, I can see it's a Lucky Strike."

Kim Li dropped the stub and kicked sand over it. Smoke still drifted from the burning end, all but buried under the mound. "What do you know of life?" she asked loftily and walked up the white glaring path past the bathhouse and up the wooden side stairs.

Kim Mee felt herself abandoned as she watched her sister's back vanish through the door. "Ugly witch!" She glanced at her feet, where the blood red toenails twinkled darkly.

Saturdays were, as long as she could remember, quiet days, heavy and slow with the gray masculine presence of their father, who spent most of the day, with Mother beside him, resting, gathering strength in his green leather chaise in the sunroom. Only his bushy eyebrows, growing in a straight line like a scar across his forehead, seemed awake. The hair there was turning white, bristling in wisps that grew even more luxuriant as the hair on his head receded and left the tight high skin mottled with discolored specks. Now and again he would speak in sonorous tones, but, chiefly, he dozed or gazed silently out of the windows which surrounded the room to the low flowering trees which Ah Chee, the family servant, tended, and, through the crisp green leaves, to his private thoughts.

They were his second family. Every Friday he drove down from Kuala Lumpur, where his first wife and children lived, in time for dinner. On Saturdays, the girls stayed home. No school activity, no friend, no party, no shopping trip took them out of the house. Their suppressed giggles, lazy talk, muted movements, and uncertain sighs constituted his sense of home, and every Saturday, the four girls played their part: they became daughters whose voices were to be heard like a cheerful music in the background, but never loudly or intrusively.

Every Saturday they made high tea at five. The girls peeled hard-boiled eggs, the shells carefully cracked and coming clean off the firm whites, and mashed them with butter into a spread. They cut fresh loaves of bread into thick yellow slices and poured mugs of tea into which they stirred puddles of condensed milk and rounded teaspoons of sugar. Ah Kong would eat only fresh bread, thickly buttered and grained with sprinkles of sugar, but he enjoyed watching his daughters eat like European mems. He brought supplies from Kuala Lumpur: tomatoes, tins of deviled ham and Kraft cheese, and packages of Birds' blancmange. Saturday tea was when he considered himself a successful father and fed on the vision of his four daughters eating toast and tomato slices while his quiet wife poured tea by his side.

"I say, Kim Bee," Kim Yee said, swallowing a cracker, "are you going to give me your blouse?"

The two younger girls were almost identical in build and height. Kim Yee, in the last year shooting like a vine, in fact being slightly stockier and more long-waisted than Kim Bee. Teatime with Ah Kong was the occasion to ask for dresses, presents, money, and other favors, and Kim Yee, being the youngest, was the least abashed in her approach.

"Yah! You're always taking my clothes. Why don't you ask for the blouse I'm wearing?"

"May I? It's pretty, and I can wear it to Sunday School."

Breathing indignation, Kim Bee shot a look of terrible fury and imploration to her mother. "She's impossible . . ." But she swallowed the rest of her speech, for she also had a request to make to Ah Kong, who was finally paying attention to the squabble.

"Don't you girls have enough to wear? Why must you take clothes from each other?"

Like a child who knows her part, Mother shifted in her chair and said good-naturedly, "Girls grow so fast, Peng. Their clothes are too small for them in six months. My goodness, Kim Yee's dresses are so short she doesn't look decent in them."

"Me too, Ah Kong!" Kim Mee added. "I haven't had a new dress since Chinese New Year."

"Chinese New Year was only three months ago," Ah Kong replied, shooting up his eyebrows, whether in surprise or annoyance no one knew.

"But I've grown an inch since then!"

"And I've grown three inches in one year," Kim Bee said.

"Ah Kong, your daughters are becoming women," Kim Li said in an aggressive voice. She was sitting to one side of her father, away from the table, not eating or drinking, kicking her long legs rhythmically throughout the meal. She wore her blue school shorts, which fitted tightly above the thighs and stretched across the bottom, flattening the weight which ballooned curiously around her tall skinny frame. Her legs, like her chest, were skinny, almost fleshless. They were long and shapeless; the knees bumped out like rock outcroppings, and the ankles rose to meet the backs of her knees with hardly a suggestion of a calf. In the tight shorts she didn't appear feminine or provocative, merely unbalanced, as if the fat around the hips and bottom were a growth, a goiter draped on the lean trunk.

Everyone suddenly stopped talking. Mother opened her mouth and brought out a gasp; the sisters stopped chewing and looked away into different directions. Kim Mee was furious because Ah Kong's face was reddening. There would be no money for new clothes if he lost his temper.

"And you, you are not dressed like a woman," he replied without looking at her. "How dare you come to the table like a half-naked slut!" He had always been careful to avoid such language in his house, but her aggressive interruption aroused him.

"At least I don't beg you for clothes. And what I wear is what you give me. It's not . . ."

"Shut up!" he roared. "You . . ."

"Go to your room," Mother said to Kim Li before he could finish. Her voice was placid as if such quarrels were an everyday occurrence. If Ah Kong's bunched-up brows and protruding veins all balled up like a fist above his bony beak put her off, she didn't show it. "Peng," she continued, sweet-natured as ever, "maybe tomorrow we can go over the cost of some new clothes. The girls can shop for some cheap materials, and Ah Chee and I will sew a few simple skirts and blouses. We won't have to pay a tailor. They'll be very simple clothes, of course, because it's been so long since I've stitched anything . . ." So she chatted on, rolling a cozy domestic mat before him, and soon, they were spreading more butter and drinking fresh cups of tea.

Kim Li did not leave the table till Ah Kong's attention was unraveled; then she stretched herself out of the chair, hummed, and sauntered to her room, casual as a cat and grinning from ear to ear. Her humming wasn't grating, but it was loud enough to reach the dining room. What could Ah Kong do about it? He had again slipped into silence, drowsing along with the buzz of feminine discussion, acknowledging that, Sunday, he would once again open his purse and drive off in the warm evening to their grateful good-byes.

But there was Saturday night and the evening meal late at nine and the soft hours till eleven when his girls would sit in the living room with long washed hair reading *Her World* and *Seventeen*, selecting patterns for their new frocks. And by midnight, everyone would be asleep.

There was Ah Chee snoring in her back room among empty cracker tins and washed Ovaltine jars. He had acquired her when his second wife had finally given in to his determined courting and, contrary to her Methodist upbringing, married him in a small

Chinese ceremony. The three of them had moved in immediately after the ceremony to this large wooden house on Old Beach Road, and, gradually, as the rooms filled up with beds and daughters, so also Ah Chee's room had filled up with the remains of meals. She never threw out a tin, bottle, or jar. The banged-up tins and tall bottles she sold to the junk man; those biscuit tins stamped with gaudy roses or toffee tins painted with ladies in crinoline gowns or Royal Guardsmen in fat fur hats she hoarded and produced each New Year to fill with love letters, bean cakes, and *kueh bulu*. Ah Kong approved of her as much as, perhaps even more than, he approved of his wife. Her parsimonious craggy face, those strong bulging forearms, the loose folds of her black trousers flapping as she padded barefoot and cracked sole from kitchen to garden, from one tidied room to another waiting to be swept, these were elements he looked forward to each Friday as much as he looked forward to his wife's vague smile and soft shape in bed. Ah Chee had lived in the house for seventeen years, yet her influence was perceivable only in a few rooms.

Ah Kong seldom looked into Ah Chee's room, which, he knew, was a junk heap gathered around a narrow board bed with a chicken wire strung across the bare window. But, at midnight, when he rose to check the fastenings at the back door and the bolts on the front, he looked into every room where his daughters slept. Here was Bee's, connected to her parents' through a bathroom. A Bible lay on her bed. She slept, passionately hugging a bolster to her face, half-suffocated, the pajama top riding high and showing a midriff concave and yellow in the dimness. Across the central corridor Kim Yee stretched corpselike and rigid, as if she had willed herself to sleep or were still awake under the sleeping mask, the stuffed bear and rabbit exhibited at the foot of her bed like nursery props, unnecessary now that the play was over. He sniffed in Kim Mee's room; it smelt of talcum and hairspray. The memory of other rooms came to mind, rooms which disgusted him as he wrestled to victory with their occupants. But no pink satin pillows or red paper flowers were here; a centerfold of the British singers the Beatles was taped to one wall and blue checked curtains swayed in the night breeze.

Kim Mee slept curled against her bolster. In a frilly babydoll, her haunches curved and enveloped the pillow like a woman with her lover. He hated the sight but didn't cover her in case she should wake. There was a time when he would walk through the house looking into every room, and each silent form would fill him with pleasure, that they should belong to him, depend on his homecoming, and fall asleep in his presence, innocent and pure. Now the harsh scent of hairspray stagnated in the air; its metallic fragrance was clammy and chilled, a cheap and thin cover over the daughter whose delicate limbs were crowned with an idol's head aureoled and agonized by bristling rollers. Again the recollection of disgust tinged his thoughts, and he hesitated before Kim Li's room. He didn't know what to expect anymore of his daughters, one spending her allowance on lipstick, nail polish, Blue Grass cologne, and this other somehow not seeming quite right.

Kim Li was not yet asleep. With knees raised up, she sat in bed reading in the minute diagonal light of the bed lamp. He stopped at the door but could not retreat quickly enough. She turned a baleful look. "What do you want?"

"It's twelve o'clock. Go to sleep," he said curtly, feeling that that was not exactly what he should say; however, he seldom had to think about what to say in this house, and his self-consciousness was extreme. Suddenly he noticed her. She had cut her hair short, when he couldn't tell. He remembered once noticing that her hair was long and that she had put it up in a ponytail, which made her unpretty face as small as his palm. Tonight, her hair was cropped short carelessly in the front and sides so that what might have been curls shot away from her head like bits of string. She's ugly! he thought and turned away, not staying to see if she would obey him.

He stayed awake most of the night. This had been true every Saturday night for many years. Sleeping through the mornings, drowsing in the lounge chair through the afternoons, and sitting somnolent through tea and dinner hours, his life, all expended in the noise, heat, and rackety shuttle of the mines during the week, would gradually flow back to being. The weakness that overcame him as soon as he arrived at the front door each Friday night would ebb away; slowly, the movements of women through the rooms returned to him a masculine vitality. Their gaiety aroused him to strength, and his mind began turning again, although at first numb and weary.

He was supine and passive all through Saturday, but by night-fall he was filled with nervous energy. After his shower he would enter his bedroom with head and shoulders erect. His round soft wife in her faded nightgown was exactly what he wanted then; he was firm next to her slack hips, lean against her plump rolling breasts; he could sink into her submissive form like a bull sinking into a mudbank, groaning with pleasure. Later, after she was asleep, his mind kept churning. Plans for the week ahead were meticulously laid: the lawyer to visit on Monday; the old *klong* to be shut and the machinery moved to the new site; Jason, his eldest son, to be talked to about his absences from the office; the monthly remittance to be sent to Wanda, his second daughter, in Melbourne; old Chong to be retired. His mind worked thus, energetically and unhesitatingly, while he listened to his daughters settle for the night, the bathrooms eventually quiet, Ah Chee dragging across the corridor to bolt the doors, and soft clicks as one light and then another was switched off. Then, after the clock struck its twelve slow chimes, he walked through the house, looking into each room while his mind and body ran in electrical fusion, each female form in bed renewing his pleasure with his life, leaving each room with a fresh vibrance to his body. So he would lie awake till the early hours of Sunday, calm yet vibrating strongly, breathing deeply, for he believed in the medicinal value of fresh night air, while his mind struggled with problems and resolved them for the next week.

Tonight, however, his sleeplessness was not pleasurable. Old, he thought, old and wasted his daughters had made him. He couldn't lie relaxed and immobile; the bodies of women surrounded him in an irritating swarm. He heard Kim Li slapping a book shut, footsteps moving toward the dining room; a refrigerator door opening and its motor running. "Stupid girl!" he muttered, thinking of the cold flooding out of the machine, ice melting in trays, the tropical heat corrupting the rectangles of butter still hard and satiny in their paper wrappers. But he didn't get up to reprimand her.

All day Ah Kong would not speak to Kim Li; this wouldn't have appeared out of the ordinary except that she sat in the sunroom with him most of the morning.

Kim Bee and Kim Yee escaped to church at nine. In white and pink, wearing their grown-up heels and hair parted in braids, they looked like bridesmaids, ceremoniously stiff with a sparkle of excitement softening their faces. The Methodist Church was ten minutes' walk away. Mother no longer went to church, but her younger daughters went every Sunday, since it was still their mother's faith, and were greeted by women their mother's age, who sent regards but never visited themselves. The pastor was especially nice to them, having participated in the drama eighteen years ago.

She's a stray lamb. Those were barbaric times after the Japanese Occupation; otherwise, she would probably not have consented to live in sinful relationship as a second wife. And, although I suppose it doesn't matter who the sin is committed with, Mr. Tang is a well-known, respectable man. Her situation is more understandable when you know how careful and correct Mr. Tang is with everything concerning himself and his family. It's a pity he is so Chinese, although, of course, divorces weren't as acceptable until a few years ago, and, even now, one shouldn't encourage it. Yet, if only he would divorce his first wife, she could return to the Church and the children . . . They're lovely girls, all of them, although the oldest hasn't been to service in a while, and the second seems excitable. The two young ones are so good, volunteering for the Sunday School Drive, singing in the choir (they have such sweet tones!) and so cheerful. A little anxious about the Scriptures. They want to know especially what has been written about the Day of Judgment, which isn't surprising seeing . . . Now, if Mr. Tang weren't a pagan, he couldn't maintain this terrible life, keeping two households in separate towns, but, of course, he's old-fashioned and believes in the propriety of polygamy. Pagans have their own faith, I have no doubt, and Christ will consider this when the Day comes, but for the mother . . .

For Kim Bee and Kim Yee, Sunday service was one of the more enjoyable events in a dull weekend. Fresh as frangipani wreaths, they walked companionably to church, for once in full charge of themselves. They radiated health and cheerfulness from the hours of imposed rest, from their gladness at meeting the friends their parents never met but still approved of, and from the simple encouraging emotions of welcome, love, and forgiveness which welled up in hymns, and which were the open subjects of the pastor's sermon.

"Love, love, love," sang the choir. "Our Father, Our Father," they murmured and flooded their hearts with gratitude, with desire. Radiant, they returned from church at noon, in time for lunch and, later, to say good-bye to Ah Kong, who drove back to Kuala Lumpur every Sunday at two.

All morning Kim Li sat cross-legged on the floor next to Ah Kong's chair. Now and again she attempted to clip a toenail, but her toes seemed to have been too awkwardly placed, or, perhaps, she had grown too ungainly; she could not grip the foot securely. It wasn't unusual for the girls to sit on the floor by Ah Kong's feet. As children they had read the Sunday comics sprawled on the sunroom floor. Or Mother would bake scones, and they would eat them hot from the oven around their father. It was a scene he particularly savored, a floury, milling hour when he was most quiescent, feeling himself almost a baby held in the arms of his womanly family. This morning, however, Kim Li's struggles to clip her toenails forced his attention. Her silent contortions exaggerated by the shorts she was wearing bemused him. Was she already a woman as she had claimed last evening? Ah Kong felt a curious pity for her mixed with anger. Yes, he would have to marry her off. She moved her skinny legs and shot a look at him slyly as if to catch him staring. If she weren't his daughter, he thought, he could almost believe she was trying to arouse him. But he couldn't send her out of the room without admitting that she disturbed him. Once he had watched a bitch in heat lick itself and had kicked it in disgust. He watched her now and was nauseous at the prospect of his future: all his good little girls turning to bitches and licking themselves.

Leaving promptly at two, Mr. Tang told his wife that he might not be coming next Friday; he had unexpected business and would call. He didn't tell her he was planning to find a husband for Kim Li. Complaisant as his wife was, he suspected she might not like the idea of an arranged marriage; nor would the girls. By midweek, he had found a man for Kim Li, the assistant to his general manager, a capable, China-born, Chinese-educated worker who had left his wife and family in Fukien eleven years ago and now couldn't get them out; he'd been without a woman since and had recently advised his Clan Association that he was looking for a second wife. Chan Kow had worked well for Mr. Tang for eight years. What greater compliment to his employees than to marry one of them, albeit one in a supervisory position, to his daughter? Chan Kow was overwhelmed by the proposal; he wasn't worthy of the match; besides, he was thirty-three and Mr. Tang's young daughter might not want him. But he would be honored, deeply honored.

Ah Kong called Mother with the match sealed. Would she inform Kim Li and have her agreeable for a wedding in July, the next month, which was the date the fortune-teller had selected as propitious for the couple? When he arrived on Friday night, he was surprised and relieved to find the family unchanged by his precipitous decision. "You did the right thing," his wife said late at night after the girls had gone to their own rooms. "My goodness, I was afraid Kim Li would yell and scream. You don't know the tantrums she can throw. Well, she took it so calmly. Wanted to know his name, his age, what he looks like. The girls were quite upset. Kim Mee is so sensitive. She was crying because she was afraid you will arrange a marriage for her also, and I couldn't say a thing to her. But you should have seen Kim Li. She was so excited about it. Started boasting that soon she was going to be a married woman and so on."

Ah Kong grunted.

"I told her a married woman has all kinds of responsibilities. She's lucky she'll have a husband who'll take care of her, but she will have to learn to get along with him. Well, she didn't like that. She wants to let her hair grow long now, and she needs some new dresses and nightclothes, of course. And we have to shop for towels and sheets for when she goes to her own house . . ."

"Spend whatever you like," Ah Kong said, and his wife fell silent. He had never said that before. She began calculating all she could buy for the other girls and for the house as well as long as he was in a generous mood.

"When am I going to meet the lucky man, ha, ha!" Kim Li asked the next morning, appearing suddenly in the sunroom. Startled, he opened his eyes with a groan. He thought he might have been asleep and had wakened on a snore. "When am I going to meet this Chan Kow?" she repeated loudly. His wife came hurrying in from their bedroom next door. He said nothing and closed his eyes again. "Ah Kong, I want to meet my husband-to-be. Maybe I can go to Kuala Lumpur with you and have a date with him, ha, ha!" Behind his shut eyes, he sensed her looming figure; her voice had grown strident.

Without opening his eyes, he said, "In an arranged marriage, the woman doesn't see the man till the day of the wedding. You can have a photograph of Chan Kow if you like."

"No, I want to go out with him first."

"Kim Li, you're having a traditional wedding. The man cannot go out with the woman until after they're married," the mother said in a mild tone. "You mustn't spoil the match by acting in a Western manner."

The other three girls huddled by the door listening to the argument. Kim Mee felt a great sympathy for her sister. It wasn't fair of Ah Kong to rush off and pick a husband for Kim Li. What about love? It was true that Kim Li was stupid and had been rude to Ah Kong, but this wasn't China. She wouldn't accept such an arranged marriage even if it meant that she had to leave home and support herself. She looked at her sister curiously. Imagine, she would be married next month! In bed with a stranger, an old man who only speaks Chinese! Kim Mee couldn't think of a worse fate.

Kim Li left the sunroom scowling; her mother couldn't persuade her that she didn't have a right to a few dates with Chan Kow. She didn't appear for tea, and, all through Sunday, she was languid; she walked slowly through the rooms as if she were swimming underwater, lazily moving one leg and then the other, falling into every chair on her way, and staring blankly at the walls. Ah Kong ignored her; she was as good as out of the house.

When he came back next Friday, Kim Li had gone through a total change. "I'm a woman now," she had said to her sisters and began using Kim Mee's makeup every day. She penciled her eyebrows crudely, rubbed two large red patches on her cheeks, and drew in wide lips with the brightest crimson lipstick in Kim Mee's collection. After every meal, she went to her room and added more color. Blue shadow circled her eyes, and her clumsy application of the mascara stick left blotches below her lids like black tearstains. She teased her short hair into a bush of knots and sprayed cologne till it dripped down her neck. Kim Mee didn't complain. Her sister who roamed up and down the house peering into every mirror and rubbing the uneven patches on her face had all her sympathy. To be married off just like that! No wonder Kim Li was acting crazy.

Ah Kong stood at the door afraid. No, he could not possibly allow Chan Kow to meet his daugher before the wedding, this painted woman who was smiling at him provocatively from her bedroom door. He could not understand from where Kim Li had picked up her behavior; in her blue shorts with her wide hips tilted, she presented a picture he was familiar with and had never associated with his home. No, his wife was always submissive, a good woman who could never suggest an immodest action. Was there something innate about a woman's evil that no amount of proper education or home life could suppress? It was good she was marrying soon, for her stance, her glances, her whole appearance indicated a lewd desire. He turned his eyes away from her and stayed in his room all night.

Lying in bed on Saturday morning, he asked the mother to take the girls to town. "I've work to do, and they are too noisy," he said. He was very tired. That he had to lie to his wife with whom he'd always had his way! He felt this other half of life falling apart. The shelter he had built for eighteen years was splintered by the very girls he supported, by their wagging hips and breasts.

"I don't wanna go," Kim Li was yelling. "I'm setting my hair."

"You must come along." Mother was patient. "We're shopping for your trousseau. You have to pick your clothes. Then we're going to the tailor shop and you have to be measured."

"All right, all right. I'm going to be a married woman, ha ha! Do you wanna know about my wedding night, Kim Mee? You have to be nice to me. I'll have all kinds of secrets then."

Only after the front door shut behind their chatter did Mr. Tang go to the sunroom, where Ah Chee had pulled down and closed the louvers. Next to his chair she had placed a plate of freshly ripened cikus. Because it grew so close to salty water, the tree usually bore small bitter fruit, but this season, it was loaded with large brown fruit which needed only a few days in the rice bin to soften to a sweet pulp. Stubbornly refusing to throw any out, Ah Chee was serving ciku to everyone every day. Mr. Tang slowly lowered himself onto his green leather chaise. Using the fruit knife carefully, he peeled a fruit. It was many years since he had last tasted one. Juice splattered onto his pajamas. He spat out the long shiny black seeds on the plate. His hands were sticky with pulp, but he kept them carelessly on the arms of his chair and let his head drop back. Gradually the cool dark room merged into his vision; Ah Chee's banging in the kitchen faded, and the silence flowed around his shallow breathing, flowed and overcame it until he felt himself almost asleep.

A body pressed against him softly. It was his wife's rolling on him in their sleep. He sighed and shifted his weight to accommodate her. The body was thin and sharp; it pressed against him in a clumsy embrace. He opened his eyes and saw Kim Li's black and blue eyes tightly shut, her white and red face screwed up in a smile. His heart was hammering urgently; he could feel his jaws tighten as if at the taste of something sour. "Bitch!" he shouted and slapped her hard. Kim Li's eyes blazed open. He saw her turn, pick something up, and turn to him again with her arms open as if in a gesture of love or hope. Then he felt the knife between his ribs. Just before he fell into the black water, he saw the gleaming fish eyes of the fish woman rise from the *klong* to greet him.

K. S. MANIAM

(Malaysia)

K. S. Maniam was born in 1942 in Bedong, Kedah. He trained as a schoolteacher in Great Britain for two years and later completed a university degree at the University of Malaysia. He began writing in the 1970s, and his works have appeared in many Southeast Asian journals. Maniam writes principally about Malaysia's large Tamil Indian minority, delving into issues of personal and communal history in a national mosaic originally complicated by British colonial interests. His inquiries hinge upon what has been called the irresistible force in every ethnic Indian's trauma of cultural identification: the question of allegiance either to Mother India's spiritual authority and rituals or to some modification of them in keeping with a new environment. His novel The Return *(1981) is uniquely expressive of such conflicts: a youthful protagonist must contend with the matter of loyalty either to his family's traditional Asian values or to the influence of his hard-won education in English with all that it entails. In "Mala," Maniam continues his inquiry into the complexities wrought by Malaysia's thorny multicultural, social, and economic problems; the story details a young country bride's harsh transition to city life. He has also written two plays,* The Cord *(1983) and* The Sandpit *(1990), which have been staged in Kuala Lumpur and Singapore. Maniam is associate professor in English at the University of Malaya and lives in Subang Jaya, Selangor.*

Mala

When Malati left school she came into full encounter with her family. Having dreamed and drifted through her education, she came to roost in her home. The neighbor woman soon branded her lazy and called her "Mala," an abbreviation of the Malay word "malas." The neighbor repeated it with the relish of an insult the more she saw the girl idle and happy. She was stuck with the name when her family began calling her Mala. There was an ugly sound to it whenever they were angry with her.

That was often enough. For some reason they felt offended if Mala hummed a tune in the bathroom or sat in the doorway reading a magazine. The father was a thin, tall man who only straightened from his stoop to deliver some unctuous reprimand. His colleagues at work never knew this side of him for he was always smiling. Mala's mother clattered through her housework with a solemnity that made desecration of a temple seem like a prayer. Her two brothers, constantly running errands for their stout mother, looked at Mala with a sense of achievement.

Parental love pursued a twisted path here; it was expressed through a terrifying ritual of silence. Her indifference grated on their self-gratifying sense of diligence. The boys spent their after-noons desultorily digging at an unyielding plot of ground. Mala watching them, noticed how the handles of the *changkul* flew away from them. There was a dull thud as the *changkul* hit the ground. Their bodies were covered with a lackluster glow. Mala's father clucked at the chickens; they squabbled restlessly, refusing to be housed for the night. Mala's mother looking on, gave some silver-ware a shine where none was necessary.

The punishment began the day they learned she had failed her final school examination. There was no show of anger or of disappointment. They withdrew into silence that froze her movements and her spirit. No talk passed between them. If they saw her they turned their heads away. Meals were swallowed in utter silence, beds made in rustling quiet. Outside the house they resumed interrupted conversations with their neighbors as if nothing had happened.

"Have I done something wrong?" Mala asked, unable to bear the cemetery quietness in the house.

They only placed their fingers on their lips and rolled their eyes in the direction of the family niche. Here resided not only pictures of gods and goddesses, but also photographs of a pantheon of dead relatives. Even on ordinary days the sight of these photographs revolted her. Now they produced a darkness in her mind. Not a day passed without their genuflecting before the staring, vacant eyes. Garlands, a week old, bordered the picture frames of these departed men and women. Mala had never helped the family string the flowers.

Mala began her own rituals. Getting up before the others did, she took a cold bath and went out into the unfenced compound. The dawn air hit her then, causing a shiver to course through a body that had just risen from sleep. The skin on her face seemed to peel away and reveal a new self. She stood under the mango tree and watched the sun rise over the hills. As the land emerged from darkness and mist she felt herself torn up and rushed toward the brightening clumps of trees and hill slopes. Perhaps to replace the singing silence of the family there rose, beyond, a resonant clamor. She turned abruptly—a door had slammed inside—toward the house.

That morning she sat in the doorway, her eyes blinking at the mystery the trees were losing. The leaves slowly turned a flat green as voices from the neighboring houses reached her in monotonous waves. A breeze stirred the loose skirt she wore. She felt a gentle slap of coolness on her calves and thighs. Her mother came out with a bucket of washing, her lips twisted in perpetual scorn. The neighbor woman appeared at the door and whooped with delight.

"Ah, showing your legs to the world, Mala!" she screamed with unrepressed pleasure.

Mala rose and went into her room.

The silence deepened. Her brothers sat in the cubiclelike living room, afraid of making the slightest movement. Mala's mother was a squatting, impassive statue on the kitchen floor. A scrappy, cold lunch, garnished by the intolerable gloom of the house, had been eaten. The afternoon passed and brought Mala's father back from his work. Her parents had a whispered conversation under a tree outside the house. The boys sat on, knees held together, biting their nails.

Mala's mother stomped back, thrust the door of the room open, and tore off Mala's clothes. She wrapped a white sari in suffocating folds around Mala's well-fleshed body. As she was dragged to the bathroom, she saw her brothers cleaning the tray and lamps at the family niche. Inside the bathroom her mother poured pail after pail of water over her loosened hair. The water came so fast, the woman held her so tightly, Mala could not breathe. But her mother didn't stop. She grunted and bent and slammed the water against Mala's hair, eyes, face, breasts, and legs until the girl was thoroughly numb. She had been reduced to a nerveless, confused girl when her mother pulled her back to the niche. A lamp had been lighted. Mala's mother pushed her down before the colony of deceased. Her father placed his hand on her head so that she would remain on her knees. Her mother branded her forehead with a streak of the holy ash.

At last, when he was tired, Mala's father removed his hand. Mala moved in a daze to her room. The sari, having wrung the heat off her body, had almost dried. Mala changed and sat on the bed. Her immersion in the punishing waters had ended the silence. There was an unnatural gaiety as the family laughed at the talk of the father. A chicken was slaughtered, a feast prepared to which Mala's father invited her with some cajolery. She remained in her room.

A fury broke upon her in the night. The snores of the well-fed and contented roused a rebellious anger within her. She wanted to get out but the thought of bodies in various postures of sleep confined her to the bed. In her restlessness she tossed and turned and then lay rigid, waiting for the dawn. At the first cockerel's crow, she stumbled toward the bathroom. She stood there, unclothed, letting the chill prick her body. Then she splashed water on herself and soaped and rubbed her body so that the blood flowed again. And she recalled the red-tinged sky of the previous dawn opening upon a landscape, miraculous and fresh. She went out into the compound and let her warm breath thaw the dew and mist around her face.

"Mad Mala," the neighbor woman said. "Standing like a ghost under the mango tree!"

The word spread. "She rubs her bad blood on her body! Stands naked in the mist!" The squat and ugly neighbor woman returned from the town, where she was believed and made its spokeswoman. The town gathered about her as if she carried, in the marketing bag on her arm, colorful bundles of mysteries. She did possess strange powers and ways of knowing, sometimes accompanied by prophetic pronouncements.

"Mangoes are ripening," she said, referring to Mala's breasts. "Keep them covered with sacking. Hands may reach out."

The warning was not heeded. Mala walked to her friend's house beyond the bridge. She had felt stifled, closeted in her room. For an hour or so Susi, her friend, talked of Kuala Lumpur. Her brother, who had a small business there, had told her of the freedom, lights, and wealth of the city.

"Nobody knows you there," Susi said. "Here everyone knows the color of your shit!"

The ugliness of Susi's words didn't jolt Mala out of the trance into which she had fallen. Had she not herself escaped, for a brief spell, from the daily torment, imprisonment, boredom, and slow dying? She returned home late to an angry mother.

"I'll burn your legs!" she screamed. "Who heard of a young girl wandering wherever her feelings took her? Haven't you brought the family enough shame?"

"Tame the goat or the rams will bristle," the neighbor woman called sagely.

There was a whispered consultation that night between Mala's parents.

A priest came to the house, when it had been washed and sprinkled with saffron water, to purify it. He sat in the living room and chanted until it was assumed that evil spirits had been cast away. Then he rose to go saying, "The dead came freely into the house." He accepted a few dollars on a *sireh* leaf and departed, mumbling, "Friday would be an auspicious day."

Preparations were begun on Thursday itself. Flowers were gathered from bushlike plants in the compound, strung together, and left overnight to be moistened by the dew. The two boys wiped the picture frames free from cobwebs and dust the following morning. Highly honored among the deceased was Mala's great-grandfather. Her father often recounted the story of his life, dwelling on his hunting activities.

"He was a wild man when he was young," Mala's father said. "Many women threw him glances until your mother's mother showed him the good life."

"Tell us about how he went into the jungle," one of Mala's brothers said.

"He disappeared for two or three nights. When he came back he carried the best wild boar meat slung on a pole across his shoulder."

"No one helped him?" the other boy said.

"There was no need," Mala's father said. "He could carry two wild boars on his thigh, unaided."

"He was never frightened of the tigers and elephants he saw out there," Mala's mother said.

"Not one word about jungles or wild boars after his marriage," Mala's father said. "He could change at the blink of the eye."

"But he never did," Mala said. "He died of the wasting disease, you told us."

"Pull your tongue out!" Mala's mother said. "That was God's

great test of patience. And your great-grandfather went like a warrior to Him."

The great-grandfather's virtues were extolled again that evening. The vegetarian meal they had had in the afternoon made them particularly receptive. Laughter had been banished for the whole day. Mala's father slaughtered three toughened cockerels that evening with sacrificial zeal. The boys caught the blood, the woman plucked the feathers, and the man chopped the meat into chunky pieces. Mala had been told to remain in her room, closeted with holy thoughts.

The cooking nearing its completion, the boys took their baths— short spurts of water thrown over their bodies. The parents wore clean, white garments for the purification. Mala was made to stand in a white *sarung* knotted at her breast while her mother repeated the punishing bath ritual. Mala's initiation into the world of the dead had been made.

Mala waited in her wet *sarung* watching her mother lay out the feast for the dead: large scoops of rice, drumsticks, vegetables, chicken curry, a bottle of stout (opened), cigars (for the deceased ladies), and cigarettes (for the dead men and striplings). The boys made the gestures first, bringing their camphor tray and incense brazier thrice around the closet of the dead. Mala's mother followed. She rubbed the holy ash at the base of her throat and struck her forehead until tears started. Mala's father made the full obeisance before the pantheon of the good, undistracted life, now dead. He took a garland that had been lying on a tray in the middle of the niche. He put it around Mala's neck and thrust her forward. She performed the ritual with brief gestures. The father then led them in favor-asking from the dead.

"May you grant us sobriety," he called to the ancestors.

The others repeated the words solemnly, Mala with distaste.

"May you grant us the strength not to take the crooked path."

"May you grant us the swiftness with which to stop the blood rising in anger, lust, and bestiality."

"May you grant us patience."

"May you grant us long life."

"May you grant that this girl, now your daughter too, does not shorten that life."

They took turns placing *kumkum* and oil and holy ash on the part in Mala's hair. She was led to her room, where she barely succeeded in keeping down the bile that rose to her mouth. For the whole week she hardly left her room, suffering a depression that left her convinced she really belonged to the dead. One evening she escaped to Susi's house, where she listened to Sanker, who had come on a holiday from Kuala Lumpur.

"O! O! The mangoes want to fall into some man's hands!" the neighbor woman remarked loudly.

She had laughed over their method of "taming" Mala. Her father reported that he heard the town laughing at him the minute he turned his back.

"Better put an end to it all," Mala's mother told him with a certain look in her eyes.

A different kind of word passed around this time. The neighbor woman was then at the peak of her career; no men came to Mala's house although it had been recurtained, redecorated, refurnished, and, in some other ways, restored. A fresh string of mango leaves hung over the front doorway.

Weeks passed. The mango leaves had curled and turned brown when a man, accompanied by his son, called at the house. Mala's father hurriedly put on a shirt and ushered them in.

"Is there anyone else coming?" Mala's mother asked, noticing the absence of women.

The man looked around him unhurriedly and shook his head.

"Aren't we enough?" he said.

His son, clothed in tight pants, a broad belt, and tapering-collar shirt, examined the various articles in the room. He paused a long while at the collection of tapes, scratched his head as he read the titles, and then turned, with a puzzled expression on his face, to Mala's father.

"No modern songs?" he asked.

"We don't sell records here," Mala's father said.

The young man sat down and laughed. The proceedings were conducted to the accompaniment of his laughter.

"As you can see, my son is educated," the older man said. "Good music makes him go mad. Now what about your daughter?"

"She has been to school," Mala's father said.

"Come, come. Even a donkey can be led by the neck to school," the man said. "Let's go to other things. Jewelry?"

"I can only afford a chain," Mala's father said.

"A mare with jingling bells!" the man said, rising to go. "I was foolish to come after hearing so much about your girl."

The next suitor came alone. From the minute he stepped into the house he would not sit down. His face was pockmarked, his eyes red, and his hair bristled like the back of an unruly bull.

"I'm a widower," he said. "I've three children. I've a lot of money. The children need a mother and I want a woman. I know all about your girl. She needs someone like me to tame her."

"Go and join a circus!" Mala's father shouted, thinking of the whole town turned out to see his daughter the mother of three children on the marriage day itself.

Mala heard the negotiations and, humiliated, thought of suicide. The eyes of the ancestors seemed to stare at her. She saw herself pinned between glass and wood, withered flowers garlanding her memory—a monument to sacrifice for the good name of the family. In that cold, hazy hour between night and morning, she let herself be peeled and revealed. She lived again, fiercely, stubbornly, in the light that spread over the country, knowing instinctively that there could be no greater darkness than despair.

"I'm going out," she said firmly when she left that evening to visit Susi.

"Don't you know about the auspicious period you've entered?" her mother asked.

"You can auction me off on the name I've got from this town," Mala said.

Susi was in a thoughtful mood. She laid aside a letter from her brother.

"Sanker is thinking of marriage," she said. "He has asked me to look for a girl."

"There must be plenty of girls in Kuala Lumpur," Mala said.

"He wants to marry in the old way," Susi said, and smiled. "I hear your parents are looking for a bridegroom."

Mala laughed but looked down shyly.

"I can't even think of it," she said. "My people are proud. They are known for their correctness in this town. I can't leave the house except with the man my father finds for me."

"My brother isn't in a hurry," Susi said. "Think about it. He can give you a good life."

There was a certain breeziness about Sanker that she liked. She had only seen him briefly, but his confidence and sense of responsibility were evident. She put her thoughts away as she approached her house. Her mother stood talking with the neighbor woman and barely gave her a glance.

Then, Vasu, a relative of Mala's father, arrived accompanied by a group of people crammed into two cars. It was an impressive show and even the neighbor woman was silenced. Perhaps she had met her match in Vasu. He had a reputation for lying, scrounging off on liquor, a habit of exaggerating, and possessed as well a sense of drama. He also had a son, of marriageable age, born out of wedlock. He got down from the car, smiling, and waited for the others to bring up the rear of the procession to Mala's house.

Several women carried trays of fruits, sweets, and clothes. Vasu inquired for Mala's father in a formal manner.

"We've come with the plenty of the season," he announced when Mala's father appeared and gestured them in.

The usual questions were asked and then Vasu jumped up as if possessed by a strange spirit.

"Don't you really know me?" he asked. "I'm the man you spat at. At that old man's funeral. What did I know about drumming?"

"I've forgotten all that," Mala's father said.

"Correctness!" the man hissed. "Each man lives differently. He has his feelings. You threw water on that fire. What's happening to your correctness? This!"

The man spat on the trays he had brought as gifts. The sweat, the various perfumes the women wore, and the man's raucous breath filled the close air in the living room with some kind of rottenness.

Mala appeared in the silence that fell over the gathering. She held a traveling bag and her eyes were red.

"I'm taking the shame out of this house!" she said and pushed past them.

She walked quickly toward the bridge.

The marriage, without any fanfare, was performed at the registry office. Mala's father gave his unwilling approval. No one else was present at the official occasion. As they traveled down to Kuala Lumpur in a secondhand car Sanker had recently acquired, Mala looked at the country flashing past her. All her mornings, after those baths, she thought, had not been useless. She was coming into her own at last. She couldn't suppress a sense of triumph.

They came to a busy row of shops, above which were flats. Sanker rented part of a flat. He had slept until then in his one-room office as a requirement of the businessman making his first million. The dust, the noise, and the traffic assailed Mala even as she mounted the steps, behind Sanker, to the rooms upstairs. They had to share the hall and the kitchen with a woman and her child. Only the bedroom provided some space for a marriage to breathe, grow, and acquire some purpose.

"Lucy," the Chinese woman said, coming out of the kitchen to meet them. "My son. No husband."

But, looking out of the dirty window, Mala saw that what had once been jungled hill and remoteness had been cut level and made a home. She smiled at Lucy and the boy, about three, whose face was still covered with the remnants of his breakfast.

"Sankah, good man," Lucy said. "Make a lot of money. Like Chinese himself!"

It might have been the car journey or the windless hall, but Mala felt giddy and looked for a place to sit.

"Better go to the room," Sanker said. "Rest."

He opened the door to the bedroom, to an unmade, stained mattress, and the barest of furniture. He ran down the steps and returned with some packages of food and hot tea in a plastic bag.

Sanker was at his office most of the day or out on assignments. Mala didn't know exactly what he was doing. He thrust some money into her hands at night, after they had made love, and told her to buy the things necessary for a home.

"All this will change," he said, "when we've more money. Just do some simple cooking. Make use of whatever we've now. Lucy manages even without a husband."

Mala had adjusted a little to the situation. A meal was there if Sanker wanted it. The days he followed his business out of his office, she ate alone. Lucy had made it clear from the first day that she didn't want her son fed by any stranger. She was, however, pleasant about other matters. Mala derived fascination just watching Lucy's transformation in the evenings. She ceased to be the sloppy, flabby woman she was in the mornings. A smart dress emphasized her suddenly ample, firm breasts, the makeup gave her a newfound vitality. The boy had an old woman to look after him on some days. When there was no one he cried and tired himself and lay curled on the cold, terrazzo floor of the hall. It was from there that Lucy picked him up, grumbling, in the early hours of the morning.

"Children, they give us no time," Lucy said around noon, when she got out of bed. "Bawl! Bawl! Bawl! All day. Prevent them."

The advice was unnecessary. Sanker had taken Mala to a doctor, who put some metal inside her. After that Sanker ceased to be gentle in bed with her. She was reminded of the way her mother had punished her with water. The slapping, the bending down, and the humiliation had followed her into marriage. There was the lethargy too, the following morning.

"We'll have children when we're better off," Sanker said to mollify her.

She cleaned the pots and pans, saucers and cups, sometimes more than once in the course of the day. She gave Sanker his tea when he ran up the stairs and burst into the hall. Dinner was soon prepared and then the waiting for her husband began. He swayed in some nights, reeking of liquor, mumbled something about "contacts," and fumbled for her in the dark.

"I'm working hard for all of us," he said the next morning, rushing through breakfast. "The ones who come later will benefit."

He got a color TV for her, raking up the money from somewhere. Once she went down to the office to clean it. It was so bare that she wondered how business could be conducted in it at all. Lucy surprised her as well. There was something common between her and Sanker. Lucy never mentioned the work she was doing, but when she stayed home she displayed her fatigue as someone proud of having slogged away. She fed her boy something that made him sleep for hours. Lucy then sat on the floor, in a thin, loose dress, flipping through a pile of glossy magazines.

"Ask your man buy furniture," she told Mala. "Share half half. This look like pig cage."

Mala passed on the word. Sanker and Lucy came to an agreement and the sofa, armchair, and coffee tables arrived. Lucy spent whole mornings on the sofa, under the dust-blackened fan that was never switched off. One afternoon a man delivered a sound system Lucy had ordered. It was an expensive, complex set. From it came all kinds of music, but mainly Chinese songs that filled the flat with militant resonance. Lucy never allowed the boy near it. Once she smacked his fingers for touching it and she wiped off the marks with a velvety, thick cloth. Mala had to distract him from his howling.

Sanker took her to an English film one night, sitting beside her with restless absorption. While he sighed in wonder, she watched with embarrassment the couple on the screen, half naked, embrace then dance in a nightclub led on by a bare-breasted woman who wriggled sensuously, and finally make love with unashamed hunger.

"See, see," Sanker muttered. "One day we could be like that."

He was full of his dreams on the way back to the flat. They

would buy a better, new car; move out to a house in a prestigious area; fly to a holiday in a foreign country.

"They showed all those things in the film," she said.

"What's there to be ashamed about?" he said, drawn out of his preoccupations.

Susi visited them for a week, dragging Mala out to the various shopping complexes. She bought a dress, makeup, and shoes.

"Have you anything to tell me?" she asked Mala confidentially.

"What do you mean?"

Susi giggled, rubbing her belly.

"He says when we've more money," Mala said.

"You should enjoy yourself," Susi said, accompanying Lucy out that night.

She left for home reluctantly. Sanker had changed during her stay. He made Mala discard her saris and wear dresses.

"Don't rub tumeric on your face," he said.

"It won't be smooth and clean," she said.

"I bought a lotion and other things," he said. "Lucy can teach you how to use them."

She submitted. Lucy worked like a magician on her face. When she showed Mala a glass, she gasped. Her face resembled that of the women she had seen at the shopping complexes.

"My! My!" Lucy said, slapping her thighs, pleased.

As Lucy removed the makeup, Mala's face felt cool and then shrunken. She cried on returning to the flat, after Sanker had her hair cut. The hairdresser had handed her the snipped hair in a bag that carried the salon's name and logo. She laid out the truncated length, once a part of her, which had reached down to her waist.

Lucy became attached to her. She described the places in the city she frequented and the food she ate, with guests, at large, crowded restaurants.

"Why you like this?" she said. "All time in here. No children. Good time taste many things. I show you."

Mala shook her head, only accepting to look after the boy when Lucy went out. Lucy was not easily put off. Sanker was angry with Mala for refusing Lucy's services.

"She only wants to show you the city," he said. "You must learn about people and their ways."

"You take me out," Mala said.

"I don't have the time," he said, sensing that she accused him of not wanting to be seen with her during the day.

"He have woman work for him," Lucy told Mala one evening. "Plenty customers. That why he marry."

Lucy did not elaborate. Sanker grumbled at dinner: "Too much work."

"Did anyone help you before?" Mala asked.

"A secretary," Sanker said. "She was too expensive. You could do some work for me. But you're afraid of leaving this flat."

Lucy's boy was proving to be too wild for Mala. He had been left so much to himself that he turned aggressive if she fed or dressed him. Mala thought about Sanker's suggestion. It was time she shed some of her fears. Lucy encouraged her.

"Go, help your man," she said. "He go mad, if not."

"I can read and write," Mala told Sanker. "Enough?"

"You must know typing, how to answer the phone," he said.

"I can learn," Mala said.

"Practice here first," Sanker told her, smiling.

He bought her a secondhand typewriter and a manual on typing. Mala spent her mornings getting in practice. The process was trying. Her fingers flew all over the keys. She aimed for speed, but only achieved mistakes. A frustrating garble met her gaze during the first weeks.

Sanker sighed. He put down the copies abruptly.

"What's the matter with you?" he asked. "Have you got sticks for fingers?"

"I haven't done this kind of work before," Mala said.

"That doesn't mean you've to spoil good, expensive paper," he said.

Mala did not cook meals that day. Sanker had to buy dinner from the shop around the corner.

Though Mala was tired, her typing gradually showed some improvement. Sanker gruffly acknowledged her progress. She kept

at it. The traffic roared past her flat. Lucy's boy bawled for attention. Lucy herself would prattle away from the sofa, but Mala heard
none of this. She was glad that she didn't have the long hair that
would fall over the machine. She had learned to write formal,
pleasant letters and correct simple mistakes when Sanker announced that she could go down to the office.

"Ask Lucy how to dress for work," he told her.

Lucy bustled about Mala. She made Mala put on a dress, then
take it off. She tried various tones of lipstick, eyebrow pencils, and
makeup. Mala saw in the dresser mirror a girl stiff and frightened.
Lucy had done good work—Mala hardly recognized herself. And
she wanted to be that way. For a moment she recalled the dawns
she had stood under the mango tree, up north. She had changed,
she realized, but into someone not of her making.

Sanker ran a packaging business. He had the rates drawn up
neatly on a card. The firm that provided the boxes had its phone
number underlined in red, and pinned on the wall facing the typewriter. Lorry owners' phone numbers were listed on a separate
card. A little black book, indexed, contained clients' names. When
Sanker sat at his table on the other side of the small office, he was
a different man.

"We aren't husband and wife here," he said on showing her
into the office one morning. "Don't bring unnecessary problems to
me. Do whatever is necessary."

He briefed her on the work at the end of which he relapsed,
for a moment, into the Sanker she knew. In bed that night he was
affectionate to her.

"It's all for our own good," he said. "Once I get my big contracts
we can start a new life."

Mala lay, consoled, on his heaving chest. When he talked about
business a certain thickness entered his voice and he moved restlessly on the bed. She had to talk to him then, guessing at his
ambitions, agreeing, and sympathetically massaging him into sleep.

In the morning he inspected her clothes, makeup, and the way
she carried herself.

"You slouch too much," he said one morning.

"Makeup mustn't be that thick" he said on another. "They might think you're a country cow."

"Clothes should follow the body, not hide it," he commented on a third.

Mala had learned to adjust herself according to his criticisms.

Always, he gave her an encouraging hug, just before they descended the steps to the office. Mala was careful to earn that affection. Though most of the time she could not understand his ferocity or that distant expression on his face, she treasured these moments of nearness. They compensated for the silence of the family she had left behind and the scorn of that gossip, the neighbor woman.

Mala began to enjoy the activities of the day. Whenever she answered the phone she sensed the pleased pause at the other end. She gave the rates, the kind of services available, and took down times and dates if the client wanted to hear from the "boss." It was strange hearing Sanker referred to as "boss"; he became someone important and unreachable in her life.

The office changed its atmosphere in the few months that Mala attended to its secretarial demands. Sanker was out most of the time, hunting down that first major contract. He spoke to her over the phone from various parts of the city. He described an individual in detail and asked if the man had shown up at the office.

"No," Mala said.

"Be nice to him when he comes," Sanker said.

In Sanker's absence, a few men called at the office. These were lorry drivers or packaging subagents. They sat on the oblong, backless settee Sanker had installed against the wall. They flicked cigarette ash into the potted plants on either side of the settee.

"The boss isn't in," she said. "He will be back at eleven."

"We can wait," the young men said.

Mala typed or answered the phone. The men sat on, crossing and uncrossing their legs.

"How's business, Miss?" one of the young men asked.

"Only the boss knows," she said, too shy to refer to her husband by name.

"Secretaries know better than their bosses," another said.

Mala went on with her work, glad if a phone call came through to break the tension.

"This one won't even talk-*lah!*" one of the young men said as they got up to leave.

Mala complained to Sanker when he returned from one of his fruitless excursions.

"Too many men come in here," she said.

"This is a place of business," he said, looking at the list of people who had rung up while he was gone.

"Lorry drivers and those other men!" Mala said.

"They may bring some orders," Sanker said. "Get on with your work."

At night he persuaded her that she must learn to take care of herself when he was absent. He emphasized how important it was for her to be courteous to them. He ended by saying, "A customer is always right."

Sanker had stacked the folded-up cartons behind his desk. An almost empty filing cabinet stood behind Mala's desk. Labels of his company were pinned on the walls along with posters of various foreign scenic landscapes. Sometimes there were busy mornings. Men came and went. Mala typed invoices, rang up lorry drivers, and made entries into the office ledger. Sanker stayed in the office on those days.

"A special client is coming today," he announced one morning as they went down to the office.

He paid more attention to her clothes and appearance during that daily inspection. She wore a tight dress he recommended. Even Lucy came out of her room on hearing Sanker talk excitedly. She whistled on seeing Mala.

"You smart girl now!" she said. "Can even do my work."

"Any woman can do your work," Sanker said.

"What does she do?" Mala asked before they reached the office.

"Nothing you can't do," he said carelessly.

Mala watched Sanker seat himself upright at his desk.

"Order some flowers," he told her, giving her the florist's number.

The flowers, arranged in a boat-shaped container, gave the office a cold, formal color. Whenever the phone rang Sanker leaned forward quickly. At last, a nasal stream of broken English came over the line. Mala handed the phone to Sanker.

"Yes, yes," Sanker said. "Any time. Come over. Everything will be ready for you."

He put down the phone and rushed out of the office.

By the time the client arrived, Sanker had brought a smaller table from the adjoining room. A caterer delivered some savory, covered dishes, three glasses, a bottle of whiskey, and a jug of cold water. The man himself came soon after, a confident smile greeting them.

"My secretary," Sanker said, introducing her.

The man shook hands with Mala, quickly, easily, in a burst of pleasure.

"Nice, nice," he said, surveying everything.

Sanker nodded at her. Mala sat at her desk, confused by the signal.

"She will serve us," Sanker said.

Mala understood and went with suppressed anger to the cloth-covered smaller table.

"No need to trouble her," the man said, his pallid face crinkling into a smile again.

Mala got used to refilling their glasses unobtrusively while they talked endlessly and the man swallowed the balls of meat or bits of steamed fish. He drank more than Sanker, but he didn't stumble on a single word. At last he rose, smiled at Mala, and moved toward the door, which Sanker held open for him. Sanker took some time returning from seeing the man off.

"We've something big here," he said.

Then he noticed Mala's expression and, breaking the office rule, came to her.

"I should have showed you how to serve the food and drink," he said. "These are things we've to do until we're well off."

They had a quarrel that night, but Sanker was adamant.

"I saved you from that black hole up there!" he said. "Is this how you show your gratitude?"

"All I want is a child," Mala said, sobbing. "Not to wait on any man who comes to that office."

Mala didn't go down to the office the following morning. Sanker pleaded with her, but she only put a pillow over her head.

"Yes, bury yourself like an insect!" Sanker shouted and stormed out of the room.

"Why make unhappiness, ah?" Lucy said, later in the morning. "Just do what he want. How I feed that boy? Obey men, that's all. Want go out? Change place, change feeling."

They wandered through the crowded, softly lighted cubicles of the shopping arcade. Mala followed Lucy wherever she was led.

Lucy stopped at a boutique and looked at the dresses draped over mannequins. The dummies had blue, vaguely staring eyes. As the two women peered through the pane of glass, a man entered the case and stripped a mannequin with brutish efficiency. There she stood, bare, imperturbable, while the man arranged the latest dress over her shoulders and between her cleftless thighs. When the man had finished, he twisted her arms into a new posture. The dummy had acquired a fashionableness which Lucy praised.

Mala was tired, but she dragged on after Lucy. They sat, at last, in a low-ceilinged snack stall. The tables were small, neat pieces resting on a thick, stained carpet. Lucy picked up a dirty well-thumbed menu and taught Mala how to choose her food. Mala went through the motions suffused by the steady, dull light and the cold that poured in via the air-conditioning vents. Mala recognized in the gestures of Lucy and in the pale smile of the special customer the day before the silent pressure of a force from which there was no escape.

KON KRAILAT

(Thailand)

Kon Krailat is the nom de plume of Pakon Phongwarapha, who was born to an immigrant Chinese family in Nakhon Pathom province in 1947. He completed elementary school but then left school and ran a coffee shop for five years. His first published story appeared when he was sixteen. He moved to Bangkok to pursue a literary career, supporting himself as a proofreader at a popular women's magazine for the first two years. With his wife, the writer Khwan Phiangphuthai, he established himself as a publisher with Youth *magazine, modeling its editorial mixture of literature and sex on Western publications such as* Playboy. *This venture led to several other sexually oriented publications, but Krailat continued to write literary fiction. He published four short story collections available in Thailand:* Fire of Life, Golden Flowers, Report from the Pung Clan, *and most recently* We Are Not Flowers, We Are Life. *"In the Mirror" was first published in* Waves of the Chao Praya, *a 1978 anthology of younger writers edited by the esteemed Thai literary figure Sujit Wongthet. Bangkok's name has become in many ways synonymous with the terrain Krailat explores in his story.*

In the Mirror

Chiwin* sits quietly in a dark corner, waiting for his moment to come. . . .

Tonight the place is packed, since it's the beginning of the month and people still have enough cash to go out and enjoy themselves. Chiwin lights up a cigarette and inhales listlessly. It's very strange, but this evening he feels lonely, moody, not himself. He's got a lot of complicated problems on his mind, among them a letter from his mother: *"Win, my dear son, your father isn't very well. The rice planting season's already here, but there's no one at home. How are things going for you in Bangkok? Have you found a job yet or not? We haven't heard from you at all. . . . "* Parts of the letters Mother wrote usually went like this. In fact, of course, she hadn't written them at all. She was illiterate, so she must have asked someone in the neighborhood to write them for her.

Actually, it's only now that Chiwin takes cognizance of how long it's been since he left home. Days turned into years before he was aware of it. In this city, where he now lives, night and day are unlike night and day anywhere else. . . .They rush by so rapidly that he doesn't have time to think about things as they happen. . . . If he does think about them, it's only cursorily, for a moment or so. . . . like a brief gust of wind which merely rustles the leaves and then vanishes without a trace. . . .

His mother's letter brings to his mind images of various people, but heaped up on one another in such confusion that he feels dizzy and disoriented. And Chiwin inhales cigarette smoke, puff after puff, one after the other. . . .

*The name Chiwin, hardly chosen at random, also means "life."

It's so dark in that corner that people can't see each other's faces. The customers sitting at the tables loom up only as obscure silhouettes. The waitresses move back and forth, some holding flashlights to guide new arrivals in search of empty tables. On the tiny stage a naked girl is dancing to the pounding rhythm of a song. Her name is Latda. She has two children, plus a do-nothing husband drunk day in day out. So she's had to come and work as a go-go girl, stripping her body for people to have a look. She'd told him all about it one day, not long after they'd got to know each other. . . . The Tale of Latda . . . cracked in pieces like the lives of all the women in this place, full of knots and problems. If one had a good and happy life, who would ever want to bare every inch of one's body for any Tom, Dick, or Harry to stare at? Chiwin reflects, like someone who thinks he understands pretty well how the people working here tick.

The last strains of the song die away. Latda steps down from the stage. There's some halfhearted clapping from a few of the customers, none of whom know why they clap. Utter silence for a second, as though the spectators sense that the moment they've been waiting for has finally arrived. The lights on the stage turn pale pink. A slow, soft melody . . . láa-laa-láa-laa-laa-laa-láa . . . strikes up. . . . Another girl, dressed in black underwear, takes her turn on the stage. She makes her appearance slowly and silently.

And now they're playing Chiwin's musical cue. He stubs out his cigarette and pushes himself to his feet. He steps out of the dark corner into the pink glow, with the lithe movements of a young man of twenty-four. Some of the male spectators who remember him stare at him now, half in scorn, half wanting to do it themselves.

"You know, it's not easy at all," Chiwin had once told one of those who spoke to him in this tone. "It's only when you're on stage that you realize it's really no piece of cake."

No one has much of an idea about the music that's now being played, and it seems as if no one has the slightest interest in finding out. Most of the spectators simply know that when it's played it's time for the house's "special program" to begin. The words, accompanied by rhythmic sighs, most likely describe the mood of a young woman on a lonely night. The girl on the stage stretches out on her back and begins to writhe and quiver as though her flesh were burning with desire. Then slowly she removes the two little bits of clothing from her body.

Her name is Wanphen. . . .

Chiwin has now stepped up onto the stage. The play of spot-lights moves back and forth between purple, blue, and red. Wan-phen's act is so well done that it makes some of the young men close by the stage almost forget to breathe. Chiwin slowly unbuttons his shirt, then shakes his head two or three times. His eyes are getting used to the lights, which keep changing color like a magic show.

A moment later and Chiwin has nothing left to himself but his bared body. It's a handsome, well-proportioned body, full of young flesh and blood. He throws his clothes in a heap in one corner. Everything takes place with the utmost slowness, as if in this piece of life time has ceased to exist. At this moment no one can think of anything else—even if the country should meanwhile collapse in ruins.

Chiwin stretches his body out alongside Wanphen and embraces her, while caressing her naked flesh with his hands. He kisses her once, and she kisses him in turn, then turns her face away and snuggles it into the hollow of his neck.

"How many times have I told you, Elder Brother Win!" he hears her whisper. "Please don't smoke before doing the show with me. It smells horrible. I can't stand the stink, and I lose the mood. . . ."

"I'm sorry," he whispers back, as he rolls his body back and forth over hers. "Something's been bothering me. I've been in a bad mood, so I forgot. . . ."

How many times now had he partnered this woman! . . . Chiwin thinks about the man with the unremarkable face who comes to wait for her every night when the bar closes. He can't imagine what the man's real feelings are. He comes to wait here in silence, and he goes home in silence. He must feel something. How could one man not understand another? But the two of us don't even know each other. And we both suffer. At least the man had once stared at Chiwin with a strange, cold gleam in his eye.

"He's my husband," Wanphen had once explained, "a real husband, you know; we're properly registered and all."

"How can he stand having you come here and do this kind of show with me?" He couldn't put the gleam in the man's eye out of his mind.

"What can you do?" she'd answered seriously. "It's a job. It's a way to make a living. If you live with a woman like me, you have to be able to take it."

She's right. That's what it is, a job. O.K. At least it's a job for me too right now. Chiwin has the feeling that he won't be able to perform well tonight. He doesn't feel prepared at all. The young man rolls over and down. Wanphen knows the signs very well, so she presses her body tightly to him. Deploying all her skills, using everything she has, she begins, with intense concentration, to arouse his desire. The play of the lights halts for a moment at pink, bathing the bodies of the couple and bringing out their beauty.

Chiwin stretches out full length and closes his eyes. The whole world darkens before his vision. The air-conditioning makes the air cold and moist, but he feels the sweat beginning to ooze from some of his pores. His ears catch the soft music . . . when the song comes to an end, it starts up again, in an endless, indolent cycle, making his thoughts drift far away, to the past, to broad rice fields and to days and nights long gone.

. . . By now the rains must have started back home. . . . Sometimes one could see the gray-white rain pouring down, moving in over the rice fields from the horizon, blurring everything in sight. The nights would be chilly and damp, and filled with the loud croaking of big and little frogs. And mornings, if the sun shone at all, its beams would be soft and tender, soon to vanish as the thick rain clouds piled up once more. In the rainy season, the earth would be turned over once again with the plow. And it wouldn't be long before the rice plants came up green, ripening later to a brilliant yellow throughout the paddies. But this isn't his work anymore. He abandoned it a long time ago. It's hard work, backbreakingly hard. Worse still, the harder you work, the poorer you get. He'd been so utterly, indescribably tired of that way of life that he'd struggled to get a better education, and with every ounce of will turned his face and headed toward Bangkok to find a new life. . . .

. . . And my little brother Wang. . . . I wonder if he's out of the monkhood yet? Mother doesn't mention him in her letter. He's been in since last Lent.* Does he really want to study in the temple to become a Maha?† Doesn't he know these days there's no road to Nirvana anymore? And what about my little sister Wan? She must be buckling down to looking after the kids she produces year in year out, giving her almost no breathing space for anything else. She got married to a boy from another subdistrict before she was even eighteen. Everyone's left the family home. Only Father and Mother still remain, and how much can they do on their own? And now Father's sick too. . . .

Last night he'd had a terrible dream. It seemed that Father was in it somehow, but he couldn't arrange the images of the dream properly. All he knew was that it was so horrible that when he woke up his heart was pounding with fear. And then he remembered that it was a long time since he'd dreamed at all. Every night he fell into a deep sleep, as though his body'd been picked up and laid casually down on the bed, feeling nothing, till a new day dawned and the time came for him to get up once again. And when the next night fell, he'd be picked up and laid down once again in the same old place. Dreams are the travels of one's soul. It's no good if one lives without dreams. It shows that there's no soul left inside. So it's a good thing he dreamed last night, even if the dream was a nightmare. . . .

Chiwin feels Wanphen's body arching up and pressing tightly to him almost all over. As she rains kisses over his chest and in the hollow of his neck, she whispers. . . .

"What's the matter with you tonight . . . huh?"

"I told you, I'm really feeling down. . . . " Chiwin embraces

*The Buddhist "Lent," which runs from mid-July to mid-October, is a time designated for religious retreat and for the ordination of new monks.

†Maha is a title awarded to any monk who has passed at least the lowest of the seven grades of the ecclesiastical examination system for the study of Pali texts.

her in turn, mechanically. "I keep thinking about my father. . . ."

"You crazy? This is no time to think about your father. . . . If you go on like this, how can we do the show? In no time at all, the crowd'll be booing us!"

Chiwin shakes his head once. Some sort of realization makes him push his body up from hers on outstretched arms. If only this night were over! The spectators are dead quiet, each pair of eyes glued to the stage. He puts everything out of his mind, draws Wanphen's body onto his, and begins to go through all the acts he usually performs on this stage.

Many of the people up front move closer and closer. Some of them even poke their faces in, right close up—as though this were the single most extraordinary thing in life, something they'd never seen from the day they were born. Some of the customers who have girls sitting with them begin to grope them obscenely. His gaze meets their eyes and in a flash he senses that in some things men may not understand other men at all. In their eyes glitter a thousand and one things—pleasure and desire. Some of the men pretend to be unaffected by the scene, though in fact their souls are seething through every vein.

"What have I become?" Chiwin asks himself. He feels like a male animal in the rutting season, brutishly copulating with a female animal, right before the eyes of a group of studmasters. The more powerfully he performs, and the more varied the couplings, the more they're satisfied.

He glances down at Wanphen for a moment. He is now fully astride her body. She is sighing and groaning, twisting and writhing her body as if she's being aroused to the limit, even though actually she experiences nothing from what she's doing. This is the first time that Chiwin understands her life clearly, and he feels a heart-rending pity for her. He wants to ask her just one question: how much does she suffer from living this way? Having intercourse with a man she doesn't love in front of a crowd. Pretending to experience so much pleasure to arouse all these people . . . in exchange for no more than a hundred baht a night. Do her children back home know what's going on? Isn't there a night when she goes back home, lies down, and cries? After all, she still has feelings, doesn't she?

Chiwin lifts his head and stares once again at the audience, as if searching for even one person with some understanding of the things that go on in the stories of the people working here. But he sees nothing but faces burning more hotly than ever with satisfaction and excitement. In fact, it looks like some of them have even reached a climax.

Chiwin begins to see the truth. . . .

All of us here are simply victims . . . Latda . . . Wanphen . . . me . . . even those people sitting there watching with such satisfied expressions. All of them feel the pressure of the society outside. So they come here for emotional compensation, to build up a superiority complex. They come to eat and drink. They come to sit and watch others expose their genitals and perform every variety of sexual intercourse. This allows them to feel contempt for people they can then regard as lower than themselves. Man has a deep abiding instinct to shove his way up over his fellow men. The truth is that we're all animals of the city, who live lives of pain and suffering in the midst of a demented society. The only difference between us is that those who have greater advantages stand on top of those who have less, and so on down the line.

"Give it to her! All the way, kid . . . !" comes a roaring cheer from a table to the left, mixed with delighted laughter from a group of friends. Wanphen clutches him still more tightly to her body. I wonder what she's thinking about now. Chiwin stares at her, but can't see her clearly. In her eyes there's an expression of entreaty. He grits his teeth, swallows his saliva down his dry throat, and gasps for breath. The sweat oozes from his forehead, back, and shoulders. A stinging drop trickles down into one eye, blurring his vision. Feeling a numb rage, Chiwin is almost at the point of jumping up and kicking out in the direction of those voices. But in fact he doesn't dare do anything, not even respond with words.

Wanphen's hands, still clasped around his back, give him a stealthy pinch. "Take it easy, Elder Brother Win." Her voice is barely audible. "Don't listen to those crazy people. I'm not a cow or a water buffalo, you know. . . ."

So that's it! He's turned Wanphen herself into a victim of his own oppression. He comes to himself at the nip of her nails and the sound of her voice. Suddenly the tears well up in his eyes, mixed with drops of sweat. He pushes his body up, leaning on his outstretched arms, and stares Wanphen full in the eyes. When he bends over and gives her a kiss, she's surprised by a touch she's never felt from him before. Just then the song ends and the stage lights dim to darkness.

Chiwin goes into the bathroom, his shirt still unbuttoned. He turns on the tap, washes his hands, and scoops up some water to rub in the hollow of his neck. As he lifts his head, he encounters his own face reflected in the little mirror above the basin.

Indeed man encounters his real self when he stands before a mirror. . . .

In the bare, empty bathroom the faint sound of music filters in. He leans on his hands, gripping the basin's edge, and stares at that face for a long time, in silent questioning.

He thinks back to his mother's letter. *How are things going for you in Bangkok? Have you found a job yet?* How can he possibly tell his mother about the kind of work that he has found? She would faint dead away. And he himself can't really say why he's struggled so hard to make a living this way. The easy answer is probably because he was hungry and had reached a dead end.

When he'd set off for Bangkok, carrying his teacher's certificate with him, who could have known that for months he'd be clutching at straws, trying to compete with tens of thousands, hundreds of thousands, of others, taking test after test? And then go home, waiting to learn the results of his applications, place after place, day after day. At first his hopes had still been bright and clear. But, as time passed, they'd faded, like a candle that melts itself completely away, dimming down to his last baht. Then a friend of his, who worked as a bartender in a go-go club, had invited him along to try this line of work.

"Don't worry . . . at first you feel a bit shy. . . . But you get

used to it after a while . . . .A good-looking guy with a nice build
like yours is just what these people are looking for. You get a
hundred a night, two or three thousand a month. It's far better
than being a teacher. You talk yourself blue in the face for nothing
but a few pennies a month." His friend had patted him on the
shoulder and said, "OK? Give it a go, to tide you over while you
wait to hear about your job applications. You want to starve? You
don't have to worry about getting picked up. The police don't make
any trouble, the people there have got connections high up."

Is this the true image of a man who's studied to become a
teacher? Chiwin stares at his reflection with a feeling of nausea.
His hair's a mess, his eyes dry and lifeless, with a timid, evasive
look. The skin on his face and lips is parched and wan with strain.
Not a shred of dignity left, though he's still young and strong. How
did a man with clear, firm hopes and goals end up as someone who
doesn't have the courage to confront even his own face?

Suddenly he feels a terrible churning deep in his abdomen. It
surges up through his insides to his throat. Chiwin clings tightly
to the washbasin, hiccups once, and then, before being conscious
of it, doubles over, arches his neck, and vomits in a torrent. All
the different foods he ate earlier in the evening, accumulated in
his belly, spout out in streams, splattering the washbasin. Once,
twice, three times. Sounds of retching follow quickly, one after the
other. Each time, he spits out what he'd swallowed earlier, till he's
gasping with exhaustion. Snot and tears join together in a dirty
stream. Chiwin lifts one forearm to wipe his mouth, and smells
the sour stink pervading everything.

The reflection in the mirror is now a murky blur, because of
the tears which well up and fill the sockets of his eyes. He feels
so dizzy that he almost cannot stay on his feet. Chiwin swallows
his viscous saliva and hiccups once again. This time what he vomits
up is a thick, clear liquid. It spouts out so violently that it seems
to carry with it his liver, kidneys, and intestines.

Translated by Benedict R. O'G. Anderson
and Ruchira Chinnapongse Mendiones

NHAT TIEN

(Vietnam)

Nhat Tien is one of Vietnam's foremost authors. Born Bui Nhat Tien in Hanoi in 1936, he was raised in the North but left for the South when the country was separated in 1954 by the Geneva accords. Until South Vietnam fell to the communists he worked as a chemistry teacher, and at carving out a literary career. He is known as an essayist, editor, and author of short stories and children's books. In 1962 Nhat Tien won the National Literature Award for his fifth book, Them Hoang, and he later became vice-chairman of the Vietnamese Chapter of PEN. Although he was permitted by the new communist regime to continue teaching, he despaired at the repression it brought to the defeated South and joined the fleeing refugees known to the world as the Boat People. While in passage, his overcrowded boat was attacked by pirates in the Gulf of Thailand, and he was stranded for more than three weeks on a deserted island with over one hundred others. He later reported on this experience in Pirates on the Gulf of Siam. Nhat Tien resides in exile in California, where he continues to write and lobby in behalf of Vietnamese refugees around the world. In the story that follows, he offers a lamentably realistic window into the vindictive nature of the bureaucratic regime that forced so many of his compatriots abroad.

In the Footsteps of a Water Buffalo

When the production unit assigned him the task of harrowing the little patch of rice field along the creek flowing past Cong Quan, Vinh was beside himself with joy. At least that was a less punishing job than carrying baskets of clay from the ends of a shoulder pole for the local brick-making cooperative.

But Vinh had not reckoned with the abnormal sluggishness of the water buffalo. Admittedly, it was an old, old beast—a scrawny thing, weaker than the other fourteen buffalo belonging to their February 3 agricultural cooperative, but a water buffalo balking at the plow or harrow—that was unacceptable behavior. So Vinh made maximum use of the bamboo whip, lashing at the beast's ash gray skin while blustering and shouting himself hoarse. The torrid sun had him sweating profusely, and his eyes were blurry. Under his feet, the paddy slosh that had been baking since daybreak was scorching hot. And the water buffalo kept plodding on his way ever so slowly and wearily. Vinh could hear its labored breathing through the gaping mouth dribbling saliva and froth. Its entire skeleton jutted against wrinkled skin, and he could count every rib.

Apparently, Old Man Thuoc had once warned everyone against overworking the water buffalo. The creatures were always being called upon to do this or that. Plowing. Harrowing. Hauling lumber. Transporting goods. Carrying tons of brick. Old Man Thuoc had spoken up at a general meeting: "You comrades should go easy on the buffalo if you want them to work for many years. Overtax their bodies and they'll give out on you in no time."

Thuoc had spoken without malice or innuendo. He only worried about the draft animals, and far from his mind were all those aged humans on whose wizened backs were saddled sundry chores in the cooperative. To his simple way of thinking, water buffalo represented the most precious capital: when one fell sick it was cause for grave concern. If a man was ill, well, that was different: he could get back to work in a few days.

The secretary of the Party branch, however, chose to interpret Thuoc's guileless words in a completely different manner. At a restricted session of the village council, which included leaders of various groups—workers, women, youth, and the supervisory board of cooperatives—he pronounced his verdict: "Old Man Thuoc holds the most reactionary views possible. All of you, comrades, must maintain your vigilance and keep to a minimum his remarks in public on any subject."

All present understood. While innocent enough, Thuoc's words unwittingly reflected the truth of their lives. Old men and women had to bend their shrunken backs hauling bricks, pushing carts, and lugging baskets of dirt with shoulder poles like beasts of burden, yet nobody dared emit one peep in their defense. Why contradict the most powerful voice in the village and court trouble? "The best thing is to sit still, and the next best thing is to say yes." So went proverbial wisdom at meetings under the socialist regime.

Thuoc's incident eventually blew over, and he avoided pursuing the issue any further. On the contrary, both he and his wife eagerly took on any task entrusted to them. So later, when their son signed up for military service, no matter how vigilant the village council wished to appear, it was obliged to offer one of its "progressive family" certificates of merit to Thuoc and his wife. Thuoc was promoted to foreman of the production unit at the brick kiln, and his wife was admitted to the Association of Elderly Women and put on the advisory committee, even though she never opened her mouth or ventured a single opinion at any meeting. From start to finish, she could be seen lifting her apron to her rheumy eyes and dabbing at them all the time.

Then one day, from out of the blue, a warrant from the district came for the arrest of Thuoc's son for desertion. Now, if a young man fell for the "artificial prosperity" of Saigon, or flinched from his international proletarian duty in fraternal socialist Kampuchea, he would hardly be so foolish as to return to his native village. In all probability, the boy had disappeared into the corrupt society of the South, but the comrades of the security police intended to carry out the directives of the district Party committee to the letter and in earnest. Flourishing their weapons, they stormed Thuoc's house as if they were hunting enemy troops. The hut was virtually bare of furniture, and there was not much worth rummaging through, but, all the same, the gang went through the motions of searching, strutting back and forth and turning the place upside down for a whole hour. During all that time Thuoc's wife sobbed and blubbered, crying again and again, "O my son! Where have you gone? Why have you left your ma?"

As for Thuoc himself, he simply squatted at the foot of a post and hugged his knees in stony silence. He was very angry with his boy. The brat might have found a refuge somewhere for himself, but he had brought disaster down on both his father and his mother. In a twinkling their so-called revolutionary contribution to the cooperative, what they had achieved over many years, went up in smoke. Thuoc and his wife would lose their positions in the community and their jobs. They would be ostracized and punished not only in reprisal but as a pointed warning to any other youngsters who might feel tempted to follow their son down the reactionary road to decadence and hooliganism.

All of a heap, man and wife became outlaws and pariahs, doomed to live apart from society. When they met someone out on the road and ventured a hello, that person would look the other way, feigning nonrecognition. A few friends or acquaintances in whom persisted some shreds of decency might bestow on them a commiserative glance, but they would at once look around nervously, as if they had committed a crime and were afraid of being observed.

What they had dreaded, and what hurt most was that from now on Thuoc and his wife would be cut off the ration-coupon system. With ration coupons they had found it possible to buy staples at official prices. Without the coupons, they would consider themselves evicted for good from the community dining table, even if what was spread upon the board was nothing more than potato and cassava.

Thuoc now had to journey all the way to the next village and beg better-off families for work on mutual-help teams. His wife was forced to search through the mire of flooded fields and creeks for crabs and snails to help eke out their meager fare. Both came to look like woebegone souls risen out of the mud. Their plight gave the Party branch secretary much occasion for gleeful gloating. He kept repeating, as if to drill a lesson into the village folks, "This is what will befall all those who go against the Party line and state policy! It's historical necessity—there's no getting around it."

At the very moment when Vinh was struggling with his old water buffalo in the slush of the rice field, Thuoc's wife was floundering in the creek with a basket for collecting snails hung on her back. She clearly heard Vinh curse the beast. She clearly saw his hand wave the bamboo whip and lash repeatedly at its wizened skeleton. But instead of hastening its pace, the buffalo slowed down little by little until it came to a standstill, trembling all over. Utterly exhausted, it seemed unable to pull its foot out of the mire for even one more step. The harrow stuck fast. The steaming paddy slosh beneath burned at Vinh's feet and drove him close to frenzy. He flogged the beast so hard he drew blood from its flank, yet still the buffalo would not budge. Its body was bathed in sweat when, stretching out its neck and rearing its head, it exhaled something like a soft moan. Then the whole mass slumped down. The decrepit animal collapsed in the paddy like some old soldier fallen on the battleground.

This unexpected turn of events stunned Vinh. At first, he stood there staring dumbfounded at the beast asprawl in the field, his every limb numb with fear. Then he flung the bamboo whip down beside the buffalo and rushed off screaming, "Comrades! Comrades! Come out, take a look—the buffalo is dead!"

As he reached the road running and screaming, Vinh bumped into Thuoc's wife, whose eyes were wide with astonishment. The wretched buffalo had been not unlike a close acquaintance to her and her husband. They knew all about it, when and where it had been born, to whom it had belonged. They knew how many cowlicks there were on its head, how many rings there were around its horns, even what made it tick. And now it was dead!

Forsaken by kith and kin, Thuoc's wife suddenly realized what the buffalo had meant to her. Never had it glowered at her with contempt or hatred since the day her wretched boy had bolted from the army. Never had it averted its gaze when she came up to it and patted it on the back. Thuoc's wife dissolved into tears, mourning a good friend.

Vinh's news struck the cooperative like a thunderbolt. They all dropped whatever they were doing and hurried toward Cong Quan. Water buffalo were more valuable than people. During the war, many people had perished, but no death had ever caused as much consternation as that of this animal.

The person most shocked and astounded was the cooperative chief, a fat, heavy man who never walked quickly, let alone run. Today he broke into a gallop, and younger folks had trouble keeping up with him. His crimson face and eyes glared fury, and in his hand he held a bamboo cane, which he flourished to make his point as he talked to the crowd clustered around him by the paddy: "Which boys are in charge of gathering hay on Team Four? Damn you all, little rascals! You were too busy with your fun and games to feed the buffalo—no wonder it's dropped dead. I'll strip those red scarves off your necks and teach you to love games and sports less!"

In principle, what the cooperative chief had said was a grave offense to the whole Ho Chi Minh Vanguard Youth Corps, an attack on its honor. Had anyone else made the same statement it would have provoked an uproar, but the Party branch secretary shared in his comrade's anger completely. Indeed, the two men differed only in the way they expressed their displeasure. While one burst into shouts and curses, the other clamped his lips tightly with a livid look on his face. Children young enough to be the cooperative chief's sons and daughters were too intimidated to make an issue of their corporate pride.

Some boys standing on the fringe of the crowd whispered among themselves:

"Whose turn is it this week to tend the buffalo of Team Four? Is it Nang's group?"

"No. It's Quy's group. And I've seen Quy and his teammates catching crabs up there around the Ong Sung fields!"

A young tattletale, overhearing the conversation, spoke out loud enough to be heard by the cooperative chief: "It's the turn of Quy's team to cut grass for the buffalo!"

The chief swung sharply toward the boy, pouncing on him as if he were a piece of irrefutable proof. On the tip of his tongue was a string of epithets unflattering to Quy's ancestors, which he was just about to rattle off before discovering in time that the culprit was a son of the village security commissioner. As the proverb says: "Before you stroke the face, beware the nose." You don't touch relatives of an acquaintance, let alone one who wields much clout. And so the cooperative chief twirled his cane once more and said, addressing no one in particular, "I don't care whose shift it is! This time I'm going to punish them all. No letters of commendation from me, not even those I've already signed!"

Then he turned to the boys and asked them to carry the beast onto the roadside. Here they found out that the buffalo, while far from well, was not dead: it had simply collapsed from exhaustion.

Relieved, the cooperative chief looked less grim. Somewhat ashamed of his outburst, he now spoke in a more conciliatory tone. "The buffalo is hungry—that's all. Give it a good day's rest and plenty of straw to eat and it'll be back on its feet in a jiffy."

So the water buffalo enjoyed a vacation without benefit of a national holiday to thank. However, the cooperative chief's veterinary assessment fit his own hopes better than it did the facts, soon to transpire, for, on being hauled back to the barn, the buffalo simply lay there like an inert hulk. It was not hungry. A trough full of tender, mouth-watering grass was placed right next to its chops, but it would not even bother to open them. A top whose spinning force runs out will drop to the ground, and the buffalo was like that. There was no way it could pick itself up and go again. It lay there lifeless in the barn, staring stupidly with the glazed vacancy of its eyes, dribbling froth and saliva out of both corners of its mouth.

The deputy chief of the cooperative made a flat statement, mincing no words: "Let's butcher the buffalo."

People who all year round had been dreaming of meat rejoiced, hollering, "That's right! Let's slaughter it now while it's still alive. In a few days we'll have to eat carrion from a dead animal!"

The idea received collective approval. Here was a rare opportunity to forget their starvation diet and feast on meat. Surely, not much more service could be squeezed out of that old water buffalo anyhow, even if it could be cured of whatever ailed it. But, with the buffalo out of commission, the cooperative had to confront and solve another problem, and to talk of butchering the beast at this moment seemed out of place; it smacked of irresponsible gluttony. So the cooperative chief refrained from giving his consent immediately.

That night he convoked an emergency session of the village council to discuss how to replace the sick buffalo. Somebody suggested, "Without the buffalo, a number of our tasks will be crippled. And our cooperative also happens to be in the period of most intense activity. Let's lay out funds and purchase another buffalo."

The cooperative chief dismissed that idea out of hand for this reason: "If the solution were so simple, why hold a special session of the village council at all?"

The truth of the matter was that, deep in his heart, he did not want to spend one damn penny from the budget on anything whatsoever. It had to be further replenished until his cooperative could afford a small automobile. He had always put forward the view that an automobile would be of critical importance to the growth of the cooperative. It would give its chief mobility, allowing him to travel one day to the district seat and the next to the provincial capital. He could keep in touch with various commissions and agencies and arrange trade or exchange for all sorts of products and commodities: seed, fertilizer, gasoline, kerosene, and whatnot. A car would be the magic key to unlock and open wide the door to the world of abundance.

The women had their say too. One comrade recommended that a set of water pumps be purchased to replace the old-fashioned system of irrigation scoops and buckets, all those *gua-dais* and *gausongs*, which not only did a slow job but also involved a large labor force—made up primarily of women.

She said, "We are living in the age of science and technology. Let's bring science and technology to bear on production!"

But one brother countered the sister's proposal with this heroic argument: "I agree with our sister that it would be better if we could use science and technology. However, let's not forget the words of our communist poet: 'Our hands turn even pebbles and rocks to rice!' "

The sister huffily retorted, "If so, then why don't you take the place of the buffalo and pull the plow yourself, brother? We'll have rice to eat just like when we still had the buffalo!"

That was it! What the sister said in pique struck the cooperative chief as a brilliant idea, a stroke of genius. He slapped his thigh and exclaimed, "Sister Tai is right on target! With determination we can overcome any and all difficulties. Like this problem of the buffalo. I propose that you brothers and sisters discuss the substitution of human strength for animal motive power as a stopgap measure."

In amazement, the sister asked, "You mean somebody will have to pull the plow?"

"What's wrong with that? Years ago, during the war, many agricultural cooperatives took that measure to make up for shortages and to push production."

No one quarreled with the idea that the problem could be solved in that fashion. But the meeting was deadlocked on who was to fill in for the buffalo pulling a plow or harrow. The women, who had always defended equal rights, preferred to forgo this privilege and pass it on to the male members of the Ho Chi Minh Vanguard

Youth Corps. But the boys had minds of their own. They would and could do anything only if they cared to. One couldn't lean too hard on them or they might sabotage the cooperative, put it out of business. The cooperative chief knew that. Nevertheless, he made a perfunctory attempt to enlist them, virtually pleading for their help. "Well, let me suggest that the comrades in the Youth Corps hold a separate session and agree among themselves to take turns substituting for the buffalo. I hope that you all will carry out in practice the spirit of your proud motto: "Where they are needed, Youth Corpsmen will be there; where the job is tough, there will be Youth Corpsmen!' "

The comrade who represented the Youth Corps realized at once that he'd been given a tough nut to crack. He suspected, and rightly, that none of the boys would take the place of the buffalo and pull a plow. Not that any of them lacked the physical strength and stamina to do it. But once you've played buffalo, how on earth can you face a girl and talk to her seriously? That would be the overriding reason for the boys' inevitable lack of enthusiasm. It was on everybody's mind but went unspoken.

Sure enough, after the local branch of the Youth Corps held two meetings and all means of persuasion were applied, no one volunteered with socialist "joy and zeal" to be cast as a buffalo. A daylong palaver failed to force the impasse.

Meanwhile, Vinh kept a close eye on the buffalo's deteriorating health and reported it hour by hour, minute by minute. The beast could no longer raise its head. It had begun to gasp for breath. Its hind legs had gone into spasms. And he would conclude each account with the refrain "Butcher it now or we'll end up picking the bones of a rotten dead buffalo!"

The next day, Thuoc could be seen cringing and fawning in the cooperative chief's office. The Party branch secretary was also present. It seemed a unique opportunity had arisen for the old man to atone for his son's sins and to earn his way back into the Party's favor. After living as an outcast for almost a year, Thuoc had learned with terror what it meant to lose ration coupons and to suffer social quarantine: the State had cut out all roots, both material and psychic, from under him. Now he begged for mercy and a second chance. "May I submit a request to the two comrades? Though advanced in years, I'm still strong enough to pull a plow. And I have my wife to lend me a hand. She may not look it, but she's as tough and resilient as a leech!"

As he said that, Thuoc glanced outside. Through the wide open window, both the Party branch secretary and the cooperative chief could see Thuoc's wife in the courtyard, squatting under a tree with her arms clasped around her knees. Beside her there was a basket for crab collecting. She sat there huddled up like a sick cat, gazing fixedly beyond the hedgerow toward a vast field where shadowy figures scurried back and forth lugging stacks of blood-red bricks.

Despite the distance, she could spot friends and acquaintances, even the teenagers as they moved bricks from the kiln to the dirt floor, piling them up in long rows. They looked like ants busily gathering materials for a nest, and they formed a community—a famished and tattered society in which the last ounce of energy was being squeezed out of each of them. But from Thuoc and his wife that society still withheld its ultimate blessing, and hope seemed far beyond their reach.

Over the past year, Thuoc's wife had never had a chance to touch and fondle sheets of ration coupons: this one good for rice, that one for potatoes, another for oil or firewood, for some thread or a needle, and, once in a long while, for a kilo of sugar or a square of cloth. And she had been denied the privilege of standing in line and jostling, of squabbling and fighting outside the state-run store, sometimes in the rain, sometimes under broiling sun, while all around the air was thick with the composite odor, sour and pungent, of many types of sweat.

When Thuoc's wife slogged through the mud for crabs in flooded fields, she often prayed to both Heaven and the Buddha that her prodigal son would come back home after he'd had his lark. At worst he might go to jail, but she would at least still have her boy. Time served, he'd be set free, and the state might then relent and restore the family to the ration-coupon system. She thought longingly of the ration-coupon sheet—her pipe dream.

Now she waited for her husband under the tree with all the anxiety and dread of a convict on whom the judge is about to pronounce sentence. As soon as he appeared in the doorway to the cooperative chief's office, she sprang to her feet. She saw him toothlessly grinning from ear to ear. Both Heaven and the Buddha had heard and granted her prayer! Indeed, her husband came running toward her, waving both his hands and shouting jubilantly, "Those gentlemen said yes! We'll take the place of the buffalo!"

Translated by Huynh Sanh Thong

CATHERINE LIM

(Singapore)

Catherine Lim began writing in Singapore in the 1970s, publishing her first short story collection, Little Ironies, *in 1978. A second collection,* Or Else, the Lightning God, *published in the early 1980s, showed her willingness to begin moving away from the sugary emotionalism still characteristic of much Southeast Asian fiction. It revealed, too, an insistence upon addressing domestic and women's issues within Singapore's rapidly modernizing and cosmopolitan society. In 1987, her third short story collection,* The Shadow of a Shadow of a Dream, *showed Lim continuing to tackle issues relating both to family and to the idea of intimacy within Singapore's densely compacted urban life. In "The English Language Teacher's Secret," which is drawn from that collection, she addresses the difficulties Singaporean women may experience within the island state's multiracial society. The genetic matchmaking scheme lampooned in the story's introduction is, of course, a matter of record, having been proposed by the government of former Prime Minister Lee Kuan-Yew. Married with two children, Lim is attached to Singapore's Curriculum Development Institute and writes English-language instructional materials.*

The English Language Teacher's Secret

When the government became alarmed by the increasing tendency among graduate women to stay unmarried and thus deprive the country of the brainy children that would form the future pool of expertise for the country's economic development, it started a matchmaking scheme whereby these women might meet the men who would lead them away from the errors of their ways.

On the morning after the Prime Minister himself, in a major policy speech, alerted the nation to the perils of this trend, single graduate women woke up to find themselves suddenly on the national center stage: everybody wanted to know why they hadn't gotten married, what they looked for in a marriage partner, were Singapore men deficient in any way, et cetera. Because these graduate women had been invested with special importance as the providers of the much-needed brains to run the country in the future, they found themselves in the unique position of being cajoled and wooed by a government not normally given to these methods of getting things done, and naturally their views were sought eagerly, and the men's not at all. The minister whose prestige was only slightly less than the Prime Minister's took upon himself the task of personally interviewing a sample of these graduate women to obtain firsthand knowledge of why the educated Singapore woman no longer wanted to marry the educated Singapore man. What he found convinced him that it was all the fault of the Singapore male, so that, after the interviews were over, he turned his attention to the male graduates, berated them for their wrong attitudes, and sternly advised them to change. For the men, despite their education, were still stubbornly clinging to the old notion that, to marry happily, a man must marry an academic notch or two below him:

a man with a university degree would do better to marry someone with A levels only, and a man with A levels had better, for his own peace of mind, seek out someone with O levels only, and so on. Only in this way could marital supremacy, so important to the Asian male, be ensured. The result was that the very large crop of female graduates produced by the university each year, a crop that was moreover becoming bigger each year with a rise in female ambition, was left largely unsought, and therefore, in the words of a concerned government official, "deprived of the primary function of womanhood."

There was another deficiency of the Singapore male, besides this chauvinism: he was woefully behind his Western counterparts in matters of dress, grooming, and social niceties. The bolder of the single graduate women whom the minister interviewed spoke bluntly about the Singapore male's lack of social finesse: one of them, a particularly articulate female in her late thirties, told the minister to his face that Singapore men were downright unattractive; they were narrow-minded and petty; behind their executive desks they talked sense but outside, in the world at large, they floundered, unsure of what to say or how to behave, and in the presence of women they were definitely gauche.

"Who wants to marry such men?" asked the interviewee rhetorically, while the minister, fingertips pressed together, studied her and concluded that, yes, she was right: Singapore women were getting too independent to tolerate anymore the nonsense of the men who had better, then, be taught to change their attitude and to acquire more social graces. The minister made a mental note that he would see the Minister of Education about whether social grooming could be built into the curriculum of the sixteen- and seventeen-year-olds in the junior colleges, and when he courteously indicated that the interview was over, and watched the lady stride out in proud determined independence, he was convinced that he had got to the root of the problem. If the minister had had his way, he would have ordered that all male bachelors would have their next promotion stopped if they continued in their recalcitrance, but the operational follow-up was handled by a very cautious and discreet senior minister who never ceased to impress upon his task force the need to keep their project, of so delicate a nature, in low profile and out of public controversy as much as possible. Called the Social Development Unit, it stayed bravely above the levity that some people, including members of parliament, were determined to reduce it to, and quietly but efficiently went about its work of collecting data about single men and women and devising a range of programs calculated to bring them together in the most convivial of settings. There were polite tea dances and chaperoned cruises, and because these were rather expensive affairs that had to be subsidized by the government, certain members of parliament rose to peevishly demand why taxpayers' money was being used for something as questionable as love-boat excursions. But these protests were less in the nature of serious inquiry than of a mild parliamentary fracas that was not at all unwelcome in a day of dull proceedings. They represented no obstacle to the progress of the Social Development Unit: the real obstacle was the determination of the singles to remain single, for, after a year in operation, the unit was able to report only two weddings.

At the level of the clubhouse and the school canteen, such a unique project was sure to generate a great deal of interest: the discussions ranged from intellectual disputations on the nature of freedom of choice of the individual to tawdry jokes about dried up, hard up spinsters, of whom the largest number was reputedly found in the schools.

In Miss Sylvie Ponniah's school alone, there were five unmarried women: Miss Ponniah, approaching forty-six, Madam Cheng, the vice-principal, who was in her fifties, Miss de Silva in her early forties, and Miss Ho and Miss Tang, both in their midthirties. They were not a particularly attractive-looking lot; in fact, beside those colleagues whose happy and prosperous marriages had invested them with a certain degree of radiant contentment expressed in various vanities of dress and grooming, the unmarried women were distinctly colorless and dowdy. Miss Ponniah was better than most, mainly because the sari, so demanding in its dictates of color and appurtenances of gold chain, earrings, and other items of jewelry, guaranteed a measure of feminine appeal, although Miss Ponniah wore only the most delicate of jewelry and the most subdued of colors, unlike Miss de Silva, who, when she chose to doff her Western dress for the sari, went all out for flamboyance and decorated her earlobes and bosom with large baubles. Not counting Miss de Silva, whom everyone thought rather loud and brassy though they always spoke warm praise for her clothes and trinkets in front of her, Miss Ponniah was easily the most presentable single woman in the school. The vice-principal, thin and haggard and always in a shapeless cheongsam, was altogether out of the running; Miss Ho Wai Chun, who was thirty-five, at an age when some women are in their bloom, looked old and worn out and shuffled around in an ill-fitting dress and sandals, while Miss Annie Tang, who was enormously fat owing to some illness, had had a pretty face whose prettiness had long ago disappeared along a ripple of chins.

The married teachers, including the men teachers, whose dreary lives in school, year in, year out, had caused male enterprise to turn inward and dissipate itself in small runnels of bitchy talk and gossip, were inclined among themselves to agree that matrimony was out of the question for their unmarried colleagues. Having agreed on that, their inquiries about whether Miss Ho or Miss Tang or Miss Ponniah had been invited on one of those fabulous matchmaking cruises had a biting piquancy. The inquiries were of course never made directly, not even of Miss de Silva, whose open pursuit of men had earned her the name of Manhunter, for, if she sensed an insult, Miss de Silva could turn waspish. Miss Ho would have blushed in painful self-consciousness, and Miss Tang would have been deeply offended and fixed her large eyes on the offender's face for a full thirty seconds before resuming her work of marking the exercise books.

And Miss Ponniah—delicate Miss Ponniah would have been so shocked by an inquiry of this kind, her gentle features would have shown so much confusion, that the inquirer would have been shamed into sheepishness. For nobody spoke to Miss Ponniah of such things. Miss Ponniah's fragility of person, accentuated by the neat, softly draping saris she wore, her soft polite voice, and, most of all, her being known never to take part in any conversation remotely approaching the coarse or the mean, were the best safe-guards against any intrusion of her privacy. Miss Ponniah was a very private person. And yet Miss Ponniah loved once—loved very deeply. More than twenty years ago, Miss Ponniah fell in love with a young man whose name was Dr. Chellam, or rather, he fell in love with her the first time he saw her, and when he wrote to tell her, that was the beginning of her love for him. They sent letters secretly to each other—in all, Miss Ponniah wrote six and received eight before her father found out and put a stop to what he thought was a disgraceful affair. He was a very strict, old-fashioned man and Miss Ponniah was his only daughter, whom he doted on. He never exactly explained why he objected so strenuously to the young man whose good family background, impressive academic creden-tials, and good character would have recommended him strongly to any family, but he remained firm about not allowing Dr. Chellam to pay court to his daughter. Miss Ponniah's aunt, who was very upset about what she regarded as an irresponsible disregard of opportunity (for Miss Ponniah, at twenty-six, was not young any-more), took him to task and even complained to the relatives that his widowerhood had made him a selfish old man who only thought of his own comfort. The young man left soon afterward for Great Britain on a course of study and Miss Ponniah never saw him again.

The years that followed were quiet years spent in dutiful at-tendance on an ailing father. Miss Ponniah never complained but in her heart she mourned the loss of her love. Possessing an inward nature that shrank from confiding secrets to anyone, including even the affectionate concerned aunt, Miss Ponniah buried her love under the daily duties of her existence as daughter and teacher, moving from home to school and back from school to home, in a serenity that belied the desperation of the earlier struggles. For alone in her room, during the lonely months after Dr. Chellam had left for Britain, without even saying good-bye, Miss Ponniah had grieved and contemplated suicide. The long struggle against dis-content, against anger at her father, was known only to herself and at last the struggle was over, and she emerged more dutiful than ever, determined to forget the past.

It was not so much forgetting her love as transmuting it into something purer. In the crucible of Miss Ponniah's suffering, the love had become purified of all dross so that it was now most precious gold, enshrined in Miss Ponniah's heart. For Miss Ponniah had heard that Dr. Chellam never married; he had returned from his studies and gone to settle in Malaysia, where he was attached to a large private hospital, but he never married. Miss Ponniah had heard of attempts by relatives to matchmake for him, but he remained resolutely unmarried. Only she understood why. He had gone away a brokenhearted man, and he returned still brokenhearted, unable to forget the woman he could not marry. Miss Ponniah's father had died at the ripe old age of eighty, by which time Miss Ponniah was forty and her sad little love affair entombed almost twenty years in her faithful heart. Knowing that her memory was also being kept alive in the loyal heart of the man who declared his love for her so long ago had invested this secret love with an almost religious quality, so that Miss Ponniah, unmarried at forty-six and pitied by some for her lonely existence, was in reality a deeply contented woman.

Every day she thought of Dr. Chellam and she reread his letters in the privacy of her room, with the reverent ardour of a devotee, and, again and again, she thought of how no woman had risen to take her place in his affections. She had left a void in his life, as he had said in his last letter, and since then, the void had remained unfilled, indeed, could not be filled because it had already been sanctified by her memory. Miss Ponniah's eyes filled with tears at the thought and they were tears of quiet joy mixed with profound gratitude.

Teaching at her school, Miss Ponniah kept the secret intact in her heart. Even her secluded innocent world was not free from malicious gossip: snippets reached her of the carefree, bachelor existence of Dr. Chellam and some of his colleagues, which was at odds with his enshrined image. But this gossip was not even disquieting to Miss Ponniah, for having long ago consecrated her love for Dr. Chellam, and his for her, on the altar of sublime love, anything that did not add to the sublimity was dismissed from her consciousness.

"I am loved," thought Miss Ponniah with a glow that radiated outward; people often remarked on the radiant serenity of Miss Ponniah's smile. It had never occurred to Miss Ponniah to consider an attempt at renewing contact with Dr. Chellam; her father being dead, there was now no earthly reason why they should not be married. Perhaps she had waited for Dr. Chellam to make the first move, and when he did not, and the years went by, she set up the little altar of their love and there placed herself and her lover, exactly as they were twenty years ago, young and ardent and pure. Removed thus from time and place, they became immortal: it did not matter that Miss Ponniah's hair had turned gray and the youthful roundness of her face and body was gone; it did not matter that Dr. Chellam too had probably grayed and that gossip hinted at debauchery relieving the loneliness of a bachelor existence. She in her world, he in his, but how close together in their lives of chosen commitment to the past!

"I am loved and I love in return," thought Miss Ponniah, the inner glow suffusing her features, and her love had the capacity of expanding to embrace the whole world. It was no longer love of a particular kind but universal love that reached to all, embracing all and sundry—her dear devoted father long gone from this earth, her caring aunt, her friends, her pupils, the principal of her school, grumpy Miss Tang, vulgar Miss de Silva, and the entire brotherhood of sniggering male colleagues. Miss Ponniah, with her secret safe in her heart, rose above the little meannesses swirling around her and could not be touched by them. Miss Ponniah, fortified by her secret from the past, escaped the tyrannies of the present and the future, and was therefore happy.

A happy secret, after a time, has need to reveal itself to the world: Miss Ponniah, teaching English language to a class of secondary school pupils, found herself abandoning the "Johns" and "Marys" and "Mr. Tans" that invariably provide the human link to the dry little bones of grammar, and instead wrote on the chalkboard "Dr. C" and spoke it aloud in the oral language practices. The first time she did it—she wrote "Dr. C advised his patient to take plenty of rest" to elicit sentences of a similar grammatical structure from her pupils—she felt a little thrill of alarm at her own daring. That was the first time she had referred directly to him by name. She read out the sentence, the pupils read it out in unison. The beloved's name was now uttered upon the air, like a charm. Like a charm, it had compelling power: Miss Ponniah made several more sentences in which Dr. C featured, and listened for it to be spoken back, and still her secret was safe, for the pupils suspected not a thing. But when Dr. C appeared in contexts that were not at all medical, when he was used to teach the Active Voice and the Passive Voice and the Direct Speech and the Indirect Speech, when he featured in a comprehension passage and also in the opening lines of a composition to be completed by the pupils— the particularity hit the more perceptive of the pupils, who whispered to one another, "Why is Miss Ponniah always writing about Dr. C? Do you think that's the name of her boyfriend?"

Thrilled by their discovery, they discussed whether to ask Miss Ponniah directly about Dr. C, and also what C stood for, but decided not to: somehow Miss Ponniah's air of fragile gentility forbade it. The boldest of the pupils, a girl name Fong Yin who had round eyes and a mischievous grin, one morning left a rose on Miss Ponniah's desk, beside which was a card with the words "From Dr. C, your boyfriend," and then everyone waited breathlessly for Miss Ponniah to come in and react to the lover's offering. Miss Ponniah's immediate reaction was to snatch up the rose and card and throw them away, for the name written in another hand was alien and alienating, and the description of "boyfriend" was crude in the extreme, but she checked herself quickly, struggled to maintain her calm, succeeded after only a minute, and then proceeded to begin the day's lesson on the use of Prepositional Phrases.

A stronger nature than Miss Ponniah's would not have been deterred by such an insensitive prank and would have, at the least, punished the offender by coolly and unconcernedly continuing to refer to Dr. C as if nothing had happened. But Miss Ponniah, at the first sign that her secret was in danger, completely shut it in again and determined to guard against its escape more vigilantly. She regretted its erstwhile escape, for now the precious name would be taken up by common girls like Fong Yin and bandied around. Miss Ponniah left the rose and the card exactly where they were on the desk; after the lesson, she glided out in a graceful sweep of sari, leaving Fong Yin looking very foolish as she quickly ran up to retrieve the flower and card and suffer the taunting giggles of some of the girls.

And now the need to keep the secret away from the impure ears and eyes of the world was more urgent than ever. When the problem of the unmarried graduate women again came up, this time ranked with such national problems as the economic downturn, there was greater pressure on the Social Development Unit to do better, with consequently revived media interest in the subject, so that single women like Miss Ponniah again came in for much unwanted attention. Miss Ponniah suspected, with a little sickening feeling, that her secret had by now escaped the walls of her classroom and gone elsewhere in the school, for although she was spared any teasing, she could tell, by the underdrift of the staff-room chatter, that some people were aware that there had once been a man in her life. Miss de Silva, whose tongue could be pure vitriol, was fortunately so engrossed in a romance which she made no attempt to conceal that she paid no attention to anyone else's affairs, and could only speak of her own. Miss de Silva, it seemed, went out of the country on weekend forays, and returned to school looking much worn out, according to the men teachers, who listened in each time Miss de Silva spoke about herself, and then adjourned to the canteen to share the titillating bits with one another. Fortunately, therefore, Miss de Silva distracted attention from Miss Ponniah.

Like the pious worshiper who would lay down his life to guard the relics of his saint, Miss Ponniah threw a cordon of tightest silence around her secret, picked up her life where it had been temporarily disrupted, and continued with the same outward tranquillity.

"I am loved and I love still," thought Miss Ponniah, but a little mournfully, for the air around her shrine had become tainted with the air of the world of Miss de Silva: Miss Ponniah found herself asking, and then reproached herself for asking, "Is it true that Dr. C has been unfaithful to me?" The floodgates of doubt were opened, and Miss Ponniah was swept along, to her horror, in the flood of myriad questions: "Why didn't I marry him then? Why didn't I have the courage to stand up to Father? Why didn't I—why did I—If only—if only—"

Miss Ponniah, aghast at the direction her thoughts were taking, gasped, looked around, was glad she was alone in the room and both her aunt and the Filipina maid were out, and took an aspirin to calm the throbbing in her head and to restore her serenity in time for the afternoon duty in school, for it was her turn to supervise the girls' reading in the library. Washing her face and combing her hair carefully, she drove back to school. The foolish girl Fong Yin walked up and stuttered with much sincerity: "Miss Ponniah, I'm sorry about what I did on Friday. I didn't mean to make you angry. I'm really sorry," and Miss Ponniah smiled and said gently, "It's all right, Fong Yin," and passed on serenely. The girl rushed up breathlessly and continued, "We know now that Dr. C is Miss de Silva's boyfriend and not yours, Miss Ponniah. She told us about him."

"What did Miss de Silva tell you, Fong Yin?"

"Well," said the girl, now smiling with the pleasure of restored amity and the sharing of confidences, "she told us that she has a boyfriend now and he's a very successful doctor—his name is Dr. Chellam and he lives in Kuala Lumpur. They're going to get married in June, and going to Italy for their honeymoon."

"That will do, Fong Yin, you mustn't gossip."

"But I wasn't gossiping, Miss Ponniah. Miss de Silva told us all that. She was very happy."

"Fong Yin, 'NEWSBOX' this week—could you handle it this week? Then it will be Seow Hua's turn next week."

"All right, Miss Ponniah."

Miss Ponniah, to her surprise, went on calmly supervising the girls in the library. The sorrow welled up, it would not be beaten down. It rose to the throat so that each time poor Miss Ponniah spoke in answer to a question from an eager young reader who wanted to know the meaning of this or that word, her voice quavered, and then it threatened to rise to the eyes and fill them. Desperately, Miss Ponniah wrenched her thoughts away to fix them on something else. She now bent her head over Quirk and Greenbaum's Grammar and tried to prepare for the next week's lesson on the Subjunctive Mood.

It was in this state of concentration that Miss de Silva found her and whispered to her, "Come to the staff room when you've finished. I've something extremely interesting that concerns you." Miss Ponniah merely lifted her calm face to say with a faint smile, "Certainly," before returning to Quirk and Greenbaum.

When the library period was over, Miss Ponniah, gathering her sari about her with graceful ease, went to the staff room, where Miss de Silva was sitting alone, waiting for her. Miss de Silva, who was the only female smoker in the school, lit a cigarette, inhaled deeply, then, jerking up her chin to emit a stream of smoke through her rounded lips, turned to look at Miss Ponniah and to survey her closely.

"I didn't know that you knew Dr. Chellam," said Miss de Silva, leaning back on her chair and inclining to one side, so that she could survey Miss Ponniah, who had taken a seat opposite, with the nonchalance of superiority.

"I knew him more than twenty years ago," said Miss Ponniah calmly, while her heart swelled with anger to hear this vulgar, cigarette-smoking woman utter the name of her beloved.

"You knew him twenty years ago, I know him now, in fact I'm going to be married to him soon," said Miss de Silva, coming straight to the point with a triumphant gleam in her eye. Present challenged past, present was seeking to destroy past, but Miss Ponniah rose to the full height of her powers by replying, in a quiet and steady voice, "He loved me then, he loves me now."

"How can you say that?" demanded Miss de Silva. "He's going to marry me. He's going to marry me next month." Miss de Silva's

tone grew strident: it was not the stridency of frustrated logic—
she was not interested in exposing the illogic of Miss Ponniah's
claim—but of fear, for Miss de Silva, two weeks before her wedding, wanted to reassure herself that the man she had spent all her
life looking for and had found at last, had no other love, past,
present, or future. Chellam's women—some of them no more than
dolled-up schoolgirls out to have a good time behind their mothers'
backs—had scattered in defeat when Miss de Silva came on the
scene, hard, determined, and totally protective, the kind of woman
that Chellam had felt to be no bad exchange for those young flighty
things that he was beginning to tire a little of. Miss de Silva van-
quished all her rivals—and then, at the moment when she thought
she had a clear field, and that this man whom from their first
meeting she had fallen in love with, was totally hers, Chellam told
her about Miss Ponniah. He had mentioned her casually, a young
gentle woman he had been in love with years ago and had proposed
to. He had indeed forgotten all about her until some chance remark
from Miss de Silva made him suddenly recollect that the school his
fiancée was in was the very same school that the woman he once
proposed to had been teaching in. He asked about a Miss Sylvie
Ponniah: Miss de Silva, who was mixing drinks, looked up sharply
and studied his expression with those narrow intense eyes of hers.
He became momentarily confused under the intensity of the look,
and Miss de Silva concluded that, contrary to what he had avowed,
this Miss Ponniah, and not herself, was his first real love. Miss de
Silva's sense of insecurity returned to unsettle her thoughts all over
again: it did not matter that all Chellam's women had been driven
from the scene; it did not matter that the future would hold no
threat for she knew exactly how to manage Chellam; what mattered,
because it was a stain on the perfection of her present happiness,
was that there was a woman from the past, and the memory of that
woman was coming between her and her lover.

All Miss de Silva's instincts of possession and protection, in
the days following the inadvertent revelation that had fallen so
innocently from Dr. Chellam's lips, were roused to extract everything about the past from Chellam himself, to give him no peace

till he told her everything, and assured her that the woman was nothing to him, he did not love her then, and he never thought of her now. The events of twenty years ago were a blur in Dr. Chellam's mind; the intervening years of gross indulgence alternating with stretches of lonely bachelor existence had no place for the woman he once proposed to. Indeed, it had needed the particularity of school names to jolt this memory, and then only did Dr. Chellam remember this woman, with a brightening expression on his usually dour face. In unusually light spirits that day, he recounted her gentle beauty, her devotion to her father, unaware that his fiancée's eyes were all the time fixed upon his in a mounting of jealousy. At the beginning, it had merely tickled Dr. Chellam's ego to witness the jealous bouts of his fiancée; it gave him the warming feeling that a man experiences when he knows that not one but two women are in love with him and are ready to fight each other for his love. But when Miss de Silva's interrogations became more persistent and peevish, the feeling gave way to irritation, and he told her finally that it was no business of hers.

Miss de Silva was now convinced that her fiancé "had something to hide," and, for the first time, they quarrelled. With the ease with which lovers' quarrels are settled, they promised never to refer to the subject again, Miss de Silva secretly planning to confront Miss Ponniah the minute she returned from her weekend in Kuala Lumpur. The weekend had been satisfactory enough: something like the novelty of first passion always entered into Miss de Silva's feelings for Dr. Chellam and made up for the tiredness of his.

"He cannot love you for he's going to be my husband. How can you say he loves you?" she demanded of Miss Ponniah.

"I have no intention of revealing my secret—least of all to you," said Miss Ponniah softly. She rose to go, with the quiet assurance of the victor.

"Wait," said Miss de Silva. "You have never seen him in all this while, and he's never seen you. Don't you think if he cared at all for you, he would have made an effort to see you again, especially since both of you were free? I say therefore that you are lying. You go around giving people the impression of a great love in your life—even the pupils know it—but all the time it is a wishful dream. Well, you'd better wake up from the dream, Sylvie. I'm going to be married to your great love in two weeks' time."

"There's no use talking to you," said Miss Ponniah with that unflappability that was beginning to drive Miss de Silva mad. "As I said, I have no intention of telling anybody my secret. Your coming marriage has nothing to do with it. It's a secret I've kept in my heart all these years. It has sustained me through much sorrow. It has been my strength. Only love has this sustaining power."

"What do you know about love?" sneered Miss de Silva, desperate to pull this woman down from the loftiness of her dreams. Desperation made her bold, cruel. She said, "You are a cold, unfulfilled dried up virgin. Pity Dr. Chellam if he had married you! He would have shrunk from your frigidity. He's such a warm, loving, giving man and lover. I should know—" Miss de Silva became querulous in her attempt to send Miss Ponniah's grand self-assurance crashing down in the ruins of defeat and despair. But still Miss Ponniah stood tall and strong with her secret intact. As long as it was untold, it remained safe, and continued to have the power of stirring Miss de Silva's soul to discontent. Miss de Silva fidgeted in her seat, her intense eyes flashing; she did not want Miss Ponniah to leave the room yet, but she was not sure how she could make her stay.

"What you told me is very different from what Chellam told me," she ventured in a scornful tone. She waited for the effect of this new gambit. Miss Ponniah was equal to it; she said, "There is no use lying. Dr. Chellam never told you anything. No matter how hard you try, he never will tell you anything. He can't; you know he can't, and it will always be our secret," and, with that, she swept regally out of the room. Miss de Silva, alone, lit another cigarette.

"What the hell—" she muttered, stubbing it out immediately. "What the hell's it all about? The man's going to marry me; he proposed to her twenty years ago, they never met after that, so

what's a damn secret got to do with anything? She's deliberately
leading me on, out of jealous spite."

The picture of Chellam, twenty years younger, idealistic, capable of lifting love to a spiritual level, fascinated her and kept
obtruding upon the picture of the man now, overweight and de-
bauched, given to long hours of solitary drinking, newly escaped
from a paternity suit, yet with that sharpness of intellect intact,
which, when combined with the irreverent wit of the rake and the
lost air of the loner, must constitute all that is appealing to an
independent, adventurous, protective woman like Miss de Silva.
Miss de Silva wished sometimes for their love to be lifted to a level
above weekend bouts and brooding silences: in her forty-second
year, Miss de Silva was ready to bid farewell to the restless, empty
years of her youth and to look forward to a life of domestic peace
blessed by true and faithful love.

The coming marriage loomed largest in Miss Ponniah's mind.
The threat of desecration of her enshrined love, which was but
vague before, now took on hard edges, for it was in the form of a
colleague in the school, the marriage was going to take place in
exactly two weeks' time, and there would be the usual collection
for a general wedding present. Miss Ponniah, surprised at her own
calm strength in the face of Miss de Silva's vicious onslaughts, was
determined to keep the votive fires at her shrine burning forever.

"I am loved," murmured Miss Ponniah, but the picture of the
chaste young man who came in supplication for her hand was
defaced by that of middle-aged lust in a hotel room in Kuala Lumpur,
so that the English Language teacher corrected the Present Tense
form of her utterance and murmured sadly instead, "I was loved."
The picture of Dr. Chellam making love to Miss de Silva in a hotel
room had a power that both compelled and repelled Miss Ponniah.
Miss Ponniah's innocent world of love had not admitted of anything
carnal; now carnality had an appeal of its own and, once admitted
into the temple of Miss Ponniah's love, it refused to leave. Miss
Ponniah woke up, panting, from a dream in which Dr. Chellam

had made love not to Miss de Silva but to her; she looked around wildly, saw only the four walls of her bedroom, and knew that her secret was still safe.

If she had insisted on marrying him against her father's wishes, what then? If they had eloped, run off on their own, spent the night in a hotel room, as a distant cousin of hers had done very long ago—Miss Ponniah gasped at the daring of it all. But once the thought was lodged inside her mind, it took on a life of its own, and ramified into a hundred scenes which Miss Ponniah watched with the helpless fascination of the captive. In one, she and Dr. Chellam made the escape in the darkness of night, by the back door, while her father was snoring in the cane chair as was his wont in the evenings; in another, he held her in his arms, comforting her, and, in yet another, their love was about to be consummated. Miss Ponniah watched each scene in her mind with mounting excitement. What might have been! What might have been! A little cry escaped Miss Ponniah's throat. What might have been, and what was. Her father prevented their marriage, that was what was. Her father was ill and he wanted her, and none other, to attend to him. He could not bear her being out of his sight for even half a day. There was one incident—oh, so long ago and so long suppressed—of her going to her father and telling him, in between sobs, how much she loved the young man and wanted to marry him. Her father looked at her hard and said nothing. Then to her horror she saw tears slowly filling his eyes. She ran to him, crying, "Father, Father, I will never leave you, I will do as you say!" and still his tears flowed till she promised to tell Dr. Chellam that she would never see him again. She told him the next day and he left, utterly broken in spirit, and she mourned her loss for twenty years. Her aunt muttered, "Your father's a selfish beast," one evening shortly after Dr. Chellam had left their lives, and they were sitting quietly together after dinner. "Your mother would never have allowed this if she had been alive," continued the aunt, holding her niece's hand. Both women shed tears, while, in the next room, the old man stirred in his sleep and said something.

"Please don't say anything bad about my father," said the young woman, freeing her hand from her aunt's and running up the stairs to her room.

Those days of desolation and wretchedness came back in their fullness of dread to Miss Ponniah, as she prepared for another weary week of school. Miss de Silva had taken leave to prepare for her wedding; that was a great relief to Miss Ponniah. That irrepressible girl, Fong Yin, who had the notion that to help a person keep her secret you should reveal to her other people's, was still trying to make up for her remissness of behavior to Miss Ponniah by passing on to her everything she knew about Miss de Silva's romance.

"They're honeymooning in Italy," she confided, "and Miss de Silva says her wedding dress costs three thousand dollars. She says she will try to have at least one baby."

"Fong Yin," said Miss Ponniah with all the severity she could muster. "How many times have I told you not to spread gossip and to mind your own business?"

Miss Ponniah, in the privacy of her bedroom, searched through the letters, found the one she wanted, found the sentence in it she wanted. Yes, he had referred to children. He said he wanted to marry her and have lots of children by her: reading the sentence, Miss Ponniah felt a warm flush spreading over her face and neck. If she had married him then, how many children would they have had by now? To have lots of children by her—Miss Ponniah read the line again and again—the choice of her body by which his seed should come to fruition in the world! There was hope in the line, and blessedness, and the promise of pleasure.

And all these dreams had come to naught because of her selfish father.

"Oh my God," thought Miss Ponniah, aghast at the thought and pressing her hands to the sides of her head as if the thought had escaped and returned to thunder in her ears. "Oh my God— how could I—I must never—" Miss Ponniah slowly removed her hands from her ears and looked around forlornly. "I'm going mad. I must not allow myself to lose control. It is vital that I remain in control."

So it was a calm Miss Ponniah who went into class for the usual grammar lesson. Apart from a little paleness on her face, there was no visible sign of the wrenching struggles that she had so lately gone through. It being the last week before the holidays, the girls were in a restive state, but Miss Ponniah told them to take their work seriously and to take life seriously. She went on to teach the Subjunctive Mood; it was not a grammatical topic calculated to hold the attention of fifteen-year-old girls a week before the holidays, but even the least interested of the pupils were soon leaving behind whatever surreptitious activities they had been engaged in and turning their attention to Miss Ponniah. The ripples of interest spread rapidly; soon everyone was turning to look at Miss Ponniah, who was standing in her usual place by the teacher's desk just in front of the chalkboard, but was talking to them in a voice that did not belong to the classroom. Miss Ponniah was pleading, laughing, crying as she taught the Subjunctive Mood.

"You want more examples?" asked Miss Ponniah, looking at them with sad earnestness, although the class had not asked for any. "I shall give you plenty. Listen. 'If I had listened to her advice, I would have been a happier person.' 'If I had not been so stupid, I would not have been so miserable.' 'If he had not been such a selfish old man—' 'If I had eloped—' If, if—" Miss Ponniah's voice rose in a crescendo of sorrow. Wild-eyed, she made her pupils repeat examples of the Subjunctive Mood after her; they complied hesitantly, nervously looking at one another to ask with their eyes what was happening to their English language teacher. The voices repeating the regrets of her life, one by one, in ragged chorus, did nothing to quell the rising tide of Miss Ponniah's bitter sorrow. She continued screaming, " 'If only I had—' 'If only he had—' 'If only I had—' " and it was at this point that the spell of awe broke, and the girls scrambled out of their seats, some rushing outside to tell the principal and the teachers that something strange was happening to Miss Ponniah, and some going up to Miss Ponniah and gently leading her to a chair. Fong Yin rushed out to get a hot drink. When the principal and vice-principal arrived, they found, to their relief, Miss Ponniah quietly sitting in a chair, sipping a drink, attended by a group of solicitous pupils. The principal glanced nervously at the chalkboard and said, with all the effort toward normal conversation, "I see you have been teaching the Subjunctive Mood, Miss Ponniah," and Miss Ponniah replied, with a weak smile, "Quite right. All my life has been the Subjunctive Mood."

"Would you like to go home and take a rest?" inquired the vice-principal gently and Miss Ponniah said gratefully, "Yes, thank you very much," gathered up her sari and her books, wiped her eyes, and prepared to leave.

GERSON POYK

(Indonesia)

Gerson Poyk was born in 1931 in Namodale, Roti, part of the divided Dutch-Portuguese colonial territory of Timor in the tropical island chain east of Java. He graduated from the Christian Teachers School of Surabaja in 1965, and taught on the islands of Ambon and Sumbawa. In 1962, Poyk began writing as a reporter for Sinar Harapan, an activity he continued until 1970. Although he had enjoyed considerable popularity as an author of fiction in Indonesia, and was familiar to readers in Malaysia and the Philippines, it wasn't until he attended the International Writing program at the University of Iowa in 1982 that Poyk gained the attention of a small group of Western writers. Among his better known works are Sang Guru (The Teacher), Matias Akankari, Oleng-Kemoleng and Surat-surat Cinta Rajaguguk (Back and Forth and The Love Letters of Rajaguguk), Di Bawah Matahari Bali (Beneath the Balinese Sun), and Poti Wolo. Poyk received Indonesia's Adinegoro Prize for literature in both 1985 and 1986, and in 1989 he was presented the highly regarded ASEAN SEA-Write Award. "Matias Akankari" may offer an overly naive view of the two extremes of Indonesia's astonishingly diverse national mosaic, but it is deliberately naive—not unlike the comic South African film The Gods Must Be Crazy: the point in each case, of course, is laughter.

Matias Akankari

It was a parachutist who produced Matias Akankari from the jungles of Irian Jaya. In the dead of night he jumped and fell back to earth and had come to rest, dangling from the branches of a tall tree. With great effort on his part he managed to extricate himself. Then he rested. And, upon regaining his strength, he set out on foot to find his companions. Before finding them, however, he met up with a young Irian male called Matias Akankari.

Matias had taken ill, and the parachutist administered some medicine whose therapeutic effect soon had Matias back on his feet again. But this did nothing to quell the parachutist's dismay when he realized that the young native was wholly incapable of speaking Indonesian. Yet it was this Matias who turned out to be an extremely dependable guide and who guaranteed the parachutist's safe return to Jakarta.

So, to be brief, it was the parachutist who first met Matias and who later brought Matias to Jakarta.

Unlike the other boys from Jakarta who had also done Irian service, the parachutist returned to Jakarta without television, icebox, or the other requisites for luxurious living left behind by the Dutch in their former colony. No, this parachutist brought back Matias. Matias, who had been his boon companion through all sorts of trials and tribulations and whose friendship he could not forget.

But keeping Matias proved to be more expensive than maintaining an inanimate luxury item. Three plates of food per sitting, a daily total of nine plates of food, were going down that alimentary canal. The parachutist grew alarmed. As a soldier on soldier's pay, how would he be able to keep up with such a rich diet?

But the parachutist was blessed with a nimble mind. He dressed

Matias in expensive haberdashery he had purchased in Irian: wool suit, dress shirt, tie, and pinching shoes of foreign manufacture. Then he and Matias rode off in a borrowed jeep toward the bustling center of the city.

Newly come to town, this being the third day of his sojourn in the capital city, Matias was agog, amazed by the brilliant neon-light show, astonished by the height and number of buildings. What was more, he was dismayed by the forest of human beings. Nobody looked like him. His eyes blinked furiously and his head twisted back and forth, left and right, as he tried to capture all that was the urban marvel scattering in the wake of the swiftly moving Soviet-made Gaz jeep.

Finally, they arrived and, at the Senen shopping district, the parachutist took Matias to a movie theater. There, for the first time in his life, Matias was going to see a film. A new experience. He focused all powers of concentration on the movie screen. Thus, when a certain parachutist casually made his exit, Matias was so engrossed he did not sense the deed.

"I want to see something," the parachutist said to a fellow parachutist who was outside the theater, waiting to see the same film. "I left Matias Akankari in there to watch the movie by himself. I want to see just how a primitive makes out in this city. Who knows? Maybe I can make some money from a book about him!" the man boasted to his peer before jumping into his jeep and zooming off.

The film ended and Matias opened his eyes wide to take in his surroundings. His heartbeat quickened, yet he did not utter a sound because he could not speak Indonesian. His means of expression were his eyes. They stood out, red against the blackness of his skin, rolling in their sockets as he scanned the jostling mass of bodies for his friend. It was hopeless. He let himself drift with the current of humanity moving out of the theater.

Outside, his heartbeat quickened more: Boom-boom! Boom-boom! Boom-boom! The parachutist, the sole mainstay of his urban existence, whom he had encountered in his friendly green jungle, had vanished. And now Matias was by himself, alone, in the middle of a forest of tall lamps, jostling human bodies, a jangling forest full of the commotion made by the whirling wheels of automobiles and pedicabs. His present surroundings could not compare with his own jungle's hospitable tranquillity. He drifted along, a lone sojourner.

Suddenly Matias heard the sound of a loudspeaker. Ah, a thing he had seen in Irian Jaya on the occasions of visiting dignitaries from Jakarta. The thing cackled fiercely. A pity though that he could not understand what it was communicating. That he drew closer to this dissonance was simply in response to the memories of a remote jungle village where people similar to himself would have drawn together around this sound giver in order to listen to their own lovely language. But the people around him now were unlike him, and their language was not his own.

For a view of the speech giver, he nudged his way slowly into the center of the human crush. He is sure to be a companion to the people who come to Irian, Matias said to himself in his own language. But, in his present straits, sound was useless. What he really needed was someone who would lead him to a home. Oh, to go home, to be under a roof, to have a place to sleep and food prepared for him to eat. . . . These were the things only a protector could guarantee.

Implausibly hopeful of such a desirable fate, Matias anticipated a helping hand. And a helping hand did condescend. A soft and friendly creature came to his aid. She spoke to him, and an alluring expression on her face made his heart beat joyfully. This invitation, for that it was, was followed by a flip of the pointed hand. A pedicab pulled up, and he and this gentle creature left for yet another unknown part of the city.

Upon entering the sleeping quarters of this feminine creature, Matias was immediately entwined and made one with her small body. Big and strong as he was, he was overwhelmed by her power and could not do otherwise since he was the one in need of a friend or a house, or even better yet a small island giving safe harbor. It was finally his! He rejoiced to pass the night sleeping next to this woman who was so kind to him. He woke early the next day. Food and drink were ready on a bedside table.

After breakfast, he was entwined and overpowered again. But there had to be a limit to this sort of human activity, which Matias had never experienced before, and, once it was reached, another form of play ensued. Sitting face to face with this woman, Matias was treated to a pantomime. His jaw slack, his mouth agape, he watched her go through a set of motions for an inordinate length of time. Only when she thrust a handful of paper at him and jabbed her forefinger at his breast and then stabbed herself in her breast with the same forefinger did he finally grasp her intent.

Matias wagged his hand and shook his head to signify that he was not in possession of such papers. The constricting habiliments he wore were the only things he had. So the woman clutched his jacket and pointed her finger at her breast. Matias understood the significance of this gesture. He took off his jacket and handed it to the woman, whereupon the soft, petite creature turned crude and rude. She pulled him over to the door, shoved him out as hard as she could, and slammed the door shut. Apparently it was time for her to rest.

Matias turned his body to the left, then to the right. There was nobody that he knew. He had been thrown back into the wilderness, and it was not friendly like his Irian jungle.

He began to walk, a remarkable thing to do in a city where walking for several hours just to walk would be a feat in itself for people used to getting through life on a set of wheels. But it was nothing for Matias; in his own, friendly, jungle he was used to walks lasting for days.

Matias continued his sojourn, and by the by he found himself at the great church just as evening was approaching. No other path seemed open to him except this one leading to the expurgation of the sin that he had unintentionally committed with that woman the night before. He entered the church to pray for Christ's forgiveness. It was dark when he came out, so he sat down on the church steps and reminisced about his village.

Once, on another island, so far away from him now, he went to church naked but for his penis sheath. He belonged to the choir, and the choir would stand before the missionary in a happy jostle and sing. He had joined the choir as a small boy. Few of its members could read or write, but church songs the world over are easy to learn by heart. It was during one of their musical offerings that Matias performed the unpardonable act that had gotten him expelled from the sheath-clad choir. Matias was at the head of the choir and, swept away by the melody of the hymn, he pulled off his penis sheath and began to wield it as if it were a pendant flute. He had drilled holes in his sheath, and now he had a flute! Avidly the congregation listened to this novel form of accompaniment before collapsing in a fit of merriment. The worshipful spirit had been destroyed. Matias was reprimanded by the missionary and inveighed against by the other members of the choir. He was kicked out of the choir. . . . Nevertheless, he liked to keep his penis sheath with him at all times. Wherever he went so did it. Presently he reached inside his shirt, took it out, and began to blow into it softly, softly, and gently.

Darkness progressed, yet Matias could see, in the distance, a bobbing figure coming his way. He observed the growing shape more carefully; it was a young man with a portfolio in hand. As the figure grew closer, Matias discerned the reason behind the man's curious gait; the soles of this person's shoes had come loose, thus compelling the man to lift each leg up high before setting it down before him. Yet, hampered as he was, this man had come to church. The man went in. After a while he came back out.

"This church is always open; it's different from the other churches in this city," the young man commented as he sat down next to Matias. Although he was carrying a portfolio, his clothes would have been better consigned to the ragpicker. Matias on the other hand was turned out in the best sort of haberdashery: an imported long-sleeved dress shirt, a tie, and woolen trousers.

Matias did not understand a word, but the young man did not know this and kept on talking. "I'm so tired. I walked all over the city today and now the soles of my shoes are flapping like lizards' tongues. I have a college degree but I can't find myself a job," he said as he tried to clamp the shifty lizards' tongues shut.

Matias observed him. Then he took off his shoes and proffered them to this unemployed college graduate. "These shoes do torture me," Matias declared in native elocution. "No shoes did I wear in the great jungle, even there, where many thorny and prickly plants grow among the trees. My feet bled not. Yet these shoes do now make my feet bleed. Here, take them away from me!"

To the young man's ears Matias's words were gibberish, but with his eyes he came to understand that a new pair of shoes was being transferred to his feet.

From the church stoop, the two men walked to Banteng Field. Wordlessly they laid themselves down to sleep under the colossal statue there of another young Irian male, who had been caught for posterity's sake in the act of breaking the shackles on his wrists. They slept soundly.

The college graduate woke early the next morning but was afraid to wake Matias. If he were to do so he would be obliged to keep him by. What a pair they'd make. They would create a sensation wherever they went. So as a manner of leave-taking, he slipped a letter into Matias's shirt pocket.

When Matias woke up, his friend was not there. He noticed that he had a piece of paper on his person. He turned the piece of paper this way and that but could make nothing of it since he was an unlettered man. He crumpled it up and threw it as far away as he could, then returned to his sleep on the cold marble tiles. Gusts of wind crossing Banteng Field feathered and chilled him in his sleep.

When he next woke, Matias found that the day had turned to night. Hunger reigned in his belly, but he could still walk.

He passed into an area full of homeless beggars. In this place he came upon a woman pregnant and lying on a heap of paper refuse. She was about to give birth. He remembered how the Christ child was born over a pile of straw and was swaddled in rags. Now here was another Christ child coming into the world, but over a pile of refuse! It started to rain as the woman waited phlegmatically for her child to come out. She was fortunate; she had a piece of plastic, which she then draped over herself. That was her roof; beneath her was still paper.

Matias peeled off his clothes, which were binding him, and gave them to this woman who was about to bring forth a child into the world. "Thank you, thank you . . . ," she said to Matias, who had returned to his original dress. His penis sheath was back in place. In this manner he waited on her. The rain, coming down harder and harder, turned into a deluge. But he waited until she came out of labor. Then he could do no more for her. He resumed his walk under the heavy downpour.

And that is how he arrived at the city's greatest thoroughfare, Thamrin Boulevard, barricaded on both sides by tall, multilayered buildings. The boulevard led him nearer and nearer to the Hotel Indonesia. His wonderment grew over the host of automobiles that were beginning to collect about him. Even though it was raining these speeding vehicles had to slow down, and some of them even stopped for a closer look at him. One of the automobiles contained a dark-colored man, a man like himself, who was wearing a suit and sitting next to a beautiful girl. As the automobile came to a stop, its passengers turned to look at him. Matias found himself staring back at a person who was like himself. He sprang onto the rear of the automobile and clung on. The automobile roared forward but to no avail. Matias had a good grip on it. The automobile rushed into the drive of the Hotel Indonesia and stopped under the porte cochere, where it disgorged the dark-skinned man. Matias had guessed wrong. The man was not one of his own people. The man was a black American.

A host of uniformed men appeared. Their bodily motions and circling tactics told Matias that they were intending to capture him. He ran back into the pelting rain. Maybe because they were afraid to get wet, the groups of uniformed men gave up the chase.

Matias had escaped, but then he sensed that he was still being pursued. Indeed, a man in a raincoat was now running after him. So, like an arrow zinging away from a taut bow, Matias ran faster down the great boulevard until he found himself before one of the great multilayered buildings. He dashed inside, sighted the small, narrow room open to him, and spurted in. The room closed, and, with him in its maw, began to rise. Finally it stopped, and, when its doors opened, another room slid into view. This room was cavernous but dimly lit except for the far end, where there was an illuminated platform with a group of women dancing on it. They wore body covering exactly the way he did, except theirs was not of the prominent sort. They were doing a wonderful new interpretation of the dances of his own village. He relished that. Matias step-hopped to the stage, just as he was, in his penis sheath, and joined the women in their dance. The sound of applause rose from the shadows.

With that episode, his sojourn drew to a close. The city dailies featured the story of how Matias was recovered by his benefactor, the parachutist. It ended in the only way it possibly could, serendipitously. In fact, Matias was given a goodly sum of money. With this he was able to secure a return to his beloved village.

At home they all wanted to hear his story. And he told them that in Jakarta the "high class" was replicating what they, in Irian, already had. Folks just like to wear penis sheaths.

Translated by Mary Lou Wang

H. JAFAR SALIJ

(Indonesia)

An American citizen now resident in Kyoto, where he teaches
English, H. Jafar Salij grew up on three continents, a fact that
often imbues his writing with diverse cultural and ethnic in-
fluences. Southeast Asia, though, has remained his paramount
area of focus, and the social and cultural settings of Malaysia,
Singapore, and Indonesia customarily come under his scrutiny.
Salij's literary preoccupation has been how daily life must be
played out, often precariously, in a rapidly changing world, and
his stories concern the idea of progress in developing Asia.
"Shadow Play," from Salij's 1982 collection of the same title,
sharply crystallizes this focus, examining the contrasts not only
between developing Asian and Western cultures but within
Indonesia's economically segregated social groups as well. An
all too familiar contemporary sight in many of Southeast Asia's
once unblemished paradise islands, the hideous daily trauma
of survival of this story's young character Saima is also remi-
niscent of much of the superb cinema and fiction produced by
Japanese and Korean artists during the periods following World
War II and the Korean War.

Shadow Play

The girl leaned over one edge of the narrow bed, cleared her throat, and spat on the floor.

"Please don't spit," he said.

With a quiet smile she turned her face toward the man beside her. In the yellow flicker of the oil lamp the smile was a grimace in a brown mask. She got up and moved toward the washroom, accompanied by her shadow on the wall and a blend of *gamelan* rhythms and rock sounds that came from somewhere in the *kampung*.

Behind the windows, covered with a gray-blue striped blanket, the voices of a soft-spoken man and an emphatic woman. They talked about places to go and places to be. The woman's voice fell and rose like a distant siren.

In the washroom, the splashing noise of water being scooped from the reservoir and thrown against skin. The rasp of a throat and the liquid splatter of saliva hitting the wet floor. More water to rinse it away.

The oil lamp shot soot toward the low bamboo ceiling.

He turned it down.

Followed by her shadow, she came back. Her bare feet slapped the damp cement of the floor. She lay down beside the man again and looked at him with a smile. The flame of the oil lamp drew patterns of sand and gold on her brown skin.

Far away and nearby, *kampung* dogs barked and howled. The ocean crashed into the beach. The wind passed through the banana trees. Cicadas pushed out their interminable, high-pitched, monotonous cry that pierced the night. Lizards screamed in strident, pounding staccatos. The *tokeh* let out its throaty call: seven times for a secret wish. Jukebox rock and *gamelan* percussion. Rumbling voices.

He caressed the girl's shoulder. He took one of her hands in his, touched the palm with his fingertips. It was as hard as granite. He rubbed the calluses. . . .

The soft-spoken man said he wasn't sure whether he liked his room or not, or the whole place for that matter. "I might go to India and stay near the Taj Mahal or take a room near the airport here and watch the planes taking off and touching down. I love airports." To which the emphatic voice of the woman responded in highs and lows, "Do whatever you feel like doing."

. . . and thought she might be one of the many who had fled the hard work of planting and harvesting and the pressure of increasing poverty. But he didn't want to think about that now. He wanted to think of this girl in relationship to himself. Soot rose from the steaming oil lamp.

He turned it down and got up.

He lit a mosquito coil. Its acrid-sweet scent spread through the room. "My name is Claude," he said. "What's yours?"

"Saima."

"A Muslim name. Are you a Muslim?"

"*Ya.* Islam good. *Bagus.*"

"I thought you were from Denpasar." He lay down again.

"*Ya.* I live there now. One month. Then I go back to Madura to my *kampung.*"

"I see." Claude looked at the girl and wondered what was hidden behind the name Saima.

The pimp she was with the night before had tried hard to make him take her on instantly. "Take her, mister. She's nice." Teeth gleaming white. Eyes shining black under a red headband.

Claude told Saima he'd see her tonight.

But, aimlessly standing about in the tepid vagueness of the Balinese night, he hadn't quite known why he was waiting there. The dark had changed everything. He no longer recognized this spot, which hours before had been blistering in the yellow sun. To his left a tourist restaurant blaring out rock music. On the right the intense dark of a narrow path.

He expected the girl to come from there.

A shape detached itself from the unclear contours of a wooden shack on the right. It came forward with hesitation and stood close to Claude. "You want hash, mister? You want girl?" Teeth like dull ivory in the distant lights. "Young girl. Only fifteen. Cheap."

"How cheap?"

"Two thousand *rupiah*. If you want whole night, five thousand."

From the right the rattling noise of a Honda approaching. A girl jumping off the back, talking to Claude: "You have room here? Where you stay?"

On the left the restaurant and several human forms. Faces flashing in the beams of motorcycle headlights.

"Take her," said the shape crouching in the dark. "Take her. She very good." He clicked his tongue. "*Bagus.*"

"You must've tried her," mumbled Claude.

The girl smiled at Claude. The recommendation pleased her and seemed to make her unsure.

"Am waiting for somebody," said Claude.

She wanted to know who.

"I don't know her name."

Persistence. Like the boys girls men women on the beach, relentlessly approaching tourists with their wares:

"Hey mister, you want dr-rink?"

"You want look at *batik*?"

"Wood carving?"

"Shirt?"

And so on.

A never-ending refrain coming from the throats of hundreds of Balinese. A ten-word vocabulary learned from secondhand textbooks and adapted to their need to survive. Art for commerce. The purpose of commerce: to appease the gods. When the gods are appeased, life will be good.

At sunset:

Tourists released from air-conditioned buses for a half hour's glance at the setting sun in Kuta and its visitor-ravaged beach. In the blood and gold of the rapidly drowning sun hawkers attack like ants crawling around a lump of sugar. Busloads of aliens surrounded by carvings, *batik,* junk, Balinese existence.

Buy souvenirs to remember what you have already forgotten.

Look at the setting sun disappearing behind ominously gray, glitter-rimmed cloud masses at the farthest edge of the gray-green ocean.

Take your pictures. Have your pictures taken and wave at those whom you'll show them to once you're back again in your daily routine.

The women of Bali glide by in the last light of the day, *batik*-filled baskets on their heads, and children carry the eternal bottles of soft drinks in buckets of melting ice, trying for a last sale, approaching sunset-dazed visitors sitting in the sand, serenely absorbing nauseous gases and the strident screams of Japanese motorcycles:

"You want dr-rink?"

"You want buy *batik?*"

Heads shaking in rejection of anything offered for sale: "No, thank you."

(Leave us alone.)

On the darkening beach people are turning into transparencies amidst the shrieks of Hondas and Suzukis spewing forth clouds of gray-blue exhaust, throwing up endless sand under spinning wheels.

Tourism and motorcycles: the irreversible trauma of progress seeping into Balinese villages and compounds, surrounded by exhausted walls that used to protect and keep out evil spirits.

The visitors go back to the comfortable chill of air-cooled buses. Next item on the program: an elegant dinner and a cultural show.

And later, when the night rests brooding on the sand and envelops the palm trees, Saima and her friends arrive. Some alone. Others behind their motorcycle pimp-friends. Love offered. Accepted or refused. A many-splendored risk on the dark beach or in a room. No way of knowing what you're buying until it's spread out before you in a semidark room under a naked light bulb or near a steaming oil lamp. Love with or without alpha-, beta-, or non-specific consequences.

They swarm into the narrow paths and alleys of Kuta Beach like bees in search of honey. Like phantoms they stand motionless in the dark, near restaurants or simply alongside the road and step forward with the suddenness of a spider jumping an insect caught in its web.

"He has date," said the girl and climbed back on the motorcycle behind her friend. Engine screaming, it shot off into the dark toward the restaurant and hopefully a customer.

A Honda emerged from the right. Engine cut: "Ah *tuan*." Saima's pimp of the night before: the smiling white of teeth and the glowing black of eyes under a white headband.

"Where's the girl?"

"Why not take her?" He pointed to the girl behind his back.

She jumped to the ground and began to stroke Claude's chest. "Take me with you, *tuan*."

He took a step back. "Where's the girl?" he asked the pimp.

"Over there. Eating." The pimp stretched an arm toward the beach. "Shall I call her?"

"Yes."

"Take her," said the form near the shack.

"Take me, *tuan*," said the girl.

Funny guys, these. No problem selling girls of fifteen: "In Indonesia, a man must have a girl, *tuan*." The shape and the pimp laughed and involved him in their conversation. And the girls talked and laughed along as if everything was normal. Maybe everything was.

The girl walked her hands over his chest. "Take me with you, *tuan*," mumbled the girl.

"I'll tell her," said the headband. He swung his bike around. The girl got on. They disappeared into the dark. The rear light swayed in red streaks from right to left and from left to right.

Saima cleared her throat. Saliva hit the cement between the
bed and the wall near the door.

"Don't spit!"

Saima smiled quietly.

Claude swatted a mosquito that had landed on his leg. Close
to the blanketed windows high-pitched voices and low voices: English and Indonesian syllables strung together to words and sentences: communication at an incredibly rapid speed.

"Who are those guys?" Perhaps they could see through the
striped blanket. You never knew. Surely everybody could see their
magnified shadows on the opposite wall of the room through the
air slots above the windows. His leg was beginning to itch. A welt
was slowly rising. "Who are they? Police?"

Saima frowned.

"Your pimp?"

Saima listened carefully, then she smiled reassuringly. "Can't
be. He's over there." She made a gesture in the direction of the
beach.

Anyway, why should he care about what was going on outside?
He ought to concentrate on the inside. The oil lamp sent a black
stream to the bamboo ceiling.

He turned it down. "Did you say you're from Madura? I've
never been there."

"You can come with me. One thousand *rupiah* on the boat from
Gilimanuk."

"What would I do there?"

Low laughter: a sort of gurgle in her throat: her mouth a bit
cramped into a friendly grimace. "I don't know."

"Would you like me to go there with you?"

"Yes." Anything he said. Five thousand *rupiah* at the end of
this play at love: a serious play mixing natural urges and the need
to survive.

The high-pitched voices had gone away. The voices of the man
and woman carried on. The *kampung* dogs continued to howl and
snarl. The repetitious rock beat and the mournful-cheerful tones

of the *gamelan* went on. So did the staccato shrieks of the lizards.

He had a sore throat from the mosquito poison that filled the room with its acrid smoke. It didn't do anything to the mosquitoes. He tried to kill another mosquito but it escaped through the thin, gray cloud rising from the smoldering coil. When Balinese were in their post-terrestrial bliss, they'd probably not be bothered by mosquitoes. The hereafter was a mere continuation of the sublunary Balinese world with its tourist-orientated sweetness of *Ramayana* ballet, *Legong* dance, *Kecak* dance, and so forth, done in glittering costumes and much-practiced contortions. But before you got to that blissful place, there were hopes and fears and offerings. Propitiations. Evil spirits had to be warded off. Ceremonies.

Like the one on the beach today for a dead man whose widow, face hard with grief, led a procession to the doleful rhythms of drums for the benefit of the dead man's soul.

Birth and Death: was there anything more to Life? The time between had to be filled with rituals for the newly born and the freshly dead, who were frequently not that fresh, having lain in the house for months losing their fluids and gradually desiccating. Or the corpses that had been embedded in the fertile soil so long they couldn't be found anymore.

Cremation was imperative.

Corpses must be burned and souls released so that they can go to the paradise every Balinese dreams of going to. Prices for cremation ceremonies were high, and the tourist had to pay for the eternal peace of the souls of the dead and the quiet of the living.

Claude was paying.

He lit a cigarette. A cloud of smoke dispersed the mosquitoes. He contemplated Saima and said, "How long have you been here?"

"Three days." She cleared her throat, but she didn't spit. She had six sisters and one brother. One morning she had packed up and left. "When I have enough money, I'll go back and give my parents the money. They don't have enough to eat. Many girls from Madura come here to work, *tuan*. And from Surabaya and Banyuwangi. Most of them go back after a while."

"How old are you?"

"Ten." She held up both hands, fingers spread. "Ten."

Ten? From the cigarette fell a fiery ash. It scorched some hairs on his chest, penetrated the skin. A sharp, brief pain. The smell of burned hair. Did ten-year-old girls have pubic hair? Saima's breasts were small, perhaps undeveloped, but what did that mean? Ten years old? He was still in school trying to solve arithmetic problems. She couldn't be ten. Fifteen maybe.

Fifteen? He was dragged to a farmhouse by two straw-blond peasant girls in hard-blue dresses and black stockings after nearly drowning in the green, slimy water of a stagnant canal. Giggling they pulled off his drenched clothes and scrubbed him until his skin was pink and tingly. They quickly gave way to his groping fingers, hurriedly taking off dresses and stockings, revealing whiter flesh than he'd ever seen.

"How can you be ten?" he said, drawing on the remnant of his cigarette. But Saima had dropped off to sleep. A smile hovered in the corners of her mouth. The soft-spoken voice and the emphatic voice were carrying on in incomprehensible words. The *gamelan* music had been joined by a chorus of howling dogs. It was the night of the *Barong,* the dancers performing at six hundred *rupiah* per tourist. The commercialized, insoluble dilemma of entranced men caught between good and evil, stabbing themselves with *kerises* to the sweeping rhythms of fast percussion and not shedding a drop of blood. At the end, the tourists would applaud.

Evil against man. Old men and women in the streets of Jakarta begging for a coin. Distorted, toothless grins. Grotesque decay amid a theater-going crowd eagerly waiting in line for an hour, two hours of screen entertainment. A man in rags, standing in the middle of a restaurant near a group of well-fed businessmen around a food-covered table. They didn't acknowledge the man's existence, despite the fact that he called out in a loud voice: "I'm hungry, gentlemen, and I want to eat!" The embarrassed owner quickly shoved the man from his air-conditioned domain.

Jakarta's new green face, carefully designed and easily maintained in the fertile heat, was pockmarked by the misery of the hungry. Nobody gave them anything. It was hopeless anyway.

Or, as Intan would say, "Why worry about it? It's part of the scene."

Intan, beautiful Intan, belonged to a family of bankers and diplomats and wanted to marry Claude: "I can't, I don't want to live without you." But he answered that it wouldn't do, not only because he didn't love her enough for that but also because he didn't have any desire to enter the world of bankers and diplomats: "I might become like your uncle in the Embassy in Kuala Lumpur."

On the top floor of the Embassy Claude had handed Intan's letter of introduction to a man in a brown suit and a brown tie sitting behind a clean brown desk. On his right he was flanked by a shiny set of golf clubs in a red leather bag on a chrome-plated pushcart.

Smiling uncertainly, the diplomat read Intan's letter, put it down carefully on the oak surface of the desk, lifted two fingers to his lips, and gazed at Claude through brownish lenses. "Haven't I seen you at an Indian doctor's house at Deepavali?" he asked. He seemed a kind man.

"Possibly," said Claude politely. Deepavali? There had been Liza, a dark Indian girl, her coal black eyes filled with a sort of reluctant surprise. Having smoked two Benson & Hedges in rapid succession, inhaling deeply, she had been less reluctant than surprised. He had seen no Indian doctor. "Possibly," he said, "but it must have been before Deepavali. Or afterward." Claude had never seen this man in his brown suit and gold-rimmed spectacles.

Intan's uncle looked confused and swallowed twice. He groped for something relevant to say, to make a connection between this man, the message, and the woman who had written it. He turned toward the shiny golf clubs. His chin rested in his left hand. Who in the world was Intan? He made a decision. He lifted a gold ballpoint from his desk and wrote something down in the margin of Intan's letter. He handed it back to Claude and said, "Give this to the man in the visa section."

A dismayed visa section official talked about regulations and return tickets. So did the rotund lady behind the counter. The official looked severe, but she smiled, indulgent and a bit oily, in Claude's direction.

"It was useless," Claude said to Intan later. "I went to a travel agent in Singapore who arranged the whole thing in less than two days. Your uncle couldn't help it, of course, but he seemed to be out of it all. I guess when you get to his level, all you're good for is receptions and parties. In other words, you have no relevance."

Intan's diamonds and sapphires, dangling in a pendant from a heavy gold chain around her slender neck, glowed softly in the vague light of an electric bulb. "Can't we ever get married?"

"I don't know," he said.

The gold bangles on her wrist whirred when she put her arms around Claude's neck. Her dark antelope eyes leaned into his. "But I love you so," she said with something like pain in her voice.

He turned the oil lamp down and got up. Saima followed him. They put on their clothes. He took some bills from his trouser pocket and put them in Saima's hands.

"*Terima kasih, tuan.* Thank you." She counted the bills and stuck them in her empty bra.

Claude walked her to the main road through the tepid early morning. A rooster crowed. Back in his room, he went to sleep immediately.

Saima's was the reality that Intan looked away from. Intan didn't believe what could be seen all around. "Don't give those beggars more than five *rupiah*," she told Claude one rainy Jakarta afternoon. "They sometimes have complete organizations to buy drugs and alcohol."

Claude looked at the deformed hand he had just put a fifty-*rupiah* coin in. "That so?"

She nodded.

"The man I just gave a coin to is a deformed freak. He's full of sores. He's dying."

"Maybe," she said.

A night or two later Saima emerged from an alley beside the restaurant where he had just had a meal. "Ah *tuan,* I came all on my own tonight." She smiled with satisfaction.

Claude looked at her and said, "I don't know, Saima. Maybe not tonight."

"Ah *tuan*. Take me with you, please." Her hands clasped his. She stood so close he could feel her heartbeat. He wished she'd drop that word *"tuan."*

"I don't know." He hesitated. "I can't pay you as much as last time." It wasn't the money, though. He felt pity, and pity wasn't the right way to feel, and he didn't feel like taking anybody along tonight.

"Up to you, *tuan.*"

He took her along.

The man with the soft voice sat in front of his room when Claude got back to the compound with Saima. His name was Lyle. Lyle was from Los Angeles and worked for a travel agent. He sat reading a magazine by the light of two oil lamps, squinting at the print. A mosquito coil glowed at his feet. He didn't look up when Claude unlocked his door.

Lyle had told Claude he'd been to the beach the other night and laid a girl there. "Oh man," he said, "she was the juiciest little thing I've ever had for my fuck'n dollar." He spoke without raising his voice or changing its soft timbre.

"How old was the girl? Not much older than fourteen?"

"No-o-o. No, no. She was at least fifteen." He laughed melodiously.

"Ever thought of the fact they do this because they're poor?"

"We did it in the dunes. Under the stars. Real nice. On my parka. I tell you she was nice." He whistled softly between his teeth and sipped from a glass of lukewarm tea.

"But if you're poor and hungry . . ."

Lyle agreed. "Sure, it's no fun to be poor. But she was still the best I've ever had." He slowly shook his head in happy reminiscence and rubbed his hands. "They're nice, these little girls. Particularly on the beach when the moon's out and the ocean's crashing into the beach." He whistled between his teeth. "I tell you she was the juiciest little thing my fuck'n dollar's ever been able to buy."

Saima slowly undressed. In the flickering light of the oil lamp her hands and body performed an immense shadow play on the plaster wall. "I was away for two days," she said, folding her dress and putting it at the lower end of the bed. "Back to Madura. There was a letter. My father's sick in the hospital. With the five thousand *rupiah tuan* gave me I could pay for the trip and give my parents the rest of the money. They're very poor." She smiled.

In the distance played the *gamelan*.

"What's wrong with your father?"

"I don't know. Something in his chest. He's in the hospital, so he can't work in the fields." She lay down on the gray bedsheet.

Lyle turned a page of his magazine and coughed. The cicadas sang their monotone. The dogs barked. A mosquito coil glowed and smoked on the damp gray floor. Saima's body shone like gold in the light of the oil lamp.

After an hour and a half they went back to the road.

"I don't want to go that way," she whispered when they got to the junction. "Too many people." She pointed to the left. Near the restaurant were many people and motorcycles, vibrating in the vague shine of the oil lamps on the tables near the entrance. "I'll go that way," she said and pointed to the right. "O.K.," said Claude. For a little while they walked through the intense dark. Then she took her hand out of his and said, "I'll go on alone now."

Standing in the middle of the path that led to the beach, he watched the little figure in the long white dress until it vanished. He turned around and walked back slowly. He had a sudden feeling of abandonment or of having lost something.

Girls approached him and retreated silently into the dark. They knew about him and Saima.

The room again and the low-burning, sputtering oil lamp.

The interminable cacophony of insects, amphibians, canines, people. The wind in the banana trees. The ocean. A lizard screaming high and shrill. Another answering. A *tokeh* uttering its mournful call. He counted them: seven times: was there a wish to be fulfilled?

The memory of Saima imprinted in the gray bedsheet.

He blew out the light, lay down, and fell asleep.

Intan arrived two days later.

They went out for walks on the beach. They took trips on a rented motorcycle to Sangeh's sacred monkey forest and the Mother Temple at Besakih. In Ubud, they walked through the museum and looked at the many paintings with their rigid mythological representations in tempera. And at night, in the dancing light of the oil lamp, she was as beautiful as the fictional figures of the stories she read. Stories about love and marriage. Stories in which the romantic dilemma of a man and a woman cried for a solution and was usually solved satisfactorily.

At this moment she was living her own story and whispered to Claude that he was handsome. "I love you," and she put her arms around his neck with a delicate jingle of the gold bangles. Their shadows appeared in gargantuan sizes on the plaster wall, and Claude looked at them, fascinated by this shadow play in which he was a puppeteer, a puppet, and the shadow of both. He looked at Intan. "You're the most beautiful woman I've ever met," he said.

She was. The sand-and-gold brown of her smooth skin, her melancholy eyes that were like dark streams of unfathomable depth, the classical Indian lines of her profile.

Looking past the soft sparkle of the diamond studs in her ears, he followed every movement the shadows made on the wall. What was the meaning of handsomeness, beauty, love? Weren't they enhanced by the insufficient lighting in which contours became fluid and deep lines were softened? Only the dark shadows on the wall assumed an aspect of reality in their one-dimensional forms, for the illusion of beauty or love did not distort them. Even Saima's poverty had seemed less acute from the shadow's point of view.

"I'm going for a bite to eat," he said. "I won't be long." He took Intan's arms from around his neck. She fell back on the pillow, her face near the oil lamp. Her dark eyes gleamed toward Claude. "Don't stay out too long, please. I don't like to be without you. Don't be distracted by the girls." Languid, she directed her gaze toward the ceiling and yawned. "Amazing how many prostitutes there are here."

He closed the door behind him.

"*Tuan!*" Saima suddenly stood before him. She put her hands on his stomach, then took his hands into hers. "Take me with you, *tuan.*"

"I can't, Saima. My friend from Jakarta is here."

"*Ya,* I saw you with her last night." She held on to his hands and stood close.

"I can't take you along, Saima. I can't take you to my room."

"Ah *tuan.*"

"If I give you money, will you go home?"

She nodded.

"Come." They walked up the path a little while until they came to some bushes. They sat down behind them.

"Too many people, *tuan,*" she whispered in disappointment and kissed Claude. Motorcycles and people going by in a steady stream. Loud voices. Laughter. A man shining a flashlight at them.

Claude put an arm around Saima's shoulders. For a while they sat like this, looking into the darkness that surrounded them.

"Too many people, *tuan.*"

"Don't worry, Saima. It's all right. Here." He put a thousand *rupiah* note in her hand.

"*Terima kasih, tuan.*" She stuck the money in her bra.

They got up and walked down the narrow path. Two girls asked her, "Where are you off to, Saima?"

"Home," she answered.

At the junction he turned left to go back to his room. At least Saima would be off the streets tonight. But what did it mean? Tomorrow she'd be out again. She had to eat. Her family was poor. Her father sick. His self-satisfaction was self-deception, perhaps even a preoccupation with possession. Her problems hadn't ended just because he had provided her with a few thousand *rupiah* in the last few days. There was no end to her problems, like there was no end to the ever-present hands stretched out toward you in the towns and cities of Java, at bus stops and railway stations, in the streets and outside restaurants. Everywhere.

He remembered his intention to eat. He turned back and walked into a restaurant. When he sat down behind one of the improvised, waggly plywood tables, he had forgotten he had been hungry. He ordered a fruit juice. What was all this about suffering? Intan suffered because she was in love. Saima had to love because she suffered. Intan put dramatics into it: jealousy and suspicion. Saima had no time to be dramatic. He drank his juice. It was too sweet. Saima simply had no time to suffer: she was too busy trying to survive. Love was the source of suffering. Nobody could do without it. Everybody made it, either spending money on it or asking to be paid for it.

In the end he was not sorry for having paid some ten thousand *rupiah* to be with Saima. He was more sorry about the thirty thousand he had spent on a wood carving, even though it was the work of a renowned Balinese artist. It was a beautiful piece of work that had been chiseled out of a solid block of ebony with great craftsmanship. But there was no life to it. The feel of the unresponding black wood was nothing compared to the touch of Saima's sensitive brown skin that shone in the flicker of the ever-higher-burning oil lamp.

Claude didn't really want the heavy thing, but the consideration that Pak Togog, the old man who offered it for sale, probably needed the money more than he at that moment made him buy it. Somebody back home might be happy with it. Perhaps he'd give it to his parents.

He had two worlds on his hands: one cluttered with deities and demons that asked to be appeased and another in which the basic need for survival was satisfied by stilling a natural urge. The world of the carving was foreign to Saima. For Saima the world meant selling candy and soft drinks by day and herself by night: the world of noxious car-and-motorcycle fumes, screaming bus horns, dusty sun-worn roads. Oppressive bus terminals and sidewalks crowded with too many people hoping to sell whatever they had to sell, including themselves. Impoverished *kampungs.*

This Balinese world of gods and carvings was eternal. Saima's world would end in disease and a toothless grin. She'd probably never go back to her *kampung.*

When Claude came back to the room, Intan was asleep, her fairy-tale face turned to the low-burning oil lamp. He looked at the stains on the floor where Saima had spat. Her short-lived spell of luck had ended with the thousand *rupiah* he had given her tonight. A *tokeh* called seven times.

SITOR SITUMORANG

(Indonesia)

Sitor Situmorang was born in Harianboho, North Sumatra, in 1924. Working as a correspondent at home and abroad until 1954, he published his first book of poetry, Surat Kertas Hijau *(Green Paper Letters), and translations and collections of short stories until his arrest on political charges in 1965. Following his release from prison, he began publishing again, and his more recent books include* Wall of Time, Lake Toba, *and* Lake Breeze. *"Holy Communion" is particularly interesting for its North Sumatran locale. Renowned for their warlike valor, the Acheh people retain a fiercely independent character that has not been dampened by Dutch colonialism or contemporary Javanese centralism. Though brief, Situmorang's story gives us a privileged glimpse into the Acheh territory's subsequent mingling of Christian, Islamic, and traditional shamanist spiritual elements, without apparent contradiction. His insight into how the Malay Achehan elder enables others to invoke his blessing is especially sensitive.*

Holy Communion

It was three o'clock in the morning. Our Land-Rover crawled in the dimness of the dying moon over the steep and winding road toward Prapat. The huge island in the middle of the lake looked like a reclining giant. Prapat sits on a promontory, her electric lights blending with the moonlight flickering off the restless waters—an ocean liner at anchor.

Emotion welled up within me—home!—but there was no joy or happiness.

By the Padang food stall, which was open round the clock, several large trucks loaded with rubber were waiting for their drivers and helpers, who were inside eating plates of hot rice. The men's weather-beaten bodies were wrapped in heavy clothes. They were heading toward the Acheh–East Coast border, toward the harbors notorious as smuggling and bartering centers with Singapore and Penang. They were hauling rubber from the Pakan Baru area, a distance of a thousand kilometers to the south, following not economic rules exactly but instead the winding roads of the black market, black like the roads to the lake at night.

"A tire now costs forty thousand *rupiah*," someone remarked, although no one had asked the question.

I wondered what the rental would be for a truckload and what they would be carrying on the return trip from the smuggling area.

My brother, who had been driving the borrowed Land-Rover since Medan, was also a truck operator. While eating he talked about prices and ended up asking for a jerry can of gasoline from one of the drivers.

I knew that we still had some gas in reserve, but we had to go clear around the lake, across the whole southern area, to get to our village in the west. We would need as large a supply as possible. The rest of the road, especially so early in the morning, would be desolate—wide grasslands alternating with heavy forests—and there would be no place to buy gas.

All through the night, till the early morning, when we were beyond Prapat, my brother had not said a single word. He concentrated on his driving, going so fast it was as if he was chasing after something. He had been driving that way since leaving Medan the day before.

It was not until around five in the morning that we encountered our first obstacle: a group of women pounding *pandan* leaves, the raw material for mats, on the roadbed. Then, at another spot along the road, a group of silent farmers on their way to their fields with farming tools in their hands forced us to slow down.

Even without an exchange of words, I knew the same picture occupied my brother's mind as did mine: Father's face. Would I still see him alive? The same question haunted us. The doctor had estimated Father's age, based on his jawbone and teeth, at one hundred thirteen years. The Old-Age Ceremony had already been held for him several times in the last few years. Each time Father had assumed that his death was near—yet he had kept on living.

But what was that to me? I didn't come for another ceremony but because my brother came to Jakarta specifically to fetch me. He said: "Father is suffering too much. He's run out of strength. It would be better if he rested forever. But that's not likely to happen till he sees you for the last time."

After my brother had finalized the purchase of a truck, we left Jakarta for Sumatra.

Towards daybreak we reached the high plateau of wide open fields. The plain, which looked golden in the early sunlight, looked even brighter now because of the glittering morning dew.

Where are the herds of horses now? I asked myself. The neighing of horses, which symbolized the freedom of the plains and the strength of these mountains, became louder in my memories. We had traveled for tens of kilometers, yet we had not seen a single horse. Times had changed, but the road was still not asphalted. It was only hardened with rocks.

Horses, the lake, the wilderness, hills soaring to the sky, sunburned humans counting the passing ages by generations, measuring their suffering against their happiness in the rice field. Father was determined not to die until he had seen me.

We stopped at a village in the middle of a forest, and I was introduced to the residents. Family! Blood relatives, descendants of the nth generation from the same ancestor. Welcome!

I gave a child a ball that I had actually bought for the children of my relatives in the village.

"Any news about Father?" my brother asked them.

"Nothing yet," several of them answered.

"But luckily *he's* here now," one of them remarked, with a glance in my direction.

We came across a lumber truck in the middle of the forest, but no one was around. My brother hit the horn of the Land-Rover. From somewhere in the forest, axes resounded several times in acknowledgment. Ships in the mist calling out to one another, a melody carrying a message. We drove on without comment.

A little while later my brother said, "That was what's-his-name's truck! Father's all right," he then added.

"How do you know?" I asked.

"That truck wouldn't be up into the mountains if something were the matter with him," he answered. "The whole western area and Samosir Island, too, are ready for Father's celebration."

He meant Father's death and the great funeral ceremony that would be held after.

"It will last four days and four nights," he said. "Seven days is too long for a celebration nowadays. Four days should be enough time for all the relatives from all over Batak Land to come to the party. A telephone-courier system has been set up so that when Father dies the news of his death can be spread quickly."

As we descended to the valley by the lake, we saw some villagers carrying firewood and lumber.

"That is the shopkeeper who is in charge of building the temporary shelters," my brother commented. "It will be like a fair with thousands of people coming from all over."

"All six of you are now here in front of me," Father said after the evening meal.

My youngest brother translated Father's words after reading the mumbling lips of his toothless mouth. Anything we had to say to Father had to be spoken into his ear slowly and loudly.

We sat cross-legged in a semicircle around him, we brothers awaiting Father's words.

"This is the first time that you are all together," he then said, referring to my presence. "I will present you with a feast. So find one of the buffalo of our forefathers from the mountains!"

We brothers looked at one another in silence, muted not only by the solemnity of the message but also by a practical question: how was one to capture a wild buffalo in the mountain wilderness, in only one night?

Father was referring to the tens of wild buffalo, remnants of the herd of hundreds our forefathers had bequeathed to him. The herd was a source of draft animals and of meat for feasts. But to capture one was difficult and usually took several days. First you had to search the jungle to find the herd, then you had to find the animal most suitable for the purpose.

Father made it clear that our ceremonial feast must take place the next day.

My eldest brother suggested allowing another day, but when this was passed on to Father, he answered curtly, "I said tomorrow."

Father then asked to be put to bed. He was tired.

The next morning Father smoked the cigar I had brought for him, and he drank the milk sent by a relative from Jakarta. On that day, as on any other day, people came from near and far to see him. Some brought an offering of food for Father, to reciprocate for blessings received, just as if Father were a holy man. Father signaled his acceptance of the offerings with a touch of his hand, but he ate nothing. When babies were placed in his lap to be blessed, he caressed their heads and smiled happily.

He requested a boiled egg from one old woman. A bottle of sulfur water from somebody else. Limes to make his bathwater fragrant from yet another person. Everybody set out to fulfill his requests. They ran home to their villages, happy that they were able to fulfill Father's final requests. It was only later that I realized that their happiness was a result of Father's generosity. Father knew that the villagers were poor, and he made it possible for them to ask for his blessings by requesting things that were still within their ability to give. He did not ask for expensive rituals.

Later that afternoon we heard cheering on the mountain slope, echoing with the sound of the Land-Rover. The men had managed to find and shoot a young buffalo cow, just as Father had requested, for the offering in the sacred meal he wished to share with us, his children. The leader of the hunt proudly reported his success to Father.

From his resting place Father cut in, "Who said that my wishes will not be fulfilled? It is you people who have no faith." Then he went to sleep.

Father was awakened that evening after the ceremonial food was ready. It consisted of all the parts of the head, chopped up and cooked together in blood: tongue, ears, brain, meat, skin, bones, and the eyes. The liver was cooked whole.

My brother's daughter, the one who usually took care of Father, roused him. "Grandpa, the food is ready." He was helped up from his bed and placed on the floor, leaning against the wall with a pillow at his back. "Are you all here?" he asked while moving his hand from left to right as if inspecting us.

"Yes, Father," said my eldest brother, already a grandfather himself.

"Where is the liver?" Father asked. One of his grandchildren pushed the plate with the steaming liver toward him. Father's favorite sharp knife was also on the plate.

"Now divide this liver into six parts," he ordered while touching the hot meat. His grandson cut the buffalo liver.

"Done, Grandpa," the grandson said. Father reached for the plate and took a piece.

"Come here," he said to us. My eldest brother came forward, then the second, the third, until finally it was my turn as the fifth son, to receive a piece of the liver of the sacrificial meat.

After waiting for each of us to finish eating our share, Father said: "You have eaten my gift of food. The six of you are my blood. And to you I command . . ." He paused like a minister at a religious ceremony. "To you I command what was taught by my forefathers to my grandfather, by my grandfather to my father, and by my father to me: to love one another, especially you as brothers, to help one another and to aid one another; to be united, to share your burdens . . .

"Remember that there are times when one who is younger or poorer might be a better leader than you. Follow him! This is my message to you." Then he signaled that he wished to lie down again.

All present were moved by Father's words and fell silent. The local minister, who was also present, commented, "Just like in the Bible." The look on the pastor's face was one of obvious relief. He must have concluded that there had been no superstitious elements in the ceremony, something he had previously feared.

The meal proceeded cheerfully, livened up by conversation and bursts of laughter. There was happiness, harmony, and peace. In the evening Father asked for *hasapi* players to play his favorite melodies. But when they began to play traditional songs with a modern beat, Father got angry. He asked for help to get up and go to bed. With guilty looks on their faces, the musicians shifted to playing the tunes in the traditional way. Father nodded happily as he listened to the lutes. But after a while he suddenly commanded the players to stop. He lifted his face as if he were going to pronounce another message. And he did: "Tomorrow . . . I want to offer a prayer to the god of Pusuk Buhit!"

Everybody was startled. The prayer to the god of Pusuk Buhit, the quintessence of Batak pagan rituals, was condemned by Christian law! Imagine, paying homage to the gods of the Holy Mountain! "Call the *gondang* players from Limbong," he said. He asked for the most famous ceremonial drum player by name, supposedly the only musician in the region still capable of correctly playing the music for the ceremony of homage to Pusuk Buhit.

Like all of Father's requests or messages, this one was a command shrouded with magic overtones to people around him. And, although it was difficult to ignore religious considerations, the command was obeyed.

That night Father called for me specifically to come and sit by his resting place. He had a message for me: "The day after tomorrow you will return. Go. I know you have lots of work."

The next night, after the *gondang* players arrived, preparations were made for the Pusuk Buhit ceremony. A number of people, at the behest of the pastor, had tried to dissuade Father but to no avail.

The ceremony—which I myself had only heard about—was very solemn and at the same time, like all pagan rituals, frightening. Although Father himself did not eat pork, the sacrifice for the ceremony was a pig, dressed and cooked in a special way as befitting an offering to the gods.

During the ceremony all fires and lights in the village were to be extinguished. No one was allowed to cross the grounds or to go in and out of the houses. All doors and windows had to be tightly closed.

The villagers knew about the ritual, and, by evening, no one dared to leave his house.

At exactly seven o'clock, the *gondang* sounded. The darkness seemed to emphasize the eerie, mystical quality of the music. Inside the house, Father, outfitted in full traditional dress, was helped to stand and lift the platter containing the sacrificial pig. He was now ready for his mystical devotion: to meet and be united with the spirits of his forefathers, creatures far beyond the reach of earthly eyes, beyond words, even feelings, on top of Pusuk Buhit.

The next morning I took leave of Father, who was lying on his sleeping place. It seemed as if Father had become a stranger to me since the previous night, but at the same time he seemed quite close to me when I took my leave and whispered in his ear. "Father. I am leaving!" He nodded and dozed off again.

I started my journey home by taking the shortcut across the lake. Arrangements had been made for the boat to pick me up in the cove of the valley of the village where I was born. The boat trip would end in Prapat, a stop for buses bound for Medan.

When the boat reached the middle of the bay, I looked back toward the village, which was still asleep in the haziness of the early morning. To the right Pusuk Buhit soared clearly into the grayish blue sky. As I lit a cigarette to ward off the cold wind, it struck me that for all my adult life Father had never talked to me except for that night when he sent me off. "Go," he had said. "I know you have lots of work!"

Translated by Toenggoel P. Siagian

B. WONGAR

(Australia)

If similarities can be drawn between the phenomena of world beat "roots" music and literature in our age, Australia's most resonant gift to the latter is surely the writing of Boro Wongar. Writing extensively on Australia's aboriginal culture in novels, short stories, poetry, and nonfiction—all of which have been influenced chiefly by his late tribal wife—Wongar concerns himself with the impact of European civilization and industrial development on tribal peoples in Australia. He is best known for his nuclear trilogy, Walg, Karan, and Gabo Djara. Wongar's writing was initially greeted by academics and critics as the work of an aboriginal genius. Later, when his Serbian origins were revealed, many such judgments were abruptly reversed, although tribal Australians continue to endorse the veracity and integrity of Wongar's vision and knowledge. Several of his manuscripts, which often relate to the controversial mining of uranium on aboriginal tribal lands, have disappeared after confiscation by the police during suspicious incidents. His work, which is usually published abroad, is curiously little known in Australia, although he has received several literary awards, among them an Unsung Writer's Award given during the 1986 PEN Congress and a Senior Writer's Fellowship grant from the Australian Literature Board. Wongar lives with a pack of dingoes on virgin bushland near Melbourne.

The Family

Our Mother has left us. She has not died or run away but has changed into a crocodile. Maybe it is better that way—not that we will see much of her but it helps to know that she is not far off; should anything like that happen to any of us we will be around in the bush together again.

I hope Padre does not find out what has happened to Mother. He says that whenever any of us leaves we go to Heaven; the white man's boss called Jesus boils a huge billy in a campfire and the people, black and white, sit around and sip tea—you can put as many lumps of sugar in your cup as you like.

What should I say to the other children? There are two more of us—Anabrn and Purelko—and they are still asleep in the sandpit behind the fire, curled together like a couple of puppies. Mother called the pit *murlg,* the shelter, though it is nothing but a sheet of corrugated iron stuck sideways into the ground; it makes no cover from the rain but is a shield from the cold winds at night.

The sun has shot spear-high in the sky—the children will be up soon; they will nag me about Mother and ask for food. I had better see to the fire. A big log lies partly sunk in the ashes with a cluster of red coals buried beneath it—a few pokes with a stick and a chunk or two of wood will make it flare up again. I'm glad that Mother thought of it when she left; I was half awake and saw her waddling over the dusty ground. Her tail was swinging around the fire, slashing the ashes now and then; a log was clamped in her jaws, then dragged and pushed over the dying coals on top of the mound of ashes.

One of the children mumbles something; it is Purelko, my brother. He struggles to move his hand through the air to . . . tell me, perhaps, that he knows about Mother too. The boy, the youngest, is often awake at night and stares at the fire. When the flames go out he calls; sometimes he jerks his limbs to make me and Mother get up and do something about it. When we find food I have to feed him, the same as Mother did—hold a piece of yam in front of his mouth and wait for his lips to stretch open. With *njuga,* the mangrove crabs, you have to break off the tough pieces and chew them for him first. Padre says the boy will never get better; once a child is crippled like that he will be no different when he grows up.

Mother will be back, for sure, not now during the day, but at night. She will sneak in to check on the fire and see that we are all properly buried in the sand to keep warm. There is a big hole dug under the chain-wire fence, just over there at the far corner of the compound where the ground makes a small rise. Lucky the ground around is sandy and it is not hard to break out. She won't be far off; perhaps she's hiding in the mangroves farther down toward the bay.

Look, Padre is already up and has gone to open the gate. He only does it once a day for us to go out and look for bush tucker, but never so early. The gate squeaks—it sounds like a possum trapped in a hollow log. Once it leaves the compound, the track forks: one path goes up the river, passes a patch of thick forest, and leads to the scrub country stretching inland; the other branch follows the shore, passes the old jetty, and swings around the water. The outline of the bay looks like a badly thrown boomerang that fell short of coming back—as if it had hit the sea and made Warngi Cliff there across the entrance to the inlet.

Padre wears a white shirt and a dark wide-brimmed hat that has swallowed half his head. I saw him dressed like that long ago when Nati, Mother's father, left. Padre must have thought that the old man was on his way to Heaven and he gave him a good farewell, but Mother says our people go a different way.

"Should I come to sweep your hut?"

Mother did so every day. She made his fire and boiled the billy for tea. Once she even climbed up on the roof of the hut to prop

up a sapling with a cross on top of it and fasten the lot with a piece
of wire.

"Don't worry about it."

"We can bring you some wood from the bush."

"You will have plenty on your hands looking after those two.
You're about grown up now."

Padre pats me on the cheek and walks slowly to our shelter.
A track of freshly disturbed sand stretched from the fire right to
that hole under the fence, but the claw marks can't be clearly seen.
Good that Mother dragged her long tail to sweep the dusty ground
behind her.

"How is the little albino; growing up?"

Anabrn steps out from the pit and allows the man to pat her
on the head. She has fair hair; where she has slept a seashell has
left a deep mark on the pale skin of her neck. Why does he call
her albino? Mother thinks it means "white," but . . . all three of
us show a bit of it. Padre says that some children will turn completely black only when they grow up; perhaps that means when
they become *bala,* initiated. It should be about time for me to go
through that now. There is a place Mother told me about, a billabong, I think, far off in the bush where the bay plunges its foamy
snoot into the land. The men from Dulbu tribe sit on the ground
in the shade of paperbark trees and sound out their *bilma,* clapping
sticks, and didjeridu loud enough to please every spirit in the country. The sound tells you that the time has come to go there and be
made into a woman. I hope there is somebody there to tell me how
to go about the ceremony when the day comes. Our Nati will be
there with his *bilma* for sure. By now he must be *marngit,* medicine
man; he will know about us coming to life.

"Here is some tea and sugar. You still have that billy, I hope."
On the ground near the fire Padre leaves two half-full jars and then
stares into the ashes for a while. Look, there are paw marks on the
ground from Mother's webbed feet; they are the same as those of
ducks and other water birds but much bigger.

Purelko is up and crawls around the fire. The boy tries to tell
us something but can't make the words; he just mumbles a sound

or two. Maybe he is asking for tucker—his face is stained with
charcoal and a layer of sand is stuck to the wet skin around his
mouth. Even though he is crippled, the boy should know that you
don't feed on sand whatever the color of your skin—black or white.

"Raunga, see that the boy is fed."

Padre walks back to his hut without saying more. He might
come out later in the day to look around and tell us what to do. I
should go up the rise there and cover that hole beneath the fence;
it might be better if Padre knows nothing about it. Even if he does
guess what has happened to Mother, let's hide the way she has
gone. The man might be angry because she has not departed the
same way as the white people do and he could set a trap to catch
her when she comes back to see us tonight. Our Nati told us that
the whites like to hunt every living soul in the bush. I have never
seen Padre kill an animal but once long ago I peeped into his hut,
and there was a stack of crocodile hides inside—I doubt whether
the beast can live after you have skinned it.

If Nati were here he could tell us a lot about crocodiles. The
animal is *marain,* sacred, to him and to all of us. The old man
hardly said anything to Padre, and when he was here he kept away
from the hut—his fire was behind that dead tree right over there
on the top of the rise. Look, it is still there; the wind has blown
off the ashes, but two partly burned pieces of wood remain on the
ground. Mother thought he had gone back to his place along the
long arm of the land stretching from here into the sea and had
walked over to Warngi Cliff where the *marngit* should be. You can
see the hill far across the bay, showing up above the forest like a
cap of dark cloud. He will be down there now sitting on the rocks,
clapping his sticks and chanting to call the spirits from Bralgu far
across the sea to come back and look after us and the animals—
the whole country. When they come, the spirits will bring *dal,*
magic power, to heal Purelko and everyone else who needs help. I
wish Nati would hurry them up; without Mother I may not be able
to feed the poor boy.

I should climb up on that dead tree and look out. I did it a
season ago and went up to the top branches. The arm of land

stretches far out into the sea and then curls around the bay and ends at Warngi Cliff—it looks like the tail of a huge crocodile swinging about to poke at a monstrous porpoise asleep on the sea.

Let's push some sand in and fill up the hole. If Mother comes back at night she will dig it out again. Crocodiles have strong claws; they can burrow into the ground like anteaters and often make hollows to lie and wallow in. Look, Nati has left his *bilma* behind; I have never heard him chanting without them, but even if he does, the spirits might not be pleased to hear the voice. The sticks—just plain pieces of wood—must mean a lot. Look, they are smooth and worn from being handled for so long. The pair have been around . . . the man before Nati, and the healers before him, must have chanted with those sticks.

Padre has come out of the hut again; I'll rush back to our fire and not let him come this way. The man has brought a bundle of rags and hands it to me: "Each one of you must make a 'lap-lap.' Girls should have a cover."

Mother wore a cover made of a burlap bag and it had a few holes where patches of dark skin showed through; she called it *maidja* and . . . a fire caught her cover once and burned a whole chunk out of it. She did not wear the bag around here but had to put it on whenever she went inside the hut.

Maybe a barge is coming today and Padre is in a hurry to clear out the hut and make room for new goodies. No boat has been here for many seasons; when it sailed in last . . . I doubt whether Anabrn or Purelko were born then. Yes, that is why Padre is dressed. I wonder how the man found out these fellows are on the way here. Perhaps Jesus came in his dreams last night and told him that goodies are on the way.

"You can have some blankets; there are a few inside."

When the boat came before, there was a tall pole behind the hut with a long piece of wire stretched to it—a magic string. Mother reckoned it went all the way up to the sky to let the white man talk to his boss. They called it "radio." Padre never had to chant and clap with sticks—he talked into the wire instead whenever he wanted a barge to be sent here.

"Where's our Mummy?" Anabrn looks down to the ground and her voice quivers.

"Raunga will tell you that."

"Has she gone to the river or the sea?" The child is shy—dashes behind me and covers her face with both hands.

Padre walks off and, passing through the gate, turns back: "If I'm not back by evening, go inside the hut."

Maybe he knows about Mother and thinks she will come tonight to snatch us all. Our Nati thinks the whites are tough on crocodiles, and Padre may not be so different from that lot. Pity, he was around here before I was born, and even before our mother was born. Only Nati remembers him coming to Dulbu country. The other old fellows would have known about it too, but all of them are long gone. They say the white man landed from the sea, washed up on a small sandy patch among the boulders on the other side of Warngi Cliff. He was stiff like a log, with no word of our lingo to tell us where he came from.

The water has slipped back from the shore, leaving behind a long stretch of mud and sand—the bay looks like a water tank with the tap left open. It will be noon or even later before the sea comes back and the first waves show up; by then I will have gathered a whole bag of *njuga*, enough for a much bigger *babaru* than the three of us.

Perhaps I should go up to the top end of the bay while the shore remains dry, and then come back to look for tucker later. The old man doesn't like to wait and the quicker I go the better it will be. If . . . let's leave Purelko under that whistling tree; without him to carry I can run.

"Rest here, boy, the sand is soft and shaded . . . Anabrn will look after you for a while."

"Can I gather some crabs?"

"Do, but . . . don't let him crawl close to the water."

Anabrn did not ask where I was going—perhaps she knew that I had *bilma* with me. The sticks are in the bottom of the dilly bag that hangs around my neck. Nati will be pleased to have them. In the bush there, far beyond the bay, the other old men will gather too; a whole flock of them will sit near the billabong to chant and . . . how can they sing without *bilma?* I've watched Nati chanting in camp many times. He claps the sticks one against the other a few times and then throws his voice high into the air so that it floats above the forest and across the bay to the land beyond. The *bilma* clap now and then to warn the spirits to be on the lookout for his call. A chant like that is magic, and when it is well sung it can not only heal humans but also bring back to life the dead trees and boulders scattered throughout Dulbu country.

Someone has just passed by here. Stretching along the shore toward the top of the bay there is a line of footprints in the wet sand: Padre—no one else around here wears shoes. Maybe he has gone for a walk. It will be quite a while before the tide comes in, and without the waves the barge will never be able to sail in. The boat has to come in right there, where those two rows of posts are stuck in the mud holding up a long platform made of saplings. There is hardly any water there now, but once the waves come back the sea will almost reach the top of the stilts. Padre calls it "jetty" and it has been there ever since I can remember. It must have been quite a job to drag all those trunks from the bush and sink them in the bay. All our fellows stuck to the job and struggled for a whole Dry to build that thing.

Mother didn't think that the jetty did any good, even though the barges called in a finger-count of time. They were loaded all right—our fellows had to drag bags and boxes of goodies ashore and then farther on up to the camp. Whenever the boat called, Padre's hut became like a hollow log packed up with honey. You only had to walk inside, look at the cross and whisper a few white man's words, then come out with a piece or two of barley sugar. I often got a handful of biscuits and learned to chant a little song, though I've never found out what the words meant. The women with small children each received a tin, not easy to open and the milk inside was too thick and hard to pour out—but it tasted nice. Mother often got a billycan full of flour; the powder had something . . . you could not tell if they were maggots or tiny weevils, but once the stuff was baked it tasted all right. Once she made *nadu,* damper, from . . . never knew whether it was dried milk or washing powder. Whatever the food came in, it always had shiny lettering on it to tell you how it should taste, but in the whole camp only Padre knew how to read.

Look, there is Padre, far away across the big bite of the bay; only his white shirt shows up, bobbing along the shore. He has gone a long way, almost to the patch of mangrove forest where the top part of the "tail" stretches out to bridge Warngi Cliff and the rest of the land. It's a tricky part of the country to go through—not so bad now, but once the tide is up the sea surges beyond the shore and moves inland through the mangroves to flood a whole chunk of the country. The water would almost cut off the whole of the cliff then if it were not for a long ridge of dunes that lies behind the mangrove forest shielding it from the open sea.

Yes, the *bilma* are in my bag all right. The sticks are our *ranga,* sacred, and when they are clapped, only old men and spirits can understand what they say. I hope Nati will not be angry with me—we all know that woman is not supposed to come to this part of the country except to be initiated. He may not be at the billabong; the spirits often go over the dunes to fish or look for oysters. If Nati is not there I will leave the sticks and . . . when I get back to the camp he might appear in my dream to tell me when I should go to the billabong again.

Should I tell Nati that the boat is about to come again? No, the old man might not like the news. The last time the barge was here it brought in a pile of timber, stacks of corrugated iron sheets, doors, windows, and rolls of wire mesh. Padre wanted to build a church—nothing like that hut but much bigger. The building was to sit on that rise in the compound, and the whisper went around that once it was up Padre would climb to the top to look right over the forest to the billabong to see what our spirits were up to. He put the wire fence around all right to make that compound but went no further. The church is still down in the bush near the jetty. You can't see much of it now; the piles of corrugated iron have been swallowed up by vines and scrub, and as for the stacks of timber—the ants have eaten the lot. The windows are still there, hiding behind a thick cover of leaves, and it is only now and then when *walu,* the sun, peeps in that the glass blinks back to say the stuff is still there.

There is not much sea here, only one arm of water that has moved in from the main body of the bay to separate the shore on this side from Warngi Cliff over there; it looks like the tongue of a panting animal. The cliff looms above, tall—almost halfway to the clouds. The rocks facing the bay go straight up like a wall. The whole hill has the shape of a whale, and it was indeed once a *warngi,* sea monster. Our Nati says that at the Dreaming, the time when the spirits were about to make Dulbu country, a huge sea beast rushed toward the land to snatch them. One of our ancestors, Crocodile Man, rushed out from the billabong over there in the bush and dived into the bay. He moved about under the water for a while, and when he showed up again his jaws were wide open and he snapped at the monster, taking out a whole chunk before *warngi* could even see him properly.

The cliff side facing that small stretch of land. . . . Look— Padre is struggling up the craggy slopes and . . . he will not have far to go before he reaches the top of the wall. Quick, I'd better leave the shore and walk through the bush; I don't want him to see me. The billabong should not be far off now, tucked somewhere in the bush between here and the edge of the mangrove marsh.

I wonder what Padre is doing here. Maybe he wants to have a good look from the cliff to see how far out to sea the barge is. The boat might be passing Dulbu county and taking goodies to some other place; he will have to shout out or wave to make the white fellows call in. Before, there was a tall pole on the rise at our camp, and every time the barge was due to call, a flag flapped on the top. It helped, but the pole has long gone and . . . Padre might take off his shirt now and wave with it from the cliff to bring his fellows this way. Yes, that is what he is doing, I can see him between the branches; his shirt must be unbuttoned—it flaps about in the wind. I wonder how long he is going to be there. The tide hasn't turned yet, but it shouldn't be long before the waves come rolling across the shore to the mangrove marsh. It will be hard to get back from the cliff then.

I'll wander through the bush and look for the billabong; it can't be far off and . . . I hope it shows up soon—I'm getting thirsty. Padre might feel that way too. There won't be much to drink among the rocks there. His fellow whites might have forgotten about him and may never come. Mother says he spoke angry words to his boss. It happened not long after the barge was here last time and something went wrong with our people. A few children died first and then a whole mob of us, young and old, got sick.

"It's a plague—could wipe us all out!" Padre used to yell into the magic wire—you could hear his voice right across the camp. "Send us bloody doctors and medicine—come quickly, for Heaven's sake." His voice was heard for days. It seemed as though he would choke himself with the loud calls, but instead he grew angry and . . . The radio was thrown out of a window and broke into pieces as it hit the ground.

"Bloody Doctors" never came. Our Nati was right when he told us that the boat would not call again because there was nothing for them to take back from our country. A few bundles of crocodile skins were sent off but that was only a small crumb against all the loads of goodies that had been brought in—so little to please Padre's boss.

I have to kneel to get some water, maybe lie on the billabong bank and lean forward for a good drink. It is quite a big pool, well tucked into the bush. Huge paperbark trees have grown sky-tall, not so much to make shade but to hide the place from outside view. The ground over there near a huge boulder looks well cleared and bare—even the rock surface seems to be smooth, perhaps touched by humans and spirits alike.

Let's step about slowly; the men could be resting and elders do not like to be disturbed. They might be behind bushes, hiding in the shade, or . . . yes, they should be resting on the bottom of the billabong as all of our spirits do. I wonder if Nati will be there or . . . no, he is likely to be farther down at the top of Warngi

Cliff. Look, there is a track going that way; the path swings around the mangrove marsh heading to the sandy ridge behind, and then a long neck of land heads toward the cliff. The old man must often come down here from the hill, chant and dance with the spirits, and then head back to Warngi—from there you can keep an eye on the whole Dulbu country.

I'd better be off. I'll just leave the *bilma* stick on top of the boulder and come in some other time when they want me. Look, something has just moved in the pool. On the surface two flower buds float; no, they are a pair of green eyes and . . . yes, the snout is over there—crocodiles often surface from underneath the lily pads to get a breath of air, and they don't show much of themselves if they want to rest in peace.

The sea is back, with the waves racing one another and rolling toward the shore. It will not be long now before the water slides over the small embankment and pours in to flood the mangrove forest behind. Padre should be down from the cliff by now if he is ever to come back. Maybe he has gone to the other side of the hill. Mother told us there are pieces of an airplane washed up on the shore there and stuck among the rocks. The metal does not rot quickly and could not be eaten by ants. The wrecked pieces have been there since "War," Mother thinks. However long ago that was, it is much further back than she remembers. When the airplane plunged into the sea it had aboard a whole bunch of white men. Maybe some of them made it to the shore farther up the coast but no one ever heard of them; we wouldn't have known about Padre either if Nati had not found him.

The sun is already hanging down from the sky; it will not be long now before it plunges into the sea. I'd better hurry back— Anabrn and Purelko will be angry with me for leaving them so long. They could already be calling for me, but children have weak voices and . . . they grow feebler when you are worn out with hunger. It would need to be like the roar of a didjeridu, not just a voice to match the howl of the sea, to reach this part of the bay.

Look, a white cloth lies washed up, the waves are still splashing against it: Padre's shirt—no, only half of it. His hat has come in too, sitting there on the water as though looking for the best spot to come ashore. Perhaps . . . Padre must have gone to see Nati and our other fellows. Good that they took him with them; he has been in our country ever since that day when Nati found him on the shore. The man must be too angry to go to his boss. Better this way; we may not see much of him, but now and then he will show up in our dreams.

I'll pick up the shirt and hat and take them down to the jetty and leave them on a log there. If the barge comes this way again the whites can have their clothes back.

BRUCE STEWART

(New Zealand)

Of mixed-blood Maori and pakeha *(foreign) origin, Bruce Stewart grew up in New Zealand's North Island Waikato region. He has worked at a variety of manual labor jobs, has eleven children, and is the founder and* kaumatua, *or elder, of the Tapu Te Rangu Marae spiritual community at Island Bay, Wellington. Stewart acknowledges his white settler ancestry with pride; his work, however, is devoted to reporting on the injustices and discrimination experienced by the Maori peoples in their struggle to keep alive a cultural heritage under constant threat of erosion. He has written for radio and television and is a past president of the Maori Artists and Writers Society.* Tama, *a collection of his short stories, was published in 1989. His seminal work, "Broken Arse," which he rewrote sixteen times, is a stunning cross-cultural addition to the genre of prison literature that is informed by Stewart's personal experiences. Its depiction of "Big House" machismo, Maori and* pakeha *racial tension, and institutional dehumanization is profoundly disturbing.*

Broken Arse

The first day Henry came into the Can we could hear him cracking funnies and whistling all the way down the wing. Even while he was being stripped and even while they shore off his yellow hair, gave him a number, a well-pissed mattress, his boob blues—he still raved on. He lined up for scoff, tall; you could hear him even when his mouth was full of tucker.

"Hey man, she's a far-out pad. More like a hotel. It *is* a hotel. When you think about it, it *is* a hotel."

And he laughed till the snot came out of his nose. He was a big man with a big laugh and made me feel good: I could see everybody's face spark up a bit. It was easy to see he was a country boy trying to sound heavy, but you couldn't help liking him.

"She's sweet here buddies, very sweet. Free keep, plus they pay me missus a wage. I'll tell yer she's a sweet one buddies, a very sweet one."

Tu and I were in the same slot. We'd come in together. He was the Kingpin. Everyone liked him. He always checked the new inmates out. After we'd finished our scoff we stopped by Henry's slot. He was hanging his boob gears on the nails behind the door. He was making his bed on the bottom bunk. He stopped for a bit when he saw his blankets were ripped and patched and his towel made up of four old towels. But he laughed again and poked his head through a ripped blanket.

"An' what's more, this patchwork stuff is big deal outside buddies, yeer big deal."

He played a photo of his missus a bit like a trump card. She looked like one of those flimsy girls you see in the big cities, one of those girls with lots of smelly stuff on her sad-looking face. Didn't seem like Henry's sort of girl, but he looked at the photo as if she was some kind of a star or something.

Tu couldn't take his randy eyes off the photo.

"You got a spunky missus bud."

"Oh. . . . Tina-Marie you mean?" He tried to look surprised. "She's not too bad—fuckin' good in the sack, yeer. Straight up and down she is, yeer straight up and down."

He went into a short trance, kept staring at the photo. "She'll wait . . . yeer she'll wait. . . ." Tu rolled a slow smoke and Henry kept on mumbling about her waiting and about seven years not being too long . . . but it was only for a moment 'cause he went outside his slot and shoved his card in its place above the door. The card said:

> HENRY ATHOL BLIGH
> SENTENCE: 7 years
> DATE OF SENTENCE: 5.1.80
> DATE OF RELEASE: 5.1.87

He stood back hands on hips.

"Seven years eh? Tha's a man's lag an' I'll do it on me fuckin' head. With ease buddies."

He punched the card and roared, "With ease."

His eyes were blue on white and bright. Brighter than any eyes I'd seen for a long time. Everyone started to look up to him 'cause he made you feel good. He looked so big. He was big. Tu looked at me with a knowing kind of nod. "Too loud," he whispered. "A bit too loud."

Henry got right into his lag. He played football, he played basketball. Most of his spare time was spent in the iron room. All sorts of stories went around the Can about Henry's muscles. Like lifting the back of the pig truck off the ground was hard to believe and so was the one about Henry tipping over the prison bull, Barney.

Tu and I went up to the iron room one Saturday to see Henry's muscles for ourselves. Tu could push more iron than anyone. We shoved our way through lots of little muscles; I say little muscles because they were standing around like apes. It was the same as being in church. The place smelt of iron and sweat and sort of stung my nose. There wasn't any sound except Henry's deep breathing; sweat dripped off his nose. He was shaping up to a great heap of iron.

"He's been building up to this for three hours," someone whispered, so's we could be up on the action. Henry moved into the heap of iron; it was more than Tu had lifted. He stood there for a long time breathing deeply and twitching his fingers. He bent down, gripped the bar like he was going to tear it apart: with a half shout, half scream hurled it up over his head.

"Chesses!"

"Fuckin' hell!" said all the little apes.

Henry ripped off his shirt in front of the mirror and struck a kind of a Mr. World pose and all the little apes oohed and aahed. His pumped-up body bulged out all over the place. His veins stuck out and looked something like the roots of an old pohutakawa tree. Henry struck pose after pose. He twitched his muscles, he made them shiver. They were shiny with sweat. Everybody watched him. He was the new champion. He looked like a great white giant. I looked for Tu. He was standing with his back against the wall rolling a long slow smoke.

Henry developed a kind of a gorilla walk; guts pulled in and up to his chest, back muscles fully flexed so's his arms hung out from his body. Wherever he walked he managed to catch a glimpse of himself in the windows. The queens loved him, specially Sandra. Tu said she did a few free blow jobs on the side to get the top bunk in Henry's slot. One day Tu found them under the stage on the badminton nets. Tu was pretty sweet on Sandra. It seemed all the strong fullas got the best queens. Sandra was a Maori—somehow I knew Tu didn't like her being with Henry. Henry always showered in front of the mirror and even when he combed his hair he'd strike a pose.

Before the mail list was called, Henry would be standing outside the guard room, waiting. I saw Piggy Screw one day censoring

Henry's letter. He sniffed the scent and ripped it open. I could tell by the way his fat face lit up and by the way he was chuckling he was really caught up with the secret bits.

Henry looked like a hurt little puppy waiting for a bone. Piggy Screw kept reading. Henry waited.

"Oh Bligh, didn't see you there. I just finished censoring your letter. Here you are."

"Th . . . thanks mister."

"She's quite a girl your Tina-Marie, ay Bligh?"

"Y . . . eah, yes mister."

"Yes . . . quite a girl."

And Henry would come swaggering up the wing offering all the boys a sniff of the scent his missus had splashed on the letter. "Every day! Every day!"

Sandra didn't mind. The letters made Henry randy; it was Sandra who slept with Henry.

Henry went back to his slot and read and reread the letter. He read in between the lines. By the time he had read it six times he was happy. He started doing his lag letter by letter, kept them all in a large cigar box with a yellow ribbon tied around. Tu found out where Tina-Marie lived. He was a trustee and drove the Can's pig truck. He called in to see her every day. Everyone knew about Tu and Tina-Marie, everyone except Henry. Also, Tu was working on something. I couldn't work out what it was, but he spent a fair bit of time in Piggy Screw's ear. No one else knew he was talking to Piggy Screw. No one talks to screws much. But Tu had a way of saying things out the side of his mouth. Piggy Screw knew how to play the game too. He'd been with crims so long he was like one himself. His best mates were crims with lots of form. He was no match for Tu though. He was like most of the other screws, thick. Thick but cunning and dangerous. Well, that's what Tu told me.

Henry often talked about farming, about plowing with horses. He'd been taught by his grandfather. He knew so much about the land. I liked his talk. When he talked about Tina-Marie though, he was sad. "She taught me everything . . . I love her so much, I miss her so much . . . it hurts. Never had a girlfriend before."

Henry got a whopping toothache when I was working with him cutting scrub in Piggy Screw's outside party. Henry was in such a bad way he could hardly speak. Plus he was too scared to see Piggy Screw 'cause Piggy Screw was starting to give him a hard time making him do the dirty jobs. He called Henry "musclehead." I said I'd go and see Piggy Screw for him.

Piggy Screw was lying down in the shade asleep. He always went to sleep in the shade while we worked in the sun. It's a wonder no one killed him while he slept. Enough fullas hated him. They always talked about it. But then he was so strong and fierce. Once he told us the best job he ever had was as a mercenary hunting niggers in South Africa. "They had spears; we had automatic rifles."

I got within ten yards of where he was sleeping. He jerked upright.

"Excuse me mister. Henry Bligh has a really bad toothache; if I could get some kawakawa leaves from the bottom of this gully it would help him mister."

"A Witch Doctor eh," he roared, and his fat stomach shook. He got up to his feet. "Might just go down there and see Bligh, the musclehead. I'm a bit of a Witch Doctor myself, a WHITE Witch Doctor." Piggy Screw looked so evil.

Or maybe he was lonely too, I didn't really know. He seemed to enjoy everyone hating him. He hated Kid Fuckers the most, that's what Tu said. By the time he got down to where Henry was he was puffing and sweating.

"Bit of a toothache, eh Bligh. Well, you just remember WHO you are and WHAT you're here for. Not a holiday camp is it Bligh? No. WHO ARE YOU Bligh? Go on, YOU tell me, who are you?" He kept prodding Henry in the chest with his forefinger.

"An' whatcha here for, go on, whatcha here for?"

Piggy Screw kept pushing Henry down the hill. Henry mumbled back and Piggy Screw told him to speak clearly. We all knew Henry couldn't speak 'cause his gum was badly swollen up.

"Speak up like a man."

I couldn't work out why he was so evil, so cruel. I couldn't stand it any longer.

"Please mister, Henry Bligh can't speak."

"Well, what have we here. Witch Doctor speaks for the Kid Fucker. A bit of a Kid Fucker lover are ya. I thought there was sompin' queer about ya. Not as bad as a genuine Kid Fucker. Should cut their balls out I reckon!"

None of us believed it. Not Henry, a Kid Fucker! We all looked at each other and then back to Henry, who was shaking his head. "No!" he mumbled, "No!"

Piggy Screw asked me to take Henry back to his slot.

"I'll send the nurse when I'm good and ready."

All the way back I was trying to work out what happened. . . . I knew Henry wasn't into little boys. . . . He had Tina-Marie and Sandra . . . not little boys. What made Piggy Screw so awful? Maybe it was something to do with Tu . . . when he talked out of the side of his mouth to Piggy Screw.

There was a story about Piggy Screw finding a sack on the side of the road. . . . It had a baby in it and it was still alive—he adopted it. The boy turned out to be a bit funny in the head, they said; had to put him in a special home. Piggy got a job as a screw, for revenge they said. He's been at it twenty-five years. He was getting old for a screw but he could still swing a pick handle.

We waited in Henry's slot for the nurse. Everyone was in from the work parties, I could hear them in the showers. Henry was in a bad way. He tried lying down on his back but the hammering would make him jolt up again. He'd start pacing around his slot. I could see the pain was hammering him stupid. He was crying. He wiped away the tears and tried to make an excuse for crying in front of me, but I told him I cried too at times, and I didn't think there was anything wrong with it. He smiled a bit through his tears.

One hundred and thirty-six speakers told us it was scoff time. I left Henry in his slot; told him I'd be back after scoff. In the dining room I could feel something was going on. Tu was the center of it all. I could tell by the sly glances.

A screw checked the muster. He whispered to one of the other screws. They both looked worried. Checked the muster again. Still one down. They checked for the third time.

"Lock the doors!"

"Who is it?"

No one knew so they called the roll.

"It's Henry Athol Bligh."

I could see Tu had it all going well. The boys were leading the screws on great guns.

"Bligh must've gone over the wall."

"Yeah he had a toothache. He probably jumped over the wall."

"Bligh's a nutter."

"He split man."

Piggy Screw came in. "Shut up alla ya." He asked the two screws where Bligh was. They said he'd gone over the wall. The Super himself was called in.

"Bligh's escaped, Sir," said Piggy Screw.

"Who is Bligh?"

"The muscle man, Sir," said Piggy Screw, trying to sound very polite. And he whispered something into the Super's ear.

"Oh God no. Not him! Look, if the papers want to know what's going on, keep it quiet. Having someone escape is bad enough. Is that clear mister?"

"Yes Sir."

It was good fun listening to it all. They seemed to have forgotten we were there. It was good too because we knew Henry was safe in his slot. Piggy had sent him there. But I couldn't work out what Tu was up to. True he was liked by everyone, they'd do anything he asked. We'd been through a lot together. He was doing ten years for trapping two cops up a blind alley and "beating the shit outta them with a chain," he said. "White trash."

Tu made out he was a bit silly, but he wasn't. He was always working something out . . . some way to get his own back. He'd always been the Kingpin, no one could match him. No screw was a match for Tu.

We were all ordered to our slots for an early lock up. Tu beat me to Henry's slot. I got there just in time to hear Tu telling Henry to keep out of sight.

"They think you've pissed off man. Play along. They'll find
you soon. And you'll get painkillers. Sweet?"

Henry nodded, he knew he had to be staunch. I could see he
was in a bad way, his teeth must've been giving him one helluva
hammering. Only wish I could have got those kawakawa leaves.

An hour after lock up, Piggy Screw found him. We could all
hear everything he said.

"B . . . Bligh, you Kid Fucking bastard. You set me up y'cunt."

"Y . . . you sent me to me slot to wait mister, f . . . for the
nurse."

"No I didn't y'bastard, don't lay that on me or I'll cut y'balls
out."

He sounded pissed and evil. We could hear him kicking Henry
in the ribs.

"That's (THUD) for saying I sent ya to your slot. Lies. That's
(THUD) for pretending to escape. So by now the police are looking
everywhere for you. (THUD) It's all over the radio, Bligh. (THUD!)
'Kid Fucker at large.' (THUD) 'Everyone is requested to lock up
their sons as Henry Bligh is loose.' That's what they'll be saying
(THUD)." We could hear a lot of scuffling; Piggy Screw was trying
to shout, but it was coming out all muffled. Henry must've got him.
It sounded as if Piggy Screw was being strangled. Henry could
break his neck easily. Then we could hear Henry smashing Piggy
Screw's head against the wall.

"Kill the bastard, Henry!" roared Tu so no one could tell where
his voice came from. Everyone started chanting. Banging the heat-
ing pipes with anything they could lay their hands on. Steel against
steel. Ringing echoing, ringing ringing. Stomping out the refrain.
It was slow at first. Deliberate. Heavy.

"Kill the bastard!"

"Kill the bastard!"

"Kill the bastard!"

It echoed and bounced from wall to wall. The whole place was
going crazy and I was too, chanting along with the rest. It was good
sticking up for Henry, he was a good guy . . . I mean, Tu reckoned

all *pakehas* are trash and yet here we were stomping for Henry, a *pakeha*.

Suddenly: I knew we were killing Henry. Because if he killed Piggy Screw, he'd get life. We weren't helping Henry at all. I looked at Tu. He was at the grill pushing everyone. Keeping it all going. He looked a bit *porangi*.

"Tu!" I had to yell. He swung around. I could see he was mad. He loved fights. He was in command of the whole prison.

"Tu!" I yelled again. "Stop them Tu, he'll get life."

"You fuck up Boy or I'll put ya down."

"Y' can if y'like but you've got to stop all this."

"Fuck up Boy, I'll . . ."

He was going to drop me—we were close friends. Screws were running down the wing. The chanting stopped. We could hear three or four screws belting into Henry. "They're kicking the shit outta Henry," yelled Tu. The screws were whispering so's we couldn't hear:

"Better get the nurse."

"No he'll live. Serve him fuckin' right. He tried to kill me."

They locked him up. They left. It was quiet again. Tu could see Henry's slot through the grill.

There's blood all over the place," he screamed. "Henry's blood. Hey you guys, Henry's nearly brown bread."*

The Can started winding up, you could feel it. You could hear it murmuring.

Tu was still in command, leading everyone. "They kicked the shit outta him. The screw bastards. SCREWS FUCK SPIDERS!"

"Fuckin' screw bastards!"

"SCREWS FUCK SPIDERS! SCREWS FUCK SPIDERS!"

It was winding up again. Not only our wing but all the wings joined in. All chanting. All stomping.

"Get Bligh the nurse."

"Get Bligh the nurse."

*Dead

"Get Bligh the nurse."

It was building up. Nervous. Ugly. And I was right there caught in the fire of it all. Bashing steel against steel. Everybody stomping.

Steel against steel, ringing echoing ringing. Piggy Screw was running up and down the wing. Yelling through the peepholes.

"Cut out y' fuckin' racket. Cut it out or I'll come in and fuckin' do ya."

But it stomped even louder.

"SCREWS FUCK SPIDERS."

"SCREWS FUCK SPIDERS."

"GET BLIGH THE NURSE."

"GET BLIGH THE NURSE."

Next thing we heard Piggy Screw on the loudspeaker. He was using his loudspeaker voice.

"Would inmates refrain from creating a disturbance. If not, we will be forced to take sterner measures. I repeat: Would inmates refrain. . . ."

The more he tried to stop us the stronger we stomped. They poked a fire hose into our slot. The force of the water slapped me against the back wall. The Can hissed back. Everyone, steel against steel, 368 of us all shouting and stomping. Tu and I stripped off naked, we danced in our madness. The prison shook. It all reached a high-pitched screaming sound.

The nurse came.

There was silence. The hate and the ugliness was there. Throbbing, but it was silent.

"Come on now son, this will kill the pain."

We could hear her making the screws run: she wanted hot water, clean sheets, and blankets. She made them clean up the mess.

"How on earth did this happen?"

"One of the inmates got him. He'll live, won't he?" It was Piggy Screw talking in a hoarse whisper thinking we couldn't hear him.

"Liar."

Tu yelled so no one could tell where his voice came from again.

"Bloody liar!" came from a dozen slots.

"You got him bashed up. Y'liar."

Piggy Screw left. We all knew he hated taking orders from a woman.

The Can never settled down that night. The stomping was still there; even when it was silent. It kept turning over. Every now and again the night shattered.

"Dirty—rotten—fuckin'—screw—bastards!" someone screamed in their half-awake fear.

I couldn't sleep—kept turning over and over and over.

By morning, Tu had a new plan. He was always working on ways of destroying . . . though I wasn't sure who he was destroying. . . . Even in his sleep I could hear him mumbling things. I knew he didn't care about Henry now, 'cause Henry was a *pakeha* . . . of the 368 inmates, 203 were Maori. Tu ruled the prison, he was the boss.

The prison had a guard placed outside Henry's slot. As soon as we were unlocked Tu called a meeting in the showers.

"We've got to tell Henry to lay a complaint outside, to a magistrate. We'll tell the newspapers and the TV, sweet?"

"Sweet!"

"We'll riot," said Tu. But there was a long silence and he could see some of us weren't ready for the kind of riot he meant.

"You've got to. You all know how the bastards smashed up Henry. We can't let them get away with it. Let's tear this hellhole apart. We'll wait till the screws are standing around at morning scoff and we'll grab them." Tu was talking fast and I could see most of his heavies were being swayed. I couldn't agree though, not about the riot I mean. We were no match for the screws.

"No riot Tu," I said.

Tu glared at me. "Let's down the bastards," he shouted.

"No. They'd get the army in," I said. "Better to have a peaceful sit-out."

"No," Tu shouted.

"Yes we can, Tu. We'll all go into the yard after breakfast and sit down. We'll do as you say, get a letter to Henry. Henry could lay a complaint. We'll let Henry know the whole boob is sitting it out." Everyone agreed. Everyone except Tu.

After morning scoff, Tu chased Sludge, one of the *pakeha* kingpins. Chased him past the guard outside Henry's slot. To the shitter at the end of the wing.

"You fuckin' thievin' white trash bastard, I'll beans ya!" yelled Tu.

"Issat so black; you'll be brown bread when I've finished with ya. All you Maori cunts are gutless. Y're only good in numbers!"

He shouldn't have said that, because it was only meant to be a decoy. Tu dropped him, he started kicking the shit outta him.

The screw took the bait and rushed down to the shitter. "C'mon you two; break it up or you'll both be charged."

I slipped a note under the door to Henry.

"Henry," I whispered, "chin up. Read this. We're all with you."

After breakfast, 136 speakers ordered us to parade for work. The screws could see something was wrong, they looked a bit scared. Piggy Screw was back on duty. He must've been expecting trouble because it was his three days off. He had an unhappy face but we knew he loved trouble. We could see him reaching for the microphone. "Would all inmates get on parade." He waited for a while till all the young screws were standing beside him. They were nervous looking.

No one moved. No one said a word. We all sat there, 368 of us all waiting. None of the screws would come out into the yard. They were too scared. They stayed close to their microphone, close to Piggy Screw. I could see him reaching for the microphone again.

"Would inmates elect a spokesman. The spokesman should come forward and inform us of your grievance."

Tu whispered, "You go Boy; Henry's more your friend than any of us."

It wasn't easy for me walking up to the guardhouse and telling them we were going to stay there until we knew Henry Bligh had got a magistrate.

"What's he want a magistrate for?"

I could see they were going to play games with me so I left the guardroom and walked across the yard.

We were strong all being together. Nothing they could do to us. It was a kind of safe feeling, 368 of us lying there in the sun. No one talking. With my eyes closed I thought of my old *koroua*,* Tane. Must be he's thinking of me too. Wish I was with him in the bush. The birds were singing in the bush outside the prison.

Sun.

Bush.

Birds.

Tane.

So gentle.

I was drifting. Dreaming. Floating. In my dream I could see myself . . . lying down there with the 368 . . . heaps of walruses . . . sunning. . . . I looked happy with my eyes closed. The *tui* in the *kowhai* were busy. Going to be a long summer. It's hard to remember all the things of *aroha* Tane taught me. He said it would take a lifetime to learn its meaning. The sun heals. Tane says *aroha* always wins. Takes a long time. But it always does. He said it is the only way.

I woke up suddenly. For a while I didn't know where I was. Kind of lost. It was Henry; I saw him limping out of the guardroom. The Super, Piggy Screw, and the four other screws were crowded into the guardroom. Smirking behind bulletproof glass. Henry was all cleaned up, bandaged, and in some new recreation gear. He limped slowly. Something was wrong.

Later on Henry told me what happened. He said he'd got our letter and he'd only just swallowed it when the screws came for

*Grandfather

him. He was marched before the Super himself. He was offered a roundie* and a cup of coffee. Piggy Screw was there, he was being really nice. "Sit down Bligh."

The Super showed Henry to a comfortable chair. "You know Bligh you're in serious trouble attempting to escape."

"But I was sent to my slot. . . ."

"It's no good going over that again Bligh. We know what you were trying to do."

Henry tried to say something.

"Listen Bligh, you're in big trouble so shut up and listen; just remember WHO you are and WHERE you are!"

Henry hung his head. "Yes Sir."

"Another cigarette? more coffee?" Henry nodded. No inmate was allowed cigarettes or coffee.

"Well, it's like this Bligh. You're doing seven as it is . . . and you've got a girl waiting for you outside, eh Bligh?"

"Yes Sir."

"And she's quite a girl judging from her letters. Well, we're taking this into consideration and we are not laying charges and I know you will not take it any further: will you Bligh?"

"No . . . no Sir."

"No what?"

"No, I won't take it any further Sir."

"That's talking sense Bligh. Now you can have this packet of cigarettes. The nurse will see you and you can sit in the sun. There's no need for you to work for the next couple of weeks. I'll fix it with the nurse."

There were 368 of us all watching Henry limping. He looked really sore. Behind the glass the screws smirked. Something was wrong. Henry stopped. He was smoking roundies.

"What . . . he's smoking roundies."

"He's fuckin' scabbed."

*Tailor-made cigarette

"Wassa score?"

"He's cracked up."

The Can started winding up again. This time it was against Henry. He just stood there on one spot. In the middle of the courtyard, shaking his head.

"I couldn't . . . sorry, but I couldn't."

"Scab."

"White trash."

"Broken Arse."

"BROKEN ARSE!"

"BROKEN ARSE!"

"BROKEN ARSE!"

The stomping started again. Henry knew he'd blown it. He looked back to the guardhouse to the Super and the screws. It was almost as if he'd wanted to take back the things he'd said. But the guardhouse was empty, the screws were gone. Henry hung his head. The stomping started building up.

"BROKEN ARSE!"

"BROKEN ARSE!"

"BROKEN ARSE!"

The more they chanted "Broken Arse" the more Henry sank to his knees. It was like a giant hand was crushing him into the ground. He wept right out there in front of everybody. He couldn't control himself. Snot and tears running down his face. And all the time the stomping beat out the refrain: "Broken Arse, Broken Arse, Broken Arse."

"Crying," said someone.

"Crying like a mad woman," said another.

"Shit, now I've seen it all, a man crying in front of everyone."

"Fuckin' hell, makes you want to throw up."

Some of the 368 took off, ran to their slots. Squirming.

"Never seen anything like it before."

I went out to see Henry. I'm not into being a hero, in fact I was really scared. But it was as if Tane was pushing me out. Helped him to his feet. Put my arm over his shoulder and helped him back to his slot. It was awful . . . the brokenness was awful.

That night they demolished Henry. They stomped for two hours. The screws pretended they never heard it.

Henry spent a week lying on his bed. He couldn't eat. I managed to get him a few scraps. He was too frightened to leave his slot. Everywhere he went they called him Broken Arse. Two weeks later when Henry went up to the iron room, they hissed at him.

"White trash."

He pretended not to hear, but it was written all over his face. He piled a great heap of iron on the bar. It was heavier than he'd lifted before. He was going to try it cold.

He walked around the bar. The hissing stopped. He stood in front, deep breathing, fingers twitching. It was his last chance to come back. He grabbed. Lifted, pushed and pushed, but it wouldn't go right up. It was lopsided, started toppling over. He fell. Screamed. He'd ruptured something in his groin. He tried to get up.

"He's fucked himself."

"Must've dropped a piston."

"He's got a broken bum bum, he he."

"The original Broken Arse."

When he got back to his slot someone had done a shit in his bed. They had thrown shit all over the walls. They had rubbed it over the photo.

Henry went to hospital. He came back on crutches ten days later. Wherever he limped he was called Broken Arse. He lived for his missus's letters, but they weren't coming every day. Sometimes it was three days before he got one, even then it was often a scribbled page. We all knew Tu was rooting his Tina-Marie.

Henry wasn't seen much now. He slid along the walls, feeling his way. His left shoulder drooped. He was always seeing the chaplain or the nurse. He didn't work. The nurse said he was too sick. He slept most of the time, didn't even read, just slept. I used to go to his slot as much as I could. He liked to see me; I liked to see him too. He always sparked up a bit when we talked about our grandfathers, about the bush, the mountains.

He couldn't keep his slot clean. He never had a shower. His

great body was withering away. On film nights Henry used to sneak in after lights out so's he'd miss the hissing. But the 368 knew. One night the film clacked on about a woman becoming tired of her man. When she finally climbs into the best friend's bed, the 368 spat out:

"An' that is Broken Arse's missus."

In the dark, Henry picked up a chair and smashed it down on Tu's head. He downed two screws. He cut a furrow through the 368, leaving a bleeding heap. And all the time making half-dog, half-man noises. He rushed back to his slot and swallowed razor blades. Henry went into hospital again. When he was well enough he was committed to the nutter. Henry's head was electrocuted. Months later he was brought back.

"Broken Arse is back."

"He's a fuckin' robot."

I saw him starting across the yard from the guardhouse. He was swinging his legs like they were dead logs. His head was screwed to one side . . . it looked crooked. The further he walked out into the yard the slower he went. He looked back at the guardhouse. Piggy Screw and his mates were just staring. The closer he got to the spot where he went down on his knees crying, the place where they chanted Broken Arse, the more he started to twitch. He couldn't go past it. He just stared at it like he was staring right into hell itself. His eyes were rolling. His head twisted . . . Evil . . . his arms twitched. His fingers were bent . . . different ways. He froze. He looked like a statue . . . like a statue of what Whiro must look like. It was not Henry at all. I went out to him, so did the others, even the screws, even Piggy Screw. My guts were burning, it was all mixed up with love and hate and anger, all at the same time. Only the whites of his eyes were showing. He was breathing all right, but it was as if he were dead. His face was twisted and frozen with a look of deep hurt . . . deep pain. Tears were streaming out of his white eyes. The tears were the only warm part I knew about him. It ripped at my guts. I was full of tears too. So were many of the others. Piggy Screw looked different, his bottom lip was quivering.

"Poor bastard," someone whispered.

"Make's you feel stink," said another.

"Make's you feel stink all right," said Piggy Screw. "I gotta boy in the nutter . . . be about the same age . . . he's got yella hair too . . . make's you feel fuckin' stink all right." Piggy Screw was hugging Henry, the tears were streaming down his face too. "Found him stuffed in a sack you know . . . no one wanted him . . . no one loved him, no one at all. . . ."

It was sad seeing Piggy Screw crying out there in front of the others. He looked shattered, even broken, right out there where Henry went down on his knees. It seemed the same giant hand that crushed Henry was crushing Piggy Screw.

Tu was standing in the shadows, up against the back wall. So were all his Maori heavies. There were about eighty of them. They seemed to enjoy the brokenness: Henry and Piggy Screw . . . hugging . . . crying.

We could all feel the stomping. It was a slow, deliberate stomp. Though there wasn't a sound. They were stomping their feet, swaying their bodies from side to side like a haka. Broken Arse, Broken Arse, they stomped. Though you couldn't hear a sound. They looked so black, so ugly, so strong.

Henry and Piggy Screw looked so pale, so weak, so broken.

Tu rolled a large slow smoke.

ABOUT THE EDITOR

Trevor Carolan *was born in 1951 in Yorkshire. His family emigrated to Canada, and he has spent most of his life there. A specialist in Pacific Rim cultural affairs, he received a master's in English from the University of California, Humboldt, in 1978 and has contributed widely since then as a free-lance journalist for publications in Canada and the United States. His cotranslation from the Chinese of* Embracing the Tao: The Book of the Heart *has been acclaimed internationally as a modern Taoist classic. A longtime practitioner of tai chi chuan, he travels extensively and has published two books of poetry. In 1988 he organized the International Literary Arts Festival during the XV Olympic Winter Games. He teaches literature and East-West comparative studies in Vancouver.*

ABOUT THE TRANSLATORS

Benedict R. O'G. Anderson *was born in Kunming, China. He studied classics at Cambridge University and Southeast Asian politics at Cornell University, where he is currently professor and director of the Cornell Southeast Asia Program.*

David Deterding *studied Chinese and taught English literature at Tunghai University in Taiching, Taiwan, from 1979 to 1981. He lives in England.*

Bruce and Ju-Chan Fulton *are well known for their definitive translations of Korean fiction and have received a number of awards for their published works, including a prestigious prize from the Korean Cultural and Arts Foundation. They live in Seattle.*

Howard Goldblatt *received his Ph.D. from the University of Indiana. He is a teacher of modern and contemporary Chinese literature at the University of Colorado, where he also edits the journal* Modern Chinese Literature. *He is one of the foremost translators and critics of twentieth-century Chinese literature and has translated more than a dozen novels and collections of short fiction, including* The Butcher's Wife *by Li Ang.*

Huynh Sanh Thong *is a language and literature scholar who directs a research and publication project for Vietnamese studies at Yale University. His translations include* The Tale of Kieu *and* The Heritage of Vietnamese Poetry.

Mark Jewel *was born in Iowa and graduated from the University of Hawaii in 1973. He received a doctorate in Japanese from Stanford University in 1985, and teaches in the School of Political Science and Economics at Waseda University in Tokyo.*

Ruchira Chinnapongse Mendiones, *coauthor of the standard Thai-English Dictionary, was born in Bangkok and taught Thai language at Cornell University.*

Bonnie S. McDougall *is professor of Chinese at Edinburgh University.*

Richard King *is associate professor of Chinese at the University of Victoria in British Columbia. His principal field of research is contemporary Chinese fiction.*

Toenggoel P. Siagian *was educated at George Williams College and Cornell University, lived for many years in the United States, and taught at the University of Wisconsin and the University of California at Santa Cruz. He now lives in Jakarta, where he is executive director of the Jakarta Christian School Association.*

Mary Lou Wang *is an Indonesian-born American. She lives and works in New Jersey.*

ACKNOWLEDGMENTS

Epigram, "Hakuin Zenji," courtesy of Gary Snyder.

Kuniko Mukoda, "Doubt," copyright © 1980 by Sei Mukoda. Translation copyright © 1984 by Dan Semour. Reprinted by permission of Sei Mukoda from *Japan Quarterly;* Asahi Shimbun Publishing Co., Tokyo, vol. 31, no. 3, 1984.

Yoshiko Shibaki, "Snow Flurry," copyright © 1986 by Japanese Literature Today. Translation copyright © 1989 by Mark Jewel. Reprinted from *Japanese Literature,* Japan, P.E.N. Club, 1989. Reprinted by permission of Japan Foreign-Rights Centre, on behalf of Kiyoshi Oshimo, and Mark Jewel.

O Chong-Hui, "Chinatown," copyright © 1989 by O Chong-Hui. English translation copyright © 1989 by Bruce and Ju-Chan Fulton. Reprinted by permission of Seal Press from *Words of Farewell: Stories by Korean Women Writers* (Seattle: Seal Press, 1989).

Bei Dao, "13 Happiness Street," copyright © 1981 by Bei Dao. Copyright © 1985 by the Chinese University Press, the Chinese University of Hong Kong. Translation copyright © 1990 by Bonnie S. McDougall. Reprinted from *Renditions* magazine by permission of the Chinese University Press, the Chinese University of Hong Kong. Reprinted from *Waves* (London, 1990) by permission of William Heinemann Limited.

Zhu Lin, "The Festival of Graves," copyright © 1987 by Zhu Lin. Translation copyright © 1989 by Richard King. Reprinted by permission of Richard King from *Mānoa,* University of Hawaii, 1989.

Li Ang, "Curvaceous Dolls," copyright © 1987 by Li Ang. Translation copyright © 1987 by Howard Goldblatt. Originally published by *Yellow Silk Journal,* 1990. Reprinted by permission of *Yellow Silk* and Howard Goldblatt.

Bo Yang, "Dragon-Eye Rice Gruel," copyright © 1983 by Bo Yang. Translation copyright 1985 by Joint Publishing (Hong Kong) Co. Ltd. Reprinted by permission of Joint Publishing Co. Ltd. from *Secrets* (Hong Kong: Joint Publishing Co. Ltd., 1985).

F. Sionil José, "Progress," copyright © 1980 by F. Sionil José. Reprinted by permission of the author, from *Waywaya and Other Stories* (Singapore: Heinemann Asia, 1980).

Jose Dalisay, Jr., "Heartland," copyright © 1984 by Jose Dalisay, Jr. Reprinted by permission of Jose Dalisay, Jr., from *Oldtimer and Other Stories* (Rizal, Philippines: Asphodel, 1984).

Shirley Geok-lin Lim, "Mr. Tang's Girls," copyright © 1982 by Shirley Lim. Reprinted by permission of Shirley Geok-lin Lim from *Another Country* (Singapore: Times Books International, 1982).

K. S. Maniam, "Mala," copyright © 1989 by K. S. Maniam. Reprinted by permission of AMK Interaksi Sdn. Bhd. from *Plot, The Aborting, Parablames and Other Stories* (Kuala Lumpur: AMK Interaksi Sdn. Bhd., 1989).

Kon Krailat, "In the Mirror," copyright © 1978 by Kon Krailat. Translation copyright © 1985 by Benedict R. O'G. Anderson and Ruchira Chinnapongse Mendiones. Reprinted by permission of D. K. Book House from *In the Mirror* (Bangkok: Editions Duang Kamol, 1985).

Nhat Tien, "In the Footsteps of a Water Buffalo," copyright © 1988 by Nhat Tien. Translation copyright © 1988 by Huynh Sanh Thong. Reprinted by permission of Huynh Sanh Thong from *To Be Made Over* (New Haven: Yale University, Southeast Asia Studies, 1988; copublished with the William Joiner Center, University of Massachusetts, Boston).

Catherine Lim, "The English Language Teacher's Secret," copyright © 1987 by Catherine Lim. Reprinted by permission of Octopus Publishing Asia Pte. Ltd. from *The Shadow of a Shadow of a Dream* (Singapore: Heinemann Asia Limited, 1987).

Gerson Poyk, "Matias Akankari," copyright © 1990 by Gerson Poyk. Translation copyright © 1990 by Lontar, Jakarta. Reprinted by permission of Lontar from *Menagerie*, 1, the Lontar Foundation, Jakarta, 1991.

H. Jafar Salij, "Shadow Play," copyright © 1982 by H. Jafar Salij. Reprinted by permission of Octopus Publishing Asia Pte. Ltd. from *Shadow Play and Other Stories* (Singapore: Heinemann Asia Limited, 1982).

Sitor Situmorang, "Holy Communion," copyright © 1990 by Sitor Situmorang. Translation copyright © 1990 by Lontar, Jakarta. Reprinted by permission of Lontar from *Menagerie*, 1, the Lontar Foundation, Jakarta, 1991.

B. Wongar, "Barbaru, the Family," copyright © 1982 by B. Wongar. Reprinted by permission of Boru Wongar from *Babaru, the Family* (Champaign: University of Illinois Press, 1982).

Bruce Stewart, "Broken Arse," copyright © 1987 by Bruce Stewart. Reprinted by permission of Longman Paul Ltd. from *All the Dangerous Animals Are in Zoos* (Auckland, New Zealand: Longman Paul Ltd., 1987).